AFTER BURN

LOST KINGS MC #10

AUTUMN JONES LAKE

After Burn (Lost Kings MC #10)
Digital ISBN: 978-1-943950-24-9
Paperback ISBN# 978-1-943950-25-6

The lure of the open road never fades.

Bumpy, cracked, and full of obstacles.

In the end, it's the cure for life's complications.

My brothers behind me and our future in front of us.

Loyalty above all else.

A vow made to my brothers.'

'Til death do us part.

A vow made to my wife.

Together we'll race the rain, chase the sun, and ride the wind.

Leave no road untaken.

An unexpected truth no one ever saw coming.

Are we strong enough to survive it, or will it incinerate everything we've built?

THE LOST KINGS MC
ULTIMATE SERIES READING ORDER

Slow Burn (Lost Kings MC #1)

Corrupting Cinderella (Lost Kings MC #2)

Three Kings, One Night (Lost Kings MC #2.5)

Strength from Loyalty (Lost Kings MC #3)

Tattered on my Sleeve (Lost Kings MC #4)

White Heat (Lost Kings MC #5)

Between Embers (Lost Kings MC #5.5)

Bullets & Bonfires (standalone in the LOKI world)

More Than Miles (Lost Kings MC #6)

Unhinged (Iron Bulls MC #5) by Phoenyx Slaughter

Warnings & Wildfires (standalone in the LOKI world)

White Knuckles (Lost Kings MC #7)

Beyond Reckless (Lost Kings MC #8)

Beyond Reason (Lost Kings MC #9)

One Empire Night (Lost Kings MC #9.5)

After Burn (Lost Kings MC #10)

After Glow (Lost Kings MC #11)

Cards of Love: Knight of Swords (standalone)

Coming Soon

Zero Tolerance (Lost Kings MC #12)

White Lies (Lost Kings MC #13)

Matches & Misfires

ACKNOWLEDGMENTS

After Burn has been a long time coming. I'm so excited to finally share it with you!

This story is everything! I love it with everything in me and I hope you do too!

This book wouldn't have been possible without my critique partners, Cara, Kari, and Ginny encouraging all the wild ideas Mr. Lake planted in my head.

I need to thank Liz Kelley, Jezzie, and Daniele for their feedback.

The Lost Kings MC Ladies. Thank you for your kindness, theories, and all the half-naked man pics. I love spending time with you!

My awesome readers, there are so many days I can't believe how lucky I am and I have you to thank for that. There are other days when I'm ready to give up, and one of you reaches out to tell me how much you love my stories. I am forever grateful.

Rock, the best imaginary friend an author could ask for. Apparently you never plan to shut up and I love you for it.

Finally, my one true love since the age of seventeen. Mr. Lake planted the seed for one of the major things that happen in this story and has been smug about it ever since. I still love him!

GLOSSARY

Welcome back to the world of the Lost Kings MC!—I've made minor changes to this glossary since Beyond Reason. You may find some of the information useful if it's been a while since you visited the Lost Kings.

THE LOST KINGS MC ORGANIZATIONAL STRUCTURE

President: *Rochlan "Rock" North.* Leader of the Upstate NY charter of the Lost Kings MC. His word is law within the club. He takes advice from senior club members. He is the public "face" of the MC. Much to his annoyance, Rock is seen as the "father figure" in the club, especially by the younger members.

Sergeant-at-Arms: *Wyatt "Wrath" Ramsey.* Responsible for the security of the club. Keeps order at club events. Responsible for the safety and protection of the president, the club, its members and its women. Disciplines club members who violate the rules. Keeps track of club by-laws. In charge of the club's weapons and weapons training. Will challenge Rock when he deems it necessary. Outside of the MC, Wrath owns a gym, Furious Fitness. He is experienced in underground MMA-style fighting.

Vice President: *Angus "Zero" or "Z" Frazier.* In most clubs, I think the VP would be considered the second-in-command. In mine, I see the VP and SAA as being on equal footing within the club. Carries out the orders of the President. Communicates with other charters of the club. Assumes the responsibilities of the President in his absence. Keeps records of club patches and colors issued. Z also co-manages the MC's strip club, Crystal Ball.

Treasurer: *Marcel "Teller" Whelan.* Keeps records of income, expenses and investments.

Road Captain: *Blake "Murphy" O'Callaghan.* Responsible for researching, planning and organizing club runs. Responsible for obtaining and maintaining club vehicles.

Prospect: A prospect is someone who has stated a clear intention of being a full patch member of the Lost Kings MC. The Lost Kings vet their prospects for two or more years. To vote a prospect in as a full patch member, the vote must be unanimous. Not all prospects will become full patch members. Some will realize the club is not for them. For others, the club will realize that the prospect is not a good fit for the club. Prospects are expected to show respect to all full patch members and do whatever is asked of them. The Lost Kings MC currently has no prospects.

Other members

Cronin "Sparky" Petek: Sparky is the mad genius behind the Lost Kings MC's pot-growing business. He is rarely seen outside of the basement, as he prefers the company of his plants.

Elias "Bricks" Serrano: We saw Bricks and his girlfriend throughout the series. One of the few members who does not live at the clubhouse, he performs a lot of general tasks for the club.

Dixon "Dex" Watts: We've also seen Dex throughout the series. He co-manages Crystal Ball with Z.

Sam "Stash" Black: Lives in the basement with Sparky and helps with the plants. He came out of the basement to help out in *White Knuckles*. Other than that, we're not really sure what he's up to downstairs.

Thomas "Ravage" Kane: We got to know Rav and his snarky humor a little bit better in each book. Ravage is a general member who helps out wherever he is needed.

THE LADIES OF THE LOST KINGS MC

Hope Kendall, Esq.: Nick-named *First Lady* by Murphy in *Corrupting Cinderella (Lost Kings MC #2)*, Hope is the object of Rock's love and obsession. Their epic love story spans six and a half books: *Slow Burn, Corrupting Cinderella, Strength From Loyalty, White Heat, One Empire Night, After Burn, and After Glow.*

Trinity Hurst: She was the caretaker of the Lost Kings MC clubhouse and the brothers. She and Wrath have a long, tattered love story full of lust, fury, and forgiveness in *Tattered on My Sleeve (Lost Kings MC #4)*. She and Wrath are also featured in *White Heat (Lost Kings MC #5)*. They finally tie the knot in *White Knuckles (Lost Kings MC #7)*.

Heidi Whelan-Ryan: Teller's little sister. Heidi is a recurring character in each of the books from *Corrupting Cinderella (Lost Kings MC #2)* on. She also has short stories in *Three Kings, One Night (Lost Kings MC #2.5)* and *Between Embers (Lost Kings MC #5.5)* she is a major character in *More Than Miles (Lost Kings MC #6)*.

Alexa Jade Ryan: Heidi and Axel's daughter.

Swan: Lost Kings MC club girl and dancer at Crystal Ball. She's recently started teaching yoga classes with Hope and Trinity as her first students.

Willow: Bartender at Crystal Ball. Has befriended Hope, Trinity, and Swan. Frequently seen with Sparky these days.

Lilly: One of Hope's best friends and frequent "booty call" of Z. While she sent Trinity a wedding present in *White Knuckles (Lost Kings MC #7)*, we haven't seen Lilly since *Between Embers (Lost Kings MC #5.5)*

Sophie: Hope's former best friend. We haven't seen her since *White Heat (Lost Kings MC #5)*.

Mara Oak: Friend of Hope. Also an attorney. She's appeared in *Slow Burn, Corrupting Cinderella, Strength From Loyalty, Tattered on My Sleeve, White Heat, and White Knuckles.* She's married to Empire city court judge, Damon Oak. Their story, *Objection,* will be available one day.

LOST KINGS MC TERMINOLOGY

Crystal Ball – The strip club owned by the Lost Kings MC and one of their legitimate businesses. They often refer to it as "CB."

"Conference Center" – The clubhouse of the Lost Kings MC. It was previously used as a high-end religious retreat and is sometimes still jokingly referred to as the "Conference Center" or "Hippie Compound."

Empire – The fictional city in Upstate NY, run by the Lost Kings.

Furious Fitness—The gym Wrath owns. Often just referred to as "Furious."

Green Street Crew – Street gang the Lost Kings do business with. Often referred to as "GSC." "Loco" is their leader and frequent nuisance to Rock.

LOKI – Short for Lost Kings.

Vipers MC – Rival and frequent enemy MC. Runs Ironworks which borders the Lost Kings' territory. Their president, Ransom, and his SAA, Killa, appeared in *Tattered on My Sleeve* and *White Heat.* Ransom had a major role in *White Knuckles.*

Wolf Knights MC – Rival and sometimes ally of the Lost Kings. Their president, Ulfric, appeared in *Slow Burn* and stepped down in *Between Embers (Lost Kings MC #5.5.)* Merlin took over as President of the Wolf Knights. Their SAA, Whisper, was a partner in Wrath's gym. Actions taken by the Wolf Knights have had a serious impact on the Lost Kings in recent times and their relationship is tenuous at the moment.

Charlotte's uncle, Merlin recently stepped down as president and Whisper took over. Merlin is now on the road living the life as a Nomad.

OTHER MC TERMINOLOGY

*Most terminology was obtained through research. However, I have also used some artistic license in applying these terms to **my** romanticized, fictional version of an Outlaw Motorcycle Club.*

Cage – A car, truck, van, basically anything other than a motorcycle.

Church – Club meetings all full patch members must attend. Led by the president of the club, but officers will update the members on the areas they oversee.

Citizen – Anyone not a hardcore biker or belonging to an outlaw club. "Citizen Wife" would refer to a spouse kept entirely separate from the club.

Cut – Leather vest worn by outlaw bikers. Adorned with patches and artwork displaying the club's unique colors. The Lost Kings' colors are blue and gray. Their logo is a skull with a crown.

Colors – The "uniform" of an outlaw motorcycle gang. A leather vest, with the three-piece club patch on the back, and various other patches relating to their role in the club. Colors belong to the club and are held sacred by all members.

Dressers – Slang for a motorcycle "dressed up" with hard saddle bags and other accessories. It's designed for long-distance riding.

Fly Colors – To ride on a motorcycle wearing colors.

Mother Chapter – First chapter of the club.

Muffler Bunny – Club girl, who hangs around to provide sexual favors to members.

Nomad – A club member who does not belong to any specific charter, yet has privileges in all charters. Nomads go anywhere to take care of business, usually at the request of the club president.

Old Lady/Ol' Lady – Wife or steady girlfriend of a club member. Has nothing to do with her age.

Out Bad –The shorthand way of saying a club member has been kicked out of the club for some kind of betrayal. Someone who is "out bad" might be in hiding from the club.

Patched In – When a new member is approved for full membership.

Patch Holder – A member who has been vetted through performing duties for the club as a prospect or probate and has earned his three-piece patch.

Property Patch – When a member takes a woman as his Old Lady (wife status), he gives her a vest with a property patch. In my series, the vest has a "Property of Lost Kings MC" patch and the member's road name on the back. The officers also place their patches on the ol' lady's vest as a sign they have agreed to always have her back. Her man's patch or club symbol is placed over the heart.

Road Name – Nickname. Usually given by the other members.

RUB: Slang for Rich Urban Biker. A term generally used by real bikers to describe a person who rides an expensive motorcycle on weekends and never very far. A poser.

Run – A club sanctioned outing sometimes with other chapters and/or clubs. Can also refer to a club business run.

DEDICATION

It's never too late to steer your future in a new direction.

CHAPTER ONE

ROCK

EVERYONE SEES WHAT you appear to be. What you allow them to see. Few people ever experience who you really are. Even fewer will ever know who you are deep down in your soul.

People who fall into each of those categories surround me tonight.

"You know she's your wife, right?" Z taps my shoulder with his fist, but it barely registers. "You look like a lion about to pounce on a ham sandwich."

I doubt she heard him over the loud music pumping through the clubhouse, but Hope drags her gaze across the room to where we're standing. The corners of her mouth turn up and pink races over her cheeks as she meets my stare.

"Christ, after all this time, you can still make her blush with a *look?*"

Fuck yeah, I can, and it's still one of my favorite things about my wife. If I still get that reaction out of her when I'm eighty and gray, I'll consider it one of my best achievements.

"Girl practically melts when she looks at you." Z shakes his head. "Just go," he says, clearly exasperated with my lack of attention. "We can talk about the run tomorrow morning."

"Thanks," I mumble before I stalk across the room, brushing past people, impatient to get to my wife. Hope doesn't break her conversation with Teller and Charlotte when I wrap my arms around her waist and mold myself to her back, but she acknowledges me by running her hands over my arms.

Not enough.

I lean down and nuzzle her neck. "Let's go upstairs."

"Rock." She squeezes the arm that's wrapped around her like a python. "Teller and Charlotte want to have us over for dinner so we can see all the work they've done to their house."

"We meant to have you over sooner but wanted everything present-able before we—" Charlotte trips over the words, stopping midsentence.

Do I make her nervous?

Charlotte's a brave girl. Stabbed her uncle when he went after her. Stood up to Wrath when he voted her down. She's a smart lawyer who spends her days arguing in court. But she always seems flustered around me. I'm not sure how I feel about that. She's makes Teller happy, though, and the club trusts her now. Those are the only things that matter.

"Whenever you're ready. Let us know."

Teller's been adamant about doing the work at his house on his own. Or from what Murphy says, Teller's been putting Charlotte's brother to work. He's the most relaxed and least obnoxious he's ever been in all the years I've known him. For that alone, Charlotte's earned my respect.

"So, does Carter have to finish all his chores before you allow him to go on this trip?" A soft laugh follows Hope's question.

"I guess I'll give him the time off." Teller smirks. "Actually, he's a hard worker, once I get him motivated."

I wait for Charlotte to defend her brother, but she shrugs. "He's never been very focused." She jerks her thumb in Teller's direction. "Mr. Discipline here has been showing him the ropes."

Hope laughs again, brushing against me in a way that sets off a fierce hunger through every muscle in my body. "Sounds like someone else I know." She squeezes my arm. "Is Teller's motto 'early is on time' too?"

Teller grins and lifts his chin at me. "I probably got that from him."

"Nah, you were always a dependable, hard worker."

Teller's eyes widen as if I've never given him a compliment before. Jesus Christ, my work never ends.

I slide my hands down to Hope's waist, my fingers digging into her hips. She responds by shifting her ass and ever-so-slightly grinding it into my already throbbing erection.

This party can wait.

I tug on her hand. "I need a word with my first lady."

Teller's mouth tips into a lazy smile. "Sure, Prez."

"Text me, Charlotte," Hope calls out as I drag her away. She runs a few steps to catch up with me, laughing the whole time. "What are you doing?"

"I need you."

She lets out an exasperated snort. "You have me anytime you want."

"Exactly."

She trots up the stairs behind me. "We have a house we can go to."

"Can't wait that long."

Inside our old room, I don't even bother flipping on the light. I press her back to the door and lean down, brushing my lips over hers. There's enough moonlight coming in through the windows to see her green eyes, glittering with amusement and love.

I pull back, fighting my own smile. "What's so funny, baby doll?"

She loops her arms around my neck and stares up at me. "Nothing. I just love you."

Heat spreads over my skin. I never tire of her saying those words. "I have something for you."

"I figured that was why you dragged me up here."

"Not that."

Slipping my hand in my pocket, I pull out a small box. "A little something for our road trip."

"Aww." She sighs. "You already gave me so much for our anniversary."

"I love spoiling my girl."

"It's too small to be a new vibrator." She grins up at me. "Unless it's a pocket rocket."

I shake my head. Fuck, my woman comes up with the craziest stuff. "You don't need that when you have me ready and willing to shove my face in your pussy every chance I get."

She *vibrates* with laughter, thunking her head against the door, which only makes her laugh harder. "Ow."

Cupping the back of her head, I rub the spot that connected with the door. "You okay?"

"I'm fine." Her green eyes meet mine. "Never happier. Can I open it?" she asks, holding the small box up between us.

"Go on."

She plucks the top off the box and her eager grin melts when she sees the patch inside.

"*Not all those who wander are lost,*" she reads. Her glittering eyes meet mine and a soft smile tugs at the corners of her mouth. She knows exactly what those words mean to me. "It's perfect. I love it."

"I thought it would go with your wanderlust patch from our last trip."

She smiles even wider. "It does. Perfectly."

For some reason, she can't stop laughing. Finally, she reaches into her pocket and pulls out a small white box of her own. "Great minds and all that."

Inside the box is a tiny metal pin with the same words engraved around a miniature compass.

"I wasn't sure if it was manly enough to go on your cut"—she waves her hands in the air between us—"or whatever, so I won't be offended if you don't want to—"

I cut her off with a kiss. "Of course I'll wear it." I tilt my head to the side. "Put it on for me."

Her eyes widen. "Am I allowed to alter your colors?"

"Yes, sass-mouth, just put it on."

She bites her lip while she concentrates on jabbing metal through leather. "I don't want to stab you in the neck."

"I'll survive a poke from your little pin."

Laughter dances in her eyes when she looks up again. "I'm used to *you* doing the poking."

Fuck, I love her. "Don't worry. I'm gonna *poke* you real soon."

"There." She fusses for a few more seconds, checking to make sure it's secure. "I hope it's okay, but I bought little pins for the guys too."

"You did?" This woman never stops surprising me with her sweetness.

One of her shoulders jerks up and she glances away. "I thought it was—"

"It's sweet. Thank you."

"Don't worry. They're manly." More confidence edges into her voice. "They have a skull on them."

"Sounds perfect." I give her a more serious look. "You okay?"

"Yes."

My beautiful wife isn't good at keeping secrets from me. There's something—a hitch in her voice, a quick glance to the side—that prickles along the back of my neck.

"Are you sure?"

"I'm a little nervous about the trip," she confesses.

There's more to it. I'm convinced, but I won't push. Not tonight anyway.

As if I wasn't already nervous about this trip.

I smile for Rock's benefit, knowing he's already stressed about the upcoming run to National.

Correction. The run with multiple stops.

First stop—Devil Demons MC's clubhouse. That, I'm not stressed about. I've met them before.

National? That scares me.

The rally we're all riding to afterward, even scarier.

Trinity hasn't seemed thrilled about any of it either. Maybe her lack of enthusiasm has colored my view of the trip.

Heidi seems to be treating the run like a grown-up carnival. Charlotte's the only one who's shown a sensible mixture of interest and caution about the events.

"Are the guys excited?" I ask.

His mouth twists. "Now that Murphy figured out their lodging, he's less of a pain in the ass." He traces his fingers over my collarbones. "Where were we?"

"Are you trying to distract me?"

"All you need to worry about is me."

"I do worry about you." The truth of those words hangs in the air between us, because the invitation to National was more of an order. This mandatory meeting of all the Lost Kings charters only happens every couple of years, and Rock was a no-show for the last one. Apparently, even the "no rules" biker lifestyle comes with a few rules that can only be disobeyed for so long.

Another wry smile from my husband. "Focus on me. I have everything handled."

There's peace in that, because I do trust Rock to take care of everything. But I always want to make things easier on him, not harder.

"Hope?" His tone conveys some exasperation that he doesn't have one hundred percent of my attention.

"Present."

A warm puff of air slips over my skin as he leans down to kiss my neck.

"Oh." I sigh and close my eyes, savoring the crisp pine-and-soap scent clinging to him.

"That's it." He strokes up and down my sides while his mouth moves lower.

He skims his fingers over my legs, spreading a tickly-shivery sensation over my bare skin as he reaches the hem of my skirt and slowly drags it up, shoving it over my hips.

Now I'm focused.

Excitement sizzles over my skin as he yanks my underwear down my legs, kneeling in front of me.

"Rock?"

"Quiet," he warns before swooping in to brush a kiss over my inner thigh. "Open."

I inch my feet apart, but not fast enough. The short heels of my cowboy boots stick on the hardwood planks.

Rock's warm hand grasps me behind my knee, pulling it up. "Shoulder," he orders.

Nervous laughter spills out of me for about a second before he leans in and silences me with a long, slow lick. I arch away from the door with a gasp.

"Jesus Christ," I breathe out, staring down at him.

He flicks his gaze up, meeting my eyes. "Nope. Just your husband."

I'm out of sassy comebacks.

He rests his other hand on my butt, pulling me closer. After some maneuvering my body the way he wants—back against the door and legs over his shoulders, he dives back in, licking and kissing.

My heart pounds, blood singing in my veins. I've been worked up ever since I caught him staring at me across the room downstairs, knowing this was exactly what he had in mind.

"Rock." I tangle my fingers in his hair, and he lets out an encouraging growl.

"Yes, yes, yes," I whisper over and over in time with his tongue.

Rough stubble brushes my inner thigh, the scratchy-tickling sensation combined with the pleasure of his mouth is almost too much. I squirm, but his big hands hold me still, heightening my excitement.

He circles my clit once, twice, three times and my body tightens, my entire existence narrowing down to my flesh against his tongue.

A blow against the door jars me out of the orgasmic bliss I'm hovering over. My fuzzy brain struggles to comprehend what's happening.

Knocking. Someone is knocking on the door I'm pressed up against. Rock's either ignoring the visitor or hasn't noticed.

"Prez!" Z calls.

Rock answers by wiggling his tongue over my clit, making me gasp.

"I know you two are in there. You're needed downstairs."

An unhappy growl rumbles out of Rock as he pulls away. "Be there as soon as I make my wife come."

"Rock!" The scolding I intended dies to a whimper as he slides a finger inside me.

On the other side, Z chuckles uncomfortably. "I don't know, Prez. Hope's kind of like a sister to me, but I mean, if you're offering—"

"Get the fuck out of here!" Rock shouts.

Somewhere between mortified and amused, all I can do is laugh.

Z bangs on the door once more. "Hurry up." His heavy steps fade down the hallway.

I stare down at my husband, and by the fire in his eyes, he has no intention of leaving this room until he's accomplished exactly what he said.

"Never going to happen now," I warn him. My body's still tingling, but the impending rush of ecstasy vanished the second I heard Z's voice.

"We'll see."

I should've known he'd take that as a challenge.

He slowly lowers my feet to the floor and stands. Before I have a chance to open my mouth and offer what we both know will be a weak protest, he lifts me up. "Hate being interrupted," he grumbles, walking us to the bed.

"What do you think he needs?"

"Don't know." He drops me to the mattress and wedges himself between my legs, working his belt loose. "Don't care."

"Rock—"

Ignoring my objection, he focuses his no-nonsense gray eyes on me. "Shirt off."

I'm pretty sure I rip the seam yanking it over my head so fast. I don't wait for another command, just toss my bra to the side too.

The slight quirk of his lips says he approves.

He stares at me for a moment, drinking all of me in—naked except for the denim scrunched up around my waist and the cowboy boots on my feet. "You look good like this."

Our eyes meet and he falls over me, leaning down to press the softest kiss against my lips. He slides a hand under my ass, tilting my hips. The second his cock nudges against me, my head falls back and my eyes close. He kisses my neck as he slowly pushes inside. My fingers dig into his shoulders, sinking into the soft leather of his cut.

Pleasure floods through me in a violent wave, pushing me to the edge again. "Oh please," I beg.

"Anything you want."

"This. This is all… right there, Rock."

He brushes his fingers over my hair and kisses my forehead while continuing to grind into me at a leisurely pace.

"More?" he asks.

"Yes."

My world spins, and I find myself on top of him. He squeezes my hips. "Best view in the world."

My skin warms from the compliment. Under Rock's appreciative gaze, I believe every word from his lips.

"Giddy-up, cowgirl," he teases, tapping his fingers against my boot.

It doesn't take long before I'm gasping with pleasure. Stars burst and spin behind my eyelids. Rock pulls me down, holding me tight while he pistons up into me. A few short, rough thrusts and he's groaning against my hair. I touch my sweaty forehead to his and stare into his eyes. "Thank you," I whisper.

We both know I mean more than thanks for the amazing sex and mind-blowing orgasm.

The softest smile my hard man is capable of spreads over his face. "Anything for you."

As soon as my pounding heart slows, I sit up, remembering Z's waiting for Rock downstairs.

"They can wait." He tugs me down beside him.

"I don't think you have time for after glow cuddles." I tickle my fingers over his stomach and he captures my hand, pressing it against his chest.

"After glow cuddles." He peers down at me. "I like that."

I reach up, tracing my finger over his lips. "I like making you smile."

He rumbles with laughter. "I only do it around you."

We indulge in a few more snuggles before I roll away from him, hopping out of bed and out of his reach. "Come on, Mr. President."

He groans and sits up.

"Look at you, still dressed." I smooth my skirt back down over my hips. It's denim, so it didn't wrinkle too bad. "And somehow I ended up mostly naked."

"The way it should be." He stands and lazily buttons his jeans and buckles his belt, watching me the entire time.

"Don't look at me like that. You have duties to attend to downstairs." I swipe my shirt off the end of the bed. Yup, just as I thought, there's a small rip under the armpit. "Look what you made me do." I hold out the shirt, shaking it with mock indignation. "I was so eager to get naked for you, I put holes in my clothes."

"I'd apologize—"

"But you're not sorry."

"You know me so well." He leans over, reaching for my bra, but I snatch it out of his grasp.

"Nice try, caveman." I glance around the room. "Where'd my underwear go?"

He gives me an innocent shrug.

"There's no way I'm running around down there in a skirt and no panties," I mutter as I rummage through one of my old dresser drawers. "Ah-ha!" I hold up my prize—a pair of blue, cotton, cheeky panties.

Rock clutches his chest, right over his heart as if it's killing him to watch me get dressed.

While I hurry to fix myself up, he seems completely unconcerned Z waits downstairs with some emergency.

"You can go ahead and see what he needs. I'll be right down," I call from the bathroom.

"Want my first lady on my arm," he rumbles in his post-sex gravelly voice from the doorway.

In the mirror, I catch his gaze roaming over my backside. "Don't get any ideas."

He doesn't deny his dirty thoughts, just leans against the door frame and continues to watch me comb my hair.

"Thank you for my new patch." Our eyes meet in the mirror and I wink at him. "I can't wait to squeeze you tight all the way to Mississippi."

A larger smile brightens his face and warms my heart. Rock worries about me on these trips, and I want to reassure him that even though I'm nervous, I'm also looking forward to being by his side.

Finally, we're both presentable and return to the party. Our guests must have assumed we'd gone home for the night. The atmosphere shifted to something more X-rated in our absence.

I spot Teller busy slow dancing with Charlotte in the corner. Quickly, I blink away the tears that prick my eyelids, pleased he's found someone who makes him happy—and less of an asshole.

Any joy I'm feeling evaporates when I catch the strained look on Trinity's face. Five seconds later Tawny's voice pierces my eardrums.

Next to me, Rock groans and sighs at the same time.

"Rock!" Sway shouts, striding over with an outstretched hand. Rock shakes it, and Sway pulls him closer, slapping his back.

"Little lady." Sway throws a smirk my way.

I smile and nod in response, not quite sure anything nice will come out if I open my mouth. Rock squeezes my hand as if he can sense my internal struggle.

"Thought we'd ride out to National with you," Sway explains.

Rock forces what could be interpreted as a welcoming smile. "Good. We're actually leaving tomorrow. Have some business to attend to on the way out."

Having no idea what Sway's relationship is with the Devil Demons MC, I leave them to discuss logistics.

"Hi, Tawny." I tap her shoulder and put on my hostess face. She squeals and embraces me as if we're long-lost sisters. I suppose in a way, we are. "It's good to have you up here again." I use my most welcoming tone, but it still sounds phony to my ears.

"How are you, sweetheart? Nervous about National?"

"A little," I confess. Anything else would be a lie, so why bother?

"Don't worry. I'll be there to look out for you and introduce you to the other old ladies," she assures me. In a lower voice she adds, "The national president's wife is such a bitch."

That's something coming from Tawny. "Thank you."

I catch Trinity rolling her eyes and wink at her. Tawny turns and wraps her other arm around Trinity's shoulders. "You too, sweetie. Oh, this will be fun."

Two weeks on the road with Tawny "looking out" for me isn't exactly my idea of fun, but I try to muster up some polite, respectful enthusiasm. Trinity seems confused to find herself in an embrace with Tawny and doesn't say much.

"Charlotte's coming too, right?" Tawny asks.

"Yup. And Heidi."

Tawny cocks her head. "What about the baby?"

"She's coming. They rented a house near—"

Tawny nods. "Good. Good." She glares across the room at her husband. "I'll be happy to sit out a few events and watch the baby so Heidi can socialize."

I glance at Trinity, who shrugs.

Tawny drops us to go say hello to Charlotte, something I don't think Teller appreciates, judging by the scowl darkening his face as Tawny squeezes in between the two of them.

"Where's Wrath?" I ask Trinity.

She tilts her head toward the front door. "Outside. Sway didn't come alone."

"Oh joy," I mumble.

Sway's gone through at least two VPs and two SAAs in the last few years, none of them impressive. Not my business until it spills over into my domain, I guess. In the back of my mind, I wonder if that's something that will be discussed at National. So many unknowns.

Wrath storms in, frosty gaze sweeping the room until he sees Trinity. Then he seems to relax and even flashes a quick smile my way.

"Everything okay, angel?" he asks, twining one massive arm around her and kissing the top of her head.

"We're fine. Tawny assured us she'll look out for us at National," she answers without laughing.

He rolls his eyes. "You'll be too busy to worry about her. Lots of other old ladies for you to hang with." He nods at me. "You too. All four of you are 'new' to the organization, so they're gonna want to meet you and size you up. Especially the president's wife."

"Oh goodie, I can't wait."

The smirk on his face makes me want to smack him. "Tried to warn ya, Cinderella."

Yes, he has, but this is so much different than any other Lost Kings event. Rock will be under a lot of pressure. I don't want to do anything to let him down.

CHAPTER TWO

ROCK

SWAY SHOWING UP out of the blue last night continues to muck up my schedule the next morning. I can't say I'm eager to have him tag along to the Devil Demons with us either.

Nor do I want him to join us for church this morning. It's customary to invite the president of a visiting charter to the table unless there is very specific business we need to discuss. So that's the excuse I plan to use if he says anything. As far as anyone knows, he hasn't emerged from his room upstairs yet. I doubt he'll care one way or another.

Wrath blows out an annoyed breath as he enters the war room and takes his seat.

Z's in a good mood for once. He grins as he rounds the table. Murphy and Teller amble in behind him with slightly less enthusiasm.

"What's with the faces?" I nod to each of them.

"Nothing." Murphy shakes his head. "Tawny stopped by to play grandma to Alexa right after you left."

"Great. I'm sure Hope's thrilled," I grumble.

"Where we at with them, Prez?" Dex asks in a low voice after Sparky shuts the door.

"Sway didn't know we were making the extra stop before National. But I think he plans to tag along."

"Fan-fucking-tastic." Wrath sighs. "Just what we need when we're trying to finalize this deal with the Demons."

"Tell me something I don't know."

"Boss! Boss! We still meetin' up with the Iron Bulls before the rally? Rebel and I are planning to swap some seeds."

"Yeah, I need to call Romeo later, but that's happening."

Bricks whistles, low and mocking. "Holy shit. Sparky's actually leaving the basement?"

"Every couple years he needs to air out," Z jokes, receiving a middle finger in the face from Sparky.

"Enough." I slice my hand through the air to call their attention to the head of the table. "Road report." I nod to Murphy.

"All clear to Kodiak. No issues there. We'll be riding with the Demons through Pennsylvania, so that's good." Preferring to plan his trips the low-tech way, Murphy shakes out the map in his hand and flips through the notebook in front of him. "You're gonna have to call the MC outside Nashville and speak to their prez to get the okay to ride through their territory. If they're dicks about it, we'll reroute through North Carolina. Only adds about four hours."

"Have you reached out to them?" I ask.

"Not yet."

"Stick around afterward."

"You got it."

I glance at the schedule in front of me. "After the Demons, we have some leeway as long as our asses are in High Noon by Thursday night."

"I'm thinking a stopover in Huntington." Murphy taps his map. "It's a good halfway point."

"That's fine."

Dex raises his hand. "We going to the rally right after National?"

"That's the plan. Meet up with the Iron Bulls and ride with them."

Z signals me and I nod. "They're probably bringing another club along."

"Friendly to us?"

"Don't see why not."

"I'll talk to Romeo about it." I glance around the table. "Anyone else?"

"We staying for the whole rally, boss?" Sparky asks. The reality of being away from his plants for two whole weeks seems to be settling in for him.

"We'll stay as long as Priest and the rest of the national officers stay."

"Solidarity, fuckface," Ravage says to Sparky.

"Priest gonna be okay with us meetin' up with another club?" Dex asks.

I shrug. "Don't see why not. Better to roll in with a large crew. Several clubs friendly to each other should put residents at ease."

"And put law enforcement on notice not to fuck with us," Wrath adds.

"That too."

Ravage throws his arms in the air and head back. "I can't fucking wait! Free, hot, random pussy wearing nothing but strings and body paint as far as the eye can see."

Everyone cracks up at his degenerate enthusiasm for the weeklong annual biker rally.

Z leers at me. "Think you'll talk Hope into a painted-on bikini?"

"Not unless I'm doing the painting and we're staying in our room."

Wrath lifts his chin in Murphy's direction. "Your situation worked out?"

"Yeah, we're gonna rent a house right outside Sunnyshore." Murphy glances at me. "Hope said she'd watch Alexa one or two nights, so we could go to some events."

"That's fine."

Teller raises his hand. "Charlotte and I are staying with them."

Murphy nods as if they already discussed it ahead of time.

"Good." I glance at every one of my brothers. "I don't want anyone on their own in Florida."

"Buddy system." Sparky bounces in his seat. "Just like in school."

"Funny how that works out." I roll my eyes and turn back to Teller. "Carter still okay driving the truck?"

"Yeah, says he's looking forward to it." Teller lifts his chin at Stash. "You gonna remember to go check on my place?"

"Fuck yeah." He reaches over and slaps Hoot on the back. "Me and Hootie got things covered here."

"Both you fuckwits better remember to feed the dogs," Z reminds them.

"Thank fuck," Birch, who's usually pretty quiet during church, says. "I thought I was gonna get stuck driving the cage."

"You're driving the van," Wrath says with barely concealed glee. Birch may have finally earned his full patch, but he's still one of the lowest ranking members and gets plenty of shit work thrown on him.

"You're gonna make me trailer my bike all over like a fucking punk?"

"Yup." Wrath grins.

"We need new prospects," Birch grumbles. That wipes the smirk off Wrath's face, which Birch doesn't miss. "Sorry."

Wrath holds up a hand. "You're right. We need to think about new blood."

"Fuck knows I'm gonna get grilled about it at National," I grumble.

"Malik's been coming around Crystal Ball more, but I don't think he's ready for a trip like this," Z says. "Too unpredictable."

"Agreed." I glance around the table again. "I'm sure I'll get chewed out at National about growing our numbers. Anything else?"

We adjourn the meeting and I stand to talk to some of the brothers on their way out. Teller, Murphy, and Wrath remain at the table.

When everyone else has left, I cock an eyebrow at Teller. His gaze darts to Murphy and Wrath before speaking. "I got the money squared away from the IPO."

"Yeah?" I pull out my chair and sit back down.

"Are we reporting it to National?" Teller asks.

I glance at Wrath and Murphy. "Why didn't you bring it up at the table?"

"I wanted to talk to you about it first." He shrugs. "Figure you tell Wrath everything anyway." He glances at Murphy again.

"Probably shoulda kept Z here too," I mutter.

"No one's gonna breathe a word of it at National, Rock," Wrath says. "No reason to."

He's right. Our charter might be part of a larger organization, but we're still tight-lipped with anyone outside Upstate. "How much did it end up being?"

Teller passes over a piece of paper that raises my eyebrows. "Jesus."

"Yeah," Teller agrees.

"National's gonna want a piece," Wrath says after checking out the figure.

"Fuck that. That was all Teller's doing," Murphy says. "We already kick up enough from Sparky's operation and Crystal Ball. We got overhead here that needs to be addressed. Members who need to help out their families. National doesn't give a shit about any of that."

"He's right," Wrath says.

I tap the paper in front of me. "Can this be traced back?"

"Not easily."

I don't like doing things behind my brothers' backs, but since this is *for* them, I figure they'll forgive me. Plus, the fewer who know, the better.

"Take three-quarters and place it in another untraceable account. Anyone asks, we'll kick up our percentage of what's left. Say it wasn't finalized yet. We'll portion out shares to everyone else over the next few months."

The corners of Teller's eyes crinkle from a sly grin. "Works for me."

I glance at Wrath and Murphy, who both nod.

"I'll talk to Z about it later," Wrath assures me.

"Thanks."

Wrath holds up a hand, stopping Teller. "Before you leave, Teller."

"What?"

"I can't ride out tomorrow," Wrath says, turning my way.

"You fuckin' serious?" I sit back, pinning him with a hard stare.

"Contractors called early this morning and cancelled on me. Re-scheduled for tomorrow. Got a couple other things I need to wrap up before I can take off."

The rebuild of Furious has been moving quicker than we anticipated, but that doesn't replace the money Wrath's losing while it's shut down. Under the circumstances, I'd be a real dick to pull rank and force him to ride out tomorrow.

"All right."

"I need Murphy too." Wrath shoves a finger in Teller's direction. "You get to play bodyguard at the Demons'."

Teller rears back. "What? Why me?"

"Murphy's staying behind with us," Wrath answers slowly as if he's explaining it to a two-year old.

I raise an eyebrow and glance Murphy's way. He throws a scowl at Wrath. "First I'm hearing about it, Prez. But that's cool."

"Carter can ride with you two, then," Teller says. "That's better than taking him to the Demons."

Wrath slaps his hand on the table. "I'll let you two make your phone calls."

I groan at the reminder. It's basic biker etiquette to call ahead if you're planning a large run through another club's territory and want to fly colors. Still fucking annoying.

Teller stands. "I'm gonna head home. Unless you still need me..."

"Nah, go on." I give his cut a once-over. "Better put some dirt on that *Brother's Keeper* patch before we get to National." I slide my gaze Murphy's way. "You too."

They both snort. Teller rubs his knuckles over the couple-month-old patch that still looks freshly stitched-on, then glances at my cut. "When do I earn one of those *Respect Few, Fear None* patches?"

"Hopefully never." That one's only earned by doing time for the club.

His expression sobers and he squeezes my shoulder briefly. "Thanks for looking out for me all these years." He glances at Murphy. "Both of us. Probably woulda ended up in prison if it wasn't for you settin' us straight."

Wrath jerks his thumb toward the door. "Should I leave? You two need some alone time?"

"Fuck off," Teller growls. "I'm serious."

As obnoxious as Wrath is, I appreciate the second of snark to collect my thoughts. "Club wouldn't be where it is without you, Teller." I glance at Murphy and then finally Wrath. "Any of you. Make me proud in Mississippi."

"We will," Teller promises.

Once he and Wrath leave, I focus on Murphy. "All right. Let's get this over with."

I THOUGHT I timed it right to be waiting in the living room when the guys were finished with church. But everyone except Rock, Wrath, and Murphy come out of the war room.

Z grabs the dogs' leashes and takes them outside, promising to return for lunch. Sparky and Stash run downstairs, bickering the entire time. Bricks and Dex stop by to say hello before heading outside to the garage. The rest of the guys wave on their way to the kitchen.

Teller drops down on the couch next to me. "How you doing, First Lady?"

"Is Murphy in trouble?"

His mouth pulls into a slow grin. "Nah. Why would you think that?"

Before I have a chance to answer, Charlotte pops into the living room. "Done already?"

Teller pulls her into his lap. "There's my girl," he murmurs against her hair.

"Puke!" Ravage shouts next to them. Teller throws his middle finger up without looking away from Charlotte.

"All set at the office?" Charlotte asks me.

"Yup. You?"

She rolls her eyes. "Judge Potter tried adjourning one of my trials until next Friday. I was like, 'No way, motherfucker.'" She laughs and pats Teller's chest. "Gonna be on the back of my man's bike for the next two weeks."

"Yeah you are," Teller answers in a low voice, narrowing the distance between their mouths.

Uncomfortable.

Ravage grins.

I clear my throat before the two of them start going at it on the couch in front of us. "Charlotte, I love that lipstick. What is it?"

Under his breath, Teller mutters, "Erection in a tube."

My gaze flicks his way, but his eyes are glued to Charlotte.

She reaches down and grabs her purse, digging through it until she pulls out a dark red tube. "Matte liquid lipstick. The color is Blood Moon," she reads before handing it to me.

"I don't think I can pull off such a dark color," I say, pulling out the wand and checking out the deep, dark red liquid. "But it's fabulous on you."

"Dick-sucking red," Ravage adds, settling down across from us.

Teller throws him a scowl and Ravage shrugs. "What? That's what guys think of when a chick they're into wears stuff like that," he explains, waving his hands at both of us.

Immune to the wild things that come out of Ravage's mouth by now, I ignore him. "I'm always worried it will wear off and I'll look like a half-deranged clown." I purse my lips and widen my eyes to emphasize the *deranged* part, making the three of them laugh.

Charlotte ducks her head, still laughing. "This one's kiss-proof, but not um, *everything* proof."

"See!" Ravage shouts, standing and pointing to Teller. "Told ya."

"Who do you think she's rubbing it off on, jackass?"

Charlotte lightly slaps Teller's cheek.

His mouth pulls into a smirk. "Sorry, Sunshine. Was that a secret?"

She huffs and slides out of his lap onto the couch. "Boys." She rolls her eyes and plucks the lipstick out of my hands. "Come here, Hope."

"What?" My gaze shoots to her fingers unscrewing the gloss. "No way."

"Sit still," she orders, grabbing a napkin from the table and dabbing my neutral pink gloss off my lips.

"What're you doing?" My words end up garbled as Charlotte smooshes my chin between her vise-grip fingers, tugging me closer. "Dammit, you're strong."

"Shit, this is kinda hot," Ravage mutters. "Are you gonna kiss her, Charlotte?"

"Shut up," Teller growls.

"Don't move. This is a bitch to get off if I don't place it just right."

"Oh goodie, please paint my face blood-moon-red, Charlotte," I mutter.

"Quiet," she orders. "Purse your lips."

"Can't we do this in the bathroom?" I protest, my eyes roaming to Ravage's too-eager expression.

"Open your mouth. Like this." She demonstrates the "O" she wants me to form with my lips.

"Is that her orgasm face?" Ravage asks.

"I'm gonna murder you," Teller snarls, jumping off the couch.

Charlotte froze the minute Ravage opened his mouth, so thankfully Teller's movements don't jostle Charlotte's hand forcing her to doodle all over my face.

"It works better with liner," Charlotte mutters after the boys race out the front door.

"I think I'm too old to pull off this color."

She rolls her eyes at me. "You're not that much older than me."

"I'm like twice your age in dog years."

Another eye roll. "You're terrible at math."

I force myself to sit still while she painstakingly drags the liquid over my lips in short precise strokes. She holds the napkin up in front of my face. "Blot."

She stares at me for a minute, making me fidget. "One more layer," she says before repeating the torturous process.

Finally, she declares me finished and hands me a compact. I study my face, unsure of this new look. "Too dramatic for me, don't you think?"

"No way."

Teller returns, staring at us for a few seconds before opening his mouth. "I'm not sure how I feel about my girlfriend and my—"

"Don't you dare," I warn him.

"—president's wife," he says, drawing out the words to cover up the fact that he likely was going to say some variation of "mother figure."

"Wearing the same sexy stuff," he finishes.

"Oh!" Charlotte paws through her purse again. "It comes with this sparkly topper color. I don't have anywhere to wear it but here." She plucks the mirror out of my hand and quickly swipes the glittery gloss over her lips and beams at Teller. "Better?"

"Much." He holds out his hand to her. "Come here. I need to see it in a different light to be sure, though."

They both laugh at the fake dry-heaving noises I make as they head upstairs.

"What's wrong, Hope?" Trinity asks, coming from the direction of the kitchen.

"Where were you?"

"Helping Swan. Why, what's wrong?"

I point to my face. "Look what Charlotte did to me."

She chuckles and drops down next to me, slinging her arm around my shoulders. "Looks good."

"And I'm pretty sure Teller left Ravage for dead somewhere outside."

She shakes with laughter. "No such luck." She tilts her head toward the hallway. "He's in the kitchen harassing Swan."

"Well, that's a relief."

"Not to Swan," she teases.

We're still joking around when the war room door opens and Wrath steps out. "How long you been waitin' for me, angel?"

"Few minutes."

"Where's Murphy?" I ask a couple seconds before he pops out of the war room.

"You worried about me, Hope?"

"I never know what trouble you'll get yourself into," I tease.

"Ain't that the truth," Wrath jokes, giving Murphy a quick shove.

"Heidi come with you?" Murphy asks, glancing around the living room.

"She's at the house trying to finish up some assignments before the trip."

Murphy's mouth twists down. "Feel bad making her miss school."

I wave my hand in the air. "She'll have her laptop to check in so she doesn't get behind."

Finally, Rock joins us and I jump up, wrapping my arms around him. He runs the back of his hand over my cheek. "Waitin' for me?" he

24

asks in a low voice.

Tipping my head back, I nod at him.

"What's going on here?" He traces his finger over my bottom lip.

"Oh." I slick my tongue over my lips. "Charlotte did this to me."

He leans in closer. "I like."

I lean up to kiss him and he pulls back. Recognizing the issue, I cup the back of his head with my hands, keeping him still. "It's supposed to be kiss-proof. Let's test it out."

"You're man enough to pull off that color, Rock," Wrath adds.

"Don't you have some work to do?" Rock asks without taking his eyes off me.

"Nah, I'm good."

Murphy chuckles uncomfortably. "Where'd Teller go?"

"Upstairs with Charlotte," I answer.

"Why don't *we* go upstairs," Rock suggests.

"Um, because Tawny and Sway stayed in our old room last night?"

"No one's seen or heard from him yet this morning," Trinity reminds us.

"Fantastic," Rock grumbles.

CHAPTER THREE

Hope

ROCK TAKES ME out on the bike several times a week if we have the time and the weather's good. Mostly short trips around Empire. A few longer rides when our schedules align.

I've come to crave the exhilaration of the wind in my hair, the speed and roar of the bike, the expert way Rock handles himself. The thrill of holding on to him while he guides the heavy machine where we need to go.

There's a buzz of excitement in our house the night before we're set to leave. Even Alexa seems to sense something big is about to happen. She's been giggling and playful all evening.

"Boy, I hope this mood continues," Heidi mutters as she runs her hand over Alexa's head. "Otherwise Carter might kill me."

"I have something that might help." Murphy grins and pulls a package from behind his back.

"What's that?" I ask.

Alexa's already squealing and reaching for the soft, denim bundle Murphy hands to Heidi. "Oh my God," Heidi says, shaking it out. Her jaw drops and she stares at Murphy.

"It's so cute." I lean over to get a better look. "When did you do this?"

Now that all of our attention is focused on him, he runs his hand over the back of his neck and shrugs. "She likes the patches." He taps a couple of the patches on the front of his cut. "Thought she should have her own." The corners of his mouth pull up. "But a more age-appropriate version."

Alexa yells even louder when Heidi spreads the tiny denim vest in front of her. She points to the biggest patch—a white unicorn with a flowing rainbow mane—taking up the back and squeals in delight. Flowers decorate the pockets, a four-leaf clover and a crown on the sides. A *100% Princess* patch sits over her heart. Murphy nudges me with his elbow and points out the one at the bottom right.

"Guns don't kill people," I read out loud. "Uncles with pretty nieces do." I snicker imagining Teller picking this one out. "Inappropriate, yet still somehow appropriate in our family."

Murphy chuckles. "Teller added that one."

"I figured."

Heidi helps a squirming Alexa into the vest. She's so excited it takes Heidi a couple seconds to wrestle it on her.

"Look at you." Rock crouches down to eye-level and Alexa twirls to show off her new prize, then holds out her arms for him to pick her up.

"It's a little big," Murphy says to Heidi. "Was hoping she'd get to wear it for a while. Bought extra patches so she has 'em for the next one."

Heidi doesn't speak. She shakes her head and wraps her arms around Murphy. He pushes her hair off her face and murmurs a few words to her.

To give them privacy, I join Rock in fawning over Alexa. "Are you going to be Uncle Carter's copilot?" I ask.

"Yeth!"

"Are you going to behave?" Rock asks in a slightly sterner than usual voice.

Alexa has to think about it and scrunches up her little nose. "Yeth?"

"Sounds about right." Rock kisses her cheeks and sets her down. She's enthralled with the vest and can't seem to decide between showing off and checking it out herself.

THE NEXT MORNING, everyone assembles in front of the clubhouse to strap gear on the bikes, perform checks, and go over the schedule one last time.

For a group of non-conformist bikers, they're extremely thorough and organized.

Wrath and Murphy join us even though they don't leave until to-morrow. Even Stash and Hoot, who have to stay behind, come out to help.

I stand by Rock's side while he announces a few last minute instructions to the brothers.

"No bullshit from any of you. Priest, Blink, and the rest of the national officers will be watching you closely. Make me proud."

"Yes, Dad!" A bunch of the assholes yell back.

"Cops will be all over us down in Mississippi *and* at the rally. Don't draw unnecessary attention our way. Don't start anything you're not prepared to finish either. Have your brothers' backs at all times. Someone breaks down or gets pulled over, I want two guys to stay with him. No one gets left behind. No one goes off alone."

"Prez, you saying we should participate in a devil's triangle?" Ravage asks with a straight face.

"Like you need my encouragement for a three-way." Rock glances at Wrath and Z. "Did I miss anything?" His gaze slides back to Ravage, almost daring him to utter another obnoxious comment.

"Don't forget to wear a rubber!" Z shouts. "And steer clear of jail-bait!"

"Fuck yeah!" Ravage cheers.

Rock sighs. "On that note, Hope has something for each of you." The *treat her with respect* is implied in his tone.

I should've done this one by one at breakfast instead of now in front of an audience. Having everyone's attention focused my way makes me so nervous, I drop my bag. Rock scoops it up, hands it to me, and winks.

Figuring I'll start from the biggest brother and work my down, I approach Wrath first.

He eyes the bag in my hand with a raised eyebrow and crooked smile. "Whatcha got, Cinderella?"

"Well, it's um, my first trip to National, so I got these for everyone." I hand over one of the tiny round pins that depict a compass with a skull in the middle and the words "Explore Wisely."

"Good advice." He actually laughs. "Clever."

Trinity grins at me.

"I have special pins for the girls too," I assure her before moving on to Z.

He leans in to peck my cheek after I give him his pin. "You know I'll be looking out for you, right?"

I squint at him. "Is that good or bad?"

"Depends on you." He hooks his thumbs in his pockets and flashes a dimpled smile.

Shaking my head, I continue on to the rest of the guys.

I arrive in front of Stash and Hoot last. They both look so bummed out. "I have pins for you too. They're teeny-tiny middle fingers since I know you're pissed about staying behind."

The silver pins actually make both of them chuckle.

Stash gives me a quick one-armed hug. "Thank you for thinking of me too, First Lady."

"Of course."

The girls are gathered around Teller's bike and I hand Trinity her pin first. "I'm so mad you're not coming until tomorrow." I give her a big hug to hide the fact that I'm only half-kidding.

Glancing down at the small pin of a white skull wearing a crown of violets, she swallows hard. "This is so cute." She drops her smile and gives me another hug. "I think you're the only ol' lady I've ever known who would think of something like this."

"Is that a compliment?" I ask.

"Yes, you nut." She pushes me in Heidi's direction.

"I'll make sure everything's off and locked up tight," Heidi promises me as she attaches her pin to her vest.

"I know you will."

Charlotte's last and I watch her bottom lip tremble as I hand over her pin. "It's just decoration, Charlotte. I'm not proposing."

"Thanks, Hope."

Sway and Tawny step out of the clubhouse as I'm finishing up. Since I hadn't been expecting the extra guests, I'm out of pins. It's something Sway might mock me for in front of everyone, so I'm glad he missed it.

"We late?" he asks, scrubbing his hand over his face.

"Just having a last-minute talk with my guys," Rock answers with a bland expression.

Sway's crew stumbles out a few minutes later, and he gives them a shorter version of Rock's speech. Tawny picks at her nails and stares at the ground the whole time.

Then it's time to go. Teller hands Alexa over to Heidi. I give Heidi and Alexa an extra hug. My chest squeezes when Alexa starts bawling.

"She's fine, Hope," Heidi says. "She always gets like this when they start up the bikes."

Rock's intense expression softens as I approach. "Ready?"

"Definitely."

I eagerly wrap myself around him and hang on tight until the Thruway, where I loosen my hold just a bit and turn slightly to catch a glimpse of Sway and Tawny on my right. Normally Wrath would be there and I miss his presence. He probably would've been bumped to a position behind us anyway as a sign of respect to Sway.

Tawny gives me a tight smile, as if I've already annoyed her this morning.

What am I going to do without Trinity until tomorrow?

About two and a half hours into the ride, Rock signals for the guys to stop at the next rest area.

Rock swats my numb rear end as soon as I get off the bike. "Don't start, caveman," I tease.

He growls and lifts me in the air for a quick spin before setting me down. "Hurry back to me."

Charlotte already disappeared inside the building, so I end up walking to the ladies' room with Tawny.

"You two are so cute it's disgusting," she says. It's not said in the same fun-loving way one of my friends would joke around with me. No, she genuinely sounds bothered.

"We try," I say in a flip manner designed to shut her up before locking myself in a stall.

As we're washing our hands at the sink a few minutes later she starts up again.

"I know you haven't been riding long. But you really shouldn't hang on to Rock so tight. It's hard for him to concentrate with a passenger who's so clingy."

And doesn't that slug me in my most vulnerable spot on this trip? As if I'm not already worried I won't measure up to all the other old ladies—some who no doubt have been involved in the club for decades.

I've never given the way I ride as a passenger any thought. Rock gave me instructions the first time he took me out and I've always adjusted according to which bike we're on and follow his lead.

"Rock's never complained," I answer with more confidence than I'm feeling.

"Well of course he wouldn't admit that. You know how our men are. Always have to act like they have things handled."

No, I don't know how that is, because when Rock assures me of something, I believe him. Maybe because he's not afraid to be vulnerable and honest with me when it counts. Something I doubt Sway is even capable of doing.

That seems too deep a conversation to have with Tawny in a rest stop bathroom.

"Besides, you're going to kill your back," she adds. "You're young now, but you'll start to feel it eventually."

Thankfully, Charlotte saves me from having to respond. "I brought the Blood Moon," she says, waving the dark red tube of matte lipstick my way. "Just in case you want to borrow it later."

I toss a grateful smile her way. "I might."

Tawny leaves and I breathe a sigh of relief. "Thank you, Charlotte."

She rolls her eyes. "Ignore her. She's obviously jealous." Her gaze darts to the door. "You'd be bitter too if you'd been married to a prick like Sway all these years."

"Probably."

In the parking lot Rock and Teller are next to their bikes talking while the rest of the guys are off smoking and razzing each other by the picnic benches.

"Everything okay?" I ask, sliding my arms around Rock's middle and staring up at him.

"He's trying to avoid the nicotine high. Since he quit years ago, he only gets the urge to smoke on the way to National," Teller answers.

Rock scowls at him and Teller holds up his hands. "Just a guess."

Charlotte covers Teller's mouth with her hand. "I thought we'd talked about this brain-to-mouth thing?" she murmurs, pulling him away from us.

"*Are* you nervous?" I ask once they're out of earshot.

Rock stares at me for a few seconds before answering. "Nervous isn't the right word. More like not in the mood to explain myself to anyone."

That sounds like my man. "Ahhh, I see."

While this big party has been described as a way for all the Lost Kings charters to get together—families and all—to hang out and catch up with each other before heading to the bigger motorcycle rally in Florida, obviously it also involves a lot of club business. Preparing for this trip has given me a better understanding of how large the entire Lost Kings MC organization actually is.

"Law enforcement down there is aware of the meeting, so they'll be hot to pull us over or just harass us in general. They tend to assume everyone with a cut is riding a stolen bike. Don't be surprised if we get stopped a bunch of times."

"I kind of figured from things Murphy's said and your warning lecture before we left."

"I want you with me as much as possible. If I'm needed somewhere, Z's gonna be looking out for you and if he can't, Birch will. You and the girls stick together when we're in church."

"We will. Trinity already scoped out a spa down there."

His mouth tips into an interested smile. "Did she?"

"Mmmhmm." I nuzzle against his chest and we stand there like that for a few relatively quiet moments before Z comes over to heckle us.

Rock jerks his chin toward the picnic area. "They done fucking around?"

"Yeah. Let's fire 'em up."

Shaking his head, Rock climbs on his bike and I situate myself behind him. I practice sitting back with my hands on my legs the way I've seen Tawny ride, but it feels weird and unnatural.

"What're you doing?" Rock shouts over the deafening rumble of his bike.

"I don't want to distract you!"

He throws me a what-the-fuck face over his shoulder.

I place my hands on his hips and he moves them to where I usually hang on.

Across the parking lot, I catch Tawny staring at us. She shakes her head as she straps on her helmet.

"You all right?" Rock asks.

"Yup."

Mad at myself for letting Tawny rattle me, but otherwise everything's perfect.

I catch Tawny glaring my way again, and this time I lift my hand. There's only one finger I actually want to flip her way, but I behave and wiggle my fingers at her in a carefree manner instead.

Then hang on tight to my man.

ROCK

STUMP'S CLUBHOUSE IS in a festive mood when we arrive. It's almost dark and the prospects at the gate hurry to open it as we approach.

It's Stump's son, Chaser, who greets us outside. "Long time, man. Good to have you."

"Thanks."

He greets Hope the same way and she immediately seems to relax.

Chaser's wife, Mallory, gives Hope a big hug. They've met less than a handful of times, but Mallory's always been a good hostess. If she hadn't grown up as the daughter of a mob boss, I'd say she's a lot like Hope.

Chaser moves on to say hello to Sway and Z ambles up next to me.

"Christ, Mallory's still smokin' hot," he mutters as he watches the girls talk.

"Are you trying to get yourself killed tonight?"

"Come on. The term MILF was created for her."

I slap my palm against his shoulder, pushing him back to get his full attention. "Keep your eye on *our* girls tonight, please."

"Who's watching your back?"

"Teller."

He nods, not insulted that I'm asking him to look out for the girls instead of standing next to me discussing club business. Not that Z won't do plenty of that too.

All of our attention is drawn to a black stretch Navigator pulling into the parking lot.

"What the fuck?" Z mutters. Teller and Dex wander over with similar questioning expressions.

I can take a guess who's going to step out of the limo, but I wait with my mouth shut.

"Oh!" Mallory turns and hurries over to the car.

Two overly muscled goons jump out as if they pulled up to a red-carpet movie premier, instead of a midlevel outlaw motorcycle club in the backwoods of western New York.

Goon number one opens the back door and Mr. DeLova—Mallory's father—steps out.

"Jesus fucking Christ," Stump grumbles as he passes us and pastes on a fake smile.

"Didn't realize we were in for a family reunion," Dex mutters.

"This can't be good," Teller says.

Hope and Charlotte are still surrounded with other old ladies of the club and probably have no idea of the significance of this visit.

I can only assume it means trouble for Stump.

I just hope my crew can stay out of the crossfire.

CHAPTER FOUR

Hope

THE EXCITEMENT OF the unexpected visit from Mallory's father seems to change the atmosphere of the party.

Oh, there's still an abundance of the usual drugs, drunken dancing, and topless girls pouring shots. I swear at this point, I'm pretty much blind to all of those antics.

Besides the debauchery, there's an air of everyone rushing around to please Mr. DeLova. And the few times I've met Stump he didn't exactly seem like the type to go out of his way to please anyone.

Mallory also went from welcoming hostess to tense and edgy the minute her father showed up. I wish I could do something to help her out, but I'm not sure what would be helpful.

Even though we've only met a few times, I'm usually able to relax around her. I never feel like she's waiting to stab me in the back.

Unlike other people I won't name at the moment.

"Hope, why don't we go in the kitchen and help out in there?" Tawny says, taking my arm and dragging me through the swinging doors before I give her an answer.

Z sort of trails behind us, and out of the corner of my eye, I catch him motioning Charlotte to follow me.

Well, at least I won't be alone with Tawny.

It's mostly club girls in the kitchen cooking and preparing drinks. Tawny takes over immediately and I admire the balls of her coming into someone else's clubhouse and immediately bossing their girls around.

A short dark-haired young woman flinches when she realizes who Tawny is, and slinks out the door.

"Ten dollars says Sway's banged her like a barn door," Charlotte whispers in my ear.

"Ew, I don't want to even… ew."

Tawny glances over. "What's wrong, girls?"

"Nothing." I jam my elbow in Charlotte's ribs, hoping she'll keep her theory to herself.

Eventually there's nothing left to do in the kitchen. Z pokes his head in and curls his finger at me. "Your man's looking for you."

"Sway out there?" Tawny calls out.

Z's face smooths into an expressionless mask. "Not sure where he is, Tawny. Probably talking to Stump."

Tawny narrows her eyes and glares at him, but his expression doesn't change. Nor does his answer.

Eager to get back to Rock, I duck out of the kitchen. Rock's sitting at the bar and he pulls me against him. "You want my chair?" he asks.

"Nope. This is nice." I run my hands over his thighs, admiring the hard muscles underneath soft, worn denim. He cocks his head and pushes some hair off my cheek. "What are you doing, baby doll?" he asks in a low voice.

"Touching you."

The corners of his eyes crinkle with his smile.

"Everything okay?" I ask.

"Hope so."

Well, that doesn't tell me anything.

He signals the girl behind the bar to bring me a drink.

"Oh! I'm so sorry about that," Mallory says, joining us. "Dad's going to kill me," she says, and it doesn't take a genius to recognize she's referring to Stump. "I had no idea my father would be stopping by tonight."

Rock grins. "Still keeping tabs on his baby girl?"

"Ugh," she groans. "Please." She turns my way. "Thanks so much for helping out."

"I didn't do much. It was mostly Tawny."

Her lips quirk as if she's familiar with Tawny's brand of "helping."

"So, Hope, did Rock ever tell you about the first time we met?" she asks with a devilish smile.

You've got to be kidding. Here I think Mallory's so nice, and she wants to share a story about how she banged my husband back in the day?

Behind me, Rock groans. "You don't have to share that story, Mallory."

She grins even wider. "Oh come on. It's cute."

Another groan from Rock. "It's really not."

My face must betray what I'm thinking, because the smile slides off Mallory's face. "It's not *that*, Hope." Her eyes sparkle with mischief again. "Chaser and I had just gotten engaged." She wiggles her left hand in my direction and I stop to stare at the stack of pretty sparklers on her ring finger.

"I've always loved this ring, Mallory."

She studies it for a minute with a secret smile. "Thank you. Anyway, Rock here came with his mentor, Grinder." Her mouth pulls down. "How's he doing, Rock?"

"Okay. Was out to see him not that long ago. We're hoping he's released soon."

She nods and seems to collect her thoughts before continuing. "So, Rock was, what?"

"Thirteen, maybe," Rock answers.

"Well, he looked at least sixteen. I didn't realize he was younger because he seemed so sure of himself." She puffs up her chest and holds up her arms in an imitation of a young, cocky Rochlan North.

Behind me, Rock snorts, but his arm around my waist tightens, drawing me closer.

"What Mallory is forgetting to mention is that *she* starred in one of the biggest music videos that year," Rock says.

She blushes and drops her gaze to the floor. "He's exaggerating, but yes."

"And *I* didn't know she was Chaser's ol' lady," Rock adds.

Chaser slides up behind Mallory, wraps his arms around her, and hugs her to his chest. He leans down and kisses her cheek before addressing us. "Is Mal telling you about the time Rock hit on her and I almost kicked his ass?" he asks with a wide grin.

Rock shakes with laughter and sits forward. "Unfortunately, yes."

"He was a little punk," Chaser adds. "But a respectful one." His easy-going manner fades and he takes on a more serious tone. "Grinder always thought highly of you, Rock. Even back then he said you'd be leading your club one day."

Rock goes completely still and a few seconds pass before he answers. "Best mentor I could've had."

Mallory's bright smile smooths over the awkward moment and she goes on to regale me with juicy stories about her time trying to make it as a young actress in Hollywood.

"I'm going to fucking kill you!" someone screams so loud it carries over the music and conversation. The four of us turn, seeking the source of the commotion.

"Always something around here," Mallory jokes, but when I turn her way, she seems troubled.

Tawny storms down the hallway with Sway right behind her. The lighting's dim, but I'm pretty sure he's buttoning his jeans as he chases her down.

"Great," I groan.

Sway catches her arm and the two of them exchange a flurry of harsh words in front of the entire clubhouse. Conversation in the room quiets as everyone watches with wide eyes or laughs and badgers the troubled couple. Thank God no one turns down the music or the scene would be even more awkward.

Tawny pulls free and slams open a side door, disappearing into the night.

"I better go check on her." I flash a smile at Mallory, feeling terrible we brought drama into their clubhouse.

Rock hasn't released his hold on me and I turn to face him. "I should make sure she's okay?" I phrase it as a question because I'm hoping he'll tell me not to worry about it.

But he nods and gives me a quick kiss. "Thank you, baby doll."

Groaning, I push my way through the crowd and out the same door Tawny stomped through minutes before.

I find her pacing along the side of the clubhouse, frantically smoking and tapping on her cell phone at the same time. Somehow she manages not to turn an ankle in her five-inch heels as she stomps over the uneven ground. Impressive.

"Tawny, are you okay?" I call out.

At first, it seems she didn't hear me, but finally she shoves her phone in her pocket and looks at me. "I never should've come."

Think. I'm a lawyer for fuck's sake. I can come up with some helpful words, can't I?

"Go back inside, Hope. I have a car coming. I'm fine," she insists.

I take a few steps closer and lightly touch her arm. "Please don't leave."

Honestly, though, won't it be a relief not to worry about her flipping out during the entire trip? I mean, this is just the first night and look what's happened. Not that I blame her. How anyone can stay married to Sway mystifies me. Together they seem so toxic. "Why don't you come back inside and talk to—"

She settles a bony hand on my shoulder, long talons lightly grazing my skin. "I'm all talked out, Hope. Just"—her gaze darts to the side— "watch your man. Put your foot down early and often. Don't let him get away with shit."

Oh please. If I thought Rock was anything like Sway, we wouldn't be together. At a loss for a response, I simply nod.

"I know you two are still in that obsessed-lovey-dovey-honeymoon stage." She blows out a wistful breath. "Believe it or not, I was in that spot once myself."

That must have been a long, long time ago.

My heart squeezes, wanting so badly to do something to make this situation better for Tawny. Even though she either intimidates me or irritates me whenever we're around each other, the pain in her eyes is almost too much to stand.

Her gaze strays to my stomach. "I wouldn't wait much longer to have those babies. Men like ours need to fully claim their woman."

That erases any sympathy I was feeling toward her. I almost choke. *Gross.* Maybe her man feels that way. Rock and Sway might both be bikers. Might both be presidents, but they're nothing alike. Rock's shown me over and over that I matter to him more than my reproductive organs. And anyway, doesn't Tawny have two kids? Doesn't seem like it helped her marriage one bit.

Thankfully, I express none of those thoughts.

A car skids to a stop on the road in front of the clubhouse.

"Are you sure you're okay, Tawny? Who did you find to pick you up at this hour?"

"Don't you worry about me. I'll be fine." She pulls me in for a hug and pats my hair. "Be careful. I'm sorry I won't be there to look out for you on this trip. But I think you'll do fine. You're property of a Lost Kings president. Do us proud."

I almost say, "Trinity will be there to make sure I don't stick my feet in my mouth," but catch myself at the last moment. No need to make Tawny feel more unwanted than she probably already does. Or point out that Tawny causes more problems than she solves.

We say goodbye one more time before she struts to the car without looking back, head held high. Her special brand of regal biker bitch on full display. Quite admirable under the circumstances, honestly.

As soon as the car's out of sight, I sigh and shake my head.

"Shit," I mutter, scuffing my boot against the crumbling asphalt, sending a bunch of little stones skittering away. A cloud of unease settles around me and I have the strongest urge to find Rock and hug him tight. To thank him for being who he is and tell him I love him.

"Thanks, Hope." The gruff voice comes out of the dark to my left and I jump.

Sway steps out of the shadows.

"Jeez. You scared the crap out of me." Why did he wait until his wife left to make his presence known? Like some killer clown from a horror movie waiting for the right moment to pounce on the hapless victim.

Without apologizing for startling me, he moves in closer. This must be what little fish feel like right before a giant shark scoops them up.

"Thanks for trying to get her to stay and waiting with her." He nods toward the clubhouse. "Lotta old ladies woulda whipped her up into even more of a frenzy." He smirks. "Or encouraged her to come slice off my balls."

Yuck. Now I'm picturing what I assume is a wrinkly, hairy...I don't want to think about Sway's balls or... anything else.

"I'm worried about her."

"She'll be fine," he says in a tired voice. "She always is."

Maybe you should treat her better.

He lifts his chin in the direction of the road. "She tell you I'm fucking Stella?"

Taken aback by the change in subject and crude question, I pause. "Uh... she's mentioned it before," I mumble like an idiot.

Where the hell is Z? Isn't he supposed to be following me around?

"I'm not." He shrugs. "Just so you know. She's not like that. It's purely business."

Good for you? "Why do you care what I think?"

"I don't," he answers bluntly. "But I'm tired of being accused of shit I haven't done. Feel free to mention it to her next time you gals chat."

Yeah, no thanks. I have zero desire to play family therapist with these two. Of course, the lawyer part of my personality decides to ignore that instinct. "You two obviously loved each other at some point."

He stares down at me and I fight the urge to twitch. I may not like or respect Sway all that much, but he's a terrifying man. I'm acutely aware of how much he towers over me.

Slowly, he slips a quarter out of his pocket and holds it in front of my face. Flashes of light bounce off the shiny coin as he twists it back and forth. "You ever hear that saying about love and hate being opposite sides of the same coin?"

I swallow hard and try to come up with something halfway intelligent that won't piss him off or insult him. "To hate someone, you have to care about them."

"I *care* about her more than she understands."

It feels more like he's using the word to mock me more than he's explaining his feelings for his wife.

"Well, I'm sorry she's not joining us for the rest of the trip." I gesture toward the clubhouse where I really want to be right now.

"It's probably better this way."

As I try to step into the clubhouse, he slaps his hand against the doorframe, blocking my path. "You're a better ol' lady than I expected."

"Uh, thanks."

"Maybe Rock's onto something with the quiet types." He reaches out and tucks a piece of hair behind my ear. "I don't picture you screaming at your man in the middle of a full party. Bet you never raise your voice to him at all."

My entire body shudders with displeasure from the unwanted touch. Did he just insinuate I'm a pushover? Somehow, I keep my spine straight and don't break eye contact. "He's a good man."

Sway's lips twitch as if he'd heard the "unlike you" I left unspoken.

"Sway," Z barks from behind us. "You're needed inside."

Oh, thank God.

Sway nods, acknowledging Z's words without taking his eyes off me. "Thanks again."

"Sure."

Gravel crunches behind me as Z approaches. Sway disappears inside the clubhouse.

I practically collapse in relief that he's finally gone. God, that was creepy.

Z's arm grazes my shoulder. "You okay?" he asks. "What was that about?"

"No idea." I throw my hands in the air. "Trust me, I didn't initiate that conversation."

He snorts as if the idea is absurd. "I figured that."

"I was waiting with Tawny, and after she left, he popped up like some creepy-ass horror-movie clown. Thanked me for talking to her." I lower my voice. "Wanted to assure me he's not banging Stella. Like I care."

The corners of his mouth turn up and he chuckles. "They've always been volatile, but it's never exploded in front of another club before."

"I feel bad, but—"

"Don't." He gives me a softer look. "I know you can't help it." Reaching past me, he grabs the door handle and pulls it open. "Come on, Rock's probably wondering where you are."

Rock is indeed wondering where I am. I spot him across the room in a tense discussion with Mr. DeLova. His gaze lands on me and a brief smile flickers over his mouth. Some of the tension in his posture slips away.

"I take it I should stay away?" I mutter to Z.

"Can't say," he says in a voice I can barely make out over the rest of the noise in the room. "DeLova's a wild card tonight."

"And the fun times keep coming," I grumble. "Is he upset Wrath's not here?"

"Maybe. Teller's doing a fine job."

My gaze sweeps over Teller, standing with his arms folded over his chest at Rock's back, eyes scanning the room. The expression darkening his handsome face moves him closer to the Wrath end of the scary-biker spectrum tonight.

"How about you?"

"Well, I let you out of my sight for five seconds."

I press a finger against my lips. "I won't tell if you won't."

He chuckles. "Mallory was looking for you."

Charlotte bumps my shoulder. "Where'd you go?"

"To talk to Tawny before she left."

Charlotte rolls her eyes. "Drama queen, that one." She tilts her head in Teller's direction. "I'm going to jump him so hard later."

Z bursts out laughing. "The fuck-off face works for you, huh?"

"Fuck yes."

I chuckle and nudge Charlotte. "How much have you had to drink?"

"Probably too much." She hands Z the rest of her beer. "I don't usually drink at all," she mumbles.

"It's fine. We're supposed to have fun on this trip." I poke her in the side to lighten her up and she laughs.

Next to me, Z shakes his head. "Why you two making my job so hard?"

I widen my eyes and gasp in an exaggerated way that forces a chuckle out of Z.

"Are you saying we're more difficult than wrangling dancers at Crystal Ball?"

"No. You're definitely... easier. It's just..."

"He can't see us naked, Hope," Charlotte finishes what Z was reluctant to say to our faces.

He holds up his hands. "She said it, not me."

Someone turns the music up even louder, and I glance at Rock, who motions me over.

He takes my hand when I reach him and pulls me to his side. Mr. DeLova has ventured into the party, so I don't have the pleasure of talking to him.

Rock leans down. "Everything okay?" he asks against my ear.

"Tawny went home and Sway... creepily thanked me for talking to her."

He pulls back, a frown darkening his face. I wave my hand between us. "I'll tell you more later."

"Yes. You will."

That bossy tone of his turns me on way more than it should. I silence any more questions with my lips against his.

ROCK

AFTER HOPE EXPLAINS her conversation with Sway, I decide he needs a punch in the face first thing in the morning.

"I know what you're thinking," Hope says without turning her head.

"Good, so it won't be a shock when I lay him out tomorrow."

"Please don't," she pleads. "We're going to be on the road with him for two weeks."

I'll ask Z how much he overheard before I make a decision on how to handle Sway.

She taps my shoulder. "What I *really* want to talk about is young Rock trying to hit on Mallory."

I snort with laughter and pull her closer. "You heard the whole story."

"Oh, I doubt that." She presses her lips against my arm. "How come you never mentioned it?"

"Honestly, I forgot about it until she brought it up." I peer down at her. "Do you really want to hear about all the women I've tried to pick up in my life?"

"Ugh, no." She chuckles and turns to face me. "Come on, though. It sounds like a cute story."

"Not to me."

"Right. The big stud struck out," she teases. She stops laughing. "Thirteen, huh? Seems young to be so sure of yourself."

Uncomfortable with the conversation, I shrug off her probing statement. "Had already been around the club for a couple years."

"You don't talk about Grinder a lot," she says softly.

"Lot of complicated feelings there, baby doll."

"You feel guilty he's still in prison?"

"Every day."

"Oh, Rock," she whispers, hugging me tighter. I wasn't looking for sympathy, but I love her up against me. And I can't deny that confessing to her lifts some of the weight off my chest.

"Let's get some sleep. Big day tomorrow."

THE NEXT MORNING, Wrath, Trinity, and Murphy join us at the clubhouse.

"How was the ride?" I hug Trinity as if it's been a month since I saw her instead of a day. "Where's Heidi?"

"Right behind us," Murphy says. "Alexa was out cold when we left, but we stopped about halfway and she was having a meltdown, so Heidi rode with them."

"Oh, poor baby."

He shrugs. "We knew that would happen. It's just nice having them with me."

A few minutes later, Murphy's pickup slides into the lot with Carter behind the wheel. Murphy jogs over to meet them.

Today a lot of the club members have their families over, so it's not unusual that Alexa's here. Mallory and her daughter whisk Heidi and Alexa away to introduce Alexa to some of the other kids.

I finish packing my bag and Birch takes it to the van. "This is the way to travel on a bike," I joke to Rock.

"Yeah?" He wraps an arm around my shoulders.

"I get to be with my man *and* bring all my girly supplies along."

"Good thing we had the van." He jerks his thumb toward Murphy's truck. "I'm sure Murphy packed Alexa's entire bedroom in the back of that pickup."

"Thank you for helping them make this work. He's really happy to have them along."

He stops and surveys the parking lot, full of brothers checking out each other's bikes and joking around. "Some guys like club life because it allows them to escape their families and responsibilities. But to guys like Murphy, it *is* the family."

"And you."

"And me," he agrees. "National will be the same. A lot of families come. That's why they rent out a whole hotel." His mouth pulls into a filthy grin. "The dirty stuff will happen in the woods behind the hotel."

"Oooh, tell me more about the *dirty* stuff."

"I'm gonna *show* you the dirty stuff." He yanks me closer. "Gonna fuck you from here to Mississippi."

"Can't wait."

"Do I need to get the hose?" Z asks.

Rock turns and glowers. "Yeah, if you want me to choke you with it."

"So hostile," I tease, leaning up on tiptoes to kiss Rock's cheek. "I'm going to talk to Mallory. No choking Z while I'm gone."

"I'll do my best."

Z winks at me as I pass him, and I mouth, "behave."

I find Mallory in the kitchen packing a cooler full of snacks for the guys.

"Do you need any help?" I ask.

"No, I'm almost done. Thanks, Hope." She peers at me over the lid of the cooler. "Excited for the rally?"

"Sort of. Rock says it's a really big one and it could get... lively."

"That's a good way to put it. But don't worry. It ends up being pretty chill. Hopefully we'll run into each other there."

"Definitely." We exchange numbers and promise to meet up for drinks.

While the Demons are busy, Trinity gathers Heidi, Alexa, and Charlotte by the guys' bikes for pictures.

Even though Alexa yowls like a distressed cat every time she hears the rumble of a Harley engine, she seems to recognize which one is Murphy's and reaches for it.

"Yes! Oh my God. Adorable." Trinity bubbles over with excitement. "Let me take a picture of her on Murphy's bike wearing her teeny-tiny, girly cut. She's so flippin' cute!"

"Blake," Heidi calls out. She tilts her head toward the bike and he jogs over.

"What's up?"

Trinity explains her vision while she throws out a bunch of instructions on how she wants the three of them to pose. Murphy wraps his arm around Alexa and sits her in front of him. She immediately stretches toward the handlebars, squirming to touch everything within reach.

"Thank God." Murphy sighs with relief. "I was starting to worry she hated it."

"Careful, Murphy. You don't want her dating bikers when she's older," Z says.

Ignoring him, Murphy pulls Alexa close and kisses her cheeks. "Don't gotta worry about that. You're never dating *at all.*"

"Da!"

"Trin, did you film that so I can show it to her when she's sixteen?" Murphy asks.

"Sounded more like she was mocking you. A baby version of 'you're so silly, daddy.' Charlotte snorts with laughter and ruffles Alexa's hair.

"No, she was agreeing with me."

Alexa flaps her hands in the air. "Yeth!"

"See?" Murphy's smug smile makes Heidi and Charlotte crack up.

"Murphy, what the fuck?" Wrath shouts. "Rock's looking for you."

"I'm right here. Your woman's holding me hostage." His complaint about Trinity's photo session is negated by the contented smile stretched across his face.

Alexa purses her lips and narrows her eyes as Wrath approaches.

"Oh, wow. It's like she knows you're the fun police." I snicker and clamp my hand over my mouth.

Wrath's unamused gaze slides my way. "Very funny."

"Here, take her." Murphy holds Alexa out for Heidi, but Wrath scoops her up instead, swinging her into his arms.

"Eeee!"

"See, she knows I'm the fun uncle."

"Don't drop her," Murphy says, walking backwards to keep an eye on Alexa, or make sure Wrath doesn't sneak up on him. Hard to tell.

"Drop her? I'm gonna drop *you* if you don't get your ass over there," Wrath threatens.

Murphy answers by holding out his arms in a "come at me" sort of gesture. An invitation Wrath can't resist. He hands Alexa to Heidi and sprints after him.

"Play nice, boys." The rest of Charlotte's warning is swallowed up by her laughter.

"Teller, control your woman," Wrath calls out.

"I hope you got your pictures, Trin. I think the guys are ready to get back on the road."

She runs over with her cellphone in her hand. "One more selfie."

One hundred and one selfies later, Rock wraps an arm around my waist and says it's time to go.

The two clubs ride out together. Rock already told me the Demons will go their separate way once we're through Pennsylvania. He didn't explain why, but I assume it's a territory issue.

All I'm worried about is the next part of our adventure.

CHAPTER FIVE

ROCK

WE RIDE FOR most of the day and stop to camp at a spot Murphy found outside Huntington, West Virginia.

"Why does Murphy get a tent?" Ravage bitches as Carter and Teller unload the bulky shelter.

"Because I don't want my baby being carried off by a coyote," Heidi shoots back, making me laugh.

When Wrath slides two more tents out of the back of Murphy's truck, Ravage really loses it.

"You shittin' me?"

"Would you shut the fuck up and quit bitching," Z says. "Christ you're a fucking pussy."

"Are one of those tents for us?" Hope whispers.

"Fuck yes."

I expect her to say, thank God, or something along those lines. But she surprises me with, "I hope Ravage doesn't drag us out in the middle of the night."

"If he tries, I'll shoot him."

Wrath and Z get a good fire going. Charlotte passes out beer and soda to everyone. We sit around talking about the ride and what's gonna go down at National until the girls pass out from boredom.

Teller nudges Charlotte awake.

"Bro, carry your girl like a real man," Wrath taunts, showing off by lifting Trinity in the air. The movement wakes her and she wraps her arms around his neck, resting her head on his shoulder.

"He picks me up plenty. Don't worry, Teller's a proper little caveman," Charlotte assures us. "You've all taught him well."

"There's nothing little about me, woman." Teller throws her over his shoulder and marches off toward their tent.

"See! Told ya." Charlotte waves and laughs the whole way.

"What'd I miss?" Hope murmurs.

"Nothing exciting."

Our tent's small, but I made sure we had an extra sleeping pad. "Getting too old for this shit," I mutter.

She chuckles as she strips down to her underwear. "This is fun. I've never been camping before."

"Never?"

"Nope." She tugs at the flap of the tent and peers out into the darkness. "I think it has something to do with peeing in the woods."

"That'll do it."

The guys are rowdy well into the night, and I relish the idea of waking their asses up bright and early as payback.

I doze for a while only to be woken up by Teller yelling from his tent. "I can hear you! Knock it off!"

Hope bursts into giggles, burying her face against my shoulder. "I can only guess."

"What a bunch of fuckwits." I hug her to me tighter. "Come on. You need some sleep."

BEFORE WE LEAVE the next morning, I pull Hope aside. "Here. Didn't want to give you this at home." My lips curl into a crooked smile. "Pretty sure it's not legal to own in New York."

"Speaking of." She pats her hands over my cut and down to my ass. "I assume you're not carrying because we're crossing state lines and all—"

I place my finger over her lips, stopping her from asking her question. "You really don't want to know."

She holds my gaze for a few seconds before nodding.

"I promise I'll keep you safe." I don't even blink in the direction of the plain black van Birch is driving where enough weapons for each brother are stored under a secret panel.

Just in case.

"And yourself out of trouble?" she insists.

"I'll do my best, baby doll."

Clearly frustrated with my nonanswers, she turns her attention to her gift.

"Kimber personal safety... What the heck is this?" she asks, flipping open the metal tin.

She plucks the plastic device out of the tin and tilts it to the side.

I ease it out of her hand and show her where the cartridges slide in. "Pepper spray blaster."

"Oooh, romantic," she teases.

"Just in case."

"You think things will be that bad?" She scrunches her nose. "I thought the purpose of the property patch was to keep guys away from me?"

"I'm not worried about National as much as I'm concerned about Florida. There will be a lot of other clubs at the rally from all over. And a lot of phony wannabe MCs that don't follow our same biker code. I want you to have something extra to protect yourself. Just in case."

"I wonder if I could sneak this into court in my briefcase?" she mutters, plucking the cartridges out of the package.

"Got a judge you want to mace?"

Her evil grin is pretty damn sexy on my wife's usually innocent face. "One or two."

"It's not a toy." I take the gun and cartridge out of her hands. "It shoots out a red gel-like substance that burns like hell when you breathe it in. Causes enough damage to stop a grown-ass man in his tracks."

"So don't test it on Wrath?"

"Only if he's being an asshole."

"What now?" Wrath asks, joining us.

"Nothing." Hope smiles sweetly at him and tucks the gun into her vest pocket.

"That thing's no joke, Hope," Wrath says. "I shot Jake with one—"

Trinity's jaw drops. "You did what?"

"He asked me to do it," Wrath explains. "For his YouTube channel. The company sent some to him to test."

"Sure they did," Hope teases. "Poor Jake."

"Poor Jake, my ass," Wrath grumbles. "What I was trying to say is be careful, Hope. You don't want to get any of that shit on you. Make sure you hold the gun away from your body and aim it at your target. Aim for the head."

The smile slides off her face. "Hopefully I won't need it."

CHAPTER SIX

ROCK

"UPSTATE, NEW YORK!" Priest, our national president, greets us as we enter the hotel lobby. "Long fucking time, brother." He pulls me in for a quick hug and slap on the back.

Here we go with the "haven't seen you in a while" bullshit.

"Who's this?" he asks as he eyes my wife up and down. Not in a disrespectful way. More of a curiosity. Which is a relief because I don't want to calculate the fine I'd face for knocking our national president the fuck out.

I make the introductions and Priest crosses his arms over his chest. "Valentina's around here somewhere. She'll entertain the girls when we sit down for business."

Can't wait. I'm sure Hope will be eager to get grilled by the national president's wife too.

I glance at her, but she seems calmer than she's probably feeling. Priest's a scary old bastard. Has been ever since I've known him, and taking the seat at the head of the national board didn't make him any cuddlier. But he's always been soft with the ladies and talks easily with Hope about our ride down. One of our old presidents might've asked her to fetch him a beer, but that's never been Priest's style. Fetching beers is what prospects are for.

"Very nice to meet you, Hope. I'm sure we'll talk more later." He glances at me. "Go get settled. Meet us down here at five."

"All right."

I check with Wrath before leading Hope upstairs. She's bright-eyed and buzzing with nervous energy. "Who knew outlaw bikers held a convention like this." She places her hands on her hips. "I find it hard to believe there won't be a single muffler bunny, though."

"Oh, they'll show up. Don't worry. Just because we didn't bring any doesn't mean others left them behind." I give her a more serious appraisal. "Sure you're okay with this?"

"I'm great. It'll be nice to meet other experienced old ladies besides Tawny. I like Mallory a lot, but she's part of a different club, so I'm not totally comfortable talking with her."

"Same rules apply here. Don't talk about shit I tell you with anyone. King's ol' lady or not."

Her face scrunches into a pissy expression that I probably enjoy too much. "Gee, that hadn't occurred to me."

"Especially Valentina."

She rolls her eyes. "I figured."

"Get over here."

She thrusts her chin up. "No."

"Don't mess with me right now. I don't have time to fuck you properly."

"Then do it improperly," she sasses back. She grabs her stuff and dashes for the bedroom, knowing I can't resist chasing her down.

PINNING MY WIFE to the shower wall and fucking the hell out of her was the only way to prepare for this meeting.

I'm certainly calmer.

This is just a brief introductory meeting where Priest and the other board members will lay out their expectations for the weekend.

Numbers. Recruitment.

I'm sure that will come up a lot.

All the patched members fill up one huge meeting room. Wrath, Z, and I end up toward the front of the room against the right wall.

Wrath leans down. "Blink's already given me the heads-up he wants a private sit-down."

"How fun for you."

His mouth twists in annoyance. Yeah, Wrath enjoys being told what to do about as much as I do. But an invitation from the national sergeant at arms can't exactly be ignored.

"I'm sure I'll get my own grilling from Priest. So don't feel too special."

"Niner's looking old." Z bumps me with his elbow and jerks his chin toward our national vice president. "Betcha he's planning to retire soon and Priest'll be looking for a replacement. Prez of the most successful charter's where he'll probably start."

I growl out my irritation at what Z's implying. "I'm not going anywhere."

Priest slams down his gavel and the room falls silent. He remains quiet, which is a good sign that this meeting will be as short as he promised.

"First, I need to give everyone a heads-up. Not that you'll be leaving the property much or have time for other activities, but there's a heavy law enforcement presence this weekend. Came in special just for us."

A few jeers and curses from the brothers in the crowd.

"Yeah," Priest agrees. "However, we are *not* to engage. Do *not* give them a reason to take you into custody. As usual, they're gonna be checking registrations and looking for stolen parts." He levels a cool stare at us. "But I know that won't be a problem for any of my brothers. Lost Kings are not thieves."

Lots of clubs were built on dealing in stolen motorcycles and parts. Our charter has never been about that. Weapons back in the day, sure. Drugs, yup. A little murder from time to time—comes with the territory. But something about stealing another man's bike always seemed too dishonorable to build an empire on.

I'm not one hundred percent positive our other charters operate the same way. Hell help the poor asshole who can't produce a clean registration this weekend.

After making himself clear on that point, Priest continues. "Local cops have teamed up with the Feds."

Louder groans and cursing fills the room.

"Yeah." The bite in Priest's tone shuts everyone up so he can finish explaining. "They're looking to identify patch-holders in leadership positions and what territory each one of you came from. I fully expect this to spill over to ol' ladies as well. I'm gonna assume any ol' lady you brought is fully informed of how to conduct herself with outsiders. So, any fuckups are on you."

Wrath and I share a glance. "Girls are going to some spa tomorrow. Sounds like I better check with Blink that's okay," he says.

I nod in Birch's direction. "Planning to send him with them, but maybe another brother should go too."

"I'll find someone." He moves closer and lowers his voice. "This is fucked up. That's serious intel he has on what the cops are up to. Not just guesses."

"I noticed." Nothing surprises me anymore. Priest's always been a crafty motherfucker. What I'm more worried about is Hope getting picked up and questioned by the cops for no fucking reason, ruining our trip before it barely gets started.

Hope

"ARE YOU SURE it's okay for us to go?" I ask Rock the next morning.

"Yeah. Just remember what I said."

"Don't talk to anyone. Stick with Birch and the prospect from Priest's club."

"You got it." He pulls me closer and kisses my forehead. "Have fun, but be careful."

I pull back. "See, when you put it that way, it makes me nervous again."

He rumbles with laughter. "Come on, let's go downstairs. Trinity's probably waiting for you."

Trinity, Charlotte, and Heidi are all waiting downstairs with Birch. Rock takes Birch aside, probably to terrorize him.

Wrath ambles up with a prospect who keeps eyeing Wrath like he's waiting for a beating. "Ladies, this is Stitch. He'll be joining you and Birch. He's on loan from Priest's club, so go easy on him."

"Thank you, Stitch. I'm sure you planned on doing something a little more fun than following us around all day."

"No, ma'am. I'm just happy to assist wherever I'm needed."

Wrath pats him on the head. "Good little prospect." He makes a circular motion at us with his finger. "All four of them are lethal. Don't let those pretty faces fool ya."

I grin at Wrath and pat the outside pocket of my purse where my little pepper spray gun rests.

"What time are the appointments?" I ask Trinity once we're on the road.

"Don't worry, we're on time…" She stops midsentence and stares out the window.

Charlotte and I both turn to see what captured Trinity's attention. Two of what look like unmarked police cars are stationed just outside the hotel's grounds. "That can't be good," she whispers to me.

"Hopefully they leave us alone," I mutter.

Trinity shakes it off and turns her phone my way. "Ramsey, party of four, expected in thirty minutes."

"I don't even know what we're having done," Charlotte says. "I'm just excited to go."

"Me too," Heidi adds.

Trinity *hmms* as she scrolls through her phone. "We're signed up for their "signature package." Body scrub and massage. Then we'll be ready for the big pool party."

"We definitely have someone following us," Birch mutters to the prospect. Stitch focuses all his attention on his side mirror for the rest of the ride.

While we were told not to wear our property patches, Birch and Stitch are wearing their cuts. Stitch's only identifies him as a Lost Kings prospect.

Does identifying who we're with make us safer or put us more at risk?

THE SPA IS small, but neat and quiet. If Trinity hadn't arranged things ahead of time, they probably wouldn't have been able to accommodate the four of us.

Rock's warning last night that we might be approached by law enforcement has me on edge. The treatments help me unwind and chase away some lingering stiffness in my back from the ride down.

By the time we're finished, I'm relaxed and invigorated. Then I'm completely shocked when we're told everything's already been paid for.

"Trinity, you didn't have to do that," I say.

"Wasn't me." She holds her hands up in the air. "I swear. It had to be one of the guys."

The receptionist hands me a Post-it note with *Mr. North* scribbled on it. "Awww. It was Rock."

Trinity nudges me with her elbow and wiggles her eyebrows. "Maybe you should go back and get a Brazilian to thank him."

"Who says I didn't?"

"That's my girl."

Birch is waiting for us outside watching the front door. He meets us halfway and walks us to the SUV. "Anywhere else today, ladies?"

"Can we find a Walmart or something?" Heidi asks. "I need to grab a few things we forgot."

"We can do that. Yo, Stitch," he yells into the truck, "find us a Walmart."

"Who needs Google Maps?" I quip as I jump in the truck. "Just ask Stitch."

He gives me a half smile in return.

"Our friend is back," Birch says as we pull into the Walmart parking lot. No wonder he's been careful not to drive a hair over the speed limit.

"Don't they have anything better to do?" I grumble. I put it out of my mind and follow the girls into the store. "Meet you up front? I need to grab some things."

"Sure." Heidi has a list of stuff, most of it for Alexa and Murphy. Should keep her busy while I explore the candy aisle.

By "some things" I meant large quantities of chocolate. I should've grabbed a cart. I drop a bag of truffles on the floor and as I bend over to grab them, they're snatched away by a hand I don't recognize.

Slowly I stand up straight and give the man in front of me a cool look. Something about him raises the hairs on the back of my neck and I step away.

And bang into a body larger than mine.

I turn and look up into another stranger's face.

Suits and ties. That's what's off about these two. They're dressed like they walked off the set of Men in Black. It's been in the high-eighties since we arrived in Mississippi. These are the first men I've seen wearing black suits.

Feds? Plainclothes police?

By their severe expressions and air of superiority, I assume they're FBI agents.

My stomach drops. Rock explained Law Enforcement would be sniffing around the meeting, but having two federal agents right in front of me is terrifying.

The only thing I'm guilty of is loving an outlaw.

The thought fires up my temper. Don't these jerks have any real criminals to harass?

"Excuse me," I say, pushing past them.

"Where you from, sweetheart?" One of them backs up, blocking my escape again. "That accent isn't from 'round here."

If I glare hard enough maybe the two of them will burst into flames. "Neither is yours."

The first man reaches for me, and I jerk my arm away. "Don't touch me."

"Ma'am, if you're in trouble, we can help."

My jaw drops. Are they crazy? "You have me confused with someone else. I'm fine."

"You're with the Lost Kings motorcycle gang, right?"

Seriously, laser beams of death should shoot out of my eyes any second. "Who are you?" I put my hand on my hip and call up my lawyer-bitch persona. "I know you can't *possibly* be law enforcement or you would have identified yourself first."

The two exchange glances.

My racing heart slows. They're not specifically here for *me, Rock's wife,* otherwise they'd know I was a lawyer. Most likely they saw us leave the hotel earlier and took a chance. Seems rather desperate, but at least they're not targeting Rock.

"Ma'am, we're investigating—"

"Fuck. Off."

"There you are." Trinity pushes in between the two men and grabs my hand. "Time to go, sister."

"Wait, we're here to help."

Trinity stops and places her hand on her hip. "No, you're not. You're trying to get information and you're looking in the wrong place." She takes my hand again. "Come on."

My legs feel like jelly and my heart speeds up again as we practically sprint to the front of the store. Heidi and Charlotte are waiting by the door. Charlotte's body is tight with tension, while Heidi seems…amused?

"Is Heidi okay? I shouldn't have left her by herself," I say to Trinity in a low voice, hoping no one overhears us, because now I'm paranoid.

"She's fine. One of those fucks tried to ask her some questions and she pretended she was deaf. Pretty damn funny, actually. The sign language classes she's been taking paid off." She glances at the conveyor belt with my purchases. "What's with all the chocolate? That time of the month?" she asks.

"God, I hope not. That would certainly ruin this trip."

"Speaking of—" She rubs her hands together with evil glee. "—I bought presents for everyone."

"Can't wait."

We finally get through the line and pay for my goodies, but I can't shake the feeling we're being watched. Sure enough, when I turn around, those two men are watching us.

"What exactly are they hoping to accomplish?" I ask Trinity.

"Who knows."

While Heidi's still amused. Charlotte seems freaked out and keeps glancing over her shoulder.

Completely unruffled, Trinity pushes us out the door. "Don't give them the satisfaction."

Birch jumps into action as soon as he sees us, telling the prospect to take our bags and load them into the back of the truck. I take him aside and point out the two agents who accosted us in the store and explained what happened.

He flips two middle fingers in their direction. "Sorry, Hope. I should've gone in with you. Rock's gonna kill me."

"It's not your fault."

"Yeah, it is. They saw you girls go in alone and it gave them an opening." His gaze slides Trinity's way. "Wrath's probably gonna kick my ass."

"I think I'm the only one they didn't approach." She pats her cheeks and grins. "It must be my resting bitch face."

I snort and shove her toward the truck.

ROCK

MONEY.

That's what Priest has on his mind as we sit down at the long, gleaming conference table.

How much each charter makes and what percentage they're kicking up to National.

Now, my club earns well. We send a hefty regular payment Priest's way every three months.

Swear to fuck our national board is the biker equivalent of the IRS robbing us for quarterly taxes.

While it's not in a biker's nature to follow rules, I don't fuck around with our club's by-laws. Mostly because I don't want anyone from

National coming around and sticking their nose in my club's business. Teller sends our check promptly every quarter.

Priest runs through each charter's business quickly. Less than half our organization is still into the kinds of risky activity that brings long prison sentences, something I'm happy to hear. One club has engaged in a bloody battle with a rival club that's brought a lot of attention. Probably some of the reason law enforcement has been so interested in this year's get-together. Some of these guys are total fuckups and I'm sure Priest will have more words for them later. Or they might have their patches stripped by the end of this weekend, depending on the attitude they give Priest.

Unease builds in my chest as Priest skips over me several times.

Finally, Sway and I are the last presidents to be addressed.

"New York. New York." Priest turns his stony eyes my way. "Been doing good, Upstate. Expanded your territory and grow op." He casts an irritated look down the table. "Lost a business but still managed to keep out of the spotlight. Looking real good. Beat that murder rap too, right?"

This is old news, so obviously Priest wants to make a point.

"It was bullshit. We handled the cause of the problem and moved on. Now we're working on securing our new territory and branching out into some new business ventures."

Priest nods slowly. "Still a small charter, Rock. What're we doing to grow those upstate numbers?"

Technically, *we* are not doing anything about it—I am. I sit back and take my time answering to make sure my tone isn't colored by my rising irritation. "I've said it before, Priest. And my position hasn't changed. We want quality prospects over quantity, and they're not easy to come by." I don't point out that taking in any old prospect is a good way to develop a snitch problem.

"I get that." He nods a little more vigorously. "Right. No one's telling you otherwise. Lost a prospect earlier in the year, right?"

"Yeah. He was a good kid too. Big loss."

"Keep doing what you're doing. Your efforts aren't going unnoticed."

Fantastic. I barely restrain the urge to roll my eyes, and I work hard to keep my expression neutral. Just what I need—to be on National's radar.

The smile slides off Priest's face as he turns Sway's way. The tension around the table rises to cut-with-a-knife levels. Shit, as irritating as he can be, I am not in the mood to watch my brother get dressed down. And I have no doubt that's what's headed Sway's way.

CHAPTER SEVEN

ROCK

"A SNITCH?" PRIEST says with deadly calm. Deadly enough to make me wish I wasn't sitting next to Sway right now. "How'd he make it to an officer's position?"

To Sway's credit, he doesn't flinch or weasel through his answer. "There were no signs, Prez. Another member vouched for him. As soon as I found out, I handled it."

"And where's the member who vouched for the rat?"

"We dealt with him."

"Something that's gonna come back on us?"

"No," Sway answers with complete calm, as if that whole situation wasn't an epic fuckup. "The problem's been handled," he repeats gravely.

Sway's always been a smooth bullshitter. Capable of telling you something's been done without divulging any actual details. It's served him well over the years.

Seems like that's about to end.

Priest settles back as if he's about to deliver a long lecture. "Law enforcement infiltrating your club—"

"They didn't *infiltrate* our club," Sway spits through clenched teeth.

Blink, national's SAA, moves in closer, which makes me think the odds of Sway walking out of this room are not in his favor. Maybe Tawny had the right idea about bailing on this trip.

"They turned a brother. A brother *you* patched into *your* club turned on every single one of us."

This sure went to shit fast.

"And I handled it as soon as I found out," Sway repeats. Shit, if he makes it out alive, maybe I'll get that printed on a shirt for him.

"Why the fuck did it take you so long to figure it out is what I want to know."

"I thought I could trust him," Sway answers. It's a weak fucking answer. Maybe that's not fair, but that's how it is in our world.

Stitching that President patch onto your cut means you're responsible for everything that happens under your watch.

"Aside from your snitch problem," Priest continues, ignoring Sway's outburst. "Earnings have been way down." He stares at Sway with a raised brow.

No wonder Sway's been nosing around my club, involving his club in riskier activities, and trying to steal my enforcer.

Yeah, I haven't forgotten that last one.

Wrath's as loyal and hardworking as a brother can be. A pain in my damn ass, sure, but he's one of the best brothers this entire organization has. I'm probably lucky other charters haven't tried to poach him from me sooner. Although, his generally grim attitude and hatred for everyone doesn't exactly make him approachable.

Sway's a hard-assed motherfucker, so the probing questions don't seem to rattle him as much as piss him off. Let's face it, being a president of an outlaw MC means you're generally not used to answering to anyone but yourself.

He sits forward and adopts an almost humble pose. Well, humble for Sway. "Rock set us up with an associate of his, and we're working on some things."

Feel free to leave me out of your excuses, Sway.

"Elaborate on these *things*," Priest demands in a smooth, not-up-for-discussion tone.

"Weapons. High-end ARs. Moving them from the south and delivering them to Rock's guy."

Priest leans forward. "You think daring the ATF to take a closer look at your club's a good idea right now?"

The correct answer is *no*. I wait to see what Sway will come up with.

"We're airtight on this one, Priest. But I have other things in the works in case we decide to end the gun deal."

"Such as?"

"Entertainment. I've invested in an independent porn production company. So far it's been profitable."

A few whistles and filthy words of encouragement go around the room.

Once again, pussy will probably save Sway's ass.

Or maybe not.

Priest adjourns the meeting. It won't be the last time we see him. For the rest of the weekend he'll probably hunt us down one by one for more individual consultations.

"Rock, stick around for a minute," Priest commands. He kicks out the chair next to him to make it clear "no" isn't an option.

I guess I'm in for a long session right now.

Sway lingers by the door, obviously bothered that Priest has singled me out first.

I'd happily trade places with the jackass.

It's not fear making me reluctant. Priest doesn't scare me, nor should he. Compared to everything else I heard today, I'm a goddamn rock star.

And that's what's bugging me.

Sometimes being too good at your job can get you in more trouble than being shitty at your job.

"You can leave, Sway. We'll talk later," Priest says without turning around. Motherfucker always had eyes in the back of his head.

Sway shuts the door behind him.

"Sit. Have a drink with me, Rock." He slides a glass my way and reaches for a bottle of whiskey, hesitates and grabs a bottle of Scotch instead.

Remembering what I drink? Fuck, if that's not a bad sign.

"Thank you," I say after he finishes pouring.

"You're not worried about why I asked you to stick around?" he asks.

"Not at all. Figured you planned to have some one-on-one conversations."

"I'm impressed."

I wait for him to expand on what exactly it is he's impressed with before speaking.

He nods as if he expected me to keep my mouth shut.

"You're a damn fine president. Earning real well for the club, which is appreciated more than you know."

"Thank you. We're not doing anything special."

"You're humble. Maybe too humble. Makes a man like me wonder what you're trying to hide."

That he's trying to catch me off-guard isn't a surprise. I take a sip of my drink and wait. He's not looking for me to defend myself.

"You're smarter." He waves his hand around, indicating the massive wood table. "Probably smarter than all of them. We could use you on the national board."

There it is. Exactly what I'd been worried might happen.

It's not a lack of ambition on my part. It's more of an I-have-a-low-tolerance-for-bullshit issue. National would leave me swimming in shit on a regular basis, not to mention my clubhouse becoming the point of contact for every other charter. Nor do I want to be taking orders from people any more than I already have to.

No fucking thank you.

"By that muscle ticking in your jaw, you're thinking 'no fucking way,' am I right?" He smirks and sits back, stretching his legs in front of him.

"It's not that I don't appreciate the compliment—"

"I don't give a fuck about stroking your ego, Rock," he says, cutting me off. "I care about keeping our organization headed in the right direction." He points to a spot at the end of the table where one of the presidents from our Washington charter had been sitting. "On paper, they should be making ten times what your club makes. Yet, we've had to bail them out twice in the last five years. Too fucking busy stirring up a war with another club over the border."

"That's bound to happen in our world, Priest."

"You think I don't know that? I understand better than most. My point is, they don't have the numbers to take over that territory. It was a stupid fucking move that brought a lot of eyes on them, so now they can't do shit without cops in their business."

A big enough bust could ripple throughout the whole organization, especially if the government tries to tack on a RICO charge. Every single one of us knows this.

"So not only are they draining us, they're putting all of us at risk."

"You plannin' to cut 'em loose?"

"Not yet. Pony took over after Simon got locked up. Swears he can fix it." He narrows his eyes, signaling the conversation's about to shift. "You also went to war with another club."

"The Vipers brought it to us."

"But you *ended* it. With minimal exposure."

"Except for them burning down one of our legit businesses, yes."

"But that's been taken care of, yeah?"

"Wrath's in the middle of the rebuild right now."

He nods and scratches his beard. It's more of a thoughtful gesture than an itch. "You've been busy making alliances with other clubs, something that benefits all of us. Befriending Iron Bulls gets us access through Arizona and New Mexico. That was a good deal."

I shrug. "Can't fight off law enforcement if we're always fighting each other."

"Exactly. Half these assholes don't get that concept. Think being an outlaw means being a lazy piece of shit who picks fights and draws attention to himself so he can prove he has the biggest dick."

"Every single one of my guys busts his ass for the club." I crack a smile. "And they're all confident in their dick size."

He actually snorts with laughter. "I don't doubt it. I know your club's small. I understand why you want it that way." His gaze sweeps over the spot Sway'd been in earlier. "How 'bout Sway's club? Would they fit in with your guys?"

Fuck no. This is a bad sign, but I keep my passive expression in place. "Some of 'em, yeah. Why?"

"This business with having a snitch isn't sitting well with me, Rock. Worse, he fuckin' lied and tried to keep it from me."

"I didn't realize that." Don't blame Sway. I probably woulda tried to keep that quiet too.

"That wife of his is volatile. Unpredictable. He's never been able to keep a leash on her. Didn't even come with him. Another bad sign."

I don't offer any excuses for Tawny or Sway because it's not my business.

"You and I both know a pissed-off female or one ill-timed snitch can cripple an entire organization," he says. "We've seen it happen with other clubs."

And in Priest's eyes, Sway has two of those problems.

A heavy awareness settles in my gut. Now isn't the time to open my mouth. I need to figure out where Priest plans to end up with this before I offer any opinions.

"What's your opinion on this porn thing he's got going on?"

An easy way for Sway to fuck a porn star? "Don't have enough information to form an opinion on it yet."

He nods slowly. "Keep an eye on it."

Just what I need.

Since taking over the upstate chapter, I've been careful to keep my club separate from Sway's. Yeah, we occupy the same state, but we keep out of each other's business. Not that we don't help each other out when we need to, but I've never been one hundred percent okay with how Sway runs things and I'm sure he thinks I'm a pussy for the way I run my club. Since neither of us have to answer to the other, it doesn't really matter.

"We are our brother's keeper," Priest says, breaking the silence. There's fire in his eyes when he finishes his thought. "But you can only help a brother swim for so long before he ends up dragging you under and you both drown."

CHAPTER EIGHT

ROCK

I LEAVE PRIEST and head up to my room. I need to see Hope bad. Not that I plan to tell her Sway might not make it through the rest of the year.

I turn the corner, headed for the elevators, and Sway's waiting, leaning up against the wall.

Fuckin' great.

Motherfucker doesn't waste time. He pushes away from the wall and crowds into my space. "What was that about?"

This isn't a conversation we should be holding out in the open.

Not a fan of anyone in my face, I hold up a hand between us, a gesture he needs to read as *back the fuck off before I knock you out.* He doesn't advance any farther, but he doesn't stand down either.

"Not your business. I'm sure you'll have your own sit-down."

"Yeah, that's what I'm worried about. Don't fucking stonewall me, Rock. Do I need to watch my back this weekend?"

The elevator doors across from us open and I grab his arm and shove him inside. After the doors close, I turn and face him. "You really need me to tell you he's pissed?"

"And?"

"And nothing. Here's my read on the situation, he wants to see how you do this year. But I gotta warn you, he's not thrilled about anything that's gonna bring unwanted attention to the club."

"Yeah, no shit." He leans past me and jabs one of the buttons. "Those guys can laugh all they want, but I'm on to something with Stella's studio. It's posting bigger profits every month. I'm working on a deal with a friend of hers now to get her up and running too."

Good for you. "That what got Tawny ready to blow?"

He levels a cool look my way. "Who the fuck knows. She's always been like that. I've been telling her less and less about club business to protect her ungrateful ass and she thinks I'm boxing her out."

I need a minute to absorb that information.

"What's your plan, to keep bankrolling small porn studios?"

"For now, yeah. These girls have been treated shitty by other studios and don't wanna work with 'em anymore. But they still have a big enough following to make some money. They just need a little assistance." He cocks his head. "Besides, you seem to have the weed trade covered."

The bitterness in his tone pisses me the hell off. No one's ever stopped him from running a similar operation. He and his crew just don't want to put in the work.

"What're you talking about? There's room to expand in your end of the state. I've offered to send Sparky down to help you set up."

"I don't got anyone on my crew as dedicated as Sparky."

And whose fault is that?

"I wanna build up my own thing, Rock. It's legitimate and will keep us out of trouble."

"Then run with it."

"I'm trying."

The elevator dings and stops on Sway's floor. I nod to him. "I'll catch you at the pool party later."

He stares at me for a few seconds before nodding.

As soon as the doors close, I spear my fingers through my hair and jab the button for my floor.

I *really* need to see my girl.

Hope

I CAN ONLY describe Rock as *grim* as he returns from his president's meeting. I don't have any notions about it being a polite corporate retreat sort of sit-down. My mind conjured up beer, cigarettes, topless waitresses, and maybe a beating or two being given out. Hopefully to Sway.

Rock's humorless laugh when I describe my version doesn't ease my anxiety.

"Maybe back in the day. Now it resembles more of a corporate meeting. Only with leather and denim instead of suits and ties."

"Darn."

"Come here." He holds out his arms, and I happily embrace him. "How was your trip?"

"Quite an adventure." I snuggle into his embrace and he rests his chin on top of my head. "Thank you for taking care of everything. That was really sweet."

"Least I can do for my girl."

I tip my head back. "You know you paid everyone's bill, right?"

His lips twitch into an amused smirk. "Yes."

"Well, thank you."

"No one bothered you, right?"

I hesitate and Rock rests his hands on my shoulders, gently pushing me back so he can see my face. "Hope? No one bothered you, right? Birch and the prospect took care of you?"

"Yes. Birch and Stitch did their jobs. We stopped at the store, though, and two plainclothes cops tried to talk to me in the candy aisle."

"The candy—what? Start from the beginning."

I relay what isn't that much of a story. "They tried to talk to Heidi and Charlotte too, I guess."

"Goddammit. Birch was supposed to—"

"Don't be mad at him. He couldn't be with all four of us at once the whole entire time. And what are you going to do, send four guys to the supermarket with us? Seems impractical."

He growls, a pissed-off, frustrated sound, and yanks his cell phone out of his pocket.

"Please don't yell at Birch."

"I'm not. Not yet anyway. I'm checking in with Wrath."

"Oh."

Their conversation is short and tense. When Rock hangs up, he seems a little less stressed.

"We're only here for two more days. I don't want you leaving the hotel unless you really need—"

"I won't. I'm all set now."

He blows out a relieved breath. "Good. I'm so sorry, baby doll. You shouldn't have to worry about shit like that."

I wrap my fingers around his bicep and squeeze. "It's not a big deal. More than anything, I was offended by their assumption that I needed their help." I point to the three blue grocery bags on the dresser. "I mean, I was buying my weight in chocolate, not exactly a damsel in distress."

"Any of that chocolate the kind I can smear on your body and lick off?"

"No." I take a step back and strike a pose for him. "Besides, I'm all polished and glowy and you didn't even notice."

"Oh, I noticed. You're fucking beautiful. Kinda wish we were back on our honeymoon island. All alone."

"Mmm, me too. Five-year anniversary trip, right?"

"Right," he agrees, sealing the promise with a kiss.

"Everything go okay for you?" I ask.

He doesn't tense up or mutter "club business" like I expect. Instead, he's quiet for a few seconds. "Yeah," he finally answers. "Got *recognized* for my club doing well and *reminded* that we need to add some prospects."

"Oh," I breathe out, startled Rock actually shared that much information with me. "It can't be easy to find people you can trust who are willing to sacrifice so much time to prospect for the club."

"Exactly." He blows out a breath. "I like things small. More like a family than a business. But I can't deny we're spread thin at times too."

"Makes sense," I whisper, not wanting to say too much and break the spell.

"As far as Sway, he came damn close to getting that beating you were daydreaming about." His mouth twists in a pained smile before slipping away. "Need to help that fucker some before he gets voted out or worse."

I'm conflicted about voicing what I think is bothering him. "You feel… guilty that you were congratulated while he was criticized?"

He sucks in a deep breath, eyes widening as if he hadn't quite realized that's how he felt about the situation. "Something like that."

"You can say you're a filthy biker all you want, but I know who you are, Rock." I rest my palm over his heart. "You're a smart businessman. Clever." I peek up at him from under my lashes. "Ruthless when you need to be. I understand the club is a brotherhood, but don't ever regret your successes because someone else can't compete. You're smarter and work harder than anyone I know."

"Regret isn't the right word, but I understand what you're saying. Thank you, baby doll."

I still don't think I expressed the right words. "You're fair and humble. You know when to speak and when to observe. You're good at what you do, but you give credit where it's due and that's the mark of a true leader. It's why your brothers respect you so much and why others will resent you. It's not sycophantic allegiance you've earned from your brothers. It's genuine loyalty and respect."

He frames my face with his hands and places a soft kiss on my forehead. "Where were you twenty years ago?" he mutters. "I would've been ruling the world by now if I'd had you by my side."

I turn my head and rub my lips against the underside of his wrist. "Well, I was in high school, so you probably would've ended up in *jail*, not supreme ruler of the universe."

He chuckles.

"Besides, a big badass biker like you wouldn't have even noticed the quiet, nerdy girl in the corner."

He rubs his thumb over my cheek. "I would've noticed you no matter what. I bet you were just as beautiful back then."

"Somewhere I have picture proof that's not the case. But thank you."

CHAPTER NINE

Rock's phone vibrates in his pocket and he groans. Reaching to grab it, he shakes his head and apologizes.

"What?" he barks into the phone. His gaze slides to me and he gives me a quick smile. "Now? Yeah, all right."

He hangs up and tosses the phone on the dresser. "That was Z. We're needed downstairs at the pool."

"For?"

"Family fun splash time? I don't fuckin' know."

"Good thing I brought a bathing suit."

Finally, I'm rewarded with a smile from him. "You have my full attention."

"Don't get too excited, it's a pretty conservative one-piece."

"Good," he growls. "Don't want you showing off for anyone but me."

"Trust me, neither do I."

He narrows his eyes and I shake my head. "I'm not putting myself down. I'm saying the only male attention I want is yours." I wave my hand at the door.

"Believe me, you have it."

Rock recently mentioned he liked me in purple. More specifically a dark purple bralette I like to wear at home. But the second I spotted this swimsuit hanging from the rack at Macy's, I knew it would be perfect for our trip.

"Give me a few seconds." He digs through his own bag while I slip into the bathroom.

After wriggling into the suit, I decide maybe conservative wasn't the right word. Compared to the outfits a lot of the girls who visit the clubhouse wear, this seemed positively matronly. Now, I'm not so sure.

Rock stares at me when I strut out of the bathroom, stopping to pose in the doorway for him.

"You're stunning." He crosses his arms over his chest and cocks his head. "That's your idea of conservative?"

"Well, it has a sarong that goes with it." I wrap the sheer purple scarf around my waist and tie a knot at my hip.

"It's not your bottom half I'm worried about."

The crochet suit has a high neck, but the woven material is almost see-through down the center and at the sides, giving it the illusion of being more sheer than it actually is. The back is mostly open with double ties that meet in the middle.

Ignoring the look he's giving me, I turn and point to the back. "Tie me up?"

He groans. "I want to tie you up all right. To that bed. While I spank your ass for torturing me and fuck you until you can't walk."

I cover my mouth with my hand to stifle my giggles. "Missing our fun room already?"

"Fuck, yes I am."

Heat from his body sears my back as he presses closer. He drags the ends of the ties over my shoulder leaving goose bumps behind. "Most of your back is bare." He strokes from my neck, down between my shoulder blades, stopping to press two fingers into my lower back, right above my butt. "I can almost see those cute little dimples I love so much."

"I don't have dimples."

"Yes you do." He presses against the spot harder. "Sexy as fuck. Gives me a nice target."

A soft moan slips out of me. "I love your filthy mouth."

"I want to put my filthy mouth on every pretty part of you." He reaches past me and picks up a bottle of sunscreen. "You feel so soft and silky. Shouldn't be putting my big, rough paws on you."

"I love those big, rough hands all over me."

He groans and tugs at my ponytail. "Pull your hair all the way up so I can get your back. I can't have my girl getting sunburned." He traces his finger between my shoulder blades making me shiver. "So soft, and delicate."

"Thank you," I whisper.

He takes his time rubbing the sunscreen into my skin, making sure not to miss an inch, knowing I'll burn before I ever tan. "All done," he finally says after working his way down my legs.

"Your turn."

He's patient while I give him the same treatment. When we're both coated, he pops the bottle in my tote bag, adds a towel, and a few other items, then holds out his hand. "Sooner we make an appearance, the sooner we can escape."

Downstairs my concerns about my suit being too revealing vanish. The outfits on the other ol' ladies are skimpy enough to make me feel like I'm wearing a parka.

Where the hell is Trinity? I scan the area and fail to find her bright blonde and blue hair anywhere. She also bought a one-piece, so at least I won't feel so out of place next to her.

Rock surveys the vast pool and picnic area with a bland expression I can't read behind his sunglasses.

"Does the owner of the smallest suit win a prize or something?" I mutter.

He laughs and shakes his head. "Z said they had a picnic table in the shade, in the far corner. Let's circulate first."

Goodie, just what I want to do.

But that's what I'm here for, so I follow Rock as he stops to greet members from other charters and their wives or old ladies.

One thing these women don't lack is self-confidence. Most are bubbly and welcoming as if I'm a long-lost sister instead of a stranger among family. It helps me pull the stick out of my ass and relax.

Since there's so much skin on display, I take the opportunity to admire the "property of" tattoos some women have branded across their backs. The small "Mrs. North" on my hip, doesn't seem so daring now.

"That something that interests you?" Rock asks against my ear.

His smooth, raspy voice heats me more than the sun beating down on us. "Maybe." I move my hair to the side and tap a spot on the back of my neck. "Something smaller, though. Maybe right there."

He makes a low, growly sound of approval and scoops me up, raining kisses over my neck and shoulder. "You surprise me every day, woman."

"Here he is," someone rumbles behind us.

Rock gently sets me down and takes my hand, turning us to face the national president. "Hello again, Mrs. North. Having a good time?" he asks.

"Oh yes. The hotel is lovely. It's great that you're able to rent the whole place for everyone." Nerves makes my cheeks heat up and I shut my mouth before I continue babbling.

Priest doesn't seem to mind. He nudges the woman at his side forward. "I wanted to introduce you to my wife, Valentina."

Valentina. A perfect name for the statuesque beauty. Long, sleek, black hair falls to her waist, and even though she's already a tall woman, she's wearing stilettos, without so much as a wobble, that I'd break my neck in. Her warm smile highlights bronzed cheeks as she pushes her large mirrored sunglasses up to rest on top of her head. While she doesn't seem as terrifying as Tawny, that doesn't make me any less leery of her intentions.

We share some introductory small talk before Priest asks Rock if they can locate Z and speak privately.

Ask is stretching it. What Priest issues is more of an order.

Valentina smiles as our husband's walk away, then turns her inquisitive copper eyes my way.

"You two haven't been married long, right?" she asks.

"We just celebrated our two year anniversary."

"Ah, nice anniversary trip," she says with enough sarcasm to make me warm up to her a whole lot more.

"It's been fun so far."

A little girl runs up and wraps her arms around Valentina's legs, begging her to go in the pool with her.

"Later, Mina. Grandma is busy right now."

Grandma? Holy shit. She certainly doesn't look old enough to be a grandmother.

Don't you dare say that out loud.

"But later this afternoon I'm all yours," she promises the little girl.

Mina only pouts for a second before racing off to play with other children around her age.

Valentina straightens up and smiles. "She'll either keep me young or be the death of me."

I chuckle but don't have a lot to offer on the subject. She takes my arm and leads me around the edge of the pool. I'm introduced me to several old ladies from around the country, giving me an even better idea of how large the Lost Kings really are. Somehow I magically keep my foot out of my mouth.

"How do you like upstate New York?" Valentina asks when we're alone again.

"Oh, I love it except for the summers and winters." I consider her question again. "Did you mean the geography or the club?"

She smiles. "Both." Her gaze searches the crowd before landing on

Rock, Z, and Priest. "My husband says Rock is national board material."

"Oh." I'm not sure what to say. "That's good."

"Our clubhouse isn't far from here. Hopefully there will be time for you to visit before the end of the weekend."

"Oh, sure."

"The national meeting usually takes place near wherever the president's club is based."

"Oh." God, I sound like a moron. Surely I can come up with a better answer. "That must mean a lot of work for you."

"It means more people stopping by. But this." She raises her hands to indicate the hotel. "The board plans this out."

Across the patio, I catch Trinity and try to wave her over. She smiles and nods before turning back to her conversation with Charlotte.

Wench.

"That's our SAA's wife," I explain.

"You're close?"

"With Trinity? Oh yes."

"That's good." She glances around the pool area. "We have our own sisterhood, right? Whether we like each other or not, we have each other's backs. But it's easier if we get along."

"There are only four of us, so we're pretty tight."

"Good. I like to hear that."

While she's pleasant about it, I can't help feeling that Valentina's judging me. Assessing whether I'm fit to be the wife of a national board member.

Just when I thought I was getting the hang of my current role.

So many questions run through my head. How long has she been married to Priest? How long has he been national president? How the fuck is she the most wrinkle-free grandmother I've ever seen? Stuff like that.

Wrath stops by and nods to Valentina. "Good to see you," he says in probably the most pleasant voice I've heard Wrath use with someone outside of our clubhouse.

"Been a while," she answers. "Good to be here and see everyone."

He rests his arm on my shoulders, giving me a reassuring squeeze that I appreciate more than he probably realizes. "You seen Trin?"

I point over my shoulder. "She was over that way with Charlotte a little while ago."

"See you ladies later."

After he's gone Valentina nods in approval. "You have the other members' respect."

"Well, Wrath hazed me pretty good at first. He didn't like that I was a lawyer." Shoot, maybe I shouldn't have said that? "Actually, I think he just didn't like me in general," I add because I'm pretty sure that's true too.

"That's his job. Protect the club and his brothers from outsiders." She stops and allows her gaze to wander over the crowd, before returning to me. "Priest's brothers gave him shit about me back in the day."

"So, it's customary?"

"No. I'm half-Mexican and they didn't care for that," she states plainly.

What the … how the heck do I respond to that? Everything I come up with in my head sounds stupid and useless. It hasn't escaped my notice how women are treated in this world, but I've never given a lot of thought to how much harder it might be for women of color.

My brain blanks on any sort of intelligent response. "But you won them over?" I say to fill the silence.

Her lips curl up. "Not exactly. Priest shot one of the brothers in the foot for calling me a *border bunny* among other colorful terms. It seemed to do the trick."

"Oh. Wow." I cover my mouth with my hand and laugh. "That's effective."

"I still get the occasional *hola, momacita* thrown at me." She shrugs. "A hard stare and firm 'fuck off' usually works."

"Damn, you're brave."

Her face hardens, losing the girls-getting-to-know-each-other look of a few seconds ago. "Don't engage, don't apologize, don't take any shit, Hope."

"The three D's?"

She smiles again. "You got it."

CHAPTER TEN

Hope

PRIEST RETURNS ROCK to me an hour or so later. Valentina takes her husband's arm and waves, promising to catch up with me again later.

"How'd that go?" Rock asks, watching them walk away.

"I like her. She's a lot less terrifying than Tawny," I whisper. Lifting my gaze, I stare him straight in the eyes. "Although I do have some questions for *you* when we're alone later."

The corner of his mouth twitches. "I can only imagine."

"Let's go find Heidi. I want to see how Alexa likes the pool."

He takes my hand and we move closer to the pool, finding Heidi in the shallow end with Alexa in her arms.

"She seems to like it," I call out to get Heidi's attention.

"Yayayaya!" Alexa babbles, reaching for my hand. Heidi floats her over to us and I playfully splash some water at them. Alexa squeals and slaps her hands in the water even faster.

"Have you seen Murphy?" Heidi asks. "He was worried she'd be scared of the water, but she's loving it."

"He's on his way," Rock assures her.

Heidi turns and points to a table in the corner. "We set up over there. Charlotte and Trinity are around somewhere. Wrath returned from where all the other Wraths went." She grins at her joke about the SAA meeting. "I'm not sure where my brother is."

We bump into Teller and Murphy on our way to the table.

"Oh my fuck, is that Heidi?" Murphy stops in his tracks, staring slack-jawed at Heidi as she carries Alexa out of the pool and over to a small group of women with children about Alexa's age.

"What the fuck is she wearing?" Teller grumbles.

I scowl up at him. "A suit that she looks lovely in."

"Did you do this to her, Hope?" he asks.

"Yup. She's almost twenty, Teller. What would you like her to wear to a pool party? A bag?"

He sweeps his gaze over me. "You're covered."

"Watch yourself," Rock growls from behind me.

I fix my stink-eye stare on Teller. "I'm also thirty-something." *Dip-shit.* "Don't make me tell Charlotte you're giving Heidi a hard time," I warn.

He laughs but doesn't have a chance to respond before Murphy slaps his arm.

The look on Murphy's face is all possessive, protective male who's not fucking around as he beckons Teller closer. "She's still self-conscious since having Alexa," he explains in a low, threatening voice. "So if you say one damn thing about what she's wearing, I will seriously fuck you up."

Teller blinks and stares at his best friend while I bite my lip and try not to laugh.

"I'm not joking," Murphy adds.

Teller holds up his hands. "Okay. Okay. I'll just pretend my baby sister's not on display in front of the entire organization. No problem, bro."

"Fuck off."

"Murphy." I grab his arm and pull him closer before he hauls off and punches Teller. I lean up on tiptoes. "I know Carter's busy, so bring

90

Alexa over to us. We'll watch her for the afternoon so you two can have some grown-up alone time if you want."

Murphy hesitates. "You sure you don't mind? Don't you want your own alone time?"

"We had alone time earlier and I'm sure we'll have more later."

Teller groans, but Murphy's already stalking over to the pool and tapping Heidi on the shoulder.

A couple of the girls try flirting with Murphy, but he brushes them off. He takes Alexa in one arm and wraps his other around Heidi's waist.

Teller shakes his head. "Can't even be mad at him since he's so good to her."

"You just like starting trouble."

"I'm a guy. I don't want to see a chick, think 'oh, she's hot,' then realize it's my baby sister." He shivers.

Rock cocks his head and stares at Teller. "What the fuck's wrong with you?"

Charlotte sneaks up behind her man and grabs his shoulders, jumping up to kiss his cheek. "Were you checking out girls?"

He turns and sweeps her into his arms, staring down at her. "No, I was looking for *you*."

Charlotte throws her head back laughs. "It's all good. You can tell me the truth. Found a couple guys who fill out their shorts quite nicely for me to look at too."

Now she has Teller's full attention. "That right?"

They take off for the pool, teasing each other while Rock and I shake our heads.

"She's probably the best thing that ever happened to him," Rock says.

"I love that she gives it right back to him." I watch them playfully teasing each other for a few seconds. "He's good for her too, I think."

"It's like having children who never grow up and leave," he says. He's smiling, though.

I lean against him and pat his chest. "You're a proud papa watching over all his cubs, aren't you?"

He snorts. "Want to go for a swim?"

I peer up at him. "Honestly, all I can think about is how many kids have probably peed in that pool already today."

He rumbles with laughter. "Me too."

In a lower voice, I add, "I will happily climb in our little Jacuzzi tub with you later, though."

"It's a date."

A few minutes later, Rock's giving me a what-did-you-get-us-into look when Murphy drops a dripping wet Alexa in his lap.

"I'll send Carter down to grab her," Murphy promises.

"We're fine," I answer, waving him away. Rock glances at me as if he had another answer in mind.

"I feel bad Carter has to be the babysitter for the whole trip."

"I think he knew what he was signing up for," Rock says.

LATER IN THE evening, it's a few degrees cooler, but the thick humidity continues to cling to the air.

"The hotel has an adult pool. Want to check that out?" Rock asks.

We were in such a hurry to make it to dinner, I left my swimsuit on under my dress. "Sure."

I follow him to a secluded pool in the shadows of the maze-like hotel. Lush bushes with large pink blooms surround the wrought iron fence. The gate whines when Rock pushes it open.

Small solar lights illuminate the stones around the pool, throwing off enough of a glow to see what we're doing. Rock strips off his shirt and wades into the pool. Turning, he holds out his hand.

"Is it cold?"

He snorts. "Compared to out of the pool, yeah." He curls his fingers, beckoning me closer. "Come on. I'll warm you up."

He watches with a hungry gleam in his eyes while I slip my light, cotton dress over my head and toss it on the chair with his shirt.

"Can you check and make sure my room key's in my wallet?" Rock asks.

I turn and bend over, searching for his wallet.

"Very nice." His intimate tone suggests this was a set-up.

"You just wanted to stare at my ass," I accuse, turning and glaring at him. Too bad I can't stop laughing.

"Hurry up," he urges, holding out his hands again.

I gingerly dip in a toe, then my whole foot, then the other.

"Dive in, it'll be easier," Rock says. An amused smile plays over his lips as he swims closer.

The water's kissing my calves when he hooks his arms around me and drags me all the way into the water, spinning us around.

"It's cold! You lied."

"It'll feel good in a minute." His lips curl into a sexy smirk. "If not, I'll warm you up."

Breaking free of his hold, I glide into the pool, swimming for the deep end.

"You trying to outswim me, baby doll?" Rock's low, rumbling voice drifts over the water.

I turn, floating on my back, gently moving my arms back and forth. "Couldn't if I wanted to."

"That's right." He captures my ankle and drags me through the water until my legs circle his waist. "We should've put in a pool at our house." He eases me up out of the water and I wrap my arms around his neck, holding on tight.

"Trinity and I were talking about joining the Y to take water aerobics. It'd be fun to have a pool so we didn't have to leave the property."

"What about water-fucking?"

"I don't think Trinity's into that—"

"Sass-mouth." He spins us in the water faster and I tilt my head back to look at the stars.

"Uh-oh, are we interrupting?" Someone calls out above us.

Rock groans and stops our movement. The tension in his body returning automatically.

The possessive, protective way he wraps his arms around me sends a shiver through my body.

"Not at all," Rock answers in a neutral tone. I squeeze my legs around him, but he doesn't so much as move a muscle. I turn to see who's joined us and smile at Priest and Valentina.

"Hi, Valentina. Good to see you again." I hope it's dark enough to hide the disappointment on my face.

But I knew this was more of a working vacation, so I smile and relinquish my husband's attention for a few more hours.

CHAPTER ELEVEN

F OR THE LAST night of the get-together, everyone's invited to a big cookout.

"Should I dress up more?" I ask Rock.

He tilts his head as if it's an absurd question.

"Some of these women don't mess around." I toss clothes out of my suitcase, searching for the right thing.

I finally settle on a short, black flippy skirt that falls just above my knees, a silky royal blue sleeveless blouse with ruffles down the front, black high-heeled sandals and my property patch.

Rock stares at me for a second before commenting. "We should just order room service."

"This sounded like a mandatory event."

He comes closer and leans down for a gentle kiss in contrast to the coarse words that come out of his mouth. "It's mandatory that I fuck my wife."

Laughter spills from my lips and I take his hand, dragging him to the door. "We'll have plenty of time for that later. I don't want you to get in trouble. Priest seems kind of scary."

"Now you want to be on time," he grumbles. He tips his head down and frowns at me. "You think I'm worried about Priest?"

"No, but I think you respect your national president too much to miss this dinner."

He groans as if he doesn't want to admit I'm right.

Downstairs, I spot Trinity and Wrath. Without waiting for Rock, I run over and grab her for a crazy hug. "I feel like I haven't seen you all weekend."

"I know," she says, hugging me back. "You've been very popular."

I duck and shake my head, embarrassed.

"We'll have plenty to talk about when we get to Florida," she assures me.

Wrath's lips curl into a sinful smirk. "There won't be a lot of talking going on."

He lifts his chin at Rock. They do their usual silent-president-enforcer-communication thing before ushering us outside.

There's a long buffet set up outside. Four huge grills are being manned by two nervous-looking prospects under Priest's watchful eye.

After scarfing down large quantities of fried crab claws, Cajun fried chicken, pulled pork, and cornbread, I'm ready to burst.

"I'm going to explode." I rub my stomach.

"Told you we take our food seriously," Valentina says.

"Totally worth the hours on the treadmill I have waiting for me when we get home."

She laughs and moves on, checking on every member and their significant other with an easy, welcoming manner.

Rock takes my hand and tugs me toward the grass.

"My hands still have barbeque sauce on them," I warn.

He answers by licking my fingers.

"Stop, stop! That tickles!" Anywhere else I might feel silly. But there's a playful, festive atmosphere surrounding us tonight. The Lost Kings must have concluded all their serious business and now they're ready to party.

We cross the yard and find Sparky sprawled out on a blanket, under a tree where the party seems to end and the woods begin. "What are you doing all the way out here?" I ask.

He peels one eye open and gives me a serene smile. "Listening to the trees. I need to get in touch with nature occasionally." He squints and lifts his arm, lazily pointing up at me. "Your panties match your shirt. That's cute."

"Asshole," Rock grumbles, kicking Sparky's thigh.

"Ow!" He rolls over and hugs his legs to his chest.

"I meant it as a compliment, boss."

"Stop looking up my woman's skirt."

"Well, all right, then," I say, holding my skirt tight to my legs and backing away. "Thank you, Sparky."

He seems to forget about his injured leg and flashes another blissful smile. "You have nice legs, First Lady."

"I like you better when you're in the basement." Rock snarls and leads me away. When we're alone he leans over and whispers against my ear, "Why are you wearing panties at all?"

"Uh, in case one of your brothers decides to look up my skirt?"

He rears back and laughs. "Good point." His laughter abruptly stops, and he pins me with a simmering stare. "But don't get used to them."

"Stop that. We still have a long night ahead of us."

"Fireworks!" One of the guys shouts. People start moving toward the empty field to set up with blankets and drinks to watch the show.

I clap my hands and bounce up and down. "Oh! I love fireworks. I can't remember the last time I saw them."

Z stops next to us and hands Rock a blanket. He leans in and says something to Rock that I can't hear over all the noise around us. A few seconds later Z's headed toward the hotel.

"He's not staying?" I ask.

"I think he plans to watch from somewhere else."

"*With* someone else?"

"I didn't ask."

I spot Wrath and Trinity up ahead, but Rock drags me over to a more secluded grove of trees and spreads the blanket out at the base of a thick maple.

He drops down to the blanket, leaning against the tree and holds up his hand to me.

"Hmmm… this is suspiciously familiar," I say as I settle between his knees with my back to him.

He traces up my legs and kisses my cheek. "One of my best days in the woods."

I shiver and wrap his arms around me, savoring his warmth.

"Cold?"

"Not anymore."

The first firework screeches into the sky and explodes overhead sending a shower of sparks raining down. A hush falls over the crowd.

One by one the rockets burst into the air. The shoot into the sky at a faster and faster rate and a dizzying array of colors. Gasps, oohs, and ahhhs from people carry over to our secret spot.

Rock's hand travels over my rib cage, stopping below my breast.

"Rock?" I whisper.

Ignoring me, he works one of my buttons loose and teases his finger over my bare skin.

I glance around. People are everywhere. Not near us, but we're not exactly invisible.

Two can play this game.

I reach back and stroke my hand over the hardness pressed against my back and he groans.

"What're you doing, baby doll?" he rasps against my ear.

He's not going to make this easy. Without taking my eyes off the fireworks display above, I reach behind me with both hands—thank you for the yoga classes Swan—and work his jeans loose enough to free his cock. Hot, hard, and smooth against my fingers.

I shift, gripping him with my right hand and slowly slide it up and down his length.

He groans and stretches his legs out. "Fuck, Hope. You better plan to finish this."

Instead of answering, I move my hand a touch faster.

Fireworks burst into the sky at a frenzied pace, meaning we probably don't have much time left. Rock growls and pries my hand off his cock. Holding my arm, he presses my shoulder back until I turn to face him.

His hands slide up under my skirt. "Been waitin' to do this all night. Fuck, you feel good. Come take care of me."

I bat my eyelashes at him. "How?"

He wraps his hand around his cock and strokes a few times. His free hand squeezes between my thighs and he presses two fingers against my damp panties. I gasp at the sensation as his fingers glide over my slit.

"Wrap this wet pussy around my cock," he invites. He hooks a finger into the material and drags it down my legs. "You won't be needing these." I step out of them and he tucks the material inside his pocket.

With his hands on my hips, he guides me down until I'm straddling his lap. "There you go. Nice and slow."

The sizzle and pop of the fireworks above us are nothing but background noise compared to our breathing and the racing of my heart. Heat sears my skin where we're connected. I take my time, enjoying the feel of the being stretched and filled by him.

"Teasing me all night," he whispers, gathering my hair in one hand to tilt my head back so he can lick and kiss my neck. "Such a bad girl. You're lucky I didn't bend you over, flip up this skirt, and take you right in front of everyone earlier." He continues whispering a steady stream of filthy, possessive words in my ear that take me higher and higher.

I tip my head forward, pressing my forehead against his so I can stare into his eyes and moan his name.

"What, baby doll?" He captures my hands and holds them behind my back while yanking my top down with his other hand.

"Rock! People around!"

"It's dark. Everyone's watching the fireworks."

He reaches down and pinches my ass. "Stop sassing me and ride my dick."

I growl my annoyance at the bossy command at the same time fire shoots through me.

His jaw tightens and his gray eyes peer straight into my soul. He lifts one hand and cups my cheek. "I fucking love you so much."

It's not an elegant declaration, but it's real and raw, laced with emotion and honesty.

Everything I need.

CHAPTER TWELVE

ROCK

YOU THINK I'D be used to the way my heart stops when I look at my wife. But something about her grabs hold of me every damn time.

She's dead to the world. Head on my chest, arm slung over my stomach and leg thrown over mine. It didn't take her long to pass out after I brought her upstairs when the fireworks display ended.

I should be exhausted. Instead, my mind's racing. Today we head to Florida for the weeklong biker rally.

Priest will definitely expect a sit-down before everyone rolls out. I already have his okay to meet up with a few members of the Iron Bulls MC and I send a text to their president to confirm the time and location.

"How are you already awake and productive?" Hope groans and throws her arm over her eyes, blocking out the sun.

"You get me all fired up." I pounce on her, peppering her face, shoulders, and chest with kisses until she's wide-awake. "Another long day ahead of us. You up for it?"

Excitement brightens her green eyes as she flips the covers back. "Can't wait."

I pat her ass as she walks by and she yelps, hurrying into the bathroom.

While she's busy, I stuff my remaining gear into my bag and shake my head at how much packing Hope has left to do.

My phone buzzes, and I pick it up off the nightstand.

Z: Priest wants us downstairs in 10.

"Hope, I gotta run downstairs for a quick meeting."

"Okay," she calls out. "I'll finish packing and be ready when you get back."

I'll believe it when I see it.

Wrath and Z are waiting by the elevator for me. "Where's Teller and Murphy?"

"Rest of the guys are waiting downstairs," Z says.

"Well, shit."

"Ready to blow this place?" Z asks.

"Fuck yeah."

Wrath glances up and down the hall before speaking. "Hoping we don't have any followers to our meet with the Iron Bulls."

"Maybe half of us should stay with the pack and half of us take off for the meet?" I suggest.

Z raises his hand. "I'll go with you to meet them. Last time I was there, hooked up with this chick—"

"Would you stop thinking with your dick for five seconds and be serious?" I bite out.

"That's *all* I've been doing all weekend." He moves in closer. "I haven't gotten laid in days. I'm genuinely concerned about my health here."

"For fuck's sake," Wrath growls.

"You two get pussy whenever you want. The rest of us have to work for it."

Shaking my head, I count to ten before speaking again. "You, Wrath, Murphy, and Sparky will come with me to meet up with Romeo's crew."

"Yes!" Z does some absurd fist pump and I roll my eyes.

"It's not an invitation to hit on their women," I remind him.

"Yeah, yeah. I'll behave."

"Why am I not reassured?"

Downstairs, Priest's in a foul mood.

"Everyone settle the fuck down!" He yells, banging his gavel against the table to get our attention.

No one's sitting for this meeting. We're all too eager to get on the road.

Once everyone simmers down, Priest lets us know why we were invited to this meeting. "Everyone knows we ain't friends with the Warthogs MC. They run the area right outside where the rally's being held. We got permission to be at the rally, wearing our colors—"

"Fuck those fat assholes!" someone shouts.

"That's exactly the kind of bullshit I *don't* want to hear," Priest snaps back. "I gave their president my word we were only there for the rally. I will put a fuckin' bullet in you myself if any one of you steps out of line and makes me look like a fucking liar. Are we fucking clear?"

The obvious answer is *yes*. A few guys are a little too slow responding for Priest's taste.

"This ain't a fuckin' joke. Law enforcement will be crawling all over this rally just waitin' for rival clubs to get into it and we're not giving them the satisfaction. They got pigs from every agency all over the country with eyes on this. Let's make it a wasted trip for them."

"So you want us to act like fuckin' pussies?" Shadow says.

Sway elbows his VP a little too late.

Priest sweeps his blazing stare over the crowd, finally landing on Shadow. "Someone steps to you first, handle it. I'm not saying otherwise. But use your fucking common sense. We're there to have a good time and conduct some business. We're not there to whip out our dicks and piss on another club's territory." He sneers at Shadow. "You understand the difference, son?"

"Yeah, I hear ya, Prez."

I'm guessing Sway didn't leave our meeting the other day and explain to his crew that the future of their charter isn't looking too bright. Even if that wasn't the case, Sway shouldn't have a VP mouthing off to our national president in front of everyone. Not unless he's developed a sudden death wish.

Hope

"I'M MILDLY INSULTED you look so surprised that I'm ready." I stare at Rock with my hands on my hips. The twitching at the corner of my mouth betrays my stern face.

He sighs and gives me a weary smile.

"What's wrong?"

"Nothing, baby. Come here."

"Excited to get on the road?" I ask.

"Yeah. We're making a stop along the way."

I peer up at him but glean nothing from his somber expression. "You're meeting up with another club, right?"

His mouth twists in amusement. "Been talking to Sparky?"

"He can't contain his excitement."

Rock rumbles with laughter and I'm happy I managed to chase away the tension he returned to our room with.

AN HOUR LATER, we're on the highway again. I never thought I'd enjoy moving from place to place every couple days, but I could get used to this.

Maybe two hours into the ride, we pull away from the rest of the pack. Priest salutes us as we exit the highway, so I assume we have his blessing to deviate off course without him.

At first, the exit appears to lead to a country road. Rock signals Murphy to take the lead and seems confident Murphy's headed in the right direction.

We pull into a huge twenty-four hour truck stop diner and travel station. Rock backs the bike into a spot off to the side where he has a view of the road and entrance to the parking lot.

The rest of the guys line up to his right.

"This okay?" Carter shouts out of the truck window and Murphy goes over to help him out.

"I probably should've told Carter to go on ahead," Teller says, glancing at Rock.

"Nah. I'm sure Alexa needs a break too." He cocks his head. "You really think he can't control his mouth?"

"Guess we'll see." Teller grins. "He's been okay so far."

"Are you planning to ask him to prospect, Teller?" I ask. Charlotte says her brother has no interest, but I also know Rock's looking to recruit members.

Teller snorts. "No."

Wrath and Z join us. Teller leaves to check on Carter.

Trinity pokes me in the side. "I'm starving. Will you grab lunch with me while they do their thing?"

My stomach rumbles at the mention of food and I nod.

"I'm hungry too," Sparky says.

"You're always hungry." Z rolls his eyes. "You're fucking king of the munchies."

Sparky rolls up his shirt and pats his stomach. "And yet somehow I stay svelte and sexy."

"Put that away before you blind someone, you pasty bastard," Wrath says.

"That lack of muscles isn't anything to brag about, Sparky," Z adds.

"You're both dicks."

I pat his shoulder. "You look fine, Sparky."

He beams at me. "Thank you, First Lady. Your opinion's the only one that counts anyway."

Rock side-eyes Sparky but remains quiet.

"Uh, okay."

"Because you're a chick." He points at Wrath and Z, who are busy laughing at us. "Why should I give a shit what they think?"

"They're just jealous they have to spend so much time working out," Trinity assures him.

The guys must be wound up from a long weekend conducting serious club business. Murphy's the next victim of their brotherly hostility.

"Whatcha got going on there, Yeti-beard?" Wrath calls out.

Murphy looks up and scowls. "Don't fuck with me, asshole."

"Oooh! What's wrong, ginger Yeti?" Z asks.

Wrath slaps Z's arm. "Good one."

Teller walks over, carrying a sleepy-eyed Alexa with Heidi, Charlotte, and Carter trailing behind him.

"There's our princess!" Z shouts.

Alexa bursts into tears.

"Now look what you did," Sparky mutters to Z.

"Aw, come here," Heidi coos.

"Mama!" Alexa wails even louder.

Most of the guys back away as if they're allergic to a crying baby.

"What's the matter, Alexa?" Rock asks, holding out his arms.

She stops crying and stares at him with wide eyes and pursed lips, then shakes her head and rests her cheek on Heidi's shoulder.

"She didn't appreciate being woken from her nap," Heidi explains, rubbing her daughter's back. "At least you got her to stop crying, Uncle Rock. Thank you."

"Why are you thanking him for terrorizing your kid into silence?" Z asks.

Heidi shoots a glare his way.

Ignoring Z, Rock nods at Charlotte and Heidi. "Go on and grab a table. Hope and Trin will join you in a few."

Carter follows them inside. When they're gone, Rock slings his arm around Murphy's shoulder and pulls him in. "Everything okay?"

"Yeah, she's just tired."

"You good?"

"I'm here, Prez."

"All right."

Finally, the loud rumble of multiple bikes reaches us and a few minutes later, a line of Harleys pull into the parking lot. They circle the building once and end up parking on the other side of the lot. Their patches identify them as two separate clubs. One black and red with an angry bull in the middle and the other green and gold with a fire-breathing dragon in the center.

My heart beats faster. Was Rock expecting the other club?

Dex nods to the group. "Dante's brother-in-law's club is riding with them."

"He's their VP?" Rock asks.

"Yeah. His dad's the president, but he's not coming. Blaise will probably take over soon anyway."

"Legacy asshole?"

"Nah, from what I hear he's a smart kid. Smarter than his old man, anyway."

Rock nods without taking his eyes off the other group. "Thanks, Dex."

The tension's so thick, I want to crack a joke about what a useful fountain of information Dex is when it comes to the local outlaw biker club scene. One glance at the grim faces surrounding me keeps my lips zipped.

The other guys take their time. We stay right where we are. Rock leans back on his bike and pulls me against him. It seems like a casual pose, but he's coiled tight with tension and I'm aware of him scanning the area every few seconds.

Apparently we're waiting for them to come to us.

The biker at the front of the line dismounts first. After a quick survey of the parking lot, he nods our way.

"Jeez. I didn't think anyone could be almost as terrifying as Wrath," I mutter.

"Good thing you said *almost* or I'd be worried I'm getting soft," Wrath says from behind me.

I tip my head back. "No. Definitely not soft."

Trinity laughs and Wrath lets out his own dirty chuckle.

"Is that his... daughter?" I ask, spotting a dark-haired girl climbing off the back of his bike.

"No. And for fuck's sake, don't say that to him," Z warns me.

"I'm not that—you know what, never mind."

Z laughs and pats me on the shoulder.

Three men and two young women approach our group. The rest of the bikers stay behind. I'm not sure if they're trying *not* to intimidate us or trying to show us they're not intimidated *by* us.

Rock shifts me out of his lap and stands to greet the other bikers, keeping me somewhat behind him. Z's shoulder brushes against mine as he moves to stand next to me.

The one I'd said was almost as scary as Wrath, is naturally the Sergeant at Arms.

His intimidating face breaks into a grin as soon as he sees Murphy. "Gingersnap!" he bellows.

Murphy groans and steps forward to accept a big brotherly embrace and hard thump on the back from the SAA. "Good to see you, Dante."

"I didn't know Murphy had another name." I rub my hands together and let out a little cackle.

"Don't get any ideas," Z says. "He really hates it. Dante's the only one who gets away with calling him that."

"Aw." I don't like Murphy being picked on and Z seems to sense it.

"He's a big boy, Hope."

"I know."

"Romeo, long time," Rock says, holding out his hand to the other president. I'm terrible at guessing ages. Romeo could either be a well-preserved forty-five years old or a road-hard twenty-nine. It's hard to say. His enforcer, on the other hand, I peg for about my age, maybe younger.

"You need to come pay us a visit one of these days," Romeo says.

Rock nods. "We've been talking about it. I'd like to get down that way again eventually."

Romeo glances over his shoulder. "Between our two clubs, we got most of Arizona and New Mexico locked down. Your club's always welcomed."

"Appreciate that."

"Wrath, you big bastard. Haven't seen you in so long. Figured Rock got sick of your mouth and shot your big ass," Romeo says with a wide grin as he shakes Wrath's hand.

"Not yet," Wrath answers with only a hint of annoyance coloring his tone.

Another biker approaches and Sparky runs over to embrace him.

"They could be twins," I say to Z, who laughs.

Unfortunately my comment draws Romeo's attention my way. Rock wraps his arm around my waist in a proprietary way strong enough to negate the need for the property patch on my back.

"Romeo, this is my wife, Hope."

He gives me a respectful nod, but doesn't offer to shake my hand, which is fine with me. Dante gives me a polite once-over and chin lift.

Wrath introduces Trinity with the same result.

"Where's your girl, Murphy?" Dante asks.

He tips his head toward the restaurant. "Inside with our daughter."

"Fuck me." Dante's eyes light up giving him a maniacal air. "There's a little gingersnap running around?"

Murphy grits his teeth while Teller shakes with laughter. This *ginger-*

snap thing might end up sticking after all.

Romeo curls his arm around the blonde at his side. "My ol' lady, Athena."

Dante introduces the brunette I thought was his daughter as Karina. Both girls are around Heidi's age. Maybe younger.

Rock gives me a subtle squeeze that I assume is my cue to take the girls inside.

"Trinity and I were going to grab something to eat," I offer. "You're more than welcome to join us."

Both girls nod and the four of us head inside.

"Aw, you really are momma bear," Trinity whispers in my ear.

"Shut up," I mutter back.

Heidi and Charlotte have a large corner booth all to themselves. Alexa's on Heidi's lap, happily shoveling Cheerios into her mouth.

"She seems much calmer," I say as I slide in next to Charlotte.

"I think she was hungry."

"Where'd Carter go?" Trinity asks.

Charlotte points toward the wall. "There's an arcade next door."

I introduce the girls and Karina smiles at Heidi. "Gingersnap's girl, right?"

Heidi narrows her eyes, maybe getting the wrong impression about Karina.

"Ah, Murphy's her fiancé," I explain. "I think your old man's the only one who calls him that."

Karina laughs and nods. "That sounds like Dante." She swings her gaze back to Heidi. "Sorry."

Heidi shrugs but seems relieved she's not about to have lunch with one of Murphy's ex-bunnies.

Our waitress stops by and we place our orders. After she leaves it's uncomfortable for a minute. Everyone seems to be waiting for me to initiate conversation.

Charlotte stands and says she's going to check on her brother. "Be right back."

"So, what do you girls do?" I finally ask. *Please don't say you're still in high school.*

"I'm pre-med at Arizona State," Karina says.

Heidi perks up. Finally, at least they'll have stuff to talk about.

"I'm a sometimes-employed actress," Athena answers in a funny self-deprecating way I can relate to.

"I thought you looked familiar!" Trinity says.

Athena blushes. "I've had a few small parts here and there."

"*Midnight Blue.*" Trinity snaps her fingers. "Right?"

"Yup. Girl Who Drowns. That's me."

"You were good, though. Looked so real, you had me holding my breath through that whole scene."

"Thank you."

"Do you have headshots?" Trinity asks.

Athena wrinkles her nose and whips out her cell phone. "Yeah, but I don't love them." She tilts the screen to show Trinity and scrolls through several photos.

"I'm a photographer. We could try to get some beach shots while we're in Florida."

"Oh my God, I'd love that!"

Trinity glances at Heidi. "I don't have all my lighting equipment, but we can make something work."

Heidi widens her eyes as if she hadn't expected this to be a working vacation, but she nods. "Sure. We'll figure something out."

Karina moves closer to Heidi so they can talk about school stuff. Alexa reminds everyone she prefers to be the center of attention by throwing her arms in the air and squeeing.

"Oh my God, you're the cutest!" Athena says, reaching over to tickle Alexa's feet.

"Watch out! She's going to have baby fever now." Karina laughs and her friend wads up a napkin and throws it at her.

I sit back, listening to the conversation around me. Feeling like I've done my job for the afternoon and wondering when Charlotte will return.

Our orders arrive and we continue talking while we eat.

The guys are still in the parking lot. I peer out the window. How long are we expected to stay here?

ROCK

"THEY GOT A police trap up ahead, so this was a good time to stop," Romeo says.

"Your guy gonna let you know when it's clear to get back on the highway?" I ask.

He turns and glances at the biker he introduced as Luck earlier. "I'll talk to Thorn. It's his contact." Luck strides across the parking lot.

"How's that working out?" Z asks, nodding at the other club.

"We don't bite," Wrath adds. "If you want 'em to join us."

Subtle for Wrath.

"We're tight now." Romeo smirks. "But I need to keep some of my business separate from their club."

Both logical and practical. Something I've always respected about Romeo.

"Makes sense," Z says.

"Word is, the Warthogs MC is supposed to lay low for this event," Dante says. "How many of us believe that?"

Wrath groans. "We got strict orders from our national prez to avoid 'em at all costs."

"We plan to do the same," Romeo says. "Don't need the headache."

I'm not sure if the Iron Bulls even have a national board like the Lost

Kings do. Not every MC operates the same way. And since it's pretty fucking rude to probe into the inner workings of another MC, I don't ask. They're a small club like we are. Only a few charters in the southwest. Even though they might not have the numbers that other clubs have, they're known for being ruthless in defending their territory. Not many clubs have tried to go up against them and lived to share the experience.

"LEO will be all over this shit. I just got us off their radar. Want to keep it that way," Romeo adds.

"Amen to that," I mutter. "How's the grow op coming along?" That I'm okay with asking about, since Sparky's the whole reason they were able to expand their fledgling operation in the first place.

Dante cuts a sideways glance in Rebel and Sparky's direction. "Had a few losses, but I think Rebel's got the hang of it now."

Luck returns, shaking his head. "Word is we should stay put for a little longer. They got some poor schmucks pulled over now."

"Aw, fuck. They got any idea who?" Murphy asks.

Luck frowns at the question. "The rest of your club go on ahead?"

"Yeah, just left our national meeting. All our charters are riding together."

"Fuck me," Romeo groans. "Sorry, brother. If I'd realized that, I woulda mentioned it this morning."

"Not your fault," I answer. It's not. Whoever was watching the road for Priest probably should've known and brought it up at the meeting this morning. I'm just glad we avoided it and hope the rest of my guys who stayed with the pack are all right.

"I'll text Ravage," Murphy says as if he'd read my mind. "Have him check in next time they stop."

"Thanks."

"Might as well see what the girls are up to," Wrath says, tilting his head toward the diner.

Z lifts his chin at the rest of Romeo's crew. "You only bring ol' ladies along?"

I barely hold back an irritated sigh and shoot a glare Z's way.

Romeo laughs. "There's a second group coming a few hours behind us. Couple unclaimed girls with 'em. You looking?"

"Always."

I pull Z back as we head into the restaurant. "What did I tell you this morning?"

"What? Just making conversation."

Wrath runs up and choke-hugs Z, probably realizing if I do it, I'll leave out the "hug" part.

Dante stops for us to catch up to him once we're inside. "Looks like everyone's getting along," he says, nodding to the girls.

"Figured they would." My wife's a damn saint and can put up with just about anyone even a couple of teenage ol' ladies.

She flicks her eyes our way and a smile I very much need to see right now brightens her face. She sits up and waves—as if she doesn't stand out anywhere she is as the most beautiful woman in the room.

"Where's Charlotte?" Teller asks.

"Next door with Carter." Hope points to the arcade entrance and he leaves to go find them.

Dante's girl jumps up and waits for him to take a seat before sitting in his lap. With their age difference, I can't decide if they're cute or creepy together. Since I don't want to fuck either of them, I suppose it's none of my business.

As soon as Alexa sees Murphy, she stands up in Heidi's lap and reaches for him.

"Da, da, da!"

Trinity slides out of the booth so Murphy can get next to Heidi and Alexa.

"You being good for mommy?" Murphy asks, taking Alexa and kissing her cheeks.

"Oh my God, she's so adorable, I can't stand it," Athena gushes, stopping to give Romeo a meaningful look.

Once everyone's settled, the waitress runs over and we order more food.

Hope fixes her gaze on me, trying I think, to figure out if everything's okay. I reach under the table and squeeze her hand, hoping it's enough to reassure her for now.

Dante's girl and Heidi seem to have taken a shine to each other and keep chatting about school. When Alexa's had enough of their conversation, she reaches over and slaps the table in front of Heidi.

"No one paying enough attention to you, cutie?" Romeo says.

Alexa stares at him for a few seconds before turning her big, questioning eyes Murphy's way. All of us laugh and Z cracks a "stranger danger" joke.

"Teaching her right from the start?" Romeo jokes.

"Trying." Murphy slings his arm around Heidi. "She takes after her mom and does whatever the fuck she wants most of the time, though."

Everyone laughs. Even Heidi.

"That's not true," Hope says. "She's always good. Right, Alexa?"

Alexa grins at her. "Tee!" We haven't decided if she's trying to say "aunt" or something else, but it's what she usually says to get Hope's attention.

Dante's gaze slides between Heidi and Hope, finally landing on Hope. "You're not grandma, right?"

Hope blinks and sits back. "No."

"Didn't think so. Too young to be *her* mom and too pretty to be Gingersnap's mom."

Hope chuckles. "I don't know about that."

Since we discussed business outside, we mostly relax and listen to the girls talk.

"Trinity's a photographer," Athena tells Romeo. "She said she'd help me get some better headshots in Florida."

Romeo nods at Wrath. "That's real nice. Thanks, Trinity."

Wrath's expression is unreadable, but it wouldn't surprise me if he asked Trinity to befriend the girl who probably has a lot of information about the Iron Bulls.

That's why he's my Sergeant at Arms.

Finally one of the guys from the other club—Savage Dragons MC— ambles in and tells us the highway should be clear for us to continue.

Since the Dragons' president isn't with them, Romeo and I take the lead when we return to I-65. Not too far down the road, a tow truck's pulled over on the side, loading up two bikes. Whoever got pulled over must've been arrested.

Only as we pass the tow trucks do I realize I recognize one of the midnight-blue-and-silver Harleys.

CHAPTER THIRTEEN

ROCK

I AM NOT in the mood to meet with Priest and the rest of National again.

But a text went out, stating the meeting was mandatory.

The only thing I'm interested in finding out is what the hell happened to Sway and if he's made bail.

Priest and Valentina have a suite at a hotel not too far from where Hope and I are staying.

Officers from each charter were asked to attend.

It's a lot of guys crammed into one space.

"Apologize for the tight quarters. I couldn't secure a bigger space until tomorrow and this needs to be said now."

The room quiets and everyone turns toward Priest.

"As some of you are aware two of our brothers were arrested and taken in on the way here."

Curses and grumbling go around the room. Wrath and I exchange a look.

"I want to repeat what I said before leaving. Stay under the radar. I'm working on finding out what they're being held for. But we know there's a possibility law enforcement's gunning for the whole club and Sway and Shadow are just the beginning.

"Jesus Christ," Z mutters.

"I don't want anyone leaving early, unless you were already planning to. Let's make our presence known. We're here to have fun and relax. And for fuck's sake, stay out of trouble."

After the room clears to only a few people, I make my way over to Priest.

"What can I do to help?"

Yeah, Sway's a pain in my damn ass, but I can't stand knowing a brother's sitting in jail.

Priest takes me aside. "Nothing to do right now, Rock. I got attorneys for each of them, but it's moving slow. I'll let you know if I hear something."

"Thanks."

He mentions something about a party downstairs, and I nod absently. Hope and I already have plans.

Outside, Wrath's waiting. "Well?"

I shake my head. "Nothing yet." I lean in closer. "Gonna call Glassman when I get back to the room and see what he can find out for me."

"He know any lawyers down in Ala-fuckin'-bama?"

"That prick knows people everywhere."

"You still coming by tonight?" Murphy asks when we meet up with him outside.

"Yup. Hope's looking forward to it."

I nod to Z and Wrath. "Check this party out Priest mentioned. I at least want some of our guys there."

"You got it," Z says.

Hope

"YOU'RE HERE!" HEIDI opens the door wider and throws her arms around me even though we just saw each other last night. "For once I get to invite you over," she says breathlessly.

I can't help smiling at her excitement. "Oh wow. The house is really nice."

She and Murphy give us a quick tour of the small beach house they rented so they could be close enough to go to the rally with us, but far enough away from the noise and crowds for Alexa.

Rock and I are at a hotel right in the thick of things with everyone else.

"It's so peaceful here. I might come stay with you," I tease.

"You can. We have an extra bedroom," Heidi says. Completely serious.

"I'm kidding. It's fine."

"You wouldn't be imposing," she insists, gesturing toward the living room. "Carter, Charlotte, and my brother are here too."

"Hey, Carter," I call out. I haven't had much of a chance to talk to him on the trip and feel bad. I don't want him to feel excluded.

He waves and goes back to his sketchbook.

"He's been very inspired on this trip," Teller says with a slight eye roll.

"That's great."

Murphy, Teller, and Rock end up grilling outside on the patio. Charlotte and I talk about the work waiting for us when we get home.

"Is it bad that I kind of want to set my office on fire when we go back?" she jokes. At least I think she's joking.

"If we don't have that fantasy once at least once a month, we'll go insane."

"When the arson investigators come knocking on our door, I'll pretend I never heard that," Carter says without lifting his head and looking at us.

"You blend in awfully well, Carter," I tease.

"Necessary skill in our family."

Charlotte's mouth twists into a grimace. "He's not wrong."

Curious about what he's been so diligently sketching on our trip, I inch closer to him on the couch. "Am I allowed to see your sketches?"

He glances up with wide eyes. "You want to? Why?"

"Well." I flick my gaze in Charlotte's direction, seeking assistance. She smiles. "Teller keeps saying how talented you are and—"

"He does?"

"Yes. And Murphy mentioned you were working on some sketches for a mural for Alexa's room."

Slowly, he turns his sketch pad around. It's a black and white sketch of a seagull on the sand with the ocean in the background that he's coloring in with pencils.

"Sketched it this morning on the beach," he murmurs.

"He's really good at everything," Charlotte gushes. "You know some artists only focus one or two things, but he's good at everything. Portraits, cartoons, drawing, painting, sculpture—"

"My sister's exaggerating," Carter says.

"Show her the one you drew last night," Charlotte insists.

He huffs and sits up. I get the feeling Carter's not pretending to be humble, but really is embarrassed by all the attention.

"I'd love to see, Carter. But not if you're not comfortable sharing your work."

He relaxes and flips through the large pad of thick paper. "I don't mind." He stops on one drawing and pushes the pad into my hands.

"Oh wow," I breathe out. It's a black-and-white drawing of a sleepy Alexa and Heidi being held in a protective Murphy's arms. Exactly the way I often come home and find them lounging in my living room late at night. "Wow, Carter. You really captured them beautifully."

He shrugs.

"I told him to give it to them as a wedding present."

"I'll get them a real present."

"This is very real, Carter," I assure him.

"Thanks."

The sliding glass door slides open and the guys come in from the porch carrying plates of grilled fish and steaks. Carter flips his pad closed and runs down the hall with it.

Heidi carries a sand-covered Alexa inside. "I'll be right back. Let me just clean her off."

"Hose her down outside, hon," Rock says, pointing to the door. "There's one right around the corner."

"Oh. Yeah that's probably better." She walks backward onto the deck and Murphy follows her.

A few minutes later Alexa's angry howls can be heard through the open windows. "I'm guessing she didn't like being hosed off," I say, staring at Rock.

He shrugs. "It can't be that much colder than the ocean."

Murphy carries a wet and furious Alexa in a few seconds later. "Go ahead and start eating. I'll be back."

Heidi-soaked to her skin-follows him down the hallway.

Teller watches them and shakes his head. "I'm not even going to ask."

The rest of the night is a little calmer. Before midnight Rock and I finally head back to our hotel, promising to meet up with everyone tomorrow afternoon.

"Murphy had the right idea," Rock says on our way to the bike.

"Jealous that we're going back to a hotel."

"Honestly, yes."

I chuckle as he hands me my helmet. "We're right near everything we came for."

"Yeah and in my twenties that would've been great. Now, it's going to be loud and annoying."

"Do you want to look for somewhere else?"

He stops and stares in the direction of the beach. "Nah, we're all settled. Just... next time."

"Oooh, Mr. President." I snuggle up close behind him. "Are you inviting me on another road trip?"

"Baby, you have a permanent invitation for every road trip for the rest of my life."

CHAPTER FOURTEEN

ROCK

I F A GOOD woman is capable of soothing a man, a great one will only make him more wild and violent.

That's exactly how I feel when a prospect from another club not-so-subtly checks out my wife.

Three days we've been at the rally without incident. This morning we came down to Main Street to check out the rows and rows of custom bikes lined up on the street.

And right there on the sidewalk in broad daylight, some fuckwit's staring at Hope's tits. As usual, my beautiful woman's oblivious to the attention.

Next to me, Wrath chuckles. "Are we scaring him? Or delivering him to his president after a solid beating?"

"Haven't decided yet." I glance at him and shake my head at the murderous gleam in his eyes. "Feeling more bloodthirsty than usual?"

"Don't like some little punk thinking he can flirt with my president's ol' lady right in front of us."

It's more than a club or respect issue for Wrath. It's a *Hope* thing. As much as he loves teasing her, he won't tolerate anyone else disrespecting her.

Hope's strained laugh jolts me into action. My eyes narrow on the hand brushing her shoulder and the uncomfortable way she takes a step back.

My instinct to protect at all costs catches fire.

"Here we go," Wrath rumbles.

I charge forward, shoving two bikers out of my way. Blood boils through my veins. I search the crowd for Z, but he's already moving toward me. Farther away, I spot Teller and Charlotte. Thank fuck Murphy's at the beach with Trinity and Heidi today. Teller pulls Charlotte away from the crowd and I nod at him.

We reach the prospect and I tap his shoulder. "You blind, mother-fucker?" I ask in a low voice.

"Rock!" Hope's eyes flare and relief softens the tension in her shoulders. Perhaps sensing my rage, she wraps her hand around my bicep and tugs. "He was just telling me about a party his club's throwing."

He turns to me with bloodshot eyes and a serene smile. "Yeah, man, you're all invited."

My gaze zeroes in on where his hand's still resting on Hope's shoulder. She shrugs it off and steps closer to me. I can't tell if he's willfully disobeying basic biker code, if he's high, or plain stupid.

"Anyone teach you not to put your hands on another man's ol' lady?" My low voice attracts more attention than I intended. Or maybe it's the sight of Wrath, Z, and I all glowering at this one lone prospect.

It finally seems to dawn on him that he made a mistake. His gaze bounces from my President's patch, to Hope's First Lady patch, and over to Wrath. "Fuck. I'm sorry. I didn't mean no disrespect." He holds his hands up and takes a step back, bumping into Z.

"Who are you with?" I ask.

"Dark Venom MC outta Georgia."

While Hope's still clinging to my arm, she hasn't said a word to try and convince me not to choke this motherfucker. Knowing how soft my girl is, how much she hates violence, I'm guessing he made her pretty damn uncomfortable. I gently nudge her behind me toward Wrath and step closer.

"And what's the penalty for touching a brother's property up in Georgia?" I ask.

His bloodshot eyes widen and he drops his hands, clasping them behind his back.

"Dark Venom? Slick Rick still in charge?" Z asks.

"What's going on?" someone to my left asks.

I turn and take in the beefy biker with the snakehead tattoo crawling up his throat and a patch that reads Vice President.

"He belong to you?" I jerk my head toward the prospect.

The VP looks me over and straightens up, widening his stance. "Who's asking?"

"I am. Your boy put his hands on my ol' lady."

The VP briefly closes his eyes before glancing at the prospect. "You fucking serious?"

"I was lettin' her know about the party like Bobby said."

"Single chicks. Muffler bunnies, not other club's old ladies. Tha fuck's wrong with you?" He gestures to Hope. "Couldn't be more obvious she ain't a fuckin' bunny." He throws a smirk Hope's way. "No offense, darlin'."

"I'm fine, really," Hope says, not bothering to move closer. Either that, or Wrath has a hold of her.

The VP nods at me. "Do what you gotta do. I ain't gonna dispute it."

Exactly what I was waiting to hear. I spot at least two other Venom brothers in the crowd, but that doesn't mean there aren't more of 'em. I'm fully confident Wrath, Z, and I can handle it, but I'd rather not start a street brawl if it can be avoided.

I pull back and punch the prospect in the face, knocking him to the ground. Blood gushes from his nose and he covers his face with his hands.

"You got off easy," the VP shouts down to him. "Woulda broke your damn fingers in our clubhouse and you know it."

The kid shakes his head and holds up his hands as if to explain he got the message.

Hope

"ARE YOU OKAY, Hope?" Wrath asks against my ear.

Too shaken to say speak, I nod.

"Hey, look at me," he persists.

I force a fake smile and turn. Concern darkens his blue eyes, making me feel weak and vulnerable. "I'm fine, Wrath. Were you worried I was going to try to stop Rock?"

He doesn't crack a smile, because I suspect he's not at all fooled by my false bravery. "You know better by now."

True. I don't love the violence. Hate that Rock needs to make his point with his fists. But it's what I signed up for. I'm firmly inside the biker world on this trip. Citizen rules of civility don't apply. And if the rules dictate the prospect gets a fist to the face for touching me, so be it. He knows what he signed up for too. Never mind that he was creepy as fuck.

What I *am* worried about is the brief altercation spilling over or escalating into more violence. Wrath's certainly warned me enough times how out of control these situations can get. I suspect that's why his arm has remained firmly clamped down on my shoulders ever since Rock stepped forward to speak to the other MC's Vice President.

Relief spreads through me and this time I glance up and give Wrath a more genuine smile. "Thank you."

He raises a blond eyebrow. "For?"

"Having my back."

"Always, Cinderella." A devious smile curves his lips. "Try to stay out of trouble for the rest of the day, okay?"

Even though he's baiting me, I cross my arms over my chest. "I didn't do anything."

"Too pretty for your own good, Hope," Z says, joining us.

"Is that supposed to make me feel better?"

"Yes," he answers simply.

Shaking my head, I turn back to the crowd, searching for Rock. He's speaking to the Vice President of the other MC. The prospect nowhere to be seen.

"Think they'll kick him out?"

"Probably," Z says. "Not really cut out to be a brother if he can't follow basic instructions."

"So glad I could serve as his litmus test," I grumble.

Rock shakes hands with the other biker and strides away at a slow, unconcerned pace. For a few seconds, I continue watching the Vice President for any signs that this isn't over before turning my attention to Rock.

The tightness around his mouth tells me his easy manner as he walks through the crowd is for show. He stops in front of me and lifts his chin at Wrath. The heavy arm on my shoulders is replaced by Rock's. He pulls me closer, dropping a possessive kiss on my lips, almost knocking me off my feet. I curl my fingers into the leather on his shoulders to maintain my balance.

Breaking our kiss, but keeping a firm hold on me, he pulls back. Deep gray eyes search my face. "You okay?"

"I'm fine."

He's silent. As if he's waiting for me to elaborate. Instead, I take his hand, wincing at the blood on his knuckles. "Let's get ice on this."

"We cool, Prez?" Z asks, nodding at the last place the VP had been standing.

"Yeah. Talked for a minute about how hard it is to find good recruits. Small club. Don't think he wants any trouble."

"Let's go grab a drink," Wrath says, steering us toward the closest bar.

I'm still too unsettled for alcohol, so I ask Rock to order cranberry juice and seven-up for me instead before heading into the bathroom.

As I'm washing up, I stare at my face in the mirror. Despite the sunscreen I slathered on this morning, my nose is slightly pink and freckles I haven't seen since high school dot my nose and chest. I pull a brush out and quickly run it through my wild and windblown hair. This humidity has made it double in volume.

The door swings open and a short woman with spiky black hair joins me. Almost as if she was looking for me.

She's wearing a brand new Harley Davidson tank top. Crisp, clean jeans, and scuff-free boots. No jewelry, but a tan line around her ring finger. Almost like she woke up and decided to dress up as "biker chick" today.

"Hey, you're a Lost Kings old lady right? I hear your gang's the one to talk to for the good shit."

"I'm not in a gang. I'm here with my husband's motorcycle club," I answer without looking away from the mirror, where I'm busy swiping gloss over my lips.

"Club. Right. Got you." She gives me this weird, exaggerated wink. "I hear your club has the hookup. Looking for some pot and," she lowers her voice. "A little meth."

"Huh?" Granted, I haven't been privy to many, okay any, drug deals in my life, but I sort of doubt it's customary to walk up to a stranger and ask for drugs in such a cavalier manner. "I'm sorry. I have no idea what you're talking about."

"Oh. Right. Okay. So your old man doesn't like you to talk about it." She puts her fingers to her lips. "Just tell me which one's holding and I'll talk to him." She reaches into her pocket and pulls out a rolled up wad of twenties. "I have the cash."

My heart beats faster, but outside I remain calm and impassive. "I really have no idea what you're talking about." I reach for the door. "If you'll excuse me."

"Is it the big dude? He seems like the smart choice to be carrying for you."

I almost snort and say something snotty like, "Yeah, march on over to Wrath and say that to his face and see what happens to you." But I calmly push past her and grab the door handle instead. "You were given bad information."

Relief washes over me as I step into the hallway. Z's waiting for me and pushes off the wall. "Everything all right? I saw that chick go in there—"

I grab his arm and pull him aside. "Something's not right about her. She kept asking if she could buy drugs from one of us."

"What the fuck?"

"Right? It was so damn weird."

He glares at the closed bathroom door as if he's considering storming inside to shake some information out of the pesky girl.

While I'm relieved to see Z, I really need Rock. I scan the bar area my gaze finally landing on him.

Rage replaces my worry.

A whole load of rage I'm about to unleash on the woman with her hand on Rock's arm.

CHAPTER FIFTEEN

ROCK

"W HAT AN AFTERNOON." Z stretches, showing off, and takes a good look around the bar.

"Why don't you just stick a sign on your forehead that says 'I need to get laid?' It'd be more subtle."

He laughs and slaps my arm. "I'm going to do a lap around the bar."

"Wear a condom," Wrath yells as Z walks away.

Z not-so-discreetly flips his middle finger in our direction.

Wrath gives the bar a more critical look. "I might call some of the guys and have them meet us here," he says watching a group of loud-mouthed men in the back corner. Their colors aren't visible, but there's a good chance they're bikers.

"If Z can manage not to hit on someone's ol' lady, no one should bother us."

"Doesn't mean shit and you know it."

"Fuck this. I'm ready to go home."

"Best thing you've said all week, Prez."

"What happened to us?"

"Uh." He glances around. "We've been here. Done this. And it's fucking old."

"*We're* fucking old."

"Speak for yourself." He levels a sterner look at me. "I ain't in the mood to carry you through some midlife crisis, Rock. So, go fuck your girl or do whatever you gotta do to reclaim your youth. But knock this shit off."

My mouth twists into a grin and I slap his chest. "That's what I keep you around for."

He shoves me toward the bar. "Buy me a drink." He wags his phone in my face. "I'm gonna make a few calls."

I step up to the bar and order our drinks, keeping my eyes on the back hallway for Hope.

"Hey there, Prez," a high, sickly-sweet voice greets. I don't recognize the voice or care for the familiar way she addresses me so I answer without even looking.

"Keep moving."

"Aw, come on. This is supposed to be party week."

Ignoring her, I tap my fingers against the bar. The movement must draw attention to my wedding ring.

"Wifey didn't choose to join you? That means it's time to party, right?"

Christ, what is it with this chick? I turn to glare at her and find five-feet-nothing of blonde hair, and big tits dressed in black leather grinning up at me.

"Not. Interested."

Persistent, she pouts and touches my arm and I shake her off. This time she's more blunt with her come on. "I can give a blow job that will blow your mind. Best you've—"

"It's a shame a girl your age has already suffered such terrible hearing loss." Hope interrupts. Even dripping with irritation and sarcasm, her warm, silky voice wraps around me and chases away my foul mood. She rests her hand on my shoulder and presses the weight of her body into my side. I slide my arm around her waist.

"Huh?" the girl says, eyeing Hope up and down.

"My man politely told you to get lost." Hope leans forward with her face inches from the shocked bunny. "Now, *I'm* telling you. Not so politely."

The girl blinks up at Hope.

"There are plenty of bikers here." Hope gestures to the area around us and then wraps her hand around arm. "This one belongs to me. Got it?"

"Uh…"

"Nod so I know you understand." Hope remains calm and focused. My stealthy lioness protecting what's hers.

The girl bobs her head. "Sorry," she mumbles before slinking away.

"Friend of yours?" Hope asks with an arched brow.

Christ. How had this never occurred to me? She's probably wondering if we'll run into some random ex-hookup of mine while we're here. "She was probably in grade school last time I was here," I growl.

She squeezes my arm. "I was teasing."

I slide my hand down, grabbing her ass until she squeals and slaps her palm against my chest. I yank her closer and nuzzle against her neck. "Love when you're all feisty and territorial."

She leans in and hums against my ear. "I felt more *violent* than feisty when she put her hand on you."

"Your hands are the only ones I want on me." This craving for my wife never seems to lessen. I lean in closer. "And your mouth is the only one I want wrapped around my dick."

Her eyes spark with desire. "That can be arranged, Mr. President."

I lean past her, pretending to check out the hallway leading to the bathrooms. "Any privacy back there?"

"Hmm," she answers, distractedly, staring across the room. I follow her line of sight to the persistent little bunny as she chats up Z. "I think I'll lose what little respect I have for Z if he invites her back to his room," she murmurs.

I snort and take the drinks the bartender places in front of me. "Surprised you still have any."

"Aw, don't pick on Z," she says, completely contradicting her earlier statement. Love her for it too. The way she looks out for and worries about all my brothers. Even the most degenerate of them. "He came to rescue me when I was in the bathroom."

My glass hits the bar with a thud. "Rescued you from what?"

"Sorry. I was so rage-blind when I saw that girl talking to you, I forgot to tell you what happened."

I snort. "Rage-blind? You're the sweetest person I know."

"Not when it comes to you." She pats her vest. "Came close to yanking my little pepper gun out and blasting her with it. But I didn't want accidentally spray you."

Laughter rumbles out of me. "Fuck, I love you."

"Oh." She leans in, lowers her voice, and explains the strange encounter with the woman who sounds an awful lot like an undercover cop. A bad one. I don't want to say that to Hope and freak her out, though.

She takes a sip of her drink and sets it on the bar. "I'm guessing she's a narc?"

I almost choke. "I don't know if anyone says *narc* anymore. But yes, sounds like it."

"Well, she was pretty obvious. Maybe they need to send her back to narc school."

I laugh even harder and she narrows her eyes. "I'm not *that* funny."

"You're fucking adorable." I rub my knuckles over her cheek. "Wanna go?"

She tips her head Z's way. "I think we should stay with him."

A few minutes later, a heavy arm lands on my shoulders, yanking me to the left. I lean back and find Z's flushed, happy face inches from mine.

"Hope fill you in?"

"Yup. You investigate?"

"Not much to do. She went out the back door and got into a black sedan and left."

"So much for the biker chick," Hope mutters.

"What else is on your mind?" I ask Z. I glance at his other arm, still draped over Hope's shoulders, hugging her to him.

"Something ain't right with that persistent little bitch," he says, tipping his head to the side.

Hope snickers and takes another sip of her drink. "Respect maintained," she mumbles.

Z quirks an eyebrow at her, then glances my way. "Should I fuck her to find out what she's up to?"

"Respect lost." Hope shakes her head. "Easy come, easy go."

"Do whatever you want with your dick," I growl, shrugging his arm off my shoulder and knocking his other arm off my wife. "Just stay alert and out of trouble."

"She's not really my type," he says, glancing over his shoulder.

"You *have* a type?" Hope deadpans.

"I'm getting more discriminating in my old age, Hope," he assures her.

She presses her index finger and thumb together, forming a circle. "Oooo-kay."

Like the asshole he is, Z shoves his finger through the hole, into Hope's hand. She laughs and pushes him away. "Rock's right. You're a degenerate."

He grins even wider. "Worked hard for that title."

"It's not a compliment," I grumble.

Z straightens up. All serious VP again. "I swear she had a "property of" tramp stamp."

Hope rolls her eyes. I fix my "don't start" stare on her and she wrinkles her nose. While she's accepted her own property patch and what it means to my club, the idea of other clubs treating girls as communal property still irritates her. This trip's illustrated many things I've tried to explain in the past.

"If she's property of another club, then definitely stay away," I warn, surprised Z would consider being so careless.

Hope still seems annoyed and I reach out to capture her hand, dragging her closer and bumping Z out of our way. "You my girl?" I say low enough for only her to hear.

She slings her arms around my neck. "Yes."

Z shuffles a few steps away from us. "This is getting annoying."

I raise an eyebrow and he shrugs. "You, Wrath, Murphy, Teller. Got no one left to—"

"Aw," Hope coos. "You can't possibly need a wingman, Z."

He rolls his shoulders and grins at her. "No. I don't."

"Where's Dex?" she asks.

"Fuck if I know. Probably in his room sulking."

Irritation about the girl who approached Hope in the bathroom and that another club might have sent one of their girls after us won't leave my mind.

Except for the brief altercation outside, we've done a good job of blending in—as much as a crew that includes several six-foot plus bikers can blend in—with the rally crowd.

Yeah, I'd had to meet up with Priest and a few other brothers, plus a few members from different clubs several times. Then there was the stress of Sway still being held in Alabama.

Shit.

"Wrath come back yet?"

Z nods over his shoulder. "He's in the corner."

"Stay with Z," I say to Hope. I stare at Z, hoping to sober him up. "Watch her."

Curious, he frowns but says, "Okay."

I kiss Hope's cheek and stalk toward Wrath.

"What's got you so worked up?" he asks.

I slide into the chair across from him and motion him closer. "Hope got approached by an undercover in the bathroom." I tilt my head to the side where the obnoxious little bunny is now hanging out with a different group of bikers. "And that one—"

"Wanted to climb on your dick?"

"Do you see me laughing?"

"What's this about an undercover?"

I relay Hope's story to him and his default scowl deepens. "That ain't good."

"Z said she left. But that combined with the tart who couldn't take no for an answer—"

"I don't like it."

"Here's my problem. Sway and Shadow got arrested—"

"No way." He slams his bottle on the table, obviously figuring out what I'm about to say. "Sway annoys the fuck outta me for sure, but he bleeds Lost Kings. I can't see him snitching."

"What about Shadow? We don't know him that well. He hasn't been a member that long. Don't forget, now he's VP."

"Murphy says he's a real asshole too."

"Interesting." Murphy's a pretty good judge of character. "Priest hasn't been able to find out shit about what Sway's being held on either."

"That's not good."

His phone vibrates against the table and he picks it up. "Trinity."

"Take it."

"I gotta go outside. Can't hear shit in here."

"Go on."

I turn to signal Z and Hope to join me, but there's a greasy, out-of-shape old biker in my way.

I lift an eyebrow. "You need something?"

He blinks and backs up at the hard edge to my question.

"You were rude to our girl when she was just trying to be friendly."

Fuck this shit.

I slide out of the chair and stand, pulling my shoulders back to emphasize how much he doesn't want this to escalate.

"Your girl needs to learn manners." I flick my eyes toward the group he's with. "Doesn't she have enough to keep her busy?"

He glances over his shoulder at his crew, then slides his gaze toward Z. A slow smile spreads over his grimy face.

If he's thinking he's got me outnumbered, I feel sorry for him. Z and I have taken on more than this ragged bunch and come out on top. Not to mention Wrath's right outside.

What I *don't* want is Hope in the middle of any of this, so for that reason alone I keep my fists curled at my side. Ready and alert.

"I'm only giving you the one warning." He puffs up his chest like he's accomplished something. "Next time be more polite."

Years of fighting instinct coil in my muscles. "Do I look like I give a fuck about your warning?" I'm still a little jacked up from the earlier fight and ready to put this guy in his place.

When his fist comes flying at my face, I'm not even surprised. The blow glances off my shoulder, but I barely feel the impact.

Instead, I pummel him with my fists.

As soon as I lay him out, two more come my way. Their hostility doesn't incite fear, it fuels my murderous anger.

Consumed with the situation in front of me, I don't even bother looking for Wrath. He'll be here any second.

The next two don't waste any words or bother with a warning. One pulls a knife, raising the stakes to our scuffle. My own knife rests in my pocket, but I don't want to squander time going for it.

Z better have hustled Hope out the door.

The asshole with the knife thrusts it at my face. I weave to the side and grab his wrist, giving it a vicious twist. The knife clatters against the floor. My foot shoots out, kicking the long, pointed blade under the table.

I'm pretty sure I broke something in his arm, but I punch him twice in the face and once in the throat just for being an asshole.

His friend launches himself at me headfirst, hitting me in the side. I grunt from the impact, but handle him by grabbing a fistful of his hair and slamming his face into the table.

Almost too easy.

Blood stains my knuckles. It's possible I'm enjoying myself a little too much.

White heat surges through my veins, heart thumping, blood pounding, my wild eyes search the immediate area, primed for the next opponent.

Z's BUSY FLIRTING with the pretty bartender when a hefty old biker takes a swing at Rock.

"Shit!" I smack Z's arm as I slide off my stool.

"Oh fuck."

"I'm gonna call the cops," the bartender says.

"Shit, Z."

That's the last thing Rock needs.

Rock seems perfectly at home knocking the guy out and the other bikers who come at him. It's honestly a little terrifying to see my husband so comfortable being so vicious.

A short scream jumps out of my throat when one of the guys pulls a knife.

Rock handles that too.

It all happens so fast.

Z tugs on my arm, trying to push me toward the back door, but I dig my heels into the dirty wood floor. "I'm not leaving without him."

"Hope," he warns.

"Where's Wrath?"

Some patrons flee out the front door, while others use the fight as an excuse to start their own trouble.

Two more bikers head Rock's way.

I pull out the little pepper blaster and Z laughs. "What the hell are you gonna do with that?"

"Shoot those guys."

"Hope," he says, grabbing my arm again. "Let's go."

"Z, I can either shoot you or them." I snap the cartridge in place and slip the extra one in my pocket. "I'd rather not shoot you, but I will if you don't let go of me."

"Goddammit," he mutters, releasing my arm. I'm halfway across the room, when Wrath bursts in the front door.

"Hope, don't." He motions me toward him. "Let's go."

But two more guys are approaching Rock, one with what looks like a broken chair leg clutched tightly in his left hand.

I aim the plastic gun in his direction first. My finger pushes the white, plastic safety to the side.

"Hey!" I shout to get his attention.

He turns, and oh fuck, I pray this stupid little thing works because he's a scary asshole and now he's coming my way.

Deep breath. Just like Rock's taught me, aim for right between the eyes and slowly squeeze the trigger.

A loud pop bursts from the gun and the glob of pepper spray lands in the middle of his scraggly, gray beard.

Huh, guess my aim is off.

The liquid spreads, soaking his beard as well as dousing the guy to his left enough to make him stop.

The one I nailed drops to the ground, clawing at his throat. The chair leg thumps to the floor.

Happy it worked, I smile in triumph and grab the second cartridge.

Wrath's already in the thick of things with Rock. I've witnessed what Wrath's capable of doing in the somewhat controlled environment of an underground fighting ring. Here, with no rules at all—he's absolutely savage.

"All right, let's go, Hope," Z says.

I can tell he doesn't want to leave. He's struggling between staying with me like Rock asked or helping his brothers.

"I'm fine. Go help them."

"Woman, I swear to—"

A bearded blur storms through the front door. "Look, Murphy's here. I'll go with—"

Too late, Murphy's already joined the brawl.

"Fuck. Stay put," Z says.

I glance at the bartender who's on the phone, probably with the police.

We're all going to end up being carted off to jail tonight.

"Bitch," someone snaps to my right and I whirl around.

The girl who hit on Rock earlier advances on me with a beer bottle in one hand.

Cold fear swirls in my stomach. I'm not a fighting type of girl. Never have been. I squeeze the gun in my hand, very aware I only have one cartridge left.

I flick my gaze to the corner where Rock, Wrath, Murphy, and Z have neutralized most of the threats. Everyone else has fled the building.

The girl in front of me seems to realize her backup is either beaten to a pulp on the floor or gone, leaving her behind.

I casually snap the cartridge into place. "Did you have something to say to me, short stack?"

She blows out a breath. "Uppity cunt."

"Not the first time I've heard that, sweetheart," I mutter, raising the gun and aiming for her mouth.

She pauses and cocks her head, maybe trying to figure out if the gray and red plastic gun is an actual threat.

"Last chance," I warn.

"Fuck you."

That seems pretty hostile. My finger twitches and the gun fires. The blob of pepper spray lands in her cleavage, spreads across her chest and drips down her shirt.

"What the fuck is that?" The girl screams, scooping up the goopy stuff with her long coffin-shaped nails.

It must sting because she shrieks even louder and dances around like a possessed marionette.

I don't feel as bad about it as I probably should. After all, I tried to warn her. Not my fault she wouldn't listen.

"What the fuck, Hope?" Teller shouts. He races over from the main entrance and grabs my hand. "We gotta go. Now."

"Rock!" I yell as Teller drags me to the door.

Breathing hard and covered with sweat and maybe a little blood, he looks up and scowls. "Get her out of here," he barks at Teller.

"Cops are on their way!" the bartender shouts. "Get out while you can."

"Go, Rock. I got this," Wrath says, shoving him away.

The group who earlier outnumbered us by quite a bit lies scattered on the floor in groaning, bloody heaps.

Teller's clamps down on my arm harder, determined to get me out of here whether I like it or not. "Ow. Watch it with the iron grip," I yelp.

He ignores me and pulls me into the parking lot.

"We gotta get out of here," he says, pulling me toward Murphy's truck.

"Where's Trinity and Charlotte?"

"Back at the beach house."

Wrath, Z, Murphy, and Rock burst out of the front door just as sirens sound in the distance.

"Move!" Rock yells, running toward us as if the bar's about to blow up.

My boots slap over the hard pavement, jarring my bones. These weren't meant for running. Teller opens the back door and lift-shoves me inside. I scoot to the other side as fast as I can to make room for the other guys and end up jammed against Alexa's car seat. Rock jumps in next, followed by Z.

Teller climbs behind the wheel and Wrath hoists himself into the passenger side.

"Where's Murphy?" I ask.

Wrath jerks his finger over his shoulder and I turn. Murphy taps the back window and gives us a thumbs-up.

"Let's roll, welterweight," Wrath rumbles.

"I'm going. Gonna be a little suspicious if I peel out of here, don't ya think?"

It's maddening, but Teller takes his time—even uses his blinker—as he slowly pulls out of the parking lot and onto Main Street.

Several police cars pass us, lights flashing, sirens blaring, but none of them slow down or turn around.

Once the police are a good distance behind us, Teller finally speeds up.

Everyone's breathing hard and excitedly recapping the night's events.

Rock grabs me by my hips and pulls me into his lap. "Are you all right?"

"I'm fine." I search every inch of his face, neck, and chest to make sure he's not hurt. He hisses when I touch his shoulder and push his leather cut to the side. I peel his shirt away and gasp.

"Jesus, Rock," I breathe out. His skin's already reddened and turning purple in places. "Can you move your arm?"

"Got you into my lap, didn't I?"

I'm too worried to joke around. "Be serious."

He shrugs and rolls his shoulders for me, clenching his jaw the entire time.

"All right. Nothing's probably broken. But we better ice it when we get back to the hotel."

"You think it's wise to go back there tonight?" Teller asks. "Everyone in that place probably saw our colors. The cops will come looking for you."

"Everyone in there also knows we didn't start that shit," Z says. "Doubt the bartender will say anything."

"What about the other club?" I ask.

"Fuck them," Wrath growls. "They want another beating, I'm happy to deliver it to them."

Rock lets out a dark chuckle. "Not quite how I wanted the night to end."

"Hope'll tend to your boo-boos, Prez," Wrath says. "Don't worry."

"Are you okay, Wrath?" I ask, twisting around to touch his shoulder.

He reaches back and pats my hand. "I'm fine. You did good, Hope."

"What about me?" Z asks, shaking out his hand.

I grab his arm and check out his scraped knuckles. "You'll need some ice too."

Rock must be tired, he doesn't even object to me fussing over Z's injuries.

ROCK

TELLER DRIVES BACK to the house where we clean up. Once she's sure Teller's okay, Charlotte disappears into one of the bedrooms with Alexa and doesn't ask any questions.

Trinity's all over Wrath the second she sees him.

We call to check in with the rest of the guys who're partying at a bar across town without issue.

When everyone's been taken care of and we're sure all of our brothers are safe, I grab a blanket and take Hope down to the beach.

"It's dark," she says, following me into the soft sand.

"We'll know when we hit the water." I point to the moon, glowing soft silver over the water. "Besides, it's not that dark."

"Oh." She stops and gasps. "It's so beautiful."

It's low tide, but I stop and spread out the blanket far enough from the water that we shouldn't get wet anytime soon.

I pull her down with me and she immediately pushes an icepack against my aching shoulder.

"You need to slow down," she murmurs, kissing my cheek. "Let me take care of you."

"It's my job to take care of *you.*"

"Well, you can't do that if you're injured, now can you?" she sasses right back.

My mouthy lawyer woman.

I run my hand over her hair. "Are you okay?"

"I'm fine." She grins. "My pepper gun worked. But I need new cartridges."

"Think we'll grab those tomorrow." I turn my head to the side and let out a dry laugh. "Obviously it comes in handy."

Her hand with the icepack falls away and she sits back. "That was… surreal. One minute we're hanging out joking around with Z and the next—"

"This is the reality of our world, Hope. Damn ugly at times."

She inhales deeply and tilts her head toward the ocean. "But sometimes it's beautiful."

"You're beautiful." And now I've further tainted her with the shit in my life, exactly what I never wanted for her.

She watches me for a few seconds before speaking again. "The violence I felt when that girl was flirting with you was nothing compared to how I felt when those men…" her voice trails off and she shakes her head. For a second I think she's about to tear up but her voice is clear and firm. "I wanted something bigger than a pepper spray gun to beat them with."

"Look at you so vicious under all that innocence," I tease, even though I don't feel like joking.

Her gentle fingers settle under my chin forcing me to look at her. "When it comes to you, yes."

As if she heard my earlier thoughts, her voice hardens. "And don't think it's because you somehow tainted me or turned me into something I'm not." She taps her chest. "That desire to do whatever I can to protect what's mine comes from deep inside."

The air leaves my lungs and I pull her closer for a kiss.

She breaks the kiss, her mouth turning down. "Unfortunately, I feel pretty useless in a situation like that."

I cup her cheek, rubbing my thumb over her lips. "You did good. I wish you'd left with Z when I asked you to, but I should've known better."

"Leave you behind." She snorts. "I don't fucking think so."

"Fuck." I take her hand, guiding it to my lap and the erection she's given me.

Her eyes light up and she squeezes gently.

"See what you do to me?"

Soft, husky laughter falls from her lips. "I'm pretty sure a stiff breeze would get you hard."

"Yeah, if it's carrying your scent." I shove my nose into the crook of her neck. Inhaling her scent like it's the cure for everything wrong in my world.

CHAPTER SIXTEEN

Hope

"I NEED YOU," Rock whispers against my skin. His lips trace my collarbone, to my shoulder, sliding my shirt down my arm.

"Rock, wasn't one brush with the law enough for tonight?"

He glances up and down the beach. In the distance someone's having a party around a bonfire, but other than that, the beach is empty.

"Rock!" someone shouts behind us. "Hope?"

Rock lets out an unholy, unhappy growl and turns. Wrath and Trinity are kicking up sand on their way over to us. Rock stands and pulls me up with him.

"We're going back to the hotel. You want to stay here?" Wrath asks.

Half an hour later, we're tucked safely inside our room and Rock's no less wound up than he was on the beach. He stalks me across the room until the back of my knees hit the bed and land on the mattress.

"I really wanted to fuck you on the beach." He strips off his shirt, slower than usual, putting on a show for me.

"Rock, is your shoulder still—"

"I'm fine." He works his belt loose. "Although, I'd start taking those clothes off if you don't want them shredded."

I crawl up into the center of the bed and watch him undress. Fire races over my skin when he tips his head up and focuses on me.

"Hope," he warns. "I'm fucking you one way or another."

"Is that right?"

He strokes his hand up and down his cock a few times and meets my eyes. "Nah, you're right. On second, thought, I'll go take care of myself." He struts off to the bathroom leaving me staring after him.

"Rock?"

I scurry off the bed and just as I turn the corner, he grabs me, lifting and flipping me in the air.

"I can't believe I fell for that," I shriek.

He tosses me on the bed. "I can't either."

This time, I slowly lift my shirt and toss it aside.

"Much better. Still too slow." He leans down and yanks my boots off, then drags my jeans down my legs. "Open your legs."

I hook my fingers in my underwear and lift up. He helps by slipping them off.

Despite his rough tone and crude words, he's achingly gentle as he covers me with is body. He cups my face with his hands and brushes a soft kiss against my lips. His steel-gray eyes take in more than my face.

He pushes inside me slow enough to make me moan for more, harder, faster.

He's controlled enough to deny my request and take his time. Gathering me in his arms, cradling me as he thrusts into me again.

I open my mouth and he captures my lips in a kiss. Every shared breath, every roll of his hips sends me spiraling.

"You're so beautiful." His hands clutch my hips, holding me tighter as he thrusts into me harder. Satisfied primal growls rumble from his throat with every roll of his hips.

"Whose pussy is this?" Rock whispers against my neck. His lips travel over my shoulder, teeth sinking into my flesh.

My mind's blank except for one word. "Yours."

"That's right." His frantic thrusts slow. "Give it to me any time I want, right, baby doll? Is that right? Tell me."

"Oh!" I scream and groan at the same time. "Yes. Don't stop."

I whimper as he sits up and captures my ankles in his hands. He spreads my legs obscenely wide and hammers into me, leaving me no choice but to twist my hands into the comforter beneath us and hang on.

"I'm not fucking stopping. Don't worry 'bout that. Look how pretty you are."

He shifts so he's holding my ankles in one hand and squeezes his free hand between my thighs to play with my clit.

"Nooo. Too much."

"No such thing. Come on."

Streaks of white-hot pleasure race down my body tossing me into my own personal blissful nighttime moonlit ocean waves. My wild moans of orgasmic joy give way to high-pitched broken laughter as the sensations overwhelm me.

Rock rides out my climax until my wild, breathless laughter turns to satisfied sighs.

He releases me, pulls out and throws himself down next to me.

"Come ride my cock, my dirty little doll."

I waste no time throwing my leg over him.

"Greedy tonight," he teases.

"Yup." My eyes squeeze tight as I take him inside me and slowly work my hips up and down.

"That's it," he encourages, running his hands up and down my thighs. "Oh fuck." He closes his eyes and throws his head back. "Keep going. Come on. Don't slow down now."

"Oh, Rock," I gasp. "I'm gonna… again… Oh!"

"There it is. Keep coming for me."

I'm breathless and limp when he pulls me down, burying my face against his neck. His arms clamp around me, holding me tight, shoving his face against my neck and sucking at my skin.

He stills and groans deep, the sound vibrating through me.

"Hope." His voice is rough-edged with both love and need.

"I'm here."

He doesn't loosen his hold on me, keeping me anchored to his body so we can trade soft kisses and murmured declarations of love.

Something thumps against the wall our bed rests against.

"I hope you're done for the night! We need sleep!" Sparky shouts.

I burst into giggles and roll to the side. "Oops. I thought they were still out."

Rock lazily tucks one arm up behind his head and turns to look at me. "You think that would've stopped me?"

"No." I slide closer and run my fingers over his chest, stopping to look at the bruises blooming over his right shoulder. "Did I hurt you?"

He blows out a breath. "You're the cure for everything that ails me."

"That's sweet, but I'm worried about you. We have a long ride home."

"I'll be fine in a day or two."

"If we stay out of trouble."

"Yes," he agrees. "If we stay out of trouble."

CHAPTER SEVENTEEN

Hope

T HE LAST DAY of the rally finds us strolling down Main Street checking out a new crop of custom bikes on display. Yesterday, Rock and I spent most of the day in bed so he could "rest" and "heal" his shoulder. Today he seems to be moving more freely and I don't catch him tightening his jaw in pain when he thinks I'm not looking.

We're a rather large, rowdy group walking down the street, which keeps people out of our way.

"Oh wow, look at this one." I point out a large Harley painted matte black and glowing green. On closer inspection, fire, devils, and ghosts shimmer in the painting. Pearl blue flames that can only be seen when the sunlight hits the paint just right dance along the fender.

Rock's mouth curls into a satisfied grin. "I recognize this one. Bricks," he calls out.

"Is this one of yours?" I ask.

"The paint. The rest the owner did himself."

"It's really beautiful."

Bricks nods. "Mixed that paint myself. Where's he at?"

"Vapor!" Dex shouts, striding over to meet a tall bearded guy and the slight woman at his side.

The man with the beard jolts and steps in front of his girlfriend.

Only when he recognizes Dex do his hard features seem to relax. The couple follows Dex to our little group.

"Vapor," Rock greets. "Was hoping we'd run into you down here. How've you been?"

"Not bad." He introduces us to his wife, Juliet, and we chat about the rally, the weather, and how long our rides home are. After a round of small talk, Rock gives me a subtle head tilt. I take it as he wants a second alone with this man for some reason.

"The girls and I were going to grab milkshakes, do you want to join us, Juliet?"

She glances at Vapor before answering. "Sure."

Trinity and Charlotte are actually up ahead, checking out some store windows. I wave to them and point to the ice cream shop.

"Phew." I fan the shop's menu over my heated skin after we step inside. "I don't know why I expected Florida to be cooler in the fall."

Juliet laughs. "It's hot pretty much year-round. We're actually thinking of moving back to New York."

"Then you have to deal with our winters."

She shrugs.

When our shakes are ready, we take seats near the window.

Alexa spills milkshake all over the front of Heidi's shirt. Stunned, Heidi stares down at the mess for a few seconds before letting out a loud sigh. "I knew I should've grabbed more napkins."

"I'll hold her, so you can clean up," Juliet offers.

Heidi glances at me as if to make sure I'm not going anywhere before handing Alexa over.

Alexa's fascinated by Juliet's long hair and immediately wraps her sticky fist in it.

"Sorry, I'll take her," I offer.

She waves me off. "It's fine. She's so adorable. Love the little vest."

"Present from her daddy."

"Oh, I bet you're a daddy's girl," she coos, and Alexa squees in response.

"We're not telling anyone yet," Juliet says in a whispery voice, "But since we just met, why not?" She rests her hand over her stomach. "We're having a baby. I found out just before we left, so we decided to make it a longer trip, since I probably won't be able to ride in a few months."

"Aw, congratulations."

Alexa seems fascinated with Juliet's bracelet—a wide, green leather cuff with what looks like daisies embossed in the middle—and keeps trying to unsnap it from Juliet's wrist.

"No, no, Alexa. Look, don't touch," I say.

"It's okay." Juliet shows her the bracelet and Alexa runs her fingers over the design. "This is the first gift Roman ever gave me. I never take it off."

"That's so sweet. How long have you been together?"

"Since high school."

I can't think of a tactful way to ask how long it's been. She doesn't look like her high school days are that far behind her, but her mannerisms are of someone much older.

"Where do you guys live now?"

"All over," she answers vaguely before changing the subject. "So, I finally met Bricks. Roman's mentioned him before, you know when he had the bike done, but I've never met him."

"Is your husband in an MC too?"

She glances away. "Not really."

What kind of answer is that? MC life doesn't seem to allow for vagueness. You're either in or out. Dex had seemed awfully familiar with the couple, so I try again. This time I'm more direct. "How do you know Dex?"

For the first time, her soft smile falters. "He was married to my cousin. He was kind of like an uncle to me when I was younger."

Holy shit. I had no idea Dex was married. Or had been married.

Wow.

"Oh," I answer lamely. Before I have a chance to ask any follow-up questions, Heidi rejoins us.

"I look like I'm ready to enter a wet T-shirt contest," she grumbles as she plops into the chair next to Juliet.

"I doubt Murphy will mind."

She snorts and holds her hands out for Alexa. "Come here you little monster." She presses kisses to both of Alexa's cheeks, making her giggle. "Was she good?"

"Oh yes. She's a sweetheart," Juliet says, tugging on one of Alexa's sandals.

"She's not so sweet at three in the morning when she decides it's time to get up." Heidi grins at her daughter. "Is it? No, it's not."

Charlotte peeks inside the shop and waves at me.

"I think that's our signal that the guys are ready to move on," I say, standing and grabbing my milkshake. "Heidi, you're soaked. Let's run next door and buy a T-shirt for you."

"I'll be okay, Hope. It's hot enough out."

The guys are still crowded around Vapor's bike. Well, Rock, Wrath, Z, and Dex are. The others seem to be scattered up and down the street. Except Sparky. He's having liquor poured down his throat by two scantily clad girls at a drink stand across the street.

"When Sparky goes on vacation he goes hard," Heidi jokes.

"There's my girls," Murphy says, coming up behind us. He cocks his head. "What happened to you?" he asks Heidi.

"Alexa."

"Ah, here, give her to me." He kisses her cheek. "Did you spill stuff on Mommy?"

"Yeth!"

"Oh my God, she's so cute." Juliet rests her hands over her belly. "I hope ours is as good as she is."

Juliet seems so calm and sweet, I imagine her baby probably will be too and I say that to her.

She glances down. "I hope so."

"Have you hit the weird cravings phase yet?" Heidi asks.

"No, everything makes me want to hurl right now."

Uncomfortable because I have nothing to add to their conversation and probably never will, I move closer to Murphy and Alexa. As if she senses my sudden melancholy, Alexa leans down and makes fishy lips at me until I give her my cheek.

"Aw, thanks, baby," I say softly, kissing her back.

The girls continue their animated conversation about weird pregnancy cravings and doctor visits. I don't want to be a downer, so I turn Murphy's way.

He gives me a pained smile. I know why their conversation depresses me, but it takes me a second to figure out why he looks so troubled. After Heidi and Axel married, Murphy took to the road for months and didn't return until after Alexa was born. He missed all the experiences Juliet and Heidi are excitedly sharing.

It's mean to even think it, but at least if Heidi has any more children, it will be with a man who'll be more than happy to go on midnight ice cream runs for her. Axel hadn't been the most sympathetic father-to-be, something that really grated on my nerves as Heidi approached her due date.

Shaking that off, I place my hand on Murphy's arm and reach up on my tiptoes to get his attention.

He bends down and gives me his ear.

"I'd say you'll get to do all that pregnancy stuff with her one day, but I don't want to encourage you two until you're in your own house," I whisper.

That does the trick. He rumbles with laughter and holds up his hand. "I can't make any promises."

I smack him lightly and he laughs even harder.

"What are you laughing at?" Heidi asks.

Murphy shakes his head.

"Ready, babe?" Vapor asks, slipping an arm around his wife.

"Whenever you are."

Rock's warm, solid body, presses against my back. He slides his arms around me and kisses my cheek. "Where's my milkshake?"

"Here." I offer mine but he declines.

"Teasing you," he murmurs, nuzzling my neck.

"I'll take it, if you're offering, Hope," Sparky says, swiping it out of my hand before I have a chance to answer.

"Well, I... okay." Too late now.

"I need to get the taste of that cheap tequila out of my mouth. Fucking nasty swill." He claws at his throat and makes a number of disgusting sounds. "Gah! It's still burning its way down my esophagus. How the hell is that legal and pot isn't?" Sparky grumbles.

"You looked like you were having fun," I say.

"The redhead wasn't wearing any panties," he explains.

"Alrighty, then," I mumble, making everyone laugh.

He tips his head back and pours the shake down his throat, guzzling it down in one long shot.

"Ow, brain freeze," he mumbles a few seconds later.

"Didn't think you had any brains left to freeze," Z jokes.

Sparky chucks the sort of empty cup at him and it lands on the sidewalk.

"That's not environmentally friendly," Z says.

One of the many cops patrolling the big biker rally casts a glance our way.

"For fuck's sake," Rock growls.

"Sparky." I glare at him until he picks up the cup. The last thing we need is to be hassled by the cops again.

"So you already have a bunch of kids, I see," Juliet whispers to me.

I burst out laughing. "Rock used to say that all the time, and I never quite understood what he meant."

To my surprise, she gives me a big hug before leaving. As they turn to head back to their bike, I notice the *Nomad* rocker at the bottom of Vapor's vest.

"Even if a nomad doesn't belong to a particular charter, doesn't he belong to a club?" I quietly ask Rock once we're somewhat alone.

"Sometimes. Vapor's a loner." Rock hesitates as if he's unsure of how much to share. "He picks up odd jobs for a lot of different MCs."

Odd jobs. Somehow I doubt Rock means raking leaves or painting fences.

"Were you trying to entice him into going steady with the Lost Kings?"

He rumbles with laughter. "Something like that. He'd be an asset for sure. Wouldn't need to prospect as long."

"I like Juliet a lot. She'd fit in well."

"Figured. Thank you for giving us a minute."

I squeeze his arm. "I know how to read you."

"Yes, you do."

How do I ask this question? "She said she was related to Dex's wife?"

Rock sighs and looks away. "I didn't know that."

Whether he means, he didn't know Dex was married—which I kind of doubt—or that Juliet was related to her, isn't clear, and he doesn't elaborate.

PART TWO

CHAPTER EIGHTEEN

ROCK

IT FEELS SO good to be home!" Hope sings and twirls around the garage as soon as she hops off the bike. "My ass is killing me."

Her words are mostly drowned out by the rumble of the other bikes pulling into the garage, but I catch her hand and yank her toward me. I bury my face against her neck. "Meet me in the hot tub and I'll take care of your ass."

She bats her lashes and smiles. "Yes, Mr. President."

"You two didn't get it on enough during the trip?" Ravage asks, walking over with his hands stuffed in his pockets.

"Rav, unload the van, and help Murphy unload the truck when Heidi gets here," I order.

"What? Why?"

"Because you're obviously bored and in need of something to do?" Hope turns her head to the side and snickers.

He grumbles, but gets to work.

SWAN RUNS OUT of the clubhouse and into the garage. The girls scream and hug each other and talk excitedly about the trip.

"I hope you're not all sick of each other. Stash and I put together a big welcome home dinner."

"What time do you want us at the table?" Z asks. "Dex and I need to run down to Crystal Ball and check on things real quick."

"Seven, does that work for everyone?"

"Sounds good. Thank you for doing that, Swan," Hope says.

Between my bike shop and club business, I'm sure there's a ton of things waiting my attention, but I'm not ready for this to be over with yet.

"You have that look," Hope teases, slinging her arms around my neck.

"What look is that, baby doll?"

"Like you already have club business on your mind."

She's teasing me, but I detect a note of vulnerability in her words.

"You're not sick of me yet?"

"Never," she says in her soft, husky voice.

Fuck if that simple word doesn't twist me up inside. Never have I loved being with anyone is much as I love being with her. Always feels good to have confirmation the feeling is mutual.

"No club business tonight, I promise. Still in vacation mode."

"I'm just teasing, if you really have stuff you need to—"

I cut her off with a kiss.

"Break it up, horndogs," Ravage shouts.

Behind Hope's back, I flip him off and keep right on doing what we're doing.

Before she can get caught up helping Swan out, Wrath drags Trinity to their house. "We'll be back later," Trinity calls out over her shoulder.

"Home sweet home!" Sparky yells. "You better not have killed my babies." He throws a glare at Stash as he runs past him and into the clubhouse.

"And that's the last we'll see if Sparky for the next two years," Z says.

"I don't know about that," Swan says. "Willow said she was coming over after the club closes."

Stash holds out his hands palms up and pretends to weigh Sparky's options. "Hot chick on one hand or his plants on the other? I don't know. That's a close one for Sparky."

"Don't pick on him." Swan playfully slaps Stash's arm and Dex cuts a glare her way from across the garage.

"Oh boy," Hope mutters.

"Let's go home and change." I grasp her hand and lead us home.

Hope

THE NEXT MORNING, Rock's alarm goes off way earlier than human decency should allow.

"Nooo," I moan, reaching for him. "Stay."

He leans back, brushing the hair off my face. "You make it impossible to leave when you're all beautiful and sleepy."

"Then stay."

"Don't you have to go to the office yourself?"

Exhaustion still pulls at me. Or maybe it's post-trip depression. I roll over and shove my head under my pillow. "I don't wanna," I mumble.

The bed shifts. I yelp as the sheet's ripped off me and cool air hits my skin. "Don't you dare," I warn, but my voice is muffled by the pillow.

For Rock my warning is more of an invitation and his hand cracks against my ass a few seconds later. He keeps his hand there, rubbing and squeezing, then lightly swats the other cheek. "You stay there like that I'm gonna find other things for you today."

I peek out from under the pillow. "Promise?"

"Thought you were supposed to meet the girls for morning yoga?"

"I guess," I grumble, rolling out of bed.

"We can always practice right here."

"Hmph."

"My girl's not a morning person is she?" he teases on my way to the bathroom.

"No."

In the bathroom, I'm struck with wave of nausea that brings me to my knees. "Shit."

What little I had in my stomach comes up. My nose stings and tears stream down my cheeks. I hate being sick.

"Rock?" I call out as I make my way over to the sink to brush my teeth.

"What's wrong?"

"I don't feel so good."

He's filling the doorway two seconds later. "Shit, babe you don't look good. Come here." He rests his hand against my forehead and cheeks, his mouth flattening into a grim line. "Come on, why don't you go back to bed."

He walks me to the bed and gently tucks me under the covers, then sits beside me. "What can I get you?"

"Water? Maybe some tea?"

"All right. I'll be right back."

I close my eyes and sort of drift back to sleep for what seems like only a few seconds before Rock's waking me up with a cup of tea and small plate of toast.

"Think you caught a bug on the trip?" he asks.

"Maybe." I sip at the tea and nibble on the toast for a few minutes with Rock watching over me, hands on his hips, concern wrinkling his forehead.

"I feel better now. Sorry." I can't ruin his whole day because I have a tummy ache.

"What are you sorry for?"

"I know you have a lot to do today."

"Yeah, and making sure my wife's okay is at the top of the list."

I reach out and take his hand. "I think this helped." I gesture to the half-eaten toast. "I feel a little better."

"All right." He seems reluctant to leave my side. "Well, finish that and see how you feel."

"Go ahead. Get ready. I'll be fine." I'm starting to feel better and a little foolish for being so dramatic.

With my stomach more settled, I lean back and close my eyes for a few minutes.

"Hope?" Rock's hushed voice pulls me from sleep. "I'm heading out. I'm gonna ask Heidi to check on you in a little bit."

My eyes blink open. "What? No. That's okay."

He leans down and presses a kiss to my forehead. "Text me when you get up or if you need me to bring anything home, okay?"

"I will," I promise.

He kisses the back of my hand. "Gonna miss having you with me today."

"Two weeks together and you're not sick of me?"

"No." His lips twitch. "You're that rare unicorn person I never get tired of being around."

I snort-laugh and get out of bed to hug him. "Same for me, you know."

"THERE SHE IS!" Trinity greets me at the clubhouse about an hour later. "For a minute I was worried maybe Rock tied you to the bed, but I saw him and Murphy ride off and know Rock would never leave you tied up and helpless."

"Har, har. Very funny." I give her a little push and she laughs.

Swan smiles, but doesn't add to the conversation.

"So how was it while we were away?" I ask to take the attention off me.

"Quieter than I expected. I think Rock told the guys no parties while you all were away. I promised Z I'd help manage the girls at Crystal Ball, so that took up a lot of my time." She rolls her eyes.

"Well, thank you for keeping an eye on everything here. We really missed you. Next time you have to come with us."

Trinity's eyes narrow as if that was the wrong thing to say, but I'm not sure why. Surely Swan could've ridden with one of the guys. She's not an ol' lady, but she's an important part of the club and I know for a fact other charters brought plenty of non–old ladies along.

Swan shrugs. "We'll see. How'd Carter do?"

"Good I think. I didn't see a lot of him, honestly. He said he got a lot of sketching and painting done, so he was happy."

"I'm pretty sure Teller gave him a few lectures about keeping his mouth shut," Trinity adds.

"Well." Swan turns toward the Champagne Room and waves over her shoulder for us to follow. "I bet you're both stiff and out of practice, so let's get going."

Trinity skips ahead to catch up. How she's so bright-eyed this morning I don't understand.

"Aren't you still exhausted from the trip?" I ask her.

"The trip, no," Swan answers for Trinity. "Wrath celebrating being home from the trip, probably."

Trinity laughs, but doesn't disagree.

"Oh wow." I gasp as we enter the Champagne Room. "You were busy while we were away."

Swan grins and points to the shelves of yoga mats, blocks, and straps that weren't there before we left. "Shh, I got Stash to put those together for me by telling him I was going to start having the dancers come up for yoga classes."

Trinity groans. "Guess we better lock the door."

She does indeed jog over and lock the door before we begin.

"I'll go easy on you at first," Swan promises.

"Liar," I mutter under my breath.

"We kept up on it for the first few days—" Trinity starts.

"One day, Trin. One day we remembered to do it."

"Okay, one day."

"Less talking, more moving," Swan snaps. For a quiet girl, she's quite bossy during class.

For the next hour we move and flow. My movements resemble a lumbering sloth more than a graceful cat. By the end of our session, I'm more exhausted than energized.

"You all right, Hope?" Trinity asks, tossing me a small towel.

"I don't know. I woke up feeling crappy. Wondering if I caught something on the trip."

"Maybe." Her expression softens from teasing to concerned friend. "Are you going back to work today?"

"I was planning to. I've already missed a lot."

"If you need something, let me know."

"I will."

I thank Swan and hug both of them before heading back to the house to change.

Heidi and Murphy are already gone for the day, so I have the house to myself. A nap is almost too tempting and I barely avoid crawling back under the covers while I slip on a loose pantsuit and heels. Definitely feels weird after wearing nothing but denim and leather for the last two weeks.

I can't say I like it.

CHAPTER NINETEEN

Hope

"FISH TACOS?" MARA asks, closing her menu and setting it to the side.

This is the first chance we've had to get together since I returned from Florida but now I'm wishing we'd gone anywhere else for lunch.

My stomach rolls. Weird, I usually love this place and their fish tacos.

"I think I just want some tea."

Mara cocks her head to the side and studies me. "Feeling okay?"

"No, I must've caught some sort of bug on our trip. I've felt like crap ever since we got home."

"Oooh! Tell me all about the big scary biker rally. It sounds so exciting!"

I snort out a laugh. "Says the woman who just came home from a kinkfest in the woods."

She blushes and arranges the napkin in her lap. "It wasn't a *kinkfest*."

I order toast and tea and Mara stares at me the whole time.

"Are you sure you're not pregnant?" she asks with wide eyes and a sly smile.

My breath catches in my throat but I laugh off the question. "I kind of doubt it."

She drums her fingers over the white table cloth as if she's not satisfied with my answer and has many follow-up questions.

"It's just a bug," I repeat.

"Okay, okay. I'm just saying. You'd be such a perfect mom and Rock would be such a good daddy."

"What's with the baby fever? Are *you* thinking of having more kids?"

"Maybe. I'm sure Damon would love to have a boy. Or another girl to spoil the crap out of." She stops and scrunches up her face as if she's seriously considering what another kid would do to her household. "I'm not sure how Cora would feel sharing our attention at this point, though."

"Aw, she must be getting so big. You have to come up again so she and Alexa can play together."

"How's Heidi doing? She's such a sweet girl. They're still living with you, right?"

I share enough details not to bore her to death, but then we move on to discussing cases we're both working on. My details aren't as thrilling as Mara's.

"I can throw you more work, if you need it, Hope."

What an unappealing thought. I'm not sure why I've been shying away from taking on more cases or clients. Maybe because I like being available when Rock wants to go on a two week trip. Maybe it's sinking in how much I really hate being a lawyer.

"That's okay. I'm good for now."

"Damon can get you in on a job correcting bar exams if you want."

"Ugh, no thanks. Taking it once was the only contact I want to have with it, thank you very much."

She chuckles.

All too soon we're finishing lunch and she's rushing back to work.

As I'm about to walk out, a wave of nausea hits me and I rush to the restaurant's restroom to retch. Eyes watering and breathing heavily, I stare at my reflection in the mirror as I splash cold water on my face.

Mara's question whispers in my head. *"Are you sure you're not pregnant?"*

CHAPTER TWENTY

Hope

A (+) sign in the round window indicates a 'pregnant' result.

Y<small>UP. T</small>HAT'S <small>DEFINITELY</small> a blue plus sign.

I'm terrified.

And a tiny bit excited.

But I tamp down any bit of excitement. After a miscarriage and ectopic pregnancy, the logical side of my brain is screaming that my chances of this pregnancy surviving are slim.

The rest of me? Afraid to admit I'm a tiny bit hopeful.

And scared to death.

Should I even tell Rock?

No.

No way.

I can't get his hopes up until I know one way or another. It's cruel.

I was so distracted by our trip I didn't think much about it. Besides, I'm so bad at math and my body has never exactly run like clockwork—go figure—I can only estimate that I'm three or four weeks late. It didn't dawn on me that I might be pregnant until the "stomach bug" I acquired on the trip didn't go away.

Doctor. I better schedule an appointment.

Downstairs, the front door opens and slams shut.

Can't I have a few spare moments to pee on a stick in peace?

Gathering up the box the test came in, the instructions and the stick, I stuff everything back into the paper CVS bag I brought it home in and shove it in the back of the bottom drawer of my vanity. Rock has no reason to go in there for anything.

"Hope?" Rock calls out.

I finish up in the bathroom. Good thing too, when I open the door, he's already striding into the bedroom.

"Hey, baby doll." His smile turns to concern as he looks over me more carefully. "Still not feelin' okay?"

"Meh. I think I might be getting a cold on top of the stomach thing." I wave off the concern. "How was church?"

Not that he usually shares much about what they discuss at the table, but the question always automatically pops out anyway.

Today, Rock doesn't give me one of his usual vague answers.

"Fuckin' clusterfuck. As usual." He narrows his eyes and takes me in. "Are you sure you're all right?" He brushes the back of his hand over my cheek and I lean into his touch. "I'm not used to you not waiting for me outside the war room," he says in a gentler voice. The warm, gentle tone he saves for when we're alone.

I want to tell him so bad. I'm used to sharing everything with my husband. *Everything.*

Not yet.

"How busy are you at the shop right now?" I ask.

He cocks his head and studies me again before answering. "Winter's coming, so we'll be slammed with everyone wanting their bike done for spring. What's on your mind?"

"I was wondering if we could get away for a few days."

"We just came back from a trip. Are you all caught up at work?"

I shrug. "I can move some things around."

One corner of his mouth lifts. "Have anywhere special in mind?"

"Not really." My lips curve up. "Have any presidential visits you need to make?"

"You really took to your first lady duties on our trip, didn't you?"

"I guess."

"No, you did." He takes my hand and pulls me over to the bed. "I know we've both been crazy since we got back. I haven't had a chance to properly thank you."

"Like what?"

"Putting up with everything. You were such a big help to me. Made me so proud having you on my arm." He runs the back of his hand over my cheek. "Smartest, prettiest woman in every room."

I lean into his touch, loving our connection. "I don't know about that," I mutter. "But I like that you think so."

"I know so." He blows out a breath. "I do have to run downtown for a quick meeting. You can come with me if you want to."

I HATE LYING to Rock, so the next day I call my doctor first thing in the morning and they squeeze me in.

"What was the date of your last period?" Doctor West asks.

My cheeks heat with the embarrassment of how careless I am.

"Uh, I'm not sure."

She raises an eyebrow. "Longer than five weeks?"

"Definitely. But I'm always late."

A hint of a professional smile ghosts over her lips. "It's not uncommon. We'll take some blood, schedule an ultrasound and estimate from there."

A spike of fear hits. I hate needles.

If I'm pregnant, I better get used to a lot more invasive things than a simple blood draw.

To my surprise and relief, the blood draw is quick and less painful than I expect. I'm bubbling over with emotions the whole time: scared, excited, so damn hopeful.

And guilty that I didn't tell Rock.

"We should have the results tomorrow. Let's get you in for an ultrasound on Friday. You're more than welcome to bring your husband."

"Will we really be able to see anything this early?"

"Yes."

"You'll be able to rule out another ectopic pregnancy?"

She hesitates and seems to think over the answer, which only further spikes my anxiety. "We should be able to from the ultrasound. If not, we'll order a transvaginal ultrasound. That will show us where the pregnancy is located. Try not to worry."

Try not to worry my ass. The entire ride home all I do is worry.

Worry about whether I should tell Rock and get his hopes up. Worry if this baby will be healthy. Finding out if I'm actually pregnant and it's a viable pregnancy is just the first step. There are so many other variables I have to worry about.

It's not like I'm in my twenties. As if I wasn't already aware of that fact, the "Pregnant After Thirty-Five" pamphlet the nurse shoved in my hand before I left drove the knowledge home.

I'm ready to explode with the need to talk about this with someone. But I can't tell anyone before I tell Rock. I just can't.

Friday. Just a couple days away. Hopefully I'll have an answer and then I'll come home and tell him. Good news. Happy news.

And if it's *bad* news, I'll tell him that too, but at least I won't get his hopes up only to crush them with the pain of losing a baby.

Again.

A baby. *Our baby.*

My hand settles over my stomach. "Please, please, please be okay," I whisper.

I'm afraid to admit to myself how much I want this baby.

CHAPTER TWENTY-ONE

Hope

CAN'T BELIEVE I might be a mother soon.

For the longest time I wasn't sure I even wanted children.

Now I can't imagine wanting anything more, which means I'm completely freaked out over every little thing.

"Are you sure you're okay, Hope?" Rock asks, breaking into my thoughts.

For the millionth time since I left the doctor's office, I consider confiding in him. I'm so damn scared, though. We weren't planning this, but in my heart, I know he'll be happy. So, it's not fear of his reaction stopping me.

It's fear of getting his hopes up and then failing him again.

Of course, when he finds out I've suspected for a while and didn't tell him, he won't be pleased either.

"Hope?"

"Yes. I'm fine. Just feeling a little funky."

"Think you need to take a sick day?"

I imagine I'll be taking a lot of time off in the near future. Maybe that's why I've been turning down new cases and slowly trying to wrap up my small caseload. Maybe part of me already knew. "No."

He pulls me in close, kissing the top of my head.

We're touching. So close and yet there's a huge gulf between us.

Does he know? Can he feel me holding back?

He places his fingers under my chin. Firm, but so gentle, he tips my head up. His steady gray eyes bore into mine.

"You seem to have something on your mind lately."

"I have lots of things on my mind."

"Anything you want to talk about?"

I duck my head. "I can't." It's not exactly a lie. My throat's so tight, I don't think I could form the words to express the storm inside me.

FOR THE NEXT two days, all I do is worry.

Rock's busy at his shop, catching up on all the custom work that piled up while we were away.

I'm busy preparing for my trial that starts on Monday.

Around noon my doctor's office calls to inform me that the blood test was positive and confirm the ultrasound for the next day.

I spend most of the afternoon looking up information about ectopic pregnancies, ultrasounds, and maybe peek at a baby name website once or twice.

Boy or girl? I try to push the thought out of my head before it fully forms.

"Hey, partner," Adam says, standing in my doorway.

I glance up, mouth already twisting with skepticism. He only calls me partner when he wants something.

"What's up?"

"Think you can handle a case for me tomorrow?"

The ultrasound's tomorrow morning. Depending on the outcome, I might not even come back to the office.

"Can't. I have a doctor's appointment in the morning and then I have to prep for my trial."

"You all right?"

"I'm fine."

He leans his shoulder against the door. "So, you never told me. How was the big biker orgy?"

I sigh and close out my latest Google search. "It wasn't an orgy."

At least not officially. I definitely saw enough things that could've qualified as an orgy. Not that I'd ever share that with Adam.

"Well, you look good. Rested and tan."

"Thanks, I think. Did I look pallid and haggard before I left?" I tease.

"Nope." He pops his fist against the door a few times. "You think Mara's interested in covering for me?"

"I don't know. Call and ask her."

He grumbles something and waves before walking away.

The rest of my afternoon goes by quickly. My client comes in so I can review the questions I plan to ask with her. I also go over a list of questions I suspect her ex's attorney will ask. As much as I try to concentrate, my mind wanders a lot throughout our appointment.

THE NEXT MORNING I arrive at the doctor's office right on time. A miracle for me if I'm being honest.

I wait around for a while before I'm finally brought in to an exam room and asked to change.

The technician looks around Heidi's age, but she's friendly and explains everything in detail.

The cool, slippery gel she spreads over my stomach is the easy part. Watching her slide the wand back and forth, while she searches and searches, finding nothing, brings tears to my eyes.

"It's okay. It might be too soon," the tech assures me. She calls someone in for a second opinion and they try again.

Nothing.

The doctor finally comes in to see me. "Well, your hCG rates are increasing. I would feel better if we'd seen the yolk sac today. But it doesn't mean anything is wrong. We might just be too early."

I swipe at the tears gathering on my lashes. "Early, that would be a first for me."

She's not unsympathetic, but she's not super-cuddly either. "Let's get more blood today and schedule you for the transvaginal ultrasound next week. That should give us a more definitive answer."

I'm good at ignoring and burying the things that bother me. After leaving the doctor's office, I return to the office and prep for my trial without crying once.

CHAPTER TWENTY-TWO

Hope

M Y TRIAL GETS adjourned at the last minute, freeing up my whole day.

Leaving me way too much time to dwell on tomorrow's appointment.

Dinner with Heidi, Murphy, and Alexa is what I need to take my mind off things. Heidi's chatter and Alexa's happy babbles more than cover up my silence.

For a little while anyway.

While Murphy and Heidi clear the table, Rock slides his hand over mine. "Everything okay?"

"I'm fine."

Of course that's not a good enough answer for Rock and he waits patiently for me to continue. When I don't, he prompts, "Rough case you're working on?"

Actually, yes. I have another case that needs my attention. I got so caught up in preparing for the trial, I've almost neglected everything else.

"Yes. The hearing's coming up Friday and I've had a terrible time reaching one of my witnesses."

One corner of his mouth lifts. "Want me to locate them for you?"

"Absolutely not." My answer comes out sterner than normal because

I don't think he's joking.

He cups my jaw, rubbing his thumb over my cheek. "Everything else okay?"

Those probing gray eyes of his are almost too much. Does he already suspect?

Keeping secrets from Rock isn't easy. Normally, I love his attention. How he's attuned to my needs and moods.

Now with him watching me so intently, it feels dangerous.

Relentless guilt settles in my belly. Claiming the need to work on my case, I retreat upstairs to escape Rock's scrutiny.

ROCK

SOMETHING ISN'T RIGHT with my girl, but I can't put my finger on it.

"Ready?" Murphy says.

Shit, I never told Hope I had to go back out tonight.

"Give me a few seconds."

"I'm going to start her bath," Heidi says, nodding at Alexa. She leans up and kisses Murphy's cheek. "Be careful."

I nod to Murphy to go help Heidi out. "Go on. I need to talk to Hope."

I find her in the room across from our bedroom. The room I thought one day might make a good... well, it doesn't matter what I thought. Since Alexa's taken over Hope's home office, Hope uses this room to review documents and prepare for court.

She's curled up in her over-sized chair, glasses on, hair up, practically swallowed whole by one of my sweatshirts. Skintight leggings with little skulls all over them cover her legs, leaving her feet bare.

So fucking beautiful I stop to watch her for a few seconds before letting her know I'm there. The pressure of knowing I'm needed somewhere else finally spurs me forward. I walk up and tickle my fingers over the soles of her feet.

She yelps and jerks her feet away. "You know feet are off-limits." Her wide smile negates the scolding tone.

"You looked so serious. Enthralling read?"

She rolls her eyes and sits up, placing the folder on the table next to her chair. "No, it's a medical report that I need an expert to explain to me. What's wrong?"

"Murphy and I are heading out."

Not that I want my wife unhappy, but I wish she didn't look so relieved that I'll be gone for the night.

"You feelin' all right, baby doll?"

Her gaze slides away. "Why do you keep asking? Do I look bad?"

"Never." It's true. No matter what she says, she's always beautiful to me.

"When will you be home?" The anxiety creeping into her voice doesn't make me feel better either.

"Not sure."

She sits forward and takes my hand. "Please be careful."

"Always. I'll try not to wake you when I get in."

"Wake me, so I know you're home safe."

I lean in and kiss her, taking a few extra seconds to show her how much I hate leaving.

"CHRIST, WAS WONDERING if you were ever gonna show up," Z bitches as soon as Murphy and I step into the garage.

"Shut the fuck up," I answer without even glancing his way. "Van loaded up?"

Wrath throws me an annoyed smirk. "Just waitin' on you, Prez."

Ignoring him, I glance around for Sparky.

"Got his list and details here," Z says, waving a little red notebook in the air.

"Well then let's stop bitching and get moving." I lift my chin at Dex. "You take the van with Hoot."

"Got it."

"At least someone knows how to listen and show respect," I grumble.

Wrath shakes his head, but for once keeps his mouth shut.

Neither Teller nor Murphy have spoken and I glance at both of them to see where they're at.

"Teller, you ride next to me."

"Rock—"

I cut Wrath off before he gets out his protest. "Shut your mouth and watch my back like you're supposed to." I stare at him for a second to make sure the order sticks. "Murphy and Bricks, behind the van."

"You got it," Murphy says. Bricks echoes the comment.

"Ass-kissers," Z mutters.

Murphy flips him off before starting up his bike, which finally drowns out Z's bitching.

The ride does little to clear my head. It's purely business. Everything that brings me pleasure is at home.

At least Loco's waiting outside behind his diner for us. If I have to drag my ass out here to meet him for every delivery, he should too.

This time Malik's with him and we nod to each other. Still haven't figured out how Loco really feels about Malik potentially joining the MC as a prospect.

"Don't say it," Wrath growls when Loco slides his gaze between Wrath and Malik.

"But it's uncanny." Loco cackles with glee.

Malik levels a slow glare at his friend. "I hate you." His serious rumble of a voice would give any sane man pause. Loco just laughs harder.

"Enough fucking around." I glance behind me, searching for Z. "Hurry up, Mr. Punctual."

Z's boots crunch over the gravel at a lazy pace and I shake my head. "Let's take this discussion inside." I nod to the back door.

Z, Loco, Malik, and I crowd into the hallway. Loco really has earned his nickname. He doesn't seem the least bit intimidated being crowded into a tight space with three men who're easily each twice his size.

Two who aren't particularly thrilled with him at the moment. A glance at Malik's somber expression says maybe my count is off.

"Damn, Rock. How you just take off for eighteen days and not tell a man? We do business together. Long time now. Don't I get that courtesy?"

"I *did* tell you." My clenched jaw does little to hold back the irritation in my voice. "I also told you when we returned that I had some things to handle."

"Well." Loco sniffs, and brushes some imaginary lint off his sleeves. "Your boy Stash took care of me."

"Good. You're the only person I gave him special instructions about."

He beams as if this is a compliment.

It's not. My instructions were: No matter how much he irritates you, don't blow his fucking head off.

"What was the problem?"

"Well, I ran low. That your boy helped me with. But I also had some clients that needed to be spoken to."

I flick my gaze at Malik and it's not lost on Loco.

"Yes, that's what Malik's for, but my other guy was on vacation and I coulda used an extra set of hands."

This is where I think Loco's gotten his wires scrambled. We're two separate entities. He is *not* part of the MC. He's someone the MC does business with and I'll help him out when and where it suits the needs of the MC. I can not and will not drop club business for him.

How to convey that without hurting his tender feelings?

Jesus Christ, working with DeLova's crew gets more appealing every day.

"This was club business, Loco. That comes first. Always. You know this. As you mentioned, we've done business for a long time."

"All right. Just got twitchy when I heard you all was visiting the Demons."

"You fuckin' kidding me?" This time I get in his face, backing him up against the wall. "Keeping tabs on my club isn't healthy for this relationship, Loco."

Feels good to finally get that off my chest.

Loco's gaze strays to Malik, who doesn't budge. Z also remains still.

"I don't owe you an explanation for where I go or who I visit," I continue. "You need to get that through your head."

"As long as you're not promising my supply to anyone else."

The balls on this motherfucker.

"What are you really worried about, Loco? You know I'm not selling to anyone but you. No fucking way am I risking my guys driving this large a quantity that far on a regular basis. Not the way the feds are cracking down on it lately. So what's really bothering you?"

"You know they're connected to mafia, right?"

"Fuck yes. Everyone knows that."

"Those kind of connections can bring a lot of trouble and complications we don't need."

"You think I don't know that?" I heave out a breath and take a step back, trying to muster up some respect. "I realize you've been in the game a long time, Loco. But I still got a few years on you. I know exactly what those connections are capable of. I'm not crawling into bed with DeLova anytime soon."

He sucks in a deep breath at the mention of the Russian mob leader's name. "Word is, he's looking for someone to move stuff for him and your club's name came up."

"Not my club. Sway's."

"That piece of shit," he mutters.

Can't say I disagree at the moment, but I won't speak badly of a brother to someone outside the club.

"What's the problem, Loco?" Z asks. "It's supposed to be a one-shot deal."

"It's never a one-off with those guys."

"Now, Loco, it's not nice to stereotype," Malik says with a straight face.

Loco shoots a glare at him and I barely restrain my laughter.

"Stop acting like DeLova's normal," Loco says. "We all know he ain't."

"He's got one foot in the fucking grave," Z answers in a bored tone.

"Like fuck he does. And even when he goes. Who's getting that business? Someone worse. That's who."

"Not my problem."

"You say that now, Rock. But in a few years it might be another story. They are ruthless, soulless fucks who'll start spilling blood if they think it gets them a foothold somewhere. We need to stick together."

He's not wrong. Part of why I worked so hard to extract my club from working with an organization very similar to DeLova's when I took over as president.

It's why even though Loco annoys the shit out of me on a regular basis—like every fucking time I see him—I'd still rather work with him over DeLova. "My ties to the Demons go back to when you were probably in diapers."

"You ain't that much older than me, Rock."

"Loco, our crews are tighter than any other business dealing I have. MC or not. You need to get over this."

Malik shifts on his feet. "What I think Rock's trying to say, is you're acting like that jealous girlfriend you wanna keep fucking, 'cept she keeps snooping in your phone and reading all your texts and shit."

Loco glares back at him. "Don't take his side."

"I'm not taking any side. I'm telling you as an impartial witness to *both* sides."

"You're supposed to be on my side!" Loco snaps. "You work for me."

Malik lets out a low, threatening growl before turning and walking away.

Z grins Loco's way. "See, Wrath woulda just knocked your teeth down your throat."

"Shut up, pretty boy."

"Enough," I bark, holding up my hands. "We done here? I got a van that needs unloading and other shit to attend to."

Loco takes a second to compose himself. "Just promise me you'll give me a heads-up if you're gonna work with DeLova."

"I assure you I have no interest working with DeLova. My crew isn't about that. Hasn't been for a long time. But I got no control over what Sway does." I cock my head at him. "Besides, aren't you the one he'd give that business to?"

Loco puffs up his chest. "DeLova don't work with color well. Don't wanna be on that motherfucker's radar and have his crew thinking they can roll on in here and take over my territory."

"Your "territory" is inside *Lost Kings territory*. He ain't gonna mess with that," Z reminds him.

I finally realize what's bothering Loco. "I don't want any piece of your action." I'm mildly offended he thinks I'd pair up with DeLova to get rid of him.

"DeLova's soldiers would love to start running girls in the capital region. All those deep-pocketed politicians. Lotta power running through this area. Only they won't be as nice about it as I am."

"They ain't gonna be doing it in Empire or Ironworks," Z assures him.

The back door slams open. "You done trying to cuddle-fuck my prez or should I stand around and wait some more?" Wrath shouts.

Surprisingly, Loco laughs. "Yeah, we done." He holds out his hand, which I'm not inclined to shake at the moment, but I do. "How was your trip?" he asks as if his jealous meltdown never happened.

"Fine. Good riding weather. Too fucking hot down south, though."

"Fuck yeah," Loco agrees. "Bunch of racist motherfuckers too."

"Now, Loco, you know we got those up here too," Z says.

Loco shifts his don't-tell-me-shit-I-already-know expression Z's way. "Fucking heat seems to make 'em multiply."

"Any other grievances you need to air out?" I ask.

He grins up at me. "I'll let you know."

"Fantastic. Can't wait."

Hope

AT SOME POINT during the night, the bed dips behind me and Rock's body warms my back. His lips ghost over my shoulder.

"I'm home, baby doll," he whispers.

"Love you," I mumble.

"You too." He presses a kiss against my back and settles down, resting his hand on my hip.

Unaware of the time, I drift back to sleep.

Seconds or hours—I can't be sure—later, a heavy queasiness wakes me and I moan. My hand slides down to rest over my stomach as my sleepy mind tries to figure out if I need to rush to the bathroom or if it will pass.

Please let it pass. I don't want to be sick now when I risk waking Rock up and making him worry.

The second I have the thought about him, he slides his hand over my hip to my thigh.

I hold my breath. His roaming hands frequently explore my body in the middle of the night. Most of the time his explorations lead to some pretty fantastic dreamy-half-awake sex.

Right now I can't think of anything worse.

My stomach lurches again. Oddly, the upset stomach ignites a spark of hope inside me.

Rock's sleepy fingers trail up over my ribs, stopping below my breast.

"Not now," I murmur, hoping he's asleep.

Instead, he buries his face in my hair, kissing my neck. Any other time, I'd turn over and be thrilled to indulge in some sleepy-middle-of-the-night-sex with my husband.

"Stop," I say a little louder.

He jerks back, then kisses my shoulder.

"Rock, not now."

My stomach rolls again. Nope. It's not going to pass.

Wriggling out of Rock's grasp, I throw the covers back and run to the bathroom.

Nothing comes up, but I wait on the floor for a few minutes, before standing and splashing some water on my pale, sweaty face.

I'm so freaking scared.

Deep breath.

The last time I didn't have any symptoms. Getting sick should be a good sign, right?

Maybe if I say it a couple hundred more times, I'll convince myself.

I slip back into bed as quietly as possible but realize Rock's not there. Figuring he went across the hall to use the other bathroom, I allow sleep to pull me under.

A few hours later, I wake again and Rock's side of the bed is still cold. I throw back the covers and grab my robe. The room across from ours is small. I use it as a reading room and there's a couch in there.

For the first time I realize it will make a perfect nursery.

That's where I find Rock.

"What are you doing?" I whisper, gently touching his arm. "Are you mad at me?"

He blinks up at me, his mouth curving into a warm smile. "Can't keep my hands off you. Didn't want to keep bugging you when you don't feel well."

"Oh stop." Now I feel even worse. If he knew I was pregnant and struggling with all-the-time sickness, he wouldn't be here.

"Come here," he says tugging on my hand.

"No. Come back to bed. I don't like you sleeping on the couch." I tug back just as hard, but he's immovable.

He pulls harder and I topple over him, rolling to my side and stretching out so we're face-to-face. He kisses my forehead. "You feeling okay?"

"My stomach was bothering me."

Truth.

"Murphy's cooking?" he teases.

Chuckling, I shake my head. "No."

Also true.

He rests his chin on top of my head and after a few minutes his breath turns deep and even.

Mine doesn't. All I can think about is the test that looms over me in the morning.

To find out if I'm having a baby or having my heart broken. Again.

CHAPTER TWENTY-THREE

Hope

LAST NIGHT CAN'T happen again.

I find Rock in the kitchen the next morning. "Finally get some sleep?"

"A little." I flick the burner on underneath my tea kettle and pull out a mug.

"How do you feel this morning?" he asks from behind me.

Shitty.

Taking a calming breath and slowly blowing it out, I turn and face my husband. "Rock?"

He's closer than I thought and I have to tip my head back to meet his eyes. He raises an eyebrow waiting for my question. "Are you busy today?"

He places his hands on my shoulders drawing me closer. "I have a project I'm behind on. Why?"

"When are you leaving?"

"In a couple minutes." His stare becomes too much for me and I glance down. "What's wrong, Hope? Do you need me?"

God yes.

My hand flutters over my stomach and of course Rock doesn't miss the movement.

"Tell me." His voice deeper, more serious than before.

Courage rises in me like a tidal wave. I can't—I shouldn't be doing this without him. What if it's bad news?

"I have a doctor's appointment," I whisper. "Do you think you can go with me?"

"Of course I will. You're scaring me, though. What's going on?"

"Nothing bad."

Please let that be the truth.

He drops his gaze to my hand over my stomach and narrows his eyes. Slowly, his gaze roams up my body, stopping at my chest. He drags his hands from my hips up over my ribs, then gently cups my breasts.

I suck in a hit of air, closing my eyes to focus on his touch.

"What time is your appointment?" he asks in a low voice as he gently kneads. His thumbs brush over my nipples and for a second I can't articulate an answer to his question.

"Eleven," I finally answer.

"Fuck, where?"

I pry my eyes open and my heart speeds up. The question he wants to ask burns in every line of his face. "Right down in Sterling."

He flicks his gaze to the clock and reaches past me to shut off the stove. "Shit, we need to leave now."

He leans down, pressing his lips against mine. Turmoil and curiosity shine in his eyes as he steps back, taking his hands off me.

"I'll feed you breakfast when we get back, but you need to eat something now." He pulls out a granola bar from the cabinet, grabs a bottle of water from the fridge and presses them into my hands.

"Thank you." I turn away, walking to the closet to grab my coat.

Rock's silent as he takes my hand and we walk over to the garage. Silent as he opens the door and helps me up. Silent as he slides into the driver's seat and starts the truck.

He glances over at me and I offer a hesitant smile.

"I need to call Bricks. Let him know I won't be down until… later or tomorrow," he says almost like a question.

A question I'm not sure he's ready for the answer.

He waits until we leave the property and are on the main road, headed toward Sterling, a small town right outside of Empire. He puts the call over the Bluetooth and I sit silently while he explains to Bricks that he won't be coming in today.

"Yeah, no problem. I got it covered," Bricks promises.

"Thanks, brother." He hangs up and grips the steering wheel tight. "Where am I going?"

"Straight on eighty-five. It's the first building after the light."

The tension between us rises and I'm halfway to a meltdown by the time he pulls into the parking lot.

"Left," I direct him around to the side of the building. He stops, shifts into park and glances over at me then at the building.

Sterling OB-GYN.

He doesn't say anything, but I wait for him to come around and open my door. He grips my hand tight and leads me inside.

"Hi, I have an eleven o'clock with Dr. West."

"Have a seat Ms. Kendall, we'll be with you in a few minutes."

Rock chooses a chair away from everyone else in the waiting area. As I sit next to him, he leans over. "Clearly this isn't your first visit here."

"Well, no. It's my regular—"

"*Don't,*" he growls in a low voice, only loud enough for me to hear. "You know *exactly* what I mean."

Although he's tight with irritation—not quite anger—and he has every reason to be, he wraps his arm around mine and laces our fingers together in a familiar, loving way.

"Are you all right?" he asks after a few minutes. "Is *everything* all right?"

My bottom lip trembles. "We'll find out today."

"Jesus, Hope," he mutters. He kicks his legs out straight, crossing them at the ankle and leans back in the chair. On the outside, he probably appears laid back and unconcerned. But tension radiates off him. The tight set of his jaw. The death grip of his hand on mine.

It kind of makes me want to jump him.

As if he knows the dirty thoughts in my head, he gives me a sideways glance. "What are you thinking about?"

"Nothing appropriate," I murmur.

He leans over, placing his lips against my ear. "Don't try to distract me with thoughts of sinking into your hot pussy. As soon as we get home, I'm stripping you down and working you over. Hard."

My breath catches.

"If you're good, I'll let you come too," he whispers.

"I'm going to come right now if you keep it up."

He sits back and lifts an eyebrow. I rub my hand over my stomach and lean into him, bringing my lips to his ear. "If I'm not nauseous, I'm horny."

He sucks in a breath and closes his eyes. My lips twitch, happy I have the same effect on him he has on me.

"First we need to discuss you lying to me," he says.

"I didn't lie—"

"Don't," he cuts me off. "When?"

ROCK

I COULD THROTTLE my wife right now.

She has me so fucking wound up. Torn. Hopeful. Scared as fuck. Pissed off. Turned on. So many emotions brewing inside, I could lose it any minute.

Since we returned from Florida, I've suspected something was going on with her. I think I understand why she didn't want to tell me, but it still pisses me the hell off.

My fingers squeeze hers and she turns, watching me but not saying anything.

"Does anyone else know?" I ask. As mad as I am she hasn't confided in me sooner, I'm more upset she's been struggling with this alone. If Trinity, or hell, even Heidi has at least been there for Hope, I'll feel better.

Her eyes widen as if it hadn't occurred to her to seek out help from one of the girls. "No. I'm not sure of anything yet. I wanted... I wanted you to be the first to know." Her gaze drops to the floor. "No matter what."

"I wish you hadn't been going through this alone," I finally say.

Her body stiffens, but she meets my eyes. "I didn't want to get your hopes up and then—"

"Baby, you know better by now." I reach up, brushing the back of my hand over her cheek. Something else occurs to me, and my mouth quirks. "Were you worried I'd hover over you even more than usual?"

She snorts softly and shakes her head. "Maybe."

"I've been worried about you."

"You know me too well."

"Yeah," I agree.

We're finally called into a room and I follow her with a hand on her back. Can't keep my hands off her. No, I have the urge to wrap her up in soft blankets and carry her everywhere.

"THIS IS SO embarrassing," she mutters as she emerges from the bathroom in a thin hospital gown.

"Why? I know you inside and out, Hope." Her cheeks turn pink and I lean down, brushing my lips against her ear. "I spend as much time inside your pussy as humanly possible. You don't have anything to hide from me."

She chuckles softly as I boost her up onto the lightly padded table.

She shifts as the paper crinkles under her and rearranges her gown. "Yes, but there isn't usually a doctor and an ultrasonic wand up my hoo-ha involved." She gestures toward the end of the table and shudders. "Or stirrups."

One corner of my mouth slides up and I pat the table. "I kind of like this. Maybe I'll put one downstairs." I stroll to the end pretending to inspect the equipment. Her gaze follows me and I wink at her. "Set up like this will give me easy access."

"Gross," she sputters through her laughter. "I had no idea you had some medical kink lurking under all your badassery."

"I have a *Hope* kink," I correct, throwing her another teasing smile. "Any way I can get you."

Her eyes gloss over and she holds out her hands. "I love you, Rock."

"Love you too, baby doll." I take her hands and pull her against my body, wrapping her up in my arms. The sweet scent of whatever shampoo she's using this week fills my nose and I bury my face in her hair, finding my way to her neck where I kiss and nibble her skin until she's laughing again.

"Good morning, Ms. Kendall," the doctor greets with a bright smile as she bustles in through the door, closing it behind her. I back away a few inches and the doctor smiles even wider. "Mr. North, I'm so glad she finally brought you."

Well, at least Hope must have made it clear I wasn't some asshole who didn't *want* to be here with her.

"Is everything okay?" I blurt out, realizing the whole time I've been trying to tease Hope to keep her mind occupied, I've also been trying to calm myself.

I'm scared shitless.

"We should find out today. We didn't find what we wanted on last week's ultrasound. This test should tell us one way or another."

My heart plummets. This might not have a happy ending after all.

The thoughts racing through my head must be evident on my face.

Hope squeezes my hand. "This will tell us if the baby's in the right place or…" She drops her gaze.

A technician joins us in the cramped room.

"I see what could be something right there." The doctor stares at the screen. "Well that wasn't hard to find today." She points to a black speck in the middle of the screen. "See the white area around it? That tells us it's a true pregnancy."

The technician moves. "Here's a different angle."

The doctor nods and points to the little bean again. "There's your little bean. Right in the uterus where it should be," the doctor says, pointing at the screen to fuzzy white jelly-bean-sized speck.

Hope bursts into a combination of tears and laughter and covers her mouth with her hand. "That's our baby?"

"That's your baby," the doctor confirms.

My lungs seize and my hold on Hope's hand tightens. I run my free hand over my chin as I stare at the monitor.

Ours.

Our baby.

"Everything looks good."

"Oh thank God," Hope breathes out.

"How far… when?" I croak out.

The doctor shrugs. "By the size, I estimate five weeks, three days." She taps the numbers into the computer and gives us an estimated due date.

I ask a few questions that make Hope blush, which the doctor answers honestly and with a straight face.

Finally, we're almost ready to go.

"This is good news today," the doctor says. "But I still need to see you in a couple days for more bloodwork. You're still a high risk pregnancy," the doctor reminds Hope.

I take Hope's hand and squeeze.

We have to go next door so Hope can have blood drawn. She holds on tight to my hand and closes her eyes the whole time.

Only then does it hit me the enormity of what she's about to go through. For us.

When we return to her doctor's office, her doctor hands me a pamphlet and winks.

I glance at the blue and white lettering on the front. "Pregnancy Sex: Seven Positions For Her Comfort."

Hope laughs and shakes her head. "Well, I guess I know what we'll be doing later," she whispers.

"Damn right."

While she schedules the next appointment, I take out my phone to make sure I can be with her.

"You don't have to come every time," Hope says on our way out.

"Yes. I do. And I will." My tone leaves no room for discussion. "I don't want you coming here alone for any reason."

I help her into the truck and get in on the other side. Before I start it up, I stop and look at her.

"Rock," she says softly, resting her hand on my knee. "I know how close we are to everyone, but I want to keep this to ourselves just a little longer."

Love expands in my chest, filling every space. The love for my wife. The love for the life we created. My desire to give Hope anything and everything she needs burns stronger than ever. I grab her hand lifting it and kissing her fingertips. "Sounds like a plan."

She relaxes, sitting back and closing her eyes.

"Are you okay?"

"Just tired."

The *frustration*—anger's too strong of a word—of her leaving me in the dark for so long returns. I let go of her hand and she places it over her stomach. Unsure of what else there is to say, I let her sleep for the short drive.

We'll have our talk when we get home.

Hope

THE ABSENCE OF moving wakes me as Rock parks the truck in the club's garage. He throws a glance at the clubhouse before opening my door and helping me out.

Even though it's the middle of the day, it's quiet at the property. Nothing but leaves rustling in the light breeze and the random hawk searching for prey breaks the air.

We walk home hand in hand. Rock's quiet. I think his silence has to do with making sure I make it safely over every pebble and pine cone in our way.

The ominous thud of the door closing behind us when we step into the house suggests his silence has more to do with something else. Still groggy, I stand there while he strips my coat from my shoulders and hangs it in the closet.

Exhausted, I turn to go upstairs.

"Where are you going?" Rock asks. His low voice holds something other than curiosity.

"I want to change."

He doesn't answer, and I continue upstairs. As my hand touches my closet door, he steps into the room. "You think we're done with this?" he asks.

"With what?" I can't see him because I'm lifting my shirt over my head, but after I fling it in my closet, he's right in front of me.

Staring down at my body.

Breathing hard.

Taking every inch of me in.

He reaches out and shuts the closet door.

"Rock, I wasn't—"

"Yes you are."

Something isn't quite right and I take a step back. He follows until the backs of my legs hit the bed and I'm trapped.

"Take your pants off."

"Well, I was trying to—"

He doesn't wait for me to finish. He reaches out, hooking his fingers into the waistband and yanking my jeans open. Roughly, he shoves them down my legs and I kick them off.

"Get on the bed."

"Rock, I—"

His eyes close and he takes a deep breath. "I love you, but I'm still furious with you. I can't decide if I want to fuck you or spank you."

Heat races over my skin for several reasons. Shame, because I know damn well why he's so angry. Desire for my husband who's the epitome of sex. Embarrassment that both options dampen my panties.

"Do I get a vote?"

"No." He takes another step, so we're pressed up tight against each other. His arms band around me, keeping me from falling back on the bed. He places both palms against my ass and squeezes. Despite how furious he claims to be, he feathers the softest kiss over my lips.

"You're everything to me, Hope," he almost whispers the words as he touches his forehead to mine. "I can't lose you."

"You heard the doctor—"

"That's not all I'm talking about. We tell each other everything. I don't want to lose *us*."

"You're happy about the baby?" I finally ask, because deep down, even though I know he'll be a wonderful father, I also know he was content with our life the way it is… *was*.

"So happy, baby doll. I won't lie to you, though, I'm worried."

"I know. That's why I waited until we could—"

"Yeah, about that."

Damn, I should have kept my mouth shut.

CHAPTER TWENTY-FOUR

ROCK

I CAN'T EVEN be angry at Hope. I love her too fucking much and I understand why she waited to tell me. Love her for it, even if I wish she'd told me so she wasn't going through it alone.

She has never looked more beautiful.

"Come here." I hold out my hand and she takes it. Her breath hitches when I yank her closer and swing her up into my arms.

"What are you doing?"

I press a kiss to her forehead and carry her into the bathroom. Setting her down in front of the tub. "What's this?"

"I want to take care of you."

"You want me wet and naked."

"That too."

I squeeze a few drops of her favorite oils into the tub and turn the taps. She stands there shifting from foot to foot. Uncertain and sweet. "Are you mad at me?" she asks in a low voice that I can barely hear over the rushing water.

She balls her hands into fists at her sides giving away her vulnerability. "No, baby doll. I love you too much."

Her lower lip trembles. "I'm sorry."

"I understand why. But, no more. I don't want you struggling or worrying about anything alone ever again."

"I love you so much. And I don't want to… I don't want you to be…"

"You matter the most to me."

A brief, beautiful smile flickers over her lips and she tips her head toward the tub. "Will you be joining me?"

"Fuck yeah," I answer, twisting the taps off. I sit on the edge of the tub and pull her between my knees, resting my forehead against her stomach. "How do you feel? Tell me everything."

She runs her fingers through my hair. "Sick in the mornings. Well, all the time really."

"How'd I miss that?" She always spends so much damn time getting ready in the morning. I never considered she might be locked in here because she was sick.

She shrugs. "What can you do? Hold my hair back for me?"

"Yes. If that's what you need me to do." I tease my fingers inside her underwear and drag them down her legs.

"I so appreciated you asking the doctor if sex was safe, by the way."

I grin up at her. "That was vital information."

Her shoulders bunch up and she lets out a short laugh. "I had already warned her that would be one of your questions."

"Did you now?" I tickle my fingers over her ribs and she laughs even harder. As she pulls away, I hook my fingers in her bra, keeping her in place.

My hand roams over her ass and she slants a look at me over her shoulder. "Is it time for my spanking, Mr. President?"

Only one person—*this woman*—has the power to erase all of my irritation and anxiety. I give each cheek a soft tap before unhooking her bra.

"Bath time," I say, taking her hand.

"There's no graceful way to climb into this thing," she mutters as I help her into the tub.

Shaking my head, I release her hand. "Good?"

"Perfect." She tilts her head. "Aren't you joining me?"

Instead of answering, I slowly work my belt loose, then strip off my shirt.

"Oh my," she mutters, staring up at me. "I don't need the slow, seductive routine, just get in here."

"What fun is that?" But I do hurry up because I'm eager to be skin on skin with her.

Once I arrange myself in the tub, I pull her against my chest. "You've had me worried," I mumble into her hair.

"I'm sorry." She turns slightly. "I haven't known that long. You know how bad I am at keeping track of things."

I laugh because that's a bit of an understatement.

"When do you want to tell people?"

"Maybe after the next appointment? I want us to get used to the idea first."

I'm ready to take action now. Plan a nursery, paint it, build some furniture, take some classes. Do whatever the fuck it is parents do when they get this news.

"Might be hard to keep it from Heidi and Murphy since they're right downstairs."

She sighs and drops her head against my chest. "I know."

"Think about it."

She sniffles and I squeeze her tighter.

"Thank you," she whispers.

After a few minutes, I rub my chin over her shoulder and kiss her neck. "Washing your hair?"

"Not now." She lets out a long yawn. "I'm sleepy."

"Doctor said you need your rest."

"Yes, dear. I'm aware."

"Can't help it. Get used to it, baby doll." My words are light and teasing even though my thoughts threaten to drag me down.

Guilt will gnaw on my flesh and bones until there's nothing left if anything happens to her.

Hope

THE WATER COOLS and eventually we drag ourselves out of the tub. Rock's quiet as he dries us off and leads us into the bedroom.

The matter of fact way he throws the covers back and nods for me to get into bed makes me tingle all over.

"You're not going to the shop?" I ask.

"Not today." He cocks his head and nudges me over to my side. "Are you going to the office?"

"I guess not."

He slides in next to me and I poke my toes against his leg. "I'm chilly."

He pulls the covers up but keeps staring at me, running his hand over my stomach.

"A watched tummy doesn't grow," I tease.

He rumbles with laughter. "I can't wait."

"For?"

The smoldering stare he responds with is pure caveman. "To see your belly carrying our child."

"Aww," I coo and run my fingers through his hair, smiling up at him. I know how much he means those words and it's why I'm able to admit how I feel about everything.

"That part freaks me out," I whisper.

He raises an eyebrow and strokes his finger over my cheek. "Tell me why."

"I've struggled with my weight forever." I run my hands over the few stretch marks I've already collected along my hips. "I'm not looking forward to adding to these."

The sexy, simmering stare turns into a scowl. "What did I say the day we met?"

"A lot of things. You were quite talkative for a guy who just posted bail."

He lets out a brief chuckle before turning serious again. "You told me you wore your wedding rings on your middle finger because you'd lost weight and I said 'don't lose any more.'"

"Oh yeah." I smile at the memory. "Pretty obnoxious considering the situation."

Rock's not offended or embarrassed. He grins. "My point is, gain whatever you need to. I'll think you're sexy as fuck no matter what and it'll be my pleasure to help you work it off when you're done nursing."

"Wow, you have it all planned out, huh?" I tease.

"That's what I'm here for." He pulls me closer. "Come here and let me hold you."

Warm and snuggly in Rock's arms, I'm hovering on the edge of falling asleep when he rumbles out a question that snaps my eyes open.

"Answer one thing for me. What if it had been bad news? Would you have told me then?"

His gentle tone doesn't disguise the anguish in his voice.

"Yes, of course." I take a deep breath and place my free hand over his. Bringing up such a painful time in my past isn't easy, but I so desperately want Rock to understand my reasoning. Understand *he's* not the reason I kept our baby a secret. I am.

"When I... miscarried, it took me by surprise. I went from being upset about the unplanned pregnancy, to getting married, and excited for the baby. Clay and I had just started preparing for this huge change and then it was ripped away."

I swallow hard, remembering the ectopic pregnancy that almost killed me a few years ago. "Then after losing *our* baby the way I did.

Almost dying. I honestly thought this," I stop and squeeze his hand that's resting over my belly, "might never happen. I didn't want to give you this possible future and then have it yanked away."

He swallows hard. "I understand."

"That first time, Clay and I had heard the baby's heartbeat at my appointment the week before. Saw the little life flickering on the screen." I have to stop to catch my breath. "We thought the baby was healthy. The miscarriage completely blindsided me. The silence after I lost the baby haunted me for so long. I wanted to spare you that if I could."

His arms wrap around me tighter, anchoring me to his body and he kisses the top of my head.

"I want to be with you for every appointment from now on." His low voice leaves no room for disagreement on the subject. "I don't want you doing any of this alone," he says.

"Thank you."

He closes his eyes, the line of his jaw tightens. "You don't have to *thank* me, Hope. It's the least of what I *need* to do for you." When he opens his eyes there's nothing but love in them. He gently sweeps my hair off my cheek. "I know how scared you probably are, even if you won't admit it. I'd do it for you if I could. I want to do everything I can to make this easier on you."

"Having you know is a huge help." I exhale a long, slow breath. "Sharing it with you has already made me feel so much better."

"Good." He kisses my forehead. "Take your nap. When you wake up let's try some of those positions in the pamphlet your doctor gave me."

"I think that was for later, when this gets in the way." I rub my hand over my belly and wiggle my eyebrows at him. "Right now *every* position is available."

CHAPTER TWENTY-FIVE

ROCK

TERROR CLAWS AT my insides, pulling me out of sleep.

It takes me a few seconds to figure out why.

I'm going to be a father.

Not the father-figure to a bunch of child-like bikers.

An actual father.

I can't believe it. Can't believe how much I want it.

It's all the *other* stuff leading up to our child's arrival that woke me. I almost lost Hope once. How the fuck did we let this happen?

Next to me she moans in her sleep and wriggles closer. My arm automatically slips around her waist and I settle my hand on her stomach.

That's how this happened. I can't keep my hands off her.

An hour later, I still can't sleep. Hope rolls over and burrows her head under her pillow.

Quiet as I can, I slide out of bed.

"Where're you going?" she asks.

"Why're you awake?"

"Not," she mumbles.

"Can't sleep. Gonna run over to the clubhouse."

"Be careful." Her standard answer for everything I do. My girl worries about me as much as I worry about her. She sighs and her breathing returns to deep and even.

Now that I've made the decision, I dress quickly and pad down the stairs. Except for a strip of light shining under Heidi and Murphy's door, the house is dark.

I'm the loudest thing crashing through the woods in the middle of the night. I'm not even sure why I decided to go to the clubhouse.

Z's in the war room and he grins when he sees me. "What's up brother?"

"Can't sleep."

His grin turns filthy. "I can think of a hundred better ways to cure insomnia than comin' over here."

"Yeah, well. She needs her rest."

He drops the smirk. "What's wrong? Everything okay?"

"Yeah. Just worry about her."

He cocks his head. "Looks like more than your usual overbearing nature. What's going on?"

Here, Hope and I agreed to keep the baby a secret for now and the first person I run into, I'm ready to spill everything. But it's not just anyone, it's Z. As much as he lives to irritate me some days, at least he'll be receptive to the news. Unlike Wrath, who's allergic to anything pregnancy or baby related. When I finally break the news to my oldest friend, it will break his damn heart.

So Z it is.

"She's pregnant." It feels weird to say the words. Weird and amazing. "We're not telling anyone yet."

"Yeah," he answers slowly. "I get it." He stands and gives me a hug and back slap. "Congratulations, that's awesome."

"It is." I pull out my chair and drop into it, feeling better already.

"Now the insomnia makes sense."

"I'll be pushing sixty when this kid graduates from high school." As soon as I say it out loud, I realize that's *one* of the things bothering me.

Z waves his hand in the air, dismissing that concern. "You're in better shape than most guys half your age. You'll be fine. How's *she* feeling?"

As frightening as he might appear on the outside, Z might be the only one of my brothers who'd think to ask that question first. "Tired. Nauseous."

"You just find out?"

My jaw tightens. "I did. She's known for a little bit."

"Aw, poor girl."

I give him a sharp look. "Poor girl?"

"It probably killed her keeping that from you. Bet she didn't want you gettin' excited in case something happened?"

"That's the gist of it."

"You better not have been too hard on her."

I snort and then laugh, amused with him for taking Hope's side.

There's a soft knock at the door and then it opens a fraction. Hope's pale face stands out against the darkness in the rest of the clubhouse.

"Am I interrupting?" she asks.

I stand and meet her, pulling her to my chair and into my lap.

She wiggles around so she's facing Z. "How come you're up?"

"I'm always up, Hope. You know that."

She laughs softly and leans back, wrapping her arms around me.

"What brought you over, baby doll?"

She lets out a loud yawn, stretching her arms overhead and then settling them around my neck. "Can't sleep without you."

Z stands, an uncomfortable laugh rolling out of him. "I have some work to do next door. I'll leave you two alone."

"Thanks, Z," Hope says as she watches him leave.

I squeeze her a little tighter. "Don't like you walking through the woods alone at night."

"I was worried about you." She nuzzles against my neck. "You smell good." Her tongue darts out, teasing over my skin. "Taste good too."

"Careful, baby doll."

"Why?" Her hand moves over my chest, sliding up to cup my cheek.

A slight turn of my head and I dip down to taste her lips. She shifts and sits up, taking the kiss deeper. "Rock."

"You want to go home?"

"Can't wait that long," she responds, voice full of urgency.

What little control I had in the first place, snaps. I slip my arms under her and stand. Setting her on the edge of the table, I push myself between her knees and brush her hair out of her face. "Do you know how beautiful you are? How much I love you?"

"Show me."

I unzip her sweatshirt and raise an eyebrow. "You came over here with nothing underneath?"

She gives me a sly smile and slips her hands under my T-shirt. We kiss again, and I slide her sweatshirt off, letting it pool around her. "Lie back for me."

"Why?" her voice nothing more than a husky whisper.

Movement to my right catches my eye and I glance at the door.

Sparky stands there, eyes wide and apparently too stunned to move. He catches the look on my face and backs out quickly.

Why can't I ever fuck my wife on the war room table without someone walking in on us?

"What's wrong?" Hope asks, balling her fists in my shirt.

"Nothing." She'll die of embarrassment if she knows Sparky stopped by. "Lie back for me."

She does as I ask, sitting up on her elbows, so she can watch me.

"No underwear either. You *are* naughty."

Her soft laughter eases all the worries I came over here with.

I pull my chair closer, and hook my arms under her knees, dragging her to the edge of the table.

"I really want your cock," she whispers.

"You'll take what I give you and love every second." I kiss her inner thigh, taking time to drag beard scruff over her soft skin. She makes this sigh-moan-laugh sound deep in her throat that's sexy as fuck.

Still wanting to drag this out as long as possible, I slide my fingers against her bare lips, adding pressure with each pass. She's slick and ready when I finally lean forward and skim my tongue along the same path.

"Oh more. Rock, more. Please," she begs. I smile against her skin. She has no idea how loud she's being. Love that.

This isn't the time or place to take my sweet time. I close my mouth over her clit, sucking hard. She bucks against my mouth and I answer by pushing a finger inside her.

A little more and she's done. Only when she's gasping for air and her voice is raw, do I let up. Her left ankle rests on my shoulder while her right foot is braced against the table, leaving everything on display under the harsh overhead lights.

"You're so fucking beautiful, Hope."

She answers by stretching her arms over her head, arching her back. Driving me even crazier with the need to have her.

I stand, pressing kisses along her thigh and behind her knee, even rubbing my cheek against her calf. She jiggles with laughter.

"That tickles."

"Hang on. I'll give you something that won't tickle."

She laughs harder and tries to sit up.

"No." I pin her with a look and she stops. "Put your hands over your head and arch your back again."

She does it, but it's not quite as natural and spontaneous as the first time.

I run my palm over her belly, up between her breasts and stop to tease her nipples until she's relaxed again.

I can't shove my pants down fast enough. I grab her ankles, spreading her legs and slide into her.

We both stop to groan. The tight wet heat of her body is almost too much. She sets me on fire. Incinerating me from the inside out.

This won't take long, but there's no way I'll come until she does one more time for me.

Savoring, every thrust and sound we make, I go at a lazy pace until her inner muscles tighten around my cock.

Fuck, being inside my wife is the only place I need to be. The second I'm with Hope, the rest of the world ceases to exist. All the complicated bullshit disappears. My worries evaporate.

"Harder," she whispers.

That's all I need to hear. I thrust harder, chasing the calmness and peace that connecting with her brings.

Her breathy sighs turn to long moans and whimpers. A never-ending stream of words begging me not to stop.

A searing rush of love and protectiveness surges inside me and I gather her closer, pressing my lips to hers. She holds on tight, digging her nails into my shoulders, setting me off.

I let go, unleashing an intense orgasm that leaves me shouting her name.

"Love you," she whispers, blinking up at me.

I drop my forehead to hers. "Love you too. Are you okay?"

She wiggles under me and I groan.

"This table's pretty hard."

"I'll show you hard."

We both laugh at the silly joke and I pull her up. She's soft and dreamy as I help her dress.

My fears of losing her haven't gone away. If anything I'm more aware than ever of how precious every moment is and what lengths I'll go to in order to protect what matters most.

CHAPTER TWENTY-SIX

Hope

ROCK MAY HAVE made a joke about hovering over me when he found out I was pregnant, but he wasn't kidding.

He's on me about everything. Rather than annoying, I find it to be a relief.

True to his word, Rock's taken me to every single doctor's appointment over the last few weeks. There's no rushing to the appointments either. Nope, he has me up an hour early. I don't have to worry about anything, honestly.

If it isn't related to incubating our baby, Rock's taken over. And frankly, even that he's very involved with.

"This really isn't necessary," I grumble after he wakes me up much earlier than my groggy body appreciates.

"We're not going to be late today." He gives my butt an affectionate slap. "Go take your shower. I'll be downstairs making breakfast."

My stomach lurches at the mention of food. "None for me," I spit out before running into the bathroom.

Rock's a warm, comforting presence at my back while I barf.

"You're supposed to eat the crackers I left by the side of the bed before you get up," he says gently, helping me stand.

"I keep forgetting."

He waits until I'm out of the shower before heading downstairs.

Forget nauseous or hungry. I'm *sleepy.* I could go back to bed right this second. I sigh and look at the bed longingly on my way to the closet. Maybe I'll throw on what I plan to wear and sneak in a quick nap.

"Hope, breakfast is ready!" Rock shouts up the stairs.

So much for nap time.

I drag a pair of jeans up my legs, throw on a T-shirt, and grab one of Rock's flannels, buttoning it as I trot down the stairs.

"Feel better?" he asks in a low voice as he meets me at the bottom of the stairs.

"A little."

His hungry gaze sweeps over me. "Love you in my shirts." He tugs on one sleeve and rolls it up, then motions for the other one. "It's like a coat on you."

Heidi, Murphy, and Alexa are already at the table. Heidi glances at my outfit. "Slow day at the office?"

"I have a doctor's appointment and then just catching up on paperwork this afternoon."

Murphy flicks his gaze between Rock and me. "Everything okay?" he asks.

"Everything's fine," Rock says, placing his hand over mine. "Eat your breakfast or you're going to be late for school," he says to Heidi. "Dropping Alexa off at your brother's?"

She nods to the *Mermaids don't wear pants and neither do I* T-shirt Alexa's wearing.

I snort and almost choke on my orange juice. "Is she over her unicorn phase?"

"No!" Alexa yells.

"That would be a *no.*" Heidi laughs. "She wants it all."

"Come here, funny baby," I say, picking Alexa up. In addition to the T-shirt, she's decked out a frilly, layered and poofy skirt in mermaid blues and greens. A tiny pair of sparkly-pink Dr. Martens boots on her feet complete the look.

"Where can I get a pair of these?" I ask, tapping my fingers against the toes of her boots.

"No!" She brushes my hands off her boots and holds onto them tight.

"I won't steal them. They're too small for my feet."

Satisfied, I won't rob her of her fancy new footwear, she snuggles into my lap and stares up at me. My heart pitter-patters and I kiss her forehead. "Is Uncle Teller going to put you to work today?" I ask.

"Yeth."

"Yeah right." Murphy rolls his eyes. "I'm pretty sure they have an exhausting afternoon of cartoons and naps."

Alexa giggles and reaches for him and I hand her over.

"Sully's gym keeping you busy?" I ask.

He shakes his head and sets down his coffee cup before Alexa dunks her fingers in it. "Nah, he's easygoing compared to working with Wrath."

"I imagine *anyone* would be easygoing compared to Wrath."

"Got that right," he mutters. "Now that he has a reopening date in mind, he's got endless to-do lists for me."

"Do!" Alexa mimics, patting his cheeks.

"Can't wait till you're big enough to put to work," he teases, kissing Alexa's cheek.

Heidi laughs. "I can totally see her helping you out in the garage."

"Gotta get her over her hatred of loud pipes first," Rock says.

Someone taps on the sliding glass door behind us and Rock groans.

Since Z's the only one who regularly uses the back door, I wave for him to come in without turning around.

"Morning," he says, thumping snow off his boots.

"You could use the front door," Rock says without turning around.

"I'm checking up on your safety and security, Prez." Z reaches over me and snags a strawberry out of the bowl in the middle of the table.

"Grab a plate." I point at the empty chair next to me and he holds up a hand.

"I'm good."

"Eeeee!" Alexa yells.

"I figure she's either trying to say Z or she's just excited to see you," Heidi says.

"She's trying to say 'favorite uncle' naturally." Z plucks her out of Murphy's lap and holds her at arm's length to check out her wild outfit. "Mermaids, huh?"

Alexa bobs her head up and down.

"Mermaids used to lure sailors off course to their death." He grins at Murphy. "Appropriate since that's what'll happen to boys who come sniffing around you when you're bigger." He says it with a grin, but Alexa squints at him as if she's not so sure she likes what he has to say about her new favorite mythical creature.

"Who knew your uncle Z was so knowledgeable about mermaids?" Heidi shakes her head at Z and takes Alexa from him.

"Well, thanks for the folklore lesson," I say, standing up and gathering the plates.

"I got that, Hope," Murphy says.

"Aw, look at you all domesticated and shit," Z snarks.

"It's called being a polite houseguest, you ogre."

"You're family, not a houseguest," I remind Murphy.

"You're a fucking saint, Hope," Z says.

Rock stands and takes the dishes from me. "Go get ready. We're going to be late."

ROCK

GETTING HOPE OUT of our circus of a house takes some effort, but I have us on the road on time.

"I hope Z and Murphy don't kill each other," Hope says.

"They're fine."

"I think I'm going to be a little sad when they move out," she says softly.

"Yeah? You won't be happy to have our house back?"

"Well, yes, but I like seeing them in the morning." She chuckles and fiddles with the radio. "Checking out Alexa's outfit for the day."

"They won't be far." I glance over. "Besides, I think we'll be busy."

I expected her to smile, but she places her hands over her stomach and winces. "I hope so."

"What's wrong? You feel okay?"

"Just queasy."

"You need me to pull over?"

"No. I don't think so."

She closes her eyes and sits back, taking long deep breaths until we arrive at the doctor's office.

"How do you feel?" I ask.

"Better." She yawns and pushes her door open.

"Wait for me."

We have a shorter wait than usual to see the doctor.

"How are you feeling today?" she asks as she comes into the exam room.

"Still nauseous a lot."

"And tired," I add.

"Perfectly normal." She runs through a list of other questions and

214

takes Hope's blood pressure.

The part I'm wound up tight about happens at the end of the appointment.

The last time we were here for a regular check-up we heard the baby's heartbeat on the fetal Doppler. This time we should be able to see *and* hear the baby with the ultrasound.

"There it is." The doctor points to the screen.

Hope sits up a little and I put my hand on her back to help. "Does everything look okay?" she asks in a small voice.

"Yes. The baby's the size I expect to see at this point. Heartbeat is strong." She rattles off a few more indicators that point to good news.

After our talk the day she finally told me she was pregnant, I understand why Hope's so anxious.

She's been here before. Heard this before and still lost everything.

When the doctor finishes, Hope reaches for me and I squeeze her hand.

On our way out, I stop the doctor. "What can I do?"

She's give me a not unsympathetic smile. "Keep doing what you're doing. It's great that you come with her to these appointments. She should sign up for a childbirth class soon. If you can go to those with her, it would be good. You'll learn a lot too."

"Okay."

"Keep her exercising and keep her stress down."

"I'm trying. She seems tired a lot, though."

"That's normal. I've checked her iron levels and she's not anemic, but that's something we'll keep an eye on. Once she gets into the second trimester she should have more energy."

"Okay. Thank you."

Hope's irritated expression as she's checking out quickens my steps. "What's wrong?"

"The stupid insurance won't cover the ultrasound."

"We knew that might happen."

"You can contact the insurance—" the receptionist starts to say, but I pull out my wallet and hand over the cash to cover it.

"Rock." Hope protests.

"I'll deal with it later." The last thing I need is her getting worked up over a couple hundred dollars.

We finish and I get her out into the parking lot. It's a crisp, cool winter morning. Hope grasps my hand as we navigate the damp pavement.

At the truck, she stops. For the first time since we heard the heart-beat, she smiles and tips her face toward the sun, resting her head on the truck window. I reach out and tuck a stray strand of hair behind her ear. "You're going to get salt and stuff all over your coat."

"Oh." She brushes off her sleeves and shrugs. "What'd you talk to the doctor about?"

"Just asked what else I can do to help."

"Oh, Rock." She bites her lip. "You're already so much… I don't think many women are as lucky as I am."

"Well, I'm in the unique position of making up my own schedule."

She curls her fingers into my leather cut and pulls me closer. "Being the man-in-charge has its perks." She leans up and whispers against my ear. "It's also very sexy."

How this woman lives to distract me. "She said we should find a childbirth class to sign up for."

Her lips curl into a pouty-smile. "That's not sexy talk."

"No, it's after-the-doctor-visit talk."

"Swan's been working on some prenatal yoga with me."

"That's not the same thing."

"Fine. I'll ask Mara if she knows of one."

"Speaking of your friend, how do you feel about telling people now?"

"Good." She smiles even wider. "Let's do it. Maybe poor Swan will stop worrying she gave me food poisoning all the time."

Hope

I CAN ONLY describe Rock as *giddy* as he hoists me into his SUV for the drive home. Well, giddy and more chivalrous than ever.

"Rock, I can get in the car all by myself," I say, brushing his hands off me.

He grins and leans in to kiss my cheek. "I don't want anything happening to my girl."

When he slides in next to me, he pulls out his phone and taps out a text.

"What's wrong?"

"Nothing. You're finally ready to tell people. I'm asking Z to assemble everyone who's at the clubhouse for an announcement."

It takes me a second to realize the "announcement" is this. Us. Our baby.

Oh my God, we're really having a baby!

Yeah, I'm still having *that* freak-out about twenty times a day.

Reaching over, I settle my hand on his arm to grab his attention. "Rock, it's not club business. They're going to overthrow you."

He sets the phone down, and shifts so he's facing me. Taking one of my hands in his, he squeezes gently. "It's an addition to the family."

I open my mouth, but he cuts me off.

"You still got it in your head we're a bunch of testosterone fueled Neanderthals—"

"Well—"

He smirks, before cutting me off. "While that's true ninety-nine percent of the time, trust me, they'll want to hear this."

He's right. Also, I'm ninety-nine percent sure he's already told Z.

"Should we tell Murphy and Heidi first?"

"If you want to."

We're almost at the clubhouse, when Rock reaches over, settling his hand over my stomach.

"What are you doing?"

"Want to see if I can feel the baby."

"You heard what the doctor said. I think it'll be a few more weeks."

He chuckles. "You never know. Any baby of mine should be pretty big."

"Caveman."

He laughs but doesn't disagree.

THE YARD IS full of bikes and other vehicles when we arrive. Rock tucks his SUV into its usual spot.

"Did you want to stop at our house first?" Rock asks as he helps me out of the truck.

"No." Now that I've had time to think about it, I'm excited about telling everyone. Nervous, though, because I'm still unsure that the guys really care about stuff like this.

"What's going on, Rock?" Wrath asks as soon as we're inside.

"Nothing." Rock's gaze skips around the room, taking everyone in. "We have an announcement."

I catch Trinity grinning at me. Her eyes widen and she mouths "oh my God" at me.

Rock catches me around the waist, pulling me tight to his side. His hand rests over my belly and he gently squeezes. "We're having a baby."

The guys whoop and shout. Everyone advances on us for hugs, kisses, back-slaps, and congratulations.

"I knew it." Trinity squeals and grabs my hands. "I didn't want to say anything, but I knew something was up." She glances down at my chest. "Your boobs are bigger than ever."

I burst out laughing until tears leak from my eyes. Throwing my arms around her, I wrap her up in a hug. "Thank you. I needed to laugh."

"I'm serious. They're huge."

Of course Wrath overhears *that* and sweeps his gaze over me to confirm his wife's observation. "How did I miss that?"

Trinity teasingly smacks his arm, while Z answers the question. "You're whipped, that's why. I noticed, just figured—"

"Do you want to die today?" Rock growls, pushing Z back.

Z grins and sidesteps Rock, taking cover behind Murphy and Dex.

"This is so good, boss. So, good. More babies means more good energy. So much good energy in the club," Sparky yells, taking the attention off Z.

Dex comes over and gives me a quick hug. "No wonder you're prettier than ever, sweetheart."

"Thank you. Are you excited to be an uncle again?"

He stares off into the distance for a minute before flashing a smile so confident, it almost hides the sadness in his eyes. "Sure am."

Murphy grins and playfully points a finger at me. "I owe Heidi twenty bucks, you know." In a lower voice, he asks, "Why didn't you say something? We would've kept it quiet."

"After...I...well...I just...we wanted to be sure before we told anyone," I stammer through an answer unsure of how much information Murphy's looking for and feeling a little guilty.

He envelopes me in a warm hug, rubbing my back quickly before letting me go. "Whatever you need, tell me, okay?" He glances over at Teller and Rock, who are busy holding their own intense conversation. "If you need us to move out—"

"Don't you dare. I was just telling Rock this morning how much I'm going to miss you guys when you move into your own house."

"Thanks, Hope. You and Rock. I really appreciate everything you've done for us."

"Murphy, are you pregnant too?" Z asks. "You look so emotional."

"Fuck off, asshole." He turns to me. "Heidi will be home in a bit.

She said she's going to buy a cake so we can celebrate at dinner."

"Oooh, cake." I rub my hands together and the guys laugh.

Z moves in, eyeing Murphy as if he's expecting a gut-punch. He leans down and gives me a quick hug. "You know Rock told me the night you came clean, don't you?" he whispers in my ear.

I laugh and pull away. "I suspected."

He runs an imaginary zipper over his lips, which Ravage notices and immediately calls everyone's attention to. "Uh-oh. Z, you're not secretly the dad, are you?"

"That's it." Murphy growls. He and Teller take off after Ravage, who sprints down the hall.

"Sorry, Hope!" Ravage yells out.

There's a crash in the dining room, followed by a thud.

Rock shakes his head. "Maybe we should've done it by text."

"Or carrier pigeon," I suggest, which cracks him up.

ROCK

I DIDN'T FEEL like our life was incomplete. Or we were missing anything. But after hearing our baby's heartbeat today and finally sharing the news with the club, I can't wipe the grin off my face.

If only Hope shared my excitement.

"You okay, baby doll?"

She's been quiet since we got roped into dinner at the clubhouse. I can't tell if she's not feeling well or it's something else.

Murphy and Heidi headed to bed a while ago.

Hope and I are settled on the couch in front of the fireplace. Her head rests in my lap and my hand idly strokes through her hair, down her side and over her hip. She lets out a contented little sigh before answering my question.

"This is nice. Do you think things will change?"

"Between us or in general?"

She sits up, drawing her knees to her chest. "Both, I guess."

"Sure. I know you think I'm a big caveman, but I'll help you."

Her lips twitch. "I already know how good you are with babies after having Alexa here."

Couldn't help it. Hard not to love that little girl. "Right. And you know the club will help. You saw how excited everyone was. They weren't faking that shit."

Now I get a full laugh out of her. "True."

"What's really bothering you, baby doll?"

Her eyes gloss over and I work not to smile. Hormones. My sweet woman's as sensitive as ever.

"I don't want anything to change between *us*."

"Everything will change. Good changes."

"Okay."

"Come here." I lunge forward and wrap my arms around her, pulling her into my lap. "Tell me what's bothering you."

"I just did."

"My feelings for *you* won't change. I love you more every day, Hope."

A soft *aww* sounds passes her parted lips and she leans in to press kisses over my cheek and to my ear. "I love you."

I settle my hand over her stomach and her mouth quirks. "You'll be doing that more and more, won't you?"

"All the time."

While she's staring down at my hand, I move and accidentally—I swear—brush the underside of her breast. The little gasp of surprise she lets out stirs me up.

"Sensitive?"

"No." She hesitates. "Maybe."

I do it again.

"Is that everything?" I ask, pressing kisses along her jaw.

She bites her lip. "I... I loved going on that trip with you. Going to National. Being by your side. We had a lot of fun. Even though things got a little crazy in Florida at the end."

My mouth quirks, little crazy's an understatement.

"Loved having you with me."

"And now I can't help feeling like that's all over with." She glances down. "You'll still have to go off and do those things. But you'll do them without me."

"Hey." I touch my fingers to her chin and tilt her head up. "I don't want to do any of that without you. Murphy made it work. So will we."

"You think so?"

"Fuck yeah."

A weight seems to lift off her shoulders and she takes a deep breath.

"Is that all that's bothering you?"

"What if you do decide to take a role on the national board? That will mean a lot more—"

"Hope, I promise you, baby or no baby, that is the *last* thing I want to do."

"Okay."

"What else?"

"Well, I already told you," she runs her hands over her hips, "I'm worried about the gaining weight thing." Her lips quirk into a smile. "But you helped me conquer that one pretty quick."

"Damn right I did." I kiss the hollow at the base of her throat, along her collarbone and up to her ear. "I'm more than willing to show you how sexy you are any time you need a reminder."

CHAPTER TWENTY-SEVEN

Hope

I NEED A nap.

A long one.

I felt like I was walking through mud all day. The drive home had never seemed so long.

While I wait for the clubhouse gate to open, I pop another ginger candy in my mouth, hoping it settles my stomach. I can't believe I have to carry around an emergency in-case-I-barf-all-over-myself bag with me now. Shirt, toothbrush, toothpaste, wet wipes, crackers, and my new favorite thing, ginger candies.

It's twilight as I pull into the clubhouse lot. Murphy and Z are silhouetted in the light spilling from one of the garages.

Murphy turns and waves, then jogs over to my car.

"Pull in there, Hope." He points to the garage in front of me instead of where I normally park. "I want to check a few things tomorrow morning."

"Okay."

Something in my tone must catch his attention because instead of returning to Z, he follows me into the garage and holds my door open.

"Everything okay?" he asks.

"Just a long day."

Z and his dogs meet us outside the garage. "How was your day, Hope?"

"Long." I stop to pet both Ziggy and Zipper, laughing when they each bump a cold, wet nose against my cheek.

Wrath steps out of the garage, wiping his hands on a towel. "I thought I heard that wussy little engine of yours," he teases.

Because I'm an adult about to become a mother, I do the only acceptable thing and stick my tongue out at him.

"Why are you all out here?" I ask.

Murphy points to Wrath and then himself. "We were actually working. I'm not sure what this clown's doing." He nods at Z.

"Working out the old-fashioned way." He pokes Murphy's stomach. "You should give it a try so you're not packing on more weight while Furious is down."

"Get off me, jackass." Murphy laughs while he shoves Z back.

Only then do I take in Z's shirtless body, glistening with sweat in the fading daylight. My heart may belong to only one man, but I can't help noticing what's right in front of me in all its spectacular glory.

"Are you eyeballing my trail of tears?" Z asks, running his hand down his inked abs and over the dark trail of hair disappearing under the waistband of his gym shorts.

"Your what?" I answer, dragging my gaze up to meet his laughing eyes. "Why would you refer to anything on your body as something sad?"

Next to me, Murphy snickers. "Why even ask, Hope?"

"Because," Z says, drawing my attention away from Murphy. "And this is the truth, Hope. Ladies cry tears of *joy* when they see the monster I'm smuggling in my pants."

Wrath and Murphy lose it, laughing at both of us.

"Rock's gonna kill you," Wrath finally sputters out.

"What? She asked."

"I've just never heard that before," I protest, averting my gaze toward the woods. "I thought guys called it their happy trail. Never mind."

"Come on, Hope. I'll walk you home," Murphy says, holding out his hand for my briefcase and the tote bag with the three-inch heels that never used to bother my feet. "You shouldn't be subjected to this."

We leave Z and Wrath in the garage trading insults at each other. Murphy shakes his head and offers me his arm. "You're such a gentleman," I say, grateful to have the assistance.

"You look tired."

"Gee, thanks."

"I didn't mean it in a bad way," he says patiently. "We all worry about you. That's all."

I snort. "Worry about me," I grumble. "Z made fun of me."

"Nah, he wanted to make you laugh."

I sigh and grip his arm a little tighter as the ground gets more uneven. "I *am* tired. I swear I took a nap at two red lights on the way home."

Murphy slows his steps and stares at me. "That's dangerous, Hope."

Realizing my mistake, I shake my head. "You're going to tell Rock I said that, aren't you?"

His mouth twists as he struggles to come up with an answer that won't be a lie or offensive to me. "Promise me you'll be careful. If you're tired, call me. I'll come get you."

"You have more important things to do than chauffeur me around." I squeeze his arm. "The big grand reopening is coming up soon."

Maybe I can take his mind off worrying about me with talk of the gym.

"Our first lady is more important."

No such luck.

Tears sting my eyes. Dammit, I'm tired of being so weepy. "Thank you, Murphy."

He opens the front door and sets my briefcase down by the staircase. "You hungry?"

"Starving."

"Heidi got lamb loin chops," he says, striding into the kitchen.

"That sounds amazing. I swear, lately all I want to eat is meat with a side of meat."

He chuckles as he pulls ingredients out and sets them on the counter.

"Let me go change and I'll help."

"Nah, why don't you go take a nap and I'll call you when dinner's ready."

I hesitate.

"Come on, you know you want to be bright-eyed when your man gets home."

"Are you sure?"

"Hope, I think it's the least I can do for you after you've let Heidi, Alexa, and me live in your house for so long."

"You're sure?"

He waves me off instead of answering, and I trudge my way upstairs.

I slip off my blazer and drape it over a chair by the door. My boots get kicked in the direction of my closet. I only mean to sit on my bed for a second to roll my stockings off, but I end up falling back and drifting off to sleep.

ROCK

THE AREA IN front of the clubhouse is lit up from both the floodlights and the open garages doors when I ride up.

I back into my usual spot and stop in the garage before heading home.

"What's up?" I lift my chin at Z and Wrath.

Z taps the wrench in his hand against the front tire of his bike. "Noticed a puff of black smoke earlier. Replacing the air filter."

"I think that shitty little gas station down the hill already switched to winter blend," Wrath adds.

Z shakes his head. "I never stop there."

"Where's Murphy?" I ask, since normally he'd be helping Z out here.

"He *was* helping me earlier," Wrath says. "But your girl drove up and he ditched me to walk her home." He points at Z. "Plus, he was being totally inappropriate telling Hope how big his dick is and everything."

I glare at Z, who throws a crumpled rag at Wrath's head. "Shut up. She knew I was messing around."

"You two are assholes," I growl. "You gonna pull the plugs tomorrow if the air filter doesn't solve it?"

"Yeah."

"Maybe you can use your dick to swab the chamber and check for oil," Wrath suggests.

I roll my eyes and blow out a long breath. "Catch you two later."

Other than a few faint sounds from the garage and the wildlife, the woods are quiet as I walk the path home.

After being confined to the garage all day, I take my time absorbing the space and open air around me.

All the lights are on downstairs. I circle around to the back and into the basement laundry area to leave my boots and change out of my grungy work clothes before heading upstairs.

The sounds and smells of dinner meet me when I step into the living room.

"Hey, Prez," Murphy calls out.

A quick sweeping glance of the open downstairs shows Murphy's alone. "What're you up to?"

"What's it look like?" He sets a stack of plates on the counter. "Will you go wake Hope? Dinner's almost ready.

"She okay?"

"Yeah, she looked really tired when she came home, so I told her to go take a nap while I made dinner."

I swallow hard and nod before thanking him. "Where's Heidi at?"

"Had a play date with a girl from one of her classes. She's got a daughter around Alexa's age."

"That's good."

"Yeah, nice girl. Single mom. Lives with her parents. She's been helping Heidi out with her Chem class and Heidi's been helping her with Anatomy."

"Probably good for her to hang out with another mom her age."

He shrugs. "I think so. We'll see."

"You meet her?" Murphy's protective streak runs as wide as mine. I don't doubt he's checked out someone spending so much time around his girls. Even if she is a young single mother.

"Couple times when I picked Heidi up from school. Kinda shy. Heidi keeps trying to talk Carter into a blind date."

I snort. "How's that working out?"

"Dunno. Don't wanna know." He glances at his phone on the counter next to him. "She should be home soon."

"You need help here?"

"Nah."

"Hey." I wait for him to look up. "Thanks for doing this."

"No problem, Prez."

I jog up the stairs, eager to see my girl. The small lamp by the bed throws a weak circle of light over Hope's half-dressed body.

Almost looks like she fell asleep as she was changing.

"Hope," I whisper, hating like hell to wake her up.

The angle she's at looks awkward as fuck, so I lift her legs onto the bed and finish taking off her stockings.

"Mmmm."

"Babe, dinner's almost ready," I try again.

She blinks a few times, then smiles at me. "You're home."

"I'm home. Missed you." I cup her cheek with my hand and she closes her eyes. "Tired?"

"Yes." She yawns and stretches. "But I feel a little better after my nap."

"Murphy says dinner is almost done."

"Aw, he's such a sweetheart. Z was picking on me earlier and Murphy came to my rescue."

"Z what?"

"Nothing." She pushes away from me and stands.

"Damn, you look good in those."

She shimmies her butt in my face a few times and I yank her closer, sinking my teeth into a cheek.

"Come on, let's feed you and then I want to take you to bed early."

"Really?" She bats her eyelashes at me. "And do what?"

"Worship the ever-living-fuck out of you."

CHAPTER TWENTY-EIGHT

Hope

NOW THAT WE'RE telling people about the baby, I figure I better let Adam know that I'll slowly be dialing back my caseload in the coming months.

"What's on your mind, Hope? You look stressed," he says when I knock on his open office door Monday morning.

"Not stressed." I perch my butt on one of his uncomfortable wood and leather chairs that always feels like it's going to tip over. "Excited, actually."

"About? Don't tell me you've found another office space you'd rather rent out? I like having you here."

"Not quite." My hand settles over my stomach. "We're having a baby. So, yes, I'll probably be winding down my cases over the next few months."

He sits back and stares at me for a few seconds. Not exactly the reaction I expected. Then again, he's a guy. Mara had lost her marbles and actually wept when I told her.

"So you're just going to quit practicing?" he finally asks.

Shocked by his tone, it takes me a second to formulate a response. "No. Well, I don't think so. But I need to focus on my health and making sure this baby's healthy."

"Some women do both you know."

"Well, that's great for them." My tone sharpens and I lift my chin. "But I've already lost two babies and I have no intention of losing this one."

His eyes widen and he sits back, reminding me that Rock's really the only one I've ever talked to about the miscarriage I had when I was married to Clay. Unfortunately, it's been on my mind a lot lately. I'm terrified that any thing wrong I do might—*no. Don't go there.*

"I'm sorry. I didn't know that. I'm just surprised. If you're happy, I'm happy for you."

"Thank you."

He stands and comes to my side of the desk, holding out his arms. Willing to set aside my irritation because of our friendship, I stand and let him hug me.

"Congratulations. Is Rock happy about it?"

The corners of my mouth twitch. "Very much so."

"That's great. Good. If this is what you want, I'm happy for you."

Not the most loving congratulations, but I can't expect everyone to be as excited about this as I am. What's a monumental, life-altering change in my life, is just another piece of news in everyone else's.

Well, except the club. The guys surprised me with their excitement and interest. And the way they congratulated Rock as if he'd solved the mysteries of the universe rather than knocked me up.

"I have a meeting downtown," Adam says. "Will you be okay here by yourself?" he asks. "I'll lock up."

"I'll be fine. I won't be here too long."

"See you later."

Unsettled, I wander into my closet-sized office. I won't call Rock and tell him Adam sort of hurt my feelings with his lukewarm reaction. He'll want to ride down here and kick Adam's ass and that's not exactly going to help our friendship.

I contemplate calling Mara instead. She'd been excited enough for ten people when I told her. She'll definitely make me feel better.

"Hey, momma-to-be," she answers right away.

"Are you busy?"

"Nope. What's up? Everything okay?"

I relay my conversation with Adam to her and she sighs.

"He's such a dude. Dudes don't get it."

"You think I'm terrible for wanting to take time off?"

"Um, *no*. Time off should be mandatory in every civilized society. Trust me. I still haven't gone back to a full-time caseload and I have no guilt what-so-ever. Cora, my husband, and my sanity come first."

"Well, your husband's a billionaire."

She chuckles softly. "Not quite. But I'm fairly confident Rock will support whatever you want to do and do everything possible to take care of you."

"True."

"Have you told him you want to take time off yet?"

"No, I'm not really sure what I want to do. I'm just… worried. What if things are rough near the end or it's… shit, now I'm starting to freak myself out."

"Relax. Deep breath. Women have been having babies since, well, forever. You'll be okay. But yes, if it will help you to relax to clear your calendar a little and you can afford to do it, then you absolutely should."

"Thank you. I feel like I'm about a decade and a half too old to be doing this."

"But just think how much older and wiser you are now. You'll have more patience, which believe me you'll need. Plus, you're more financially and emotionally stable."

"I'm not sure about that last one lately."

She laughs softly. "It's a roller coaster for sure."

"I'm noticing."

"You also have a partner who I have a feeling will be very support-ive."

"He is."

"Hey, do you want to get together Friday afternoon? You can bring Alexa so the girls can play?"

I quickly check my calendar and we make a plan to meet at her house.

As we're saying goodbye, my phone beeps. Caller ID says it's my mother. Strange, since I haven't heard from her since a random phone call on New Year's Day. I haven't told her I was pregnant yet, but maybe this is a sign that I should.

"Hey, Mom," I answer.

"Hope, it's me... it's Bruce."

My skin prickles. My stepfather hasn't called me once in the decade or so he's been married to my mother. "Hi, how are you?"

He clears his throat and I brace myself for what's coming next, because obviously it's not good.

"Hope, I'm really sorry to have to say this over the phone, but your mother passed away early this morning."

Numbness, a serene sort of shock settles over me. My mother isn't that old. When was the last time I saw her? Guilt rubs against the numbness. Why didn't I make more of an effort?

Because she hurt you every time you tried, a small voice reminds me.

"What happened?" I finally ask.

"She had a heart attack." He sighs. "Last night she said she wasn't feeling well before she went to bed. But nothing alarming. She was in the shower this morning and I heard a crash. By the time the paramedics arrived, it was too late." He makes a choking sound between a gasp and a sob. That's what finally breaks me. *His* grief, because I'm still not even sure what I feel.

"I'm so sorry."

"I made all the arrangements. The funeral will be Wednesday, Hope. I know she'd want you there."

As if I wouldn't go.

"Of course I'll be there." I would've spent more time with her if she'd shown any indication that she gave a damn about me at all.

Am I upset that my stepfather's apparently already taken care of everything without any input from me? Not really. He knew her better than I did. Honestly, I'm relieved not to have the additional stress right now.

I unconsciously rub my hand over my stomach. *You'll always know how much you're loved. Always, little bean.*

I reach for a pen and write down the information he gives me. A few awkward minutes later, we hang up.

My gaze fixes on the wall across from me. How white and plain it is. Maybe I should hang something there. Maybe someone else will hang something there one day. If I leave, will Adam rent this office out to some other young attorney trying to find her way?

Why am I worried about that? It doesn't matter.

I pick my phone back up and call Rock.

"I was just thinking about you," he answers.

I close my eyes, picturing his handsome face, smiling as he tucks the phone between his ear and shoulder so he can finish whatever he's working on while we talk.

"Hope? What's wrong?"

"My..." my voice trails off, unsure of how to word it. "My mother died." Saying it to Rock makes it real and my voice cracks. "My stepfather called. Sometime this morning she—"

"Where are you?" he asks. In the background his heavy boots slap over concrete and tools clatter against metal.

"At the office."

"Stay there," he orders. "I'll be there in a few minutes."

ROCK

SOMETIMES I SWEAR it feels like we attend a funeral every couple months.

Or bury a body.

Even though she keeps saying she's fine, I plan to spend the whole day with Hope so she's not alone.

"Do you want us to come with you guys?" Trinity asks quietly while I'm making breakfast.

"No, it's okay. I don't think she's close to her stepfather."

"She's hardly ever mentioned him."

I stopped trying to encourage Hope to pursue a relationship with her mother during our engagement when it became obvious the woman didn't give a fuck about her daughter. I saw how much that indifference hurt Hope every time she reached out and got slapped down.

Although I stand by my decision, I still wish things had been different for both of them.

"Hey," Hope calls as she comes down the stairs.

Trinity rushes over to her. "I'm so sorry, Hope."

Hope accepts an embrace from Trinity and mumbles, "It's fine, really."

The two of them talk at the dining room table while I finish breakfast.

"You need to eat all of it." I kiss the top of her head as I set the plate in front of her.

"So bossy," Trinity teases.

Hope wrinkles her nose and stares at the plate. "It looks so good, but my stomach… ugh"

"Start with the toast."

"That's a spiffy looking bacon, spinach, and egg frittata," Trinity says. "I see you're putting that Fit Pregnancy subscription to use, Rock."

"Thank you for that," Hope mumbles around her piece of toast. "I think he's read it more than I have."

"Aw," Trinity winks at me. "That's what I love about you, Rock. You're in the kitchen cooking for your woman while she incubates your baby. And if someone dared imply it makes you less of a badass, you'd knock their fucking teeth down their throat. That's a real man and true love rolled into one."

Hope snort-giggles. "I *am* wildly spoiled."

I bring two more plates to the table, setting one in front of Trinity. "Don't give me any I-already-ate bullshit, Trin."

"I don't even like coffee all that much, but I miss it," Hope says, leaning over to inhale my cup.

"I'll make you decaf."

"It's not the same. I'll just sniff yours."

Trinity taps on Hope's arm to get her attention. "I came up with a great idea for your next bump session."

Apparently this is a thing. Every month, Trinity claims Hope *has* to take a photo of her baby bump. She's already annoyed about missing the first two months, so she's been relentless about scheduling and planning all future ones with Hope.

"You're going to continue this after the baby's here, aren't you?" Hope says.

Trinity grins for an answer, making Hope laugh.

After that, Trinity entertains Hope with funny stories about some of her photo shoots. "So Wrath wanted me to take a few shots at Sully's place and I can't remember if you've met Sully's girlfriend, but she's like this big." Trinity holds her hand a little higher than the dining room table.

"So, she comes up to about Wrath's knees?"

"Exactly. She's such a sweetheart, though, I didn't want to make her feel bad. I had to like stand on the desk to get them both in the shot."

Hope holds out her hand like a waiter carrying a loaded dinner tray. "You could've posed them with her sitting in his hand."

"Oh! That actually would've been really cute." She drums her fingers over the table, deep in thought. "I'll have to float that concept by them next time I'm out there."

"You're very secure. I wouldn't want Rock's hands on anyone else's ass. Work or not," Hope says.

Under the table, I tap my fingers against Hope's leg. "Why are you dragging me into this?"

Trinity *pffts* and waves her hand in the air. "Please, have you seen my ass?" She twists in her chair and pats her hip. "I don't have anything to worry about."

Hope chuckles and I lift my chin at Trinity, thankful she came over this morning to keep Hope distracted before the grim morning ahead of us.

THE FUNERAL IS brief. Apparently Hope's mother left lengthy instructions for what she did and didn't want. None of it included wasting money on frills. I can respect that, I guess.

A few friends from her mother's job make an appearance. Everyone seems to know who Hope is, so at least it's not like the woman pretended she didn't *have* a daughter even if she treated Hope like she didn't exist.

Hope's stepfather is a quiet man. Everyone grieves differently—I've been made painfully aware of this over the years—but he's almost robotic in his words and movement.

"Does he have any other family?" I ask Hope.

"Two sons a little older than me, but they live in Texas, I think. At least they used to."

"Hope," Bruce says, coming closer. "I'm so glad you came."

Hope steps forward to give him a hug, which I don't think he expected because he stares at her for a few seconds before giving her an awkward embrace.

"I'm so sorry," she murmurs.

He glances down at her stomach as if he's trying to decide if he should ask if she's pregnant. I realize it's her stepfather and he's not being inappropriate. I still don't like the way he looks at her and I move in closer, curling my arm around her waist and hugging her to my side.

"Bruce, this is my husband, Rochlan North. I sent mom an invitation to the wedding... but."

He shakes his head. "You know how forgetful she could be. I think she set the invitation aside and meant to send you something," he rattles off a list of lame excuses while his cheeks turn red.

"It's fine," Hope says. She rubs her hand over her stomach. "We're expecting...I was planning. Well, when you called the other day, I thought it was mom and I was..." her voice trails off and her eyes shine with tears. She sniffles and shakes her head.

"I'm sorry, Hope," Bruce says. "Let me know before you're ready to leave, I have some things of your mother's for you."

"Oh, okay."

Bruce steps away to talk to someone else, and Hope shakes her head. "I'm kind of ready to leave *now*."

"What do you think he has?"

"Who knows. She either lost or got rid of all my dad's things years ago. I doubt it's money. Anything she had would go to Bruce."

We stay for a few more minutes, but it's painfully awkward. Hope's tired and I'm more worried about her health than sticking around an "appropriate" amount of time.

I tap Bruce on the shoulder. "We have to leave. Did you want to walk us out?"

"Sure, sure." Finally, he seems a little more animated as he follows us outside.

In the parking lot, he pulls two medium-sized gray plastic totes that smell like mothballs out of the back of his car. "Some things of your mother's I thought you'd want."

"Oh." Hope stares at the bins. "Thank you."

I shove the boxes into the back of the SUV for Hope to deal with later. Or never since she doesn't seem at all interested in the contents.

LATER AT HOME, she's exhausted. "Do you want me to carry these upstairs and put them in the spare room so you can go through them later?"

"Sure."

I tuck her into bed first, then bring up the boxes. For a few minutes, I stare at the space. Hope and I haven't talked about where we're going to put the baby yet. This room's the only one that makes sense right now.

Unless we build an addition. I left room on this side of the house just in case we wanted to expand for some reason in the future.

I guess the future is here now.

After checking on Hope one more time, I head downstairs and run into Murphy.

"Everything go okay?" he asks.

"Yeah. We didn't stay long."

He lifts his chin toward the staircase. "How's she doing?"

"Taking a nap."

"Think you can come over to the house site with me for a few minutes?"

"Sure."

Knowing her phone's on silent, I send Hope a text to tell her where I am and head out with Murphy.

"What's on your mind?"

"What isn't?" he answers, pointing toward the back of the concrete slab. "The windows. We were talking about doing a curtain wall of windows for the view. But now that I'm thinking about it, I'm worried they'll be a pain in the ass maintenance-wise down the road."

"I think you're right. They look sleek, but they're made up of a lot of component pieces. If one or two end up defective, with the kind of winters we get up here, you could have a mess of leaks and damage."

"That's what I thought."

"If you decide you still want something like that, we'll find you a professional window installer. I don't want to trust that to the contractor."

His gaze shifts at the mention of the professional installer. Money's a concern for Murphy. Given everything he's taken on this last year, I'm more than willing to help him out. Problem is, he's a proud, stubborn bastard—like the rest of us—who doesn't want to accept help.

"I feel like it's something I should do myself," he says.

"Why? That's not your specialty."

He gives me an uncertain look.

"You start taking your bike to a mechanic, I'll call you a lazy pussy. You hire the right person to build your house, you're a smart man. See what I'm getting at?"

Finally, he cracks a smile. "Yeah, I get you, Prez."

"Better to do it the right way the first time than try and fix shit you cheaped out on later. So if you need help—"

"I'm not taking money from you. You've done enough for me—"

"You'll do whatever your president tells you to do and shut your mouth."

"Rock, you can't always pull the president card. That's not fair."

"Life's not fair."

"No shit." His face smooths into something more serious. "You've got your own kid coming. You can't be helping me out too."

A childhood spent not knowing where your next meal's coming from seems to do two things to people, either they're impulsive and piss money away the second they get their hands on it or they hang on to it with an iron grip, knowing you can't count on it to always be there. Murphy falls into the second category, which I respect.

"You heard Teller, we're all going to be sitting a little prettier once we can start accessing the cash from his tech investment. Your first payout alone should cover the house and then some."

"You know I don't like to spend money before it's in my hand, Rock."

"And who taught you that?"

He smirks at me.

"Listen," I say a little less sternly, "I know you. You're not gonna suddenly get greedy and put solid gold fixtures or some crazy shit in the house, so do what you need to do and don't worry about it. One way or another I'll make sure you're covered."

He swallows hard and nods. "Thank you, Rock."

"Any time."

His phone buzzes and he checks it. "Heidi's on her way home."

"Good. Let's head back so you can meet her. And I want to check on Hope."

At the house he stops. "Thank you again."

"Come here." I pull him in for a quick hug and slap his shoulder. "You've got this. No doubt in my mind. Proud of you."

He nods and continues through the woods to meet Heidi at the clubhouse.

The house is quiet, and I assume Hope's still asleep. I can't help checking on her, so I toe off my boots and head upstairs.

I find her in the sitting room going through the boxes her stepfather gave her.

"Hey," she says, giving me a soft smile. "How'd it go at the house site?"

"Fine. Murphy just had a few concerns." I lift my chin. "What do you have there?"

She beckons me closer. "Picture proof I was a pudgy, awkward teenager."

I take the framed photo she hands me and study it, not seeing anything she mentioned. A younger version of Hope—with fuller cheeks, fuzzier hair, and incredibly sad eyes stares back at me.

"I definitely would've tried to talk you into a ride on my '76 Super Glide to see if I could get you to smile."

"There wasn't a lot to smile about that year. We moved around a lot. I still missed my dad something awful. My mother wasn't always the calmest, most reassuring person in the world." She takes a deep breath. "She was never someone I could count on."

She touches her fingers to the glass. "I want to go back in time and tell *this* Hope that one day she'll be happy, but first life will make her stronger."

The wistful catch in her voice kills me. I never want her to feel that kind of uncertainty or fear again. I swallow hard and rest my hand on her more noticeable bump. "You and I will reassure our child of that every time they need to hear it. Together. I promise."

CHAPTER TWENTY-NINE

Hope

I'M STILL FEELING down the day after the funeral. It's dinner night at the clubhouse and I consider asking Rock if we can skip it, but he's already dressed and waiting for me when I get home.

"Hey, baby doll." Soft country music spills from the speakers in the living room and he wraps an arm around my waist, twirling me into the house.

"What's gotten into you?"

"Can't I be happy to see my girl?" He spins me again and yanks me against his hard chest.

I can't help laughing. "I'm clumsier than ever."

"More beautiful than ever," he counters. "Dance with me, pretty girl."

So for two more songs we gently swing and sway to spry, twangy music while Rock softly sings lyrics of loving my troubles away in my ear.

The heaviness in my heart lifts with each turn and dip.

Behind us, the front door opens. "Damn, Prez. Had no idea you had moves like that," Murphy says.

We turn and I realize I'm laughing.

"Where's Trinity?" I ask as Rock pulls out my chair at the dining room table.

"Post office run," Wrath answers. "She'll be here any minute." He turns and glances out the window. "There she is."

"Dinner will be out in ten," Swan calls out.

Each brother's here and I spend a few minutes catching up on what everyone's been up to.

"Hey!" Trinity greets everyone. She slaps a pile of mail on the table and throws herself into the chair across from me. "Just came back from the post office." She tosses a catalog my way. "Here, Hope." She gestures toward Murphy, then Wrath, and finally Rock. "Since Murphy's started a beard trend around here, I thought you might enjoy that. And for some reason there were three of them stuffed in our box."

"That sounded incredibly dirty," Ravage points out.

"Shut it," Sparky mumbles.

I pluck the catalog off the table and flip through pages of high-end beard and shaving products featuring meticulously groomed manly men in various stages of sexy chores like chopping wood and fixing cars. "Well, this isn't realistic." I shake my head. "There isn't a ripped jean or smudge of dirt anywhere on these guys."

"Posers," Z snarks, looking over my shoulder. "I bet that dude's never touched an ax in his life. That's probably a prop tool."

"You're a prop tool," Stash says, flinging a pen at Z's chest.

Z catches it and flips Stash off in one motion.

"Their beards *are* impeccably groomed," Trinity adds, tapping one of the pages. "The company isn't far from here. Wonder if they need a photographer," she mutters.

"Oooh, the Outlaw-scented beard oil. It features scents of"—I read off the description from the catalog that ends with the line—"known to work as an aphrodisiac."

"On who?" Charlotte asks. "Them or us?"

I reread the description before answering. "Doesn't say."

"Think it over, Hope," Wrath warns. "You want to risk him jumping you more than usual?" He nods at Rock, who punches his arm. Wrath doesn't even seem to notice the hit, he's laughing so hard.

"I dunno," Ravage says. "These days Rock might be the one getting worn out."

"Haven't you run your mouth enough today?" Rock growls.

"Hmm, church must've been interesting this morning," I mutter, returning my attention to the catalog.

From the corner of my eye, I catch Heidi squirming in her seat, which makes Ravage zero in on her immediately. He rounds the table and leans down over her shoulder.

"What's wrong, princess?" The wide grin stretched across Rav's face makes Murphy narrow his eyes.

"Nothing." She puts her hand out for the catalog and checks the cover. "I bought Murphy one of those sets for St. Patrick's Day." She reaches up and strokes the back of her hand over Murphy's beard. "It's good stuff. Smells really nice."

"So metrosexual of you, bro," Rav snarks at Murphy.

Heidi squints up at Ravage. "Do people still say that?"

Murphy shrugs and slaps Rav's hand off the back of Heidi's chair. "I dunno. I use whatever she puts in front of me."

"No surprise there," Dex mutters, rolling his eyes.

Someone—Z, if I had to guess—makes a whip-crack sound and Murphy shakes his head as he's not at all embarrassed to at the insinuation that he's pussy-whipped. "Jealousy's an ugly color, bro."

Charlotte wiggles her eyebrows and elbows Heidi. "Did *it* work?"

Teller groans. "Seriously?"

"What?" Charlotte spreads her hands in front of her gives us an innocent shrug. "We could have a false advertising suit on our hands."

"Hey, they have a kid. They probably need the help in that department," Ravage adds with a false-sympathetic tone.

"Do you want to die today?" Teller growls, sounding an awful lot like Rock, which makes me chuckle.

"What?" Ravage touches his chest. "I don't discriminate. I'm equally obnoxious to all the ol' ladies."

I pick my head up and confirm his assessment. "It's true. He told me I'd make a good porn star the other day."

This time the growling comes from Rock's side of the table.

"See," Rav says without a hint of shame. "It wouldn't be fair if I treated Heidi differently because she's your sister, Teller."

Heidi scrunches up her nose. "Uh, thanks. I think."

"No one here needs the aid of an aphrodisiac," Swan says, setting out a king-sized bowl of spaghetti and meatballs. "What else do they have, Hope?"

Ravage slings his arm around her neck and gives her a quick hug. "Why, thanks, darlin'."

"No one coupled-up requires it," she amends with a cheeky smile. "Who knows *what* you single guys need."

"That hurts." Rav puts on a fake pout.

I reach over and pat his arm. "It's okay. It'll happen for you one day."

He raises his eyebrows. "What's gonna happen to me?"

"You'll find someone," Heidi explains.

"Nope. No thanks." He gestures around the table. "I love our family just the way it is." He shoots a glare at Z and then Dex. "We have a pact to remain single."

"That has to be the gayest thing you've ever said, bro" Stash says. "And you've given us *plenty* of material over the years."

"Speak for yourself," Z says, glancing at Dex, who looks away.

"Are there any more balls?" Stash yells toward the kitchen.

Z picks up a stray pot holder Swan left behind and smacks Stash with it. "Can't you go ask like a normal human?"

"No."

"Maybe we should get a to-go bag," I grumble.

"Aw, I haven't seen you all day. Don't leave." Trinity says.

"It's family dinner night, *dad*," Wrath adds.

I suspect Wrath hasn't been too thrilled about the mandatory family dinner nights Rock added sometime after Teller's accident when he came home from rehab.

Even though Teller's moved out and into his own home with Charlotte, the family dinner night managed to stick.

"I bought a chocolate cake," Swan says in her enticing-us-to-stay voice. She sets a huge bowl of meatballs smothered with red sauce in front of Ravage. "With the thick fudgy frosting, Hope."

My eyes widen in delight. "We'll stay." I point to Ravage. "If you behave."

"I'd love to, Hope. I'm not sure I know how."

"Fuck, if that's not the smartest thing you've ever said," Rock agrees.

There's hardly anything left after dinner. I offer to help Swan clean the table off, but Trinity, Charlotte, and Heidi go instead, telling me to stay put.

"Well, I still need to pee," I mutter. Rock stands and offers his hand.

"You need me?" he asks.

"To help me pee? Not yet. Give me another month or two." I rub my hand over my belly and he laughs.

"Hurry back."

ROCK

"CAREFUL, ROCK. DON'T get too worked up." Z says as soon as Hope leaves the dining room.

I drag my gaze away from my wife to cut a look at Z. "About what?"

He lowers his voice. "The no sex thing."

"What no sex thing?"

Wrath frowns. "Have you lost your mind, Z?"

Z gestures toward Hope's empty chair. "The baby."

"What about the baby?"

"She's showing more. Aren't you worried? You must, I don't know—"

Wrath explodes with laughter. "He's asking if you're worried about poking the baby with your dick."

"Shut up," Z snaps. "It's a legit question."

When I finish laughing, I answer him honestly. "The baby's perfectly fine and protected. The doctor assured me."

"Oh shit!" Ravage yells. "You really asked that?"

"Fuck yeah, I did. That's what the doctor's for."

"Poor Hope was probably mortified." Wrath chuckles.

Z shrugs and looks away. "Just figured she must be tired or whatever."

"Uh, no. For once, she's the one waking *me* up in the middle of the night."

Naturally Hope chooses that moment to rejoin us. My dickhead brothers grin at her. "Why don't you just tell her what we were talking about? It'd be easier, jackasses," I growl under my breath.

Hope's wary gaze sweeps over everyone before settling on Z, Wrath, Ravage, and finally me. "Hmm, what were you discussing?"

Ravage chooses that moment to pipe up. "Z asked if you're only blowing Rock now so the baby doesn't get a concussion."

Hope's jaw drops, which would be pretty damn cute under other circumstances.

"That's not what I said, dickhead." Z reaches across the table and punches Ravage's arm.

"Ow! Fucker."

"It's nothing that bad, Hope." Wrath smirks. "Prez was explaining the miracle of life to Z, because apparently the fancy private school he went to didn't offer sex ed."

"Shut up," Z grumbles.

Hope snorts, her cheeks turn a tad pink. "Which miracle? The joy of holding my hair when I puke? My aching feet that need his big, manly hands to rub them every night?"

Z grins. "Getting warmer."

Hope shoots me a look, a brief twitch at the corners of her mouth shows she's more amused than pissed. "Ahh, the rapture of I-need-his-assistance-in-the-bedroom-five-times-a-day."

"Five times." Z whistles. "Go easy on him, Hope. Rock's not a young stud anymore."

"No, he's better." She perches on my lap and runs her fingers through my hair.

"You guys are disgusting," Stash says.

Murphy chuckles and the guys look his way.

"What?" Ravage says.

Murphy flicks his gaze my way and for a second, I think he's going to rib me about dancing in the living room with Hope this afternoon.

"Nothing," Murphy says. "I was just thinking how sad it is that you're gonna die alone."

"Fuck that," Ravage says. "I'm going out in a blaze of glory."

Trinity carries out a huge chocolate cake and sets it in front of us. Hope's eyes widen and she rubs her hands together in anticipation while

I cut her a slice.

"Sex and chocolate cake," Wrath teases. "Now we know what does it for pregnant ladies."

"Is there any peanut butter?" Hope asks, sliding into her own chair and ignoring Wrath. She glances at the rest of us. "You guys better pray Swan bought more than one cake. I'm about to inhale this thing."

Heidi sets a jar of peanut butter in front of Hope and she grabs it, unscrewing the top and dipping in her spoon. "Thanks, Heidi."

Swan brings out a vanilla cake with white frosting. Hope gives it a brief glance and wrinkles her nose. "Keep the vanilla down there."

"Someone's kinky!" Ravage shouts.

Hope sputters. "What?"

Ravage nods at the cake. "Vanilla? Never mind."

"You're a douche," Wrath says.

"Everyone already knows about their basement room of kinkery," Z adds.

Heidi gags and covers Alexa's ears. "Isn't traumatizing me enough? Must you corrupt my daughter too?"

"There's not… we don't have," Hope stutters.

I rest my hand over hers. "Let it go, Hope. Just let it go."

MY CHEEKS ARE still warm and I glare at Z, who quickly looks away.

Heidi seems to pick up on my discomfort. "Trust me, Hope. Nothing will cure embarrassment like having your legs in the air and everyone sticking their face in your hoo-ha," she says, using her arms to demonstrate the *wide in the air* part. "Just wait."

Trinity snorts and I glare at her.

"Maybe I *should* be knocked out." I shovel another forkful of cake in my mouth and rethink my birthing plan.

"Well, but then you don't know *who's* been up in your business," Heidi says. "So afterward, every time someone comes in the room you have to wonder…"

"All right. That's enough," I say holding up a hand to stop her. "You're freaking me out." I grab Rock's hand. "You can't leave my side."

"Don't plan to." He glances at Heidi. "Especially after those visuals."

Wrath's laughing so hard the plates on the table rattle.

I glare at him too. "It's not funny."

"No, it's not." He shifts and mutters, "I won't be able to get it up for a week."

Trinity shushes him. "Continue, Heidi, this is *the best* birth control reminder ever." She leans in, whispering in Wrath's ear and he nods.

"There it is." He gives me a cocky wink. "We'll just double up."

"I hate you guys," I grumble, rubbing my hand over my stomach.

Murphy shakes his head quick, like he's trying to dislodge the words we just polluted his brain with. "I don't want anyone's face in your business," he says to Heidi.

"Well," she answers slowly. "I guess you should stop trying to impregnate me, then."

Trinity and Wrath lose it, laughing so hard my ear drums are in danger of bursting.

Charlotte's hand tightens around Teller's as he glares at Murphy.

"What?" Murphy shrugs. "She said it."

"Yes, but you're the one *doing* it."

Charlotte turns to the side and bites her fist, trying not to laugh.

I can see Murphy weighing in his head which snarky response he wants to throw at his best friend. And while most days I enjoy how much Murphy's grown up and the way he stands up to Teller, tonight, I'm too exhausted.

I lean my head on Rock's shoulder. "I'm too tired for this. Can you two go beat each other up somewhere else?"

Rock rubs a hand over my belly. "Too much cake?"

"No way, I could eat the rest of that thing right now. I just don't need the sugar rush."

At the other end of the table, the guys start up again.

"You're destined to die alone," Dex says to Ravage. "There might be some hope for you." He points Z's way.

"If I die, it's going to be in a pile of hot women living to serve my every need," Ravage boasts.

A whole lot of eye-rolling goes on.

"Find a girl and treat her the right way and it'll be better," Teller says.

"You have to say that, 'cause your girl's sittin' right there," Ravage shoots back.

"Fuck that shit," Stash says. "Then it's all missionary fucking and kissing. Giving head to get a little head. No thanks."

"I'm not sure what you're describing, but it's not marriage," Rock says.

I poke my elbow in his side and his deep, rumbly laughter warms me all over.

"Stop being such a selfish dipshit," Dex says.

"Maybe he just hasn't found *the right* person," Murphy adds. "You can't force it." In a lower voice he adds, "Or find a woman desperate enough to put up with him."

"I heard that, ginger Yeti."

"Oh great." Heidi rolls her eyes. "I'm glad that's becoming a thing."

"I said it first," Z reminds us.

"Brag about it, that makes it less idiotic," Teller says.

"My fiancé has a point," Charlotte says as she spoons ice cream onto her cake.

"What's that?" Ravage raises his eyebrows.

"That sex is better if you're with the right person." She squints like she's trying to remember something. "I think they say only eleven percent of women regularly achieve orgasm with one-night stands." She slides her hand through the air in an upward gesture. "But the longer a couple's together the more orgasms the woman has."

"In that case, Rock must be knocking Hope's socks off 'round the clock," Z says.

"Yes he does," I mutter.

"I got a list a mile long of ladies who'll tell you that's not true," Stash says with a smirk.

"They're faking it." Dex really seems to be enjoying bursting bubbles tonight.

"That's the chick's problem." Ravage shrugs and sits back. "Long as I get off. That's all I'm worried about."

"And *that's* why you're gonna die alone," Dex says.

"Well," I announce, pushing my chair back and standing up. Rock quickly stands and helps, wrapping his arm around me so I can lean into him. "This has been fun." I cast a glance at Ravage. "And disturbing." I stare up at Rock. "But maybe we can take some of that cake home."

"Oooh!" The guys make all sorts of horny cat noises at us, which we both ignore.

The slow smile that spreads over Rock's face warms me from head to toes. He leans down and presses a kiss to my forehead. "Let's go."

CHAPTER THIRTY

Hope

ANOTHER DAY IN court that utterly kicked my ass. I'm exhausted. Emotional.

Horny the second I see my husband.

By the gleam in his eyes, the feeling is mutual.

I stand still by the front door closet, waiting for him to prowl over.

His steel-gray eyes capture mine. The intensity of his stare electrifies my skin.

"What are you doing to me?" Rock asks, coming closer.

I glance down and clasp my hands behind my back. "What?" I ask as if I have no idea what's on his mind.

His gaze roams over my body and his pace slows. Becomes predatory.

"You know how I feel about you in that naughty librarian getup. Hair up. Glasses on."

Oh, that's actually not what I expected him to say.

"Lawyer, not librarian." I run my hands over my skirt. "This barely fits, so get your jollies now. Probably the last time I'll get to wear it for a while."

Ignoring my comment, he places his hands on my hips and yanks me closer.

He buries his face against my neck, breathing me in. "Didn't think you could be any sexier, but all dressed up." He places the palm of his hand flat my becoming-quite-noticeable bump. "And carrying our baby." He shakes his head. "Damn, woman."

"I'm not feeling very sexy," I whisper. It's true. As much as I want him, I'm not feeling worthy of his admiration at the moment.

"We'll work on that." He unbuttons my blazer, sliding it off my shoulders and handing it to me to hang up in the closet. His fingers toy with the buttons on my blouse for a second before he untucks it from my skirt.

"Rock," I protest. Getting naked in the foyer isn't the best idea.

"They're out for the night," he says, neutralizing my concern before I even voice it.

"Oh."

He kisses my neck and whispers in my ear, "Upstairs or downstairs?"

Heat pools in my belly. "Downstairs," I whisper.

He growls in approval and nips my earlobe. "Take your shoes off."

I kick off the low heels, toeing them out of the way. I'd be a liar if I didn't admit Rock's intense appreciation of my body and all its new curves doesn't turn me on.

He takes my hand and I follow him to the door that leads to the basement.

It's not really a basement. Rock made sure the space has nine-foot ceilings. To the right is an open storage room and another storage room that remains locked at all times.

The largest room, to our left also remains locked at all times.

But for different reasons.

I'm a fluttering mess of need by the time we reach our room. I want his body pressed against mine. Skin to skin. His mouth on mine.

My body shivers with anticipation as Rock keys in the code and pushes the door open.

"After you."

ROCK

SOME COUPLES ENJOY punishing each other with pain. Hope and I prefer to punish each other with pleasure.

At least that's the only explanation I can come up with for the determined look on her face and teasing swing to her hips as she makes her way to the playroom. Barefoot, blouse untucked and unbuttoned, she's damn tempting.

After I close and lock the door behind us, she slips her blouse off and hangs it on a hook by the door, then faces me.

"Skirt too."

She turns, showing me the zipper down the back. "Will you help me?"

As if she has to ask.

I step up behind her and kiss her shoulder before tugging the zipper down.

"If I'd known I was in for this treat, I would have worn sexier underwear."

"You get any sexier, I'll explode from looking at you."

She smiles over her shoulder and wiggles out of her skirt, purposely bending over to shove her ass against my crotch. There's a hanger on one of the hooks, just for days like these when I pounce on her at the front door and we end up down here. A small closet to our left holds some clothes and robes for both us. For afterward.

Deciding to speed things up, I flick the hooks of her bra open and she hangs it up next to her blouse.

My fingers trace the red lines left by her bra and she sighs. "I've already gone up two cup sizes."

"Fucking love it. But I *don't* like the marks this left." I slide my hands around to cup her breasts. "Think I'll come with you to work and keep you supported. Just like this."

She laughs softly and leans back against me. "My own personal hand bra."

"Mmhmm." I sweep her hair out of the way and nuzzle against her neck.

She sighs and reaches back to run her fingers through my hair.

I strip the rest of her clothes off, needing to have her soft skin under my rough hands.

When I came up with the idea for this room, I wanted something simple and straightforward. No windows. Soft, recessed lighting. My gaze sweeps over the space. Four-poster king-sized bed. A leather swing suspended from the ceiling. A sex couch.

And my personal favorite, what I plan to use in about ten seconds, a hook suspended from the ceiling in the corner of the room.

Keeping on arm around her waist, I reach for the cabinet door.

"Oh my," she breathes when I pull out the bundle of soft blue rope. Her body softens against me even more as I unwind the thick strand.

We're on the same page, because she holds out her arms, wrists facing us.

The simple gesture amps me up even more. The trust she places in me does it every time. The excitement in the way her breathing picks up. I drop my head and trail my lips over her shoulder while I rub the rope over her chest, down the soft slope of her breasts. She gasps wen I drag the taut threads over her stiff nipples. So I do it again.

"Rock." She sighs.

"What do you say if you want me to untie you?" I whisper in her ear.

"Too kinky."

"Good girl."

With the rope in one hand, I grasp her by the wrists and lead her to the couch. She only needs a gentle nudge to lie down on her back and offer her wrists again.

I wrap the doubled over rope twice, cross it, steadily working up her forearms. She bites her lip as she watches me pull the bright through the loop, knowing I'm almost finished. When I'm satisfied the rope won't tighten down on her wrists, I help her up and over to the hook.

I'm so fucking hard it hurts.

"Rock? When did you put a mirror in here?" She angles her shoulders forward, trying to hide herself. Which is exactly *why* the mirror is here. It's a damn big wall mirror too. Obviously she was too focused on *us* to notice it right away. I want to bring her back to that mindset.

"I always meant to put one in this spot."

"But—"

I place my finger of her lips and she scowls.

We stare at each other for a few electrifying seconds before I hold out my hand and she gives me her bound wrists.

The hook's up far enough that she has to stretch her body to reach, but not so high it puts her on tiptoes. There's a swivel, so I can spin her however I want, which comes in handy.

"Beautiful."

She averts her eyes.

I place my hands over her rounded stomach, then stroke her sides and hips. "So soft."

With her arms above her head, she's beautifully stretched out and exposed for me. No way to hide or cover all those generous, beautiful curves.

Tonight she's tense. Wary as she watches us in the mirror. "Don't move." I have something to help her with her nerves.

I return to the cabinet and pull out a blindfold. Before returning, I dim the lights to a more seductive level. This is supposed to be fun and romantic, not a clinical inspection.

Her curvy silhouette stops me in my tracks and she turns. "What?"

"I'm admiring my wife."

The corners of her mouth tug up, but she pulls away when I approach with the blindfold.

"Why?"

"I want you to relax and enjoy what I'm doing to you instead of worrying about what you look like."

She doesn't move again and I secure the fabric over her eyes.

A soft "Oh" falls from her lips when I mold myself to her back and slide my hands up and down her body. Caressing every inch before stopping to lift each breast. My fingers tease and tug on her nipples and she lets out a moan.

"That's better."

"It'd be even better if you were naked and I could feel your skin on mine," she says.

I step back just enough that she can barely feel the whisper of fabric against her back as I strip off my shirt.

Eager, she turns and tries to press against me, but I move just out of reach.

A soft whine from her lips as she strains, but can't quite touch me.

"You're the kind of beautiful that fucks with my self-control." I reach out and brush my knuckles over her cheek. "Especially now."

"Then come fuck me," she sasses back.

Every part of my body hardens and heats up at her words. I love pushing her to say what she wants me to do to her.

I curl my fingers around her neck, her pulse jumps against my thumb as I pull her closer. Need throbs below my belt when her tongue darts out to lick her lips. My cock strains against my zipper.

"This is everything I've ever wanted." I trace my fingers over her hip. "My name inked in your skin. My ring on your finger. Your stomach rounded with my child."

I lower to my knees, allowing my hands to roam over every inch. Worshipping every curve and dip. Kissing, licking, and stroking soft skin. Her nipples tighten, her breaths grow shallow as I kiss her belly, her hip, her thighs. My hands slide between her legs, grabbing her ass and yanking her to me.

"You're wetter than ever."

Her leg muscles strain as if she's trying to hide herself from me again. I sink my teeth into her flesh, a light warning nip.

I could easily spend all night with my face buried in her pussy. But I'm worried about her arms getting fatigued or straining her back. By this point, I think she's too far gone to tell me if she's hurting right away.

Using my thumbs, I spread her lips, licking and sucking until her legs shake. Within seconds she wildly comes on my face, rolling her hips, grinding herself against my mouth, panting all sorts of breathy little noises.

I'm so fucking turned on I could come in my pants right this second.

She's so damn sensitive, she jumps when I tease her clit and giggles when I pepper kisses along her inner thigh. I stand, trailing my fingers over her legs and ass. Gripping her hips, I turn her so she's facing the mirror.

"Fuck me." I run my hand over my chin.

"What?"

"Nothing. The view is even better than I expected. It's probably good you can't see *me*, though."

"Why?"

"Because I look like I'm going to eat you alive."

She tugs on the rope. "You just did." More soft laughter from her.

I lightly tap her ass, then slide my hand around her body, stroking down her belly and between her thighs. Finding and lightly pinching her clit. She dances on her toes, pressing her ass against me again.

"Please."

"You think you can take more?"

"God, yes."

I hate leaving the warmth of her body for even a second, but I make quick work of my belt, stopping to trail the end over her ass, teasing her with the thick leather.

"Rock?"

"Mmm?"

I stroke my hand up and down my cock and grab her hip with the other.

"I… I want to see."

Better than I'd hoped for.

I untie the blindfold, allowing it to fall to the ground.

Our eyes meet in the mirror, hers hazy with desire, mine downright feral. I wrap my arm around her chest. "Look how flushed and pretty you are."

"Mmm."

She pushes her ass out, swinging her hips from side to side. Taunting me. Hurrying me along when I want to take all night. As soon as my cock bumps against her backside, she goes up on tiptoes, giving me better access. Normally, I'd have her dressed up in a pair of the for-bedroom-use-only heels stored down here, but I was worried about her balance.

I dip and bend to get the right angle and finally slowly sink inside. A deep groan I can't control vibrates in my throat and I brush my nose against her cheek.

"More," she begs.

"Give me a second."

The intensity, her heat, the sounds she makes, it's absolute heaven on earth.

I band my arm around her chest and the other under her belly, holding her tight while I thrust into her at a staggering pace.

Having her tethered is actually getting in my way, so I slow down, reach up and unhook her. She grasps the arm I have over her chest. With both hands.

"That's right. Hold on."

She doesn't smile or laugh. There's only white-hot excitement burning in her eyes. I drive into her deeper, harder. Her body responds and she pushes back against me.

"Good girl." I kiss her cheek and watch her face in the mirror.

The angle isn't quite right. I should've put a platform or something in this spot to account for our height difference.

Yeah, that's perfect. I already worship the fuck out of this woman, so putting her on a pedestal so I can fuck her better seems appropriate. That'll be my next addition.

"Why...are...you...laughing?" Her body sags as if she can't hold herself up another second.

"Too much?"

She shakes her head. "Don't stop."

I pull out and lift her up.

"What're you doing?"

"Over here," I carry her to the specially curved, black leather couch in the middle of the room. The first time we used it, we fucked so relentlessly, one of the short wooden legs snapped, almost sending us to the floor. I've removed the legs since then and fixed it so it's sturdy. Can take a good pounding. It has a high curve at one and swoops lower at the opposite end with a valley in the middle. I stretch out and invite her to climb on me. She's a little unsteady at first, but I guide her all the way down.

"There you go," I whisper.

My fingers tug at the ropes around her wrist, unwinding them as she starts to rock back and forth on my cock.

"Fuck" I squeeze my eyes shut. "Fuck, that's good."

She moan-mumbles something unintelligible and grinds down on me harder. She's so slick and hot, I can feel every flutter and pulse as she throws her head back and braces her palms against my chest.

"That's it. Come for me." Love her on top of me, giving me full access to her body. Ravenous desire guides me to tweak her nipples, then pull her down to suck one into my mouth. Her frenzied bucking slows, but it's her last long, low, satisfied moan that sends me over the edge. My hips jerk up and every pleasure zone in my body bursts.

"Come here." I twist my fingers in her hair and drag her down against me, taking her mouth, kissing her, devouring her while our frantic movements slow.

"Oh," she half moans, half laughs as she sits up and slowly stands. The absence of her heat around me makes me groan.

"You all right?"

She wobbles on her feet and that snaps me out of my stupor. "Come here, baby doll."

"I'm drunk on your dick." She snort-giggles.

"I can live with that." I take her hand and tug her over to the bed. Best thing I put down here. We can fuck ourselves to exhaustion and not have to worry about crawling upstairs into bed. I move to pull the covers back and she stops me.

"I'm already overheated."

"Hottest fucking woman I know." I tap her ass with my hand. "Go on."

Once she's situated, I slide next to her. I hold her hands, checking her wrists, then rub her arms. "Feel okay?"

"So good."

"I don't want to be too rough with you."

Her gaze slips down my body. "You're so much bigger than me. In every way. Your body, your hands, your voice, your personality."

I bite my tongue waiting to see where she's going with this.

"You could overpower me whenever you wanted. But instead you use all that strength to be so affectionate, loving, and protective of me." She snuggles closer and I wrap my arms around her. "And to pleasure me."

"Nothing I love more."

We snuggle like that for a while, slowly stroking our hands over each other. She throws her leg over my hip.

"Did you have a good day," I ask.

She takes a minute to answer. "Not really."

"Tell me."

She tips her head back, putting some space between us.

"I'm just tired and feel so fuzzy-headed sometimes. I keep forgetting stuff."

"I don't think I like you driving if you feel that bad."

She bites her lip, which isn't a good sign.

"Hope?"

"I've been winding down my cases. And it's actually taken less time than I expected."

"Okay?"

"I think I want to stop." She rubs her hand over her belly. "Focus on more important things."

Thank fuck. "I think that's a good idea."

"You're not disappointed in me?"

"What? No."

"I wish I could be like Heidi and do it all, but—"

"Hey, we didn't think that this," I place my hand over hers, "Would be possible after what you went through. It's a fucking miracle."

I spend the next few minutes, stroking the back of my hand over her cheek, staring into her eyes.

"I don't want to be a burden or make you feel—"

"Stop right there. I can more than take care of us." I stare down at her harder. "And no, I don't need to rob a bank to do it, sass-mouth."

"That's not what I was thinking."

"You won't be bored around here." I point at the ceiling. "You have a nursery to decorate, research and shopping to do. You'll be plenty busy."

CHAPTER THIRTY-ONE

Hope

"I THOUGHT I was done with this." My vision's blurry, but I'm definitely staring down at toilet water.

Behind me, the bathroom door clicks open and Rock's heavy boots thud over the floor. "Baby doll, are you okay?"

"No," I moan, unable to lift my head.

He sits on the floor behind me, wrapping his body around mine. He threads his fingers into my hair, pulling it back from my face. "What can I do?" he murmurs against my shoulder.

"Let me barf in peace."

His warmth seeps into my body, driving out the nausea that brought me to my knees fifteen minutes ago. I heave out a deep breath and sag against him.

"Better?" he asks.

"I think so."

He moves to pull us off the floor and my stomach lurches.

"Nope. Not okay." My head spins as I rush back to the toilet. Not much comes up since I've barely eaten all day.

Rock brushes a hand over my forehead, then smooths my hair away from my face. He touches his lips to the back of my neck. "I'm so sorry, baby. You know I'd do this for you if I could."

"I know," I whisper.

When I'm finished, I lean my head against his shoulder and let him rock me back and forth.

"How about now?" he asks.

I lift my head, waiting for the queasiness to return. "I think it's passed."

He unfolds himself from the floor, then gently lifts me. "Let's get you cleaned up."

This is a purely perfunctory shower, but Rock takes his time cleaning me and toweling us dry.

"I think I've got it now," I protest when he opens one of my dresser drawers.

He throws me a look over his shoulder. "Let me do this for you, please."

The flannel jammies he picks out are thick and warm. Everyone told me pregnancy would make me hot all the time, but I'm usually freezing. Rock bundles me up and tucks me in to bed without any lingering touches.

"What's wrong?" he asks, studying my face.

"This is the end of everything. You didn't try to cop a feel once."

He laughs softly. "Trust me, it's not easy." His expression darkens and he squeezes my hand. "But I'm still shaken from finding you sick on the floor."

"Sorry."

"You want me to start a fire?"

"Please."

Another sensation stirs inside me as I watch Rock light the fire— such a simple caveman act—and slip on a pair of shorts. The hotter I need the room, the fewer clothes Rock wears. Win-win for me all around.

"Why are you smiling like that?" he asks as he pulls the covers on his side back.

I rub my hand over my belly and grin. "Just thinking of my pregnancy perks."

He gives me the side-eye. "Like what?"

"Well, I hate being cold all the time, but I do enjoy you being mostly naked."

He rumbles out a laugh and shakes his head before climbing in next to me. "Silver lining?"

"Yup."

"How do you feel now?" he asks as I snuggle up against him.

"Better."

"Good."

I turn and look at the clock. "It's so early. I don't want to be one of those couples who goes to bed before nine o'clock."

He slowly strokes his hand over my hair and down my back. "You need your rest."

"But you're a night owl," I murmur.

"This is nice. I'm not complaining."

ROCK

THE WEIGHT OF Hope's soft naked body on top of mine wakes me from sleep.

She straddles me, hugging my hips with her knees and rubbing her hot, wet pussy against my half-hard cock. Even sound asleep, my body recognizes and responds to her.

"Hope?"

"Shh. Let me have my way with you." She places a finger over my lips and I suck it into my mouth. The searing heat from her center pulls me fully awake. I shift flat onto my back and grab her hips.

By far my favorite way Hope's ever woken me up.

"Rock." She yanks at my shorts, not even bothering to pull them off before her pussy squeezes down my length. I groan as she takes me completely inside her.

My eyes open, taking in the beautiful sight on top of me. Dark shadows and slices of light play over her pale skin, enough to highlight the curves of her breasts, her hips, the line of her neck, slope of her shoulder to her fingers digging into my chest. She rocks forward, moving up and down.

I grip her ass, rocking her faster. A raspy groan pulls from my throat. Mist of sleep still surround us, giving the moment a dreamlike quality.

Coming fully awake, I circle my hands around her waist, shifting our bodies until I'm sitting up with my back to the headboard.

"Rock," she whispers, voice full of urgency.

"Right here." I tighten my hold on her, continuing to guide her up and down my length.

Her nails dig into my shoulders as she works herself harder and harder.

"Oh." She gasps and grinds her hips into me harder.

"Fuck you're beautiful when you come."

"Wow. That was intense." She blinks at me and I roll us to the side.

"I'm about to show you intense."

INTENSE IS RIGHT. But then again, everything with Rock is intense.

He turns me on my side and gathers me in his arms. He nuzzles against my neck as he slides back into me.

"Rock," I gasp.

He tightens his hold on my hip and groans in my ear as he lets go.

"Fuck, I planned to last longer than that." He kisses my cheek, but makes no move to release me.

"No complaints here." I wriggle against him and he presses another sleepy kiss to my shoulder.

I'm on the verge of falling asleep when a quick pulsing sensation wakes me.

My eyes blink open and I stare into the dark. Did I imagine it?

There it is again. A fluttery-quiver unlike anything I've ever felt before.

"Rock," I whisper.

"Hmm?"

I grab his hand and place it over my bump where I felt the movement.

"Holy shit," he says, coming fully awake. "Is that? Is that the baby?"

"I think so." Laughter bubbles out of me from the excitement of feeling the baby move.

"Oh my God." The wonder in his voice makes me tear up. Few things in this world have the power to awe my husband.

I trail my fingers through his hair while he runs his hands over me, trying to feel another kick.

"Here." I move his hand to a different spot.

"Did we wake you, baby?" he asks as he kisses his way down my belly. "Sorry." He smiles against my skin. "But not really."

"Don't tire yourself out too much. Big day tomorrow," I say to the baby. "We want to know if you're a boy or a girl, so we can stop calling you "it.""

Rock rumbles with laughter and I think our little bean likes his voice, because there's more fluttering.

"Oh my God. That's amazing." Tears run down my cheeks. This is real. This is really happening. And it's amazing.

"Why you crying, baby doll?" Rock asks, settling down next to me and kissing my tears away.

"I'm so happy," I whisper.

It takes a while to fall asleep after that. We keep waiting and check-ing but there's no more movement.

"She must've gone back to sleep," Rock mumbles. "You too. You need your rest." Even half asleep his tone leaves no room for discussion.

CHAPTER THIRTY-TWO

Hope

"OH MY GOD! Are you guys *so* excited today?" Heidi squeals first thing in the morning.

"We'll see. The doctor said we might not be able to tell the sex right away." I hesitate, remembering how scary the first ultrasound was. "I'm keeping my expectations low."

"What are you hoping for?" Murphy asks Rock.

"Don't care as long as they're both healthy." He squeezes my hand.

Our appointment isn't until later in the afternoon. Before that, Trinity asked me to stop by so she could take some photos for the "bump album."

Although I would never say it to Trinity, at first I thought the whole bump photo thing was silly and cheesy, but now I kind of look forward to the sessions.

Since the beginning, I've tried to make sure all my doctor's appointments were scheduled on Thursday or Friday. The idea was that would help me to remember when they were. But Rock's taken care of that by going to each one with me. We usually make a day of it. Only today, we're adding in the stop for the photos.

"I'll see you later at Trinity's," Heidi says, packing up the rest of her stuff.

"You dropping Alexa off at Teller's?" Rock asks.

"Yup."

"I'll walk over to the garage with you," Murphy says.

"Bye!" Alexa yells and waves as Heidi carries her out of the house. "Bye!"

"Bye, Alexa. Be good for Uncle Teller," I call out. The door closes, but the front windows are open, so we can still hear her happy baby talk through the woods. "She's so darn cute. I'm going to miss them when they move out."

"Yeah, we'll be emptying our nest and filling it right back up."

"You really think they'll be out by the time the baby's here?"

He shrugs. "Depends. Weather's been shit for construction."

"Well, I hope he knows there's no rush."

"Do you think this makes me look too earth-mothery?" I ask twisting from side to side. The long sky-blue floral maxi dress swirls around my feet, tickling my bare toes.

He stops and looks at me. "Is there such a thing?"

"You know what I mean."

"I don't." He motions me to come sit at the table. "You look beautiful."

"Thank you."

He teases a finger along the cleavage displayed by the dress. "I especially like this."

I smile as his hand brushes over my breasts. "I was worried it's a little much to wear to the doctor, but I wanted to look nice for photos. And," I tug at the tie under my boobs. "It's a true-wrap. Easy on and off."

"I definitely like the sound of that." He sweeps my hair to the side and kisses my neck.

"Mmm." My eyes close and I lean back.

"Oh Christ." A muffled yelp from the back door. "At breakfast?"

We both look up to find Z at the sliding glass door waving at us. "Let me in."

"There's this thing called knocking," Rock says as he flips the lock and lets Z in.

I glance down, checking to make sure my boobs haven't escaped the confines of my dress. Lately I swear Rock can undress me with a look.

"Good morning, Hope. You're radiant this morning," Z says, ignoring Rock's glowering and dropping into the chair to my left.

"Come on in. Make yourself at home," Rock grumbles. "Can I get you anything?"

"He's being sarcastic, isn't he?" Z mock-whispers to me.

"I wouldn't ask for pancakes if I were you."

He laughs and eyes Rock. "Coffee?"

"Are your hands broken? You see I'm busy, right?"

"I dunno. Looked like you were molesting your wife a few seconds ago."

"Like I said, busy."

I silently laugh at their banter. "I think we're definitely only having the one baby."

Z grins even wider. "Shit, can you imagine if we'd grown up together?"

"Maybe he would've gotten it all out of his system by now," I suggest.

Rock sets a bowl of oatmeal and berries in front of me. "Doubtful."

He thunks a mug of coffee on the table in front of Z and I lean over for a whiff.

"Sorry, Hope. You want me to go drink it over there?" he asks.

"Aw, you're so sweet. No. I'm fine."

He pushes his chair back and rests his foot on his opposite knee. "Heidi said you're gonna find out if it's a boy or girl today?"

"Fingers crossed."

Rock sets my ginger tea in front of me, then takes the chair on my left with his own plate.

"You're cute all domesticated, Rock," Z says.

Rock takes a few bites of his steak and eggs before responding to Z. "Did you come over here for a reason? Or just to annoy me?"

"Is, I miss both of you a good enough reason?" he asks with wide eyes.

"Aww." I reach over and pat Z's leg.

Rock growls and attacks his eggs.

Z lifts his chin at me. "You nervous?"

"About today? Not really." A slight fluttering sensation stops me and I close my eyes, resting my hand over my stomach.

There it is again. Fleeting and gentle. A soft twitch.

"What's wrong, Hope?" Z asks.

Rock's hand brushes up against mine. "You feel the baby again?"

"I think so. It's so subtle." I laugh, almost giddy from the connection.

I open my eyes and find Rock watching me intently with his hand still resting over my belly.

Z's staring at us with a curious expression and without thinking, I grab his hand and place it where I felt the last flutter.

"Is that it?" he asks, confusion clouding his expression.

I shrug. "Well, it could be gas."

He yanks his hand away and I laugh. Rock squeezes my fingers gently before finishing his breakfast.

"Rock could feel it better last night," I explain. I gesture to my dress. "There weren't all these layers in the way." I laugh a little harder, still excited by the baby's movement.

"Keep your dress on, I don't want to die today, Hope." He throws a wary glance at Rock.

"Hɪ!" Tʀɪɴɪᴛʏ ᴘᴜsʜᴇs open the back door, holding it for me until I'm inside. Rock follows me and Trinity strides to the front of her studio.

"Your dress is perfect," she says. "I thought we'd do a blue and pink theme, since you're finding out the sex today." She crosses her fingers and holds them in the air.

I can't help laughing at how excited she is. I've never probed too much about why Trinity doesn't want children. I try to be sensitive to my non-mom friends. I don't want to be that annoying pregnant mom who won't shut up about every detail whether they want to know it or not. But Trinity's been almost as excited as I am, which has made things easier.

She presses her hands together. "Your dress is perfect. Come here."

We stand in front of one of the mirrors and she gives my hair a quick fix, tucking fly away pieces into place and fluffing the long waves. "Perfect."

Trinity snaps a dozen or more pictures of me by myself before asking Rock to join me.

"Rock, can we get a little more enthusiasm, please?" Trinity asks.

While he's attentive in every single way that counts—feeding me, taking me to the doctor, tending to pretty much every need and weird craving I have—Rock's limitless patience ends at making goofy faces for cheesy maternity photos.

Unsatisfied, Trinity adjusts the lighting before taking a few more shots.

"Pretend I'm leaving and you're about to have your way with Hope right there on my prop couch," she suggests.

Rock turns the predatory eyes that have the power to liquefy my insides on me and Trinity hums in approval.

"Much better," she mutters. "Should've started there."

When she finishes, Rock still has me in his arms and seems reluctant to let me go.

"Sorry, I can't make good on that, Rock," Trinity says. "I have someone coming in at one."

"Bait and switch, Trinity." He gives her a teasing glare. "I'll remember that."

Heidi rushes in the back door. "I'm sorry I'm late, Trin."

"No problem. Just finishing up."

Poor Heidi seems so frazzled. "What's wrong, Heidi?" I ask.

"Nothing, I just got held up after class and traffic was a bitch getting over here."

"It's cool," Trinity assures her. "I got your text. We have a little time before the next one."

We say our goodbyes. In the parking lot, Rock takes my hand. "I'm sorry if that was too much," I say.

He cocks his head but doesn't say anything.

Once we're in the car, I try again.

"What are you apologizing for?" he asks.

"Just, all the cheesy photo stuff. I know that's not your thing."

He taps his thumbs against the steering wheel a few times. "Some days I just feel like maybe I'm too old for this," he waves at the studio, "stuff."

This is the first time Rock's expressed any apprehension about impending fatherhood to me and my heart squeezes.

He shrugs. "Last night, feeling those flutters… every day it gets a little more real."

"It does," I whisper.

"I wasn't trying to ruin it for you," he says.

"You didn't. Not at all. I'm sorry. I'll tell Trinity we should just do some simple shots up at the clubhouse—"

"Nah, don't do that because I'm being a grouch." He looks at the studio again. "I've known Trinity a long time. Proud of her."

I'm cut off from asking any follow-up questions by the buzz of his phone.

"Fuck," he grumbles. "They know not to bother me today."

He groans even louder when he looks at the screen. For a moment it looks like he's going to send it to voicemail, but then he answers with a terse, "What?"

I can't tell who's on the other end or what they want, but Rock's definitely not pleased about the interruption.

ROCK

"NO, I CAN'T do it today."

On the other end, Loco whines some more. "Rock, I need someone to help Malik with this gig."

"And I'm not available." No way am I explaining my plans. I don't answer to this fuck.

Hope looks out the window, pretending she's not hearing every word. I reach over and take her hand, attempting to reassure her I'm not going anywhere.

"You need to get it through your head, I don't work for you."

"Rock, I do a lot to help you out in Ironworks."

"I know. And I appreciate that. I'll check with my guys and see who's available."

"Try Wrath first."

"That's probably not happening, Loco."

"I need someone scary."

"All my guys are scary." He keeps pissing me off he's gonna witness first hand how scary my guys can be.

"Or at least send someone I can pay in pussy."

"I think my guys prefer cash."

"Yeah, yeah."

"I'll have one of them call you if they can do it. Either way, I'll have Z check back with you. I'm unavailable the rest of the day."

"Now you got me all curious, Rock."

"Bye, Loco."

Hope chuckles as I hang up. "You're so friendly."

"He's a pain in my goddamn ass."

"What does he need?"

"You really don't want to know." I dial Z. "Give me one second."

"'Sup, Rock?" Z answers.

"Can you touch base with Loco? He needs someone today and I'm busy."

He groans. "Jesus, I'm stretched thin here as it is. He needs to hire some of his own people and stop this shit."

"No kidding. He threw in the reminder of how much he helps with Ironworks as an incentive."

"Fuck. Wrath and Murphy are out. They're at Sully's place and then Wrath's meeting with the bank about Furious."

"Teller's got Alexa."

"You can't trust Ravage to behave. Look what a pain in the ass he was at dinner the other night."

We go back and forth and finally decide Stash gets to go play hooker bodyguard for the afternoon. I doubt he'll be too upset about it.

"Sorry, baby doll." I toss my phone in the middle console, not giving a fuck who needs to get ahold of me.

CHAPTER THIRTY-THREE

Hope

"WHAT ARE YOU reading to her tonight?"

We're having a girl!

Rock tips the book my way so I can see the front. "Machiavelli? Seriously? Not *Good Night Moon* or something more fetus appropriate?"

I could stare at his handsome face smiling up at me all night. "Nah, this is a classic map of how to achieve power."

His answer amuses me. I'm not terribly surprised, though. "Are you grooming our daughter to take over the MC?"

Another feral grin. "Maybe." Slowly the laughter slips away. "No matter how much we shelter her, our daughter's going to grow up in a brutal, unfair world." He waves a hand in the direction of the clubhouse. "And I don't just mean the MC."

I wait for him to continue, expecting him to say he'll murder anyone who hurts his daughter or something along those lines.

When he remains silent, I say, "Lately, I think it's worse on the outside." At least inside the confines of this club, I'm protected and cherished as I know our daughter will be.

He hums a grave sound of agreement. "I want her to grow up believing nothing is unavailable to her because she's a girl."

"Oh," I breathe out.

I reach for him, running the back of my hand over his bristly cheek. His internal struggle is clear. Maybe more to me than him. It's the same one I struggle with sometimes now that I'm a part of a world that openly values women as property.

"And," he adds, a sly note creeping into his tone. "Anyone who puts his hands on her without her permission is getting fucking murdered."

"Ah, I was wondering when you'd get to that."

His savage expression slips away and he rubs his hand over my belly again, pushing my tank top out of his way. "I *should* tell her the story of the lonely, unapologetic criminal who seduced the sweet, innocent lawyer."

Laughter bubbles out of me. "Maybe when she's older."

He spreads soft kisses over my tummy and stares at my bump with so much love.

Perfectly content in this moment, I reach down and run my fingers through his hair. "Rock?"

"Hmm?"

"We haven't talked about baby names yet. What do you think of calling her Grace?"

"My mother's name?"

"Yes," I whisper. "Would that be…if you don't…"

"No, I love it." He presses another kiss to my belly, then kisses his way up my body to lie down next to me.

He strokes his fingers over my cheek. "You're already giving me such a wonderful gift." His voice comes out husky with emotion and I swoop in to kiss him.

He presses his forehead to mine, creating a cocoon of safety. I slide my hand over his, entwining our fingers and he kisses my knuckles. "Any thoughts on middle names?"

Actually, I have been thinking about it a lot. I lean over and pick up my copy of *The Second Sex* off my nightstand. "Simone?"

His lips curve up in recognition, but his gaze slides away. "I think that book was banned by the priest at my mother's church."

"Oh, really?"

He shrugs, but his eyes remain distant as if he's lost in the past. "She was a rule-breaker."

"Why doesn't that surprise me?"

"Grace Simone North?" He rolls the name off his tongue a few times, testing it out. "I like it. It's different but simple."

"Easy to spell too."

I run my fingers through his hair while he rests next to my belly, reading softly to the baby. His voice rumbles through me, lulling me into a peaceful, happy state.

Probably the most content I've ever been.

CHAPTER THIRTY-FOUR

ROCK

BRICKS HAS A garage full of bikes to be worked on when I finally drag my ass in the next morning.

We're having a girl!

Impending fatherhood gets more real every day.

Grace Simone.

I can't wait to hold her in my arms.

"Everything okay, Prez?"

I wipe the goofy grin off my face and adjust my mind to work time. "Yeah, it's good. How's it going here?"

"Backed up." He runs a hand through his hair, a sign he's nervous about asking me something.

"Spit it out, Bricks. What's the matter?"

"My family. Down in Puerto Rico. House is still a mess. I need to go down and help my ma out. Fix shit up."

I'm not a complete inconsiderate ass. I've asked him a few times now if he needed to go visit and help out. He just couldn't work it into his schedule with the kids. "Yeah, of course. You need help?"

"Jesus Christ, I think you got enough going on here, Prez."

I laugh, because, yeah, I'm a little busy, but when a brother needs help, it's hard not to offer. "Okay. You need money?"

He hesitates before shaking his head. "Nah, I'll be fine. Winter and the kids are coming down too."

"Shit, you're coming back, right? I can't afford to lose you."

He chuckles. "You fuckin' kidding me? After a few days of hard labor and guilt trips about all my wasted potential, I'll be more than ready to come home."

The throaty rumble of a truck that can only belong to Teller rolls down the quiet street, and pulls into the driveway.

"Teller gonna help us out?" Bricks asks.

Teller has lots of talents. Art isn't one of them.

"Doubt it." No, Teller's bringing Carter by to see if he wants to learn how to do some custom paint work from Bricks.

Teller couldn't have picked a better day to bring by his almost-brother-in-law. The timing of Bricks' trip couldn't be worse, but no way am I stopping him from doing what he needs to do for his family.

If he can get Carter up and running, it'll be easier to absorb the loss of Bricks. And honestly, I have enough work that Carter can stay on when Bricks returns.

Teller swears the kid is trustworthy. I guess we'll find out. He behaved well on the trip. Didn't give anyone lip that I know of. Maybe Carter's just mouthy with Teller because he doesn't like him molesting his older sister every five seconds.

"Hey, Knucklehead," I call out.

Teller's mouth curls into a smirk because he knows the nickname's said with affection. Most of the time.

"Hey, Prez. You remember Carter."

"Good to see you, Carter. Thanks for coming over."

He shakes my hand but has trouble meeting my eyes. "Hi, Mr. North."

I haven't suggested he call me anything else yet. Mr. North works fine.

"You did some good sketches down in Florida. Some nice paint work at the one show. Think you're up to doing it on a more regular basis?"

"Here?" He steps back, gaze darted between Teller and me. "For you?"

"Yeah," I answer slowly, amused by his reaction. "Bricks is leaving me for a couple months—"

"Couple *weeks*, Prez," Bricks interrupts. "Jesus."

I lift my chin at Bricks to let him know I'm messing with him.

"I'm slammed right now. Need another talented artist."

He cocks his head and crosses his arms over his chest. "If I fuck up, you gonna cut off my fingers?"

Teller smacks him in the back of the head. "What did I tell you?" he mutters.

When I stop laughing, I grin at the kid. "Think you're gonna fuck up that often?"

"No."

"Few things can't be unfucked, Carter."

He seems to think that over. "I guess."

Teller shoots a pleading look my way, as if he's worried I might kill Carter this afternoon. He shouldn't be so worried. I kinda like the kid. He's got a brain-to-mouth malfunction that rivals Teller's when he was younger, no doubt about that. But I prefer honesty and Carter doesn't sugarcoat a thing. I'm not sure he even knows how.

Bricks takes Carter over to his section and starts explaining the job to him. I sling my arm around Teller's shoulders and steer him into the side yard.

"You sure about this, Rock?" he asks, stopping in his tracks.

"That mouth the worst thing about him?"

"I guess so." Teller seems to think it over. "He's clever. Has a good way of thinking through things from a different angle. He works hard. Honestly, once you have him set up, he'll get into a groove. You'll probably have to tell him when it's time to stop or he'll keep going." He glances at the garage again. "I just wouldn't let him speak to your customers too often."

"Wasn't planning to."

Hope

WINDING DOWN MY workload turns out to be easier than I expected. Even telling the court I wouldn't be accepting any more assigned cases went smoothly. I almost feel bad about how easy it is to walk away from something I worked hard for and once thought I'd do for many years.

No, I guess I feel bad about how little it bothers me. I'm much more excited about this next phase in my life. And I can always go back to practicing law later. I'll only have this pregnancy once.

I'm busy cleaning out my sitting room. It finally dawned on us that we might want to think about a nursery soon. I like the idea of keeping the baby—*Grace!*—in a bassinette close to us for the first few months. Rock was less enthusiastic about that approach.

My phone rings, and when I see it's Adam, I almost swipe to send it to voicemail. I don't want to discuss work stuff.

"Hey, Adam. How's it going?"

"I need you to come into the office." Adam's grave tone sends a trickle of anxiety traveling down my spine.

"Why? What's wrong?"

"It'll be easier to talk to you about it in person."

"All right. Give me a couple hours to find someone to drive me down there."

I'm not sure what to make of the sigh that comes over the line. "I'll be here."

Turns out I don't need a few hours. Rock's coming in the door as

I'm slipping on my coat.

"Where are you going?" he asks immediately.

"Adam needs me to come see him."

"Why?"

I shrug. "He was vague, but it sounded important. I assume it's about one of my clients."

He crosses his arms over his chest and regards me with an expression that suggests he's contemplating saying something I won't like. "I don't want you upset."

"I know you just got home, but do you mind taking me?"

That seems to appease him. His stern expression softens and he takes my hand. "Of course I'll take you anywhere you need to go."

If he expected me to argue, he's wrong. My hand settles over my stomach. All my independent urges have been muted in favor of doing what's best for the baby. No matter how far along I am or how many reassurances the doctors give me, I'm still so damn worried I'll lose our child.

Once we're on our way to Adam's, Rock fills me in on a few of the projects he's working on at his shop.

"How did Carter work out?"

"Not bad, honestly. He's a hard worker. He gets so wrapped up in a project, I don't even think he knows where he is half the time. I'll have to remember to make him take a break every couple hours."

"Aww, you're so sweet."

"Sweet my ass. I'm protecting an asset. With Bricks headed out of town soon, I can't afford to lose another artist."

I chuckle, because God forbid Rock ever take credit for any of the positive things he does. He always assigns some ulterior motive to his goodness.

"You don't have to prove you're a badass to me, Rock. I know you have a heart of pure gold under that black leather."

He reaches over and takes my hand. "You're the only good thing my heart's made of."

My breath catches and I squeeze his hand, too overwhelmed to respond.

In the parking lot of Adam's building Rock pats my leg before stepping out and coming around to open my door. My feet barely touch the pavement when his phone goes off.

He growls a bunch of annoyed noises as he pulls out his phone.

"It's fine, Rock. I should only be a minute. Take your call."

He leans over and kisses my forehead. "I'll be in as soon as I deal with this."

I cringe as he barks out a greeting to the poor soul on the other end and make my way into Adam's office.

"Look at you," Adam says, holding his arms open for a hug.

"I'm huge. I know."

"Stop. You look great." He gives me a quick squeeze and then glances over my shoulder. "Oh God, is some scary biker man going to break my arms for touching you?"

I'd laugh if I thought he was making a joke. "No, smartass. Rock's in the parking lot on a phone call."

His mouth flattens at the mention of my husband's name. Something, I can't say I really care for. "What's wrong?"

"Nothing. Come have a seat."

Now I'm really not liking this, but I follow him into his office and take the chair he offers me.

Without any warm-up conversation, he pulls out a thick manila envelope. "Don't be mad. I don't get a lot of mail for you anymore, so I didn't look at who this was addressed to before I opened it."

"Oh," I say, still not understanding why he seems so dramatic today. He opened something from the court. No big deal.

I part my lips to say exactly that, but he cuts me off.

"Is everything okay? I'm worried about you."

Huh? "I'm fine." I rest my hand over my belly. "I'm taking it easy and watching my diet."

"No, I mean *you*."

I huff out a laugh. "This is me, now, Adam."

"God, Hope. What happened to you?"

"Excuse me?"

"You were like uber-feminist in law school, I never thought you'd be the type to turn into some breeding wife-bot."

Well, that's not going to help my blood pressure. "What the hell is that supposed to mean?"

"I worry about you. Do you really want to be dependent on him for everything? What if he leaves you or something happens to him?"

"Adam, where is this coming from?"

"Have you thought this through?"

"Thought *what* through? Having a child with my husband? Yes." I take a few deep breaths before continuing. "You know feminism is about every woman being able to make the choices that are right for *her*, right?"

He opens his mouth to interrupt me and I cut him off.

"As you pointed out, you've known me a long time, so you also know I've never loved being a lawyer." I settle both hands against my stomach. "The hustle you like so much? I hate it. The constant need to network is torture for me." I take a deep breath. "*This* makes me happier than I've ever been. My family brings me joy. That's where my focus needs to be. As for my marriage, Rock's not going anywhere."

"Hope." He sighs and I feel like he didn't hear a word of what I said. "He's already been in jail once."

"And I survived. The club will take care of us." I hold up a hand to stop whatever else he's going to say. "I get that you don't understand the club thing. But even if I didn't have the club, I'd be fine. I survived when my life fell apart before. I can do it again."

"I know you did." He sighs and stands, coming around the desk to lean over and give me a hug. "I'm sorry."

"What's gotten into you?"

Another heavy sigh eases out of him, and he drops into the chair next to me. He reaches over and snags the envelope from the desk and hands it over.

"What is it?"

"It's a petition for a paternity test."

"For one of my clients?"

He huffs out a sad laugh. "Not exactly."

I pull out a thick petition on fancy cream-colored paper with the familiar blue backer. I don't recognize the name of the law firm, but I recognize the name of the parties.

INGA MARCH v. ROCHLAN NORTH, WYATT RAMSEY, ANGUS FRA-ZIER, et al.

"What the hell is this? Is she suing the club for something?"

"Oh yeah. She's suing them for something all right."

"What?"

"Child support."

CHAPTER THIRTY-FIVE

ROCK

HOPE AND ADAM'S many years of friendship is the only thing that stops me from beating the fuck out of him when I overhear him questioning my marriage.

There are days I wonder if I've brought too many changes to Hope's life. She was on a much different path before we met. A part of me has a twisted need to know she's truly happy with where our life has taken her.

Hearing her vehemently declare how much she trusts me, trusts the club, and *wants* our future is a reassurance I need.

But once they finish *that* part of the conversation and I learn what really prompted Adam's concern, it's time for me to step in.

I rap my knuckles against his slightly-ajar door and push my way inside.

Adam stands and backs away from Hope. Doesn't offer to shake my hand like he normally would.

Can't say I blame him.

"You two can use my office. I have some stuff to take care of out there," Adam says, edging toward the door.

"No, stay for a second, Adam," Hope says.

The grim set of her mouth flickers into a quick, brave smile and she pats the seat next to her. "Inga's back," she says in an almost teasing way.

I take the chair next to her and she reaches over to squeeze my hand before addressing her friend. "Adam, you read this already?"

"I glanced at it. When I realized who it involved," he flicks his gaze my way, "—I called you." He gives me another look I don't care for. "This woman claims she had a long-term relationship with *you.*" His lip curls in contempt. "As well as several of your bros and one of you fathered her child," he finishes while staring me down. One thing I've always respected about Adam, he's not a coward. And since his irritation with me seems to stem from the false belief that I cheated on his friend, I allow his disrespectful attitude a pass.

For now.

"Jesus Christ," I hold out my hand for the petition and Hope doesn't hesitate to hand it over.

It's all legalese, but the gist of it is exactly what Adam said. The dates and time frame are way off for me to be the father of Inga's kid and I breathe out a sigh of relief. Hope and I had just gotten engaged when this child was conceived. My dick hadn't been anywhere near Inga in well over a year. "It's not—"

"I know," Hope answers, squeezing my leg. She lifts her gaze to Adam. "It's not Rock's child. And I highly doubt it's any of his brothers'."

Christ, the love I have for this woman. Emotion burns the back of my throat at the way she doesn't hesitate, doesn't even question me or have a doubt in her mind about my fidelity.

That emotion turns to anger. Anger that once again my past behavior is tainting her life. At a time when I want her to have the least stress possible *this* utter fucking bullshit has to happen.

Busy with my internal struggle, I miss most of their conversation.

"I think that's best too. Okay, Rock?" Hope asks.

"I'm sorry, baby doll."

She pats my leg again. "It's okay, we'll discuss it on the way home." She struggles to stand and I jump up to help her.

"Are you all right, Hope?" Adam says.

"I'm fine."

Adam's glare is a little less intense as I wrap my arm around Hope's waist, but he still doesn't shake my hand on our way out.

Once we're back inside the truck, Hope turns to face me. "What's going on in your head, Rock?"

"That I've never wanted to hurt a woman in my life, but if Inga was in front of me right now, I'd probably kill her."

"I figured." She turns serious. "Listen, as galling as this is, I think it's best that we just take the test, prove her wrong and move on."

We. God, I love her. "Hope, I'm so sorry."

She snorts. "It's not your fault she's nuts."

Yeah, it is because I never should've been involved with Inga in the first place. Fuck, if I'd known Hope was in my future I would've lived like a fuckin' monk my whole damn life.

"Rock," she says, settling her hand over mine. "I read the dates. I'm not worried the child is yours. I hope you know that."

"I do."

"And if for some reason, addition and subtraction aren't Inga's strong suit, I'd fight like hell to make sure we were involved in your child's life. Nothing changes how I feel about you."

Someone who didn't know her might think she's subtly trying to say if there's a possibility I cheated on her, she forgives me. But that's not what I take from her words at all. No, my woman would definitely slice off my nuts if I cheated on her. Considering how many women I've known over the years *before* Hope, I appreciate the sentiment. I'm probably lucky I haven't been slapped with one of these petitions earlier, and I almost think *that's* what she's trying to tell me. It wouldn't matter to her.

Unconditional love. That's my Hope.

"Now," she says in a brisker changing-the-topic tone. "How do we explain this to the rest of the guys? Poor Wrath. His head is going to explode. I don't think he liked Inga very much."

I huff out a laugh, amused that Wrath's state of mind is her first concern. "I'll take care of it. I don't want you answering the petition. I'm fucking livid she sent it to you in the first place. She knew damn well Glassman represents Crystal Ball."

"How?"

Fuck me. Why can't I keep my mouth shut? "She sued for unemployment after she got out of rehab."

Hope snorts. "She did? I wouldn't think dancers are covered?"

"Some are. She wasn't because she only appeared there on a semi-regular basis. It's why she lost."

"Huh. I'm starting to wonder if her kid's even real."

"You and me both." I turn, tracing my fingers over her cheek so she meets my eyes. "Now more than ever, I don't want you off the property without one of the guys."

"Trinity's pretty badass."

"I'm aware."

"Inga's all the way in California."

"I know, but this really bugs me."

She grabs my hand, kissing the back. "Okay. I won't go anywhere without one of the guys with me."

"Thank you. I'll tell them today."

"Boy, they're really going hate me," she mutters.

"You know that's not true. There's not one brother who wouldn't drop what they're doing to help you out. You've earned everyone's respect, Hope. Not just because you're the president's wife."

"I know," she says quietly. "I was kidding."

"I'll call Glassman when we get home."

"No," she says. Out of the corner of my eye, I catch her vigorous head-shake. "Fuck that and fuck her." I don't even have a second to laugh or tease her for the language. "I will *not* let her think she rattled me or give her crazy little brain a chance to concoct some story that you're hiding this from me. She doesn't get to think she won or that she wormed her skinny little body between us in any way. I'll be the one to handle it."

"Hope. I love you for saying that, but you have more important things to worry about right now." I reach over and settle my hand over her the curve of her stomach and barely choke out the next words. "I can't have you upset. Not now."

"Rock," she says, mimicking my patient tone. "The only thing upsetting me right now, is knowing how much this upsets *you*, because you're worried about *me*. See what a vicious cycle we're spinning in here?" She rests her hand over mine. "Just let me handle it."

"Christ, what a mess. I'm so sorry."

Her soft laughter actually reassures me more than you'd think. "Oh, come on. We were due for a little extra excitement in our lives, don't you think?"

CHAPTER THIRTY-SIX

ROCK

CHURCH SHOULD BE fun today.

On the way home, I call Wrath and tell him to get everyone ready to meet. Not an unheard-of request in the middle of the day, but unusual enough that Wrath's immediately suspicious.

"What's wrong?"

"I don't want to discuss it over the phone, but it's important. Everyone needs to be there."

He hesitates for a second. "You okay, Rock?"

"I'm fine."

"All right. Well, Z's at Crystal Ball."

"I'm not far from there. I'll stop and talk to him."

After we hang up, I turn to Hope. "You mind making a quick stop?"

"Nope. I'd like to say hi to Willow anyway."

"Thanks."

Z's busy supervising a bunch of contractors working to expand the stage.

"Didn't you just finish a bunch of renovations?" Hope asks as he leans down to give her a peck on the cheek.

He winks at her. "I have some special events coming up."

"I'm afraid to ask."

Z glances my way. "What's up? You never come visit anymore."

"Let's talk in your office."

His expression hardens and he puts his hands on his hips. "What's going on?"

"I'm calling everyone up to the club for church, but I need to speak to you now."

"Rock, I'm in the middle of—"

The hard stare I give him stops him cold. "Yeah, all right."

We follow him into the office, which has changed quite a bit since the last time I was here. "Things look good, Z."

"Thanks. You didn't come down here and you sure as fuck didn't drag Hope here to give me a pat on the head, so what's going on?"

I'm not quite sure how to say it and Hope's waiting for me to speak first. The moment of hesitation makes Z frown.

"Is everything okay?" He glances at Hope and a more concerned expression darkens his face. "With the baby? Are you all right?"

"The baby's fine," she assures him. "It's not about the baby. Well, not mine, anyway."

Z starts shaking his head. "What are you—"

"Inga's suing the club. For child support. She's requested a paternity test from a bunch of us, including you."

"Are you fucking kidding me?" He jumps out of his chair and paces behind the desk a few times before stopping dead. "Oh fuck me."

"What?" Hope asks.

"She called not that long ago." He lifts his chin at me. "Looking for you."

"Jesus Christ, why? What the fuck for?"

"I don't know. But Willow ended up talking to her."

"Get her down here," I say.

Z picks up the phone and a few minutes later a there's a hesitant knock on the door.

"What's up, Z?"

She smiles when she sees us and closes the door behind her. "Hi, Hope!"

Hope gives her a patient smile and Willow's happy expression falters. "What's going on?"

"You talk to Inga when she called?" Z asks.

"Yeah, I told you I did." She turns her head my way. "She wouldn't stop asking about you. I told her you and Hope were really happy and having a baby, so she needed to get over it and move on." He gaze skitters between the two of us. "Was that wrong?"

I open my mouth to say, "Yes" but Hope pats my hand and speaks first.

"No, Willow. That's fine."

"Is she causing trouble now? I'm sorry. I didn't mean to start anything. It's just been so long, you know?"

"It's okay."

Z lifts his chin. "Thanks, hon. Go on."

After Willow shuts the door, Hope sits back and closes her eyes.

"I'm sorry," Z says. "I'll talk to her about blabbing about personal shit."

"It's not her fault," Hope says.

"I—"

"Rock," Hope says, cutting me off. "Inga would've done this one way or another. She would've found out eventually. Yes, I would prefer that Willow leave me out of all future discussion with your exes, but it's not her fault."

Z seems relieved Hope doesn't want Willow's head on a stick. "Let me finish up with the contractors and I'll be there for church."

I stand and help Hope up. "Don't take too long."

He gives Hope a hug. "I'm so sorry, sweetheart. You shouldn't have to put up with this. Not now. Not ever."

His words and body language are all brotherly affection, but it still pushes my buttons. A short growl bursts out of me.

"Easy, caveman." He laughs. "I'll see you guys in a few."

"Was that necessary?" Hope teases on our way out.

"Yes."

She squints at me. "Don't take this out on the guys."

"Why not? I swear to fuck if this kid belongs to one of them, I'm gonna straight up murder—"

In a swift move, she covers my mouth with her hand. "Please don't tell me about future crimes you plan to commit."

"How can you keep your sense of humor?"

"What do you want me to do, Rock? Cry? Get mad? She's not worth it. She doesn't deserve my energy. Or yours. Let's just get this done, over with and move on."

"That's the problem, though. When do we get to finally move on? When is it enough and these things stop happening?"

She shrugs. "That's life. We don't get the one we want, we get the one we're given. The only thing we can control is how we react to things out of our control." She grabs a fistful of my shirt and yanks me closer. "I'm not letting anyone steal my joy. Or yours. We'll get through this."

I'm so stunned by her passionate words that I can't find any of my own.

"Let's get home so you can talk to the guys. Then when you're done I'm going to call this quack and we'll find a lab to get the tests done as soon as possible."

"Jesus," I breathe out, utterly awed by how calm and rational she's being, when I'm feeling the exact opposite.

"It should be a simple cheek swab," she continues. "Nothing too invasive. But I want a reliable place. Everyone needs to go in personally and have the lab take the sample so the chain of custody is clear and can't be contested. That little bitch isn't going to keep coming at us. I want to slap her down now. Hard and fast so she doesn't know what hit her."

"I don't know what's hotter, when you're all sweet and soft or pissed and passionate."

"Well good thing you've got all of me for the rest of your life to figure it out." She takes my hand and leads me toward the car. "Come on. Let's get this first part over with."

CHAPTER THIRTY-SEVEN

ROCK

"Everyone's here. You gonna tell me what this is all about now?" Wrath says as soon as we walk in the front door of the clubhouse.

"Inga's suing him," Hope says in a way-too-chipper-for-the-situation voice. "Rock will give you all the glorious details."

Wrath slides his confused gaze between the two of us. "What?"

Hope turns to me. "I'm exhausted," she says in a lower voice. "I'm going to go upstairs and take nap—"

"Go home and—"

"No. I want to make that phone call today. If the guys have any questions, have them stick around and I'll answer the best I can."

She reaches up on tiptoes and gives me a quick kiss on the cheek. "An hour enough time? I'm going to set my alarm."

"Give me an hour and a half."

"You got it." She pats Wrath's arm on the way upstairs.

"What the hell is she talking about?" Wrath asks. "Why are we even talking about Inga?"

The basement door opens. Sparky and Stash stumble into the living room, clearly high-as-fuck. I'm irrationally irritated with Sparky, since it's his stoner ass that's responsible for Willow visiting the clubhouse and getting chummy with my wife.

"Can't you go a day without getting fucked up?" I snap at him.

The smile slides off his face. "What's wrong, boss?"

"Church, now."

"Yeah, we heard," Stash says. "That's why we're here. We're testing the new—"

"I don't want to hear it."

"Rock," Wrath says. "What crawled up your ass?"

"Where is everyone?"

"On their way."

"Get 'em in here."

TWENTY MINUTES LATER all the brothers are seated around the table. I'm still furious, but I set it aside.

"Hope received some legal papers today. Inga's suing us for child support."

"Whoa!" Ravage practically jumps out of his chair. "What the fuck?"

"How pissed is Hope that Inga's dragging your ass into family court?" Dex asks. "Poor girl doesn't need this right now."

I sit up and fling the envelope with all the legal papers at him. "I ain't goin' alone, brother."

I tip back in my chair, cover my face with my hands, and laugh. "Fuck, at the moment I think Hope's amused more than pissed."

Dex passes the papers to Wrath, who explodes when he gets to the part of the summons with his name. "I never fucked that bitch. Why the fuck is she draggin' me into this bullshit?"

"Probably to get at me. Or she genuinely doesn't remember who she fucked."

"Wrath's kinda hard to forget," Sparky says.

"Uh, not just you, brother," Dex points out. "She's dragging Z,

Teller, Stash, Ravage, Sparky, and *me* in too."

"Holy fuck." Stash whistles. "Way to let the whole world know you're a whore. Why now?"

"Who the fuck knows? She probably ran out of money and can't do porn anymore," Dex says.

I glare at Z, who leans forward to explain.

"Uh, actually Rock and I solved that mystery earlier." He turns to look down the table so he can see Sparky. "Your girl Willow had to brag to Inga all about Hope being pregnant. Inga musta gotten her panties in a twist."

"Willow ain't my girl and she wouldn't..." Sparky trails off. "She's been into planning all the girly baby shower shit with Trinity and Swan, so yeah. Maybe."

"She flat out said she did," Z informs him.

"This isn't helping," Dex says. "Doesn't matter *why*. What the fuck do we do about it?"

"Track her down and kill her?" Ravage suggests.

"Don't think I didn't consider it," I grumble.

"Rock, *you* actually fucked her. Over a long period of time," Bricks says.

I snarl his way. "Thanks for the reminder."

"What are you gonna do if the kid's yours? How's Hope gonna feel 'bout that?" Bricks asks.

"I've asked myself that all afternoon." I mumble from behind my hands, deciding to keep my conversation with my wife private. "*If* Inga's telling the truth, her timeline doesn't add up for me to be the father. I hadn't been near her for more than year at the time she's saying she got pregnant." Setting my hands on the table, I toss a smirk at the rest of my brothers. "If it's a baby King, it's one of yours."

Wrath shakes his head. "Jesus Christ. You know how much Trinity hates Inga? How am I supposed to explain this fuckery to her?"

"Don't," Z says.

Wrath glances at me. "Yeah, 'cause Hope's gonna keep that one to herself. It's not like I'm gonna turn her in for breaching client confidentiality."

Z snickers. "Look at you with the big words today."

"Fuck you. What about you? You've stuck your dick in every bitch down at CB."

"That's not true, asshole."

Wrath stares Z down and Z shakes his head. "I fucked her friend Peach. Never touched Inga." He glances at me. "Didn't seem right."

"Your observance of *bro code* warms my heart." I sneer.

Z doesn't laugh at my sarcasm.

Hell, no one's laughing.

"Couple times. Sorry, Prez," Dex admits.

Sparky taps his fingers on the table, then raises his hand. "I did. Sorry, boss."

"It's fine." Like I give two fucks.

Teller squirms in his seat. "I don't think I did, but I was pretty wasted that one night she was up here."

Sparky snickers. "You didn't do her in any way that would necessitate a paternity test, Teller."

"Thanks for the visual, Sparky," Dex says.

He shrugs. "Tryin' to be helpful."

All of us turn to look at Murphy. "How the fuck did you get left out?" Wrath asks.

"Well, one I never touched her. And two, I don't think she remembers me that well. I didn't spend a lot of time at CB when she worked there."

"Maybe she doesn't fuck gingers," Ravage says.

Murphy flips him off. "Bricks got left out too."

"Yeah, I'm okay with that," Bricks assures us. "Never touched her."

"Maybe she doesn't do Mexicans," Ravage jokes.

"I'm Puerto Rican, you fucking moron."

Rav raises his hand. "Not even gonna try to lie. I totally stormed her pink fortress."

After we finish laughing, he continues, "Kid better not be mine. I'll be fuckin' pissed as fuck if I missed out on the first couple years of my kid's life."

All of us stop and stare at him. Not exactly something we expect to come out of Rav's big mouth.

"Fuckin' A," Z mutters. "That's fuckin' bullshit. She better hope whoever the dad is doesn't fuckin' kill her when he finds out."

Now *that's* something we expect out of Z and no one so much as lifts an eyebrow.

"Can we fight this?" Wrath asks.

"Hope says yes. But it'll be easier to just take the fucking test and be done with it."

"Wow. Brave woman, right there," Dex says with a lot of admiration in his voice.

"She must believe you, Prez," Ravage says.

I'm not really interested in my brothers dissecting my marriage for me.

Z glances across the table at Wrath. "Maybe have Hope talk to Trinity for you?"

Wrath doesn't bitch Z out. Instead, he nods at me. "Yeah. Whatever."

Teller raises his hand. "Uh, anyone want to help me explain this to Charlotte?"

"Doesn't she do family law? I think she knows how the process works," Z snarks.

"That's not helpful, asshat."

"Anyone else in the organization she coulda been with? If the kid really is one of ours, we take care of our own," I say, shifting my gaze around the table to stare at each one of my brothers. "I honestly don't give two fucks. She was never my ol' lady, so don't be shy. You're not gonna hurt my feelings."

"Nah, we were prospects," Birch says, elbowing Hoot in the side. "Wrath barely let us in the clubhouse, let alone in the Champagne Room."

"You're welcome," Wrath says.

I snort and shake my head. "What a clusterfuck. I can't believe this shit."

"Fuck her, she's doing this to be a spiteful bitch. Kid could belong to anyone from here to fuckin' California."

"Simmer down," I growl at Wrath, then turn to the rest of the club. "I'll have Hope set the testing up. She wants it done at a court-approved testing facility. Don't give her any bullshit. When she gives you your appointment time, you get your fucking ass there and do what she says. Are we clear?"

"Wait a minute." Dex holds up a hand. "You're making Hope represent us on this, Rock?"

I glare at him until he sits back. "I'm not *making* her do anything. I'd honestly rather not have her involved at all. But Inga sent the papers *to* Hope—"

Stash snaps his fingers twice. "Now, that's a cunt move right there."

I finish without acknowledging Stash's interruption. "She knows damn well Glassman represents Crystal Ball, but yeah, she did it to be spiteful. Hope insists on handling the case and not backing down." I swallow hard, thinking of Hope's fierce determination to stand by me no matter what.

"Damn, brother," Dex breathes out.

"She wants to face this fuckery head-on, so Inga doesn't keep coming at us."

Someone whistles a swift, high-pitched sound of approval. "That's some woman, Prez."

Underneath my fury, guilt also stirs inside me. "Let's get this done and out of the way. I feel responsible here—"

"Actually, it's my fault," Wrath interrupts, quieter than I'd expect considering how pissed he is. "I'm the one who allowed her to come up here." He flicks his gaze at Z and Dex. "Encouraged it, really."

"Aw, see, and now you love Hope, almost as much as your own ol' lady," Sparky says with a ridiculous grin on his face. He may spend every waking moment high on his own product, but even he's aware Wrath only invited Inga up here hoping it would scare Hope away.

Wrath just snorts. "Whatever. We'll beat this and move on." The corner of his mouth turns up. "We know if it's a boy? Maybe he and Alexa—"

"Don't you finish that sentence," Murphy says.

Teller cocks his head. "What the fuck's wrong with you? What if it's *my* kid, you asshole?"

Sparky clears his throat. "Seriously, bro, you can't knock a chick up—"

"All right," I snap. "Enough with the biology lessons. Let's move on."

Before I end the meeting, I give everyone a hard look. "I have a favor to ask. Except for this bullshit with Inga." Fuck, I even hate saying her fucking name. "Hope's closing out her cases and stepping back from practicing."

"She okay?" Dex asks.

"Yeah, she just wants to concentrate on the baby. I'm going to ask the club to look after her if I'm not here."

"You know we will," Sparky says, almost sounding like I hurt his tender feelings.

"Thank you. All right now. Hope will be around if you have any questions for her about the case. Be honest with her. She's seen and heard all of you doing something disgusting at one time or another. Nothing surprises her anymore."

"Real quick," Z says, holding up his hand.

"Sway has those dates scheduled, and he really wants us there to make sure the set is secure."

Wrath glares across the table at Z.

"Not you," Z says. "Sway doesn't want to scare the poor girl."

"I volunteer as tribute!" Ravage says, jumping out of his chair.

"He also doesn't want someone who's gonna hit on her."

A slow smirk spreads over Murphy's face. "Well, then Wrath should definitely do it, he hates porn stars."

"I don't hate... never mind. Yes, I do."

Z turns his please-be-reasonable eyes my way. "He really wants you on this. At least the first time."

"Fuck, how many times is she gonna be doing this?"

I really need to reevaluate my life. There's way too many porn stars in it.

"Don't know. She travels a lot, though. If Sway can't go with her, he asked if that's something—"

"No."

"He knows *you* won't," Z finishes.

I glance at Teller and Murphy, who suddenly find the floor fascinating. "What's with you two? Couple years ago you woulda been jumping at this."

Z raises his hand. "I told Sway I'd do it."

"Oh, come on!" Stash bitches. "Why does Z always get the hot chicks?"

"Because I'm better looking than you," Z says without turning Stash's way.

"Anything else?" I ask, looking around the table.

"You still going out to Stump's to chat with DeLova?" Dex asks.

"Fuck me. Yeah. Not for a few more weeks, though." Shit. I don't want to be taking any long trips toward the end of Hope's pregnancy.

Wrath seems to sense my hesitation. "I'll go with you. It'll be like old times."

"You worried about DeLova?"

"Don't like that I wasn't there last time. Fucker needs to remember—"

"Trust me, no one forgets your scary ass," Z quips.

"All right." I take a breath and consider my next words. Fuck it, I don't really care what they think. "After that run, I'm done for a bit. I don't want to be on the road when Hope goes into labor and I sure as fuck don't want to be away—"

"Gotcha, Prez," Z says. "Don't blame you."

"I'm not dropping anything else, I'm just saying long runs are out for a bit."

"Prez, I'm just messing around. I'll go wherever you need me to," Ravage offers in the most serious tone he's used all day. Hell, maybe all year.

Teller glances at me. "You've always been fair about giving each of us a break when we need it. You deserve the same. I'm up for whatever you need."

"Aw, is Charlotte gonna unbox your balls and let you have them back?" Ravage asks.

Wrath cracks up.

"Fuck off," Teller says.

Wrath lifts his chin at Murphy. "You got a lot going on, plus I need you here to help with Furious."

"I'm not going anywhere." Murphy glances at me. "Unless you really need me to."

"No, you got plenty of shit here to keep you busy."

The guys laugh and I end our meeting.

The war room erupts into lots of loud discussions, everyone bitching about Inga.

I cock my head at Wrath. "Why are you still here?"

Z answers before Wrath has a chance to open his mouth. "He's afraid to tell Trinity he might have fathered Inga's spawn."

Wrath throws a scowl at him. "I'm not afraid of anything and there's

308

no way her kid is mine."

When we walk out of the room, Hope and Trinity are waiting for us. Trinity's wearing one hell of a pissed-off expression, but she rushes over to hug Wrath as soon as she sees him. "Hope told me what's going on. I can't believe she's trying to hurt the club like this."

I don't miss the relief on Wrath's face. I grip his shoulder briefly, then take a seat next to my wife. "How'd it go?" she asks.

"Well, there're fewer possibilities than I expected," I answer.

She chuckles and shakes her head. "Poor Inga."

"Poor Inga, my ass," Wrath says, dropping down next to Hope and pulling Trin into his lap. He glares at Ravage and Teller. "It better not be one of yours. Or yours," he says, pointing at Dex. "I'm liable to kick your asses for bringing her back into our lives."

Teller grinds his teeth and won't meet any of our eyes.

"So, I take it you narrowed it down to you three?" Hope says, nodding at the guys.

"And Sparky," Wrath adds helpfully.

"Go Sparky," Hope mutters, then snickers.

"You're finding my brothers' struggles awful amusing, baby doll."

"Oh, I know." She presses her hand against her chest and pouts. "Banging porn stars. What a struggle."

Ravage busts up laughing. "Fuck, you're funny, Hope." Then he glances at me. "She would've made a great porn star. She has that nice, classy girl-next-door thing going on."

I think my wife senses I'm about to choke the fuck out of Ravage, because wraps her fingers around my wrist. "I doubt it. I barely knew what a blow job was before I met Rock."

Wrath chokes on his laughter. "Jesus Christ, Cinderella. I've heard you say some funny fucked-up shit, but that has the be—"

"The worst," Teller finishes.

"Uh, yeah." Murphy points to himself and Teller. "We prefer to pretend Mom and Dad don't do that stuff."

I push some hair off her shoulder and kiss her cheek. "You do just fine, baby doll."

She slants a look at me through her lashes. "Thank you, Mr. President."

"Don't start," Wrath warns.

"Oh God. Aren't pregnant women horny all the time?" Ravage asks. "Are you going to go at it right here?"

"Anyway, so that's it? No one else?" She settles her questioning eyes on Murphy.

"Nope." Murphy grins at her. "Guess I'm not as disgusting as you thought." He seems like he's joking, but I sense he honestly wants her approval.

"I've never thought you were disgusting, Murphy." She tilts her head and her lips twitch. "Generous with your time and attention—"

"Generous with his dick," Ravage adds.

"That's 'cause mine's so generous in size," Murphy taunts, punching Ravage's arm.

Hope rolls her eyes. "I'm going to try to set the four of you up first, so we can find out as soon as possible." She settles her hand on my leg. "Actually, I want *you* to go first."

Fuck, I hate that I'm putting her through this.

"You're the one she's gunning for," she reminds me.

Sparky taps Murphy's arm. "You really never fucked Inga?"

Murphy's clearly not amused by the question. "Not that I know of, dick."

"This is some fucked-up shit," Dex says, staring at the ceiling.

"This is *karma*." Sparky flails his arms in the air. "We don't treat bitches right, and now we're all gonna pay."

"Speak for yourself, you little stoner-fuck," Dex snarls. "I was always nice to her. Treated her well."

"Guys, seriously, relax," Hope says. "It's going to be fine. If it turns out the child belongs to one of you, we'll handle it."

"That's it," I say, standing up and offering Hope my hand. "I've had enough for today. I need my wife."

"Sounds like Hope's going home to practice her oral skills," Trinity teases.

Hope leans over and playfully shoves Trin, knocking her out of Wrath's lap.

Outside, Teller and Murphy catch up to us.

"What?" I ask.

Murphy elbows Teller. "Go on. Tell Dad your problem." He snickers while Teller throws a punch at him.

"Knock it off with the dad shit."

Teller stops me with a hand on my arm. "Can we not tell my sister—"

"What? That you're degenerate prick?" Murphy asks, laughing so hard, we barely understand him.

"Fuck you, assclown."

Hope's not stupid. She knows Teller's really asking *her* not to say anything to Heidi.

"Of course not, Teller." She takes a step closer and wraps him up in a motherly—although I'd never say that to her—hug. "It's going to be fine. One way or another. Try not to stress too much, please?"

Her words seem to lift some of the weight off him. "I will. I just hate the idea of having a kid out there I don't know about." His gaze strays my way. "All of us do, I guess."

CHAPTER THIRTY-EIGHT

Hope

MAYBE THE HORMONES are making me ragey, but I can't remember the last time I was so furious.

And kind of skeeved out. I like to think I'm not judgmental, but *four* of them might possibly be the father? Really?

I held it together at the clubhouse to reassure the guys that everything would be okay. Now that it's just the two of us, I can't stop thinking about the audacity of that woman.

As soon as we're inside the house, Rock stops and faces me. He reaches up and tucks my hair behind my ear. "What's going on in your head? Tell me."

"Honestly?"

He sighs. "Yeah."

"That your brothers are kinda disgusting."

He laughs.

And laughs.

"*And* I don't like judging other women's sexual choices, but jeez." I actually shiver with disgust.

When Rock stops laughing, he takes my hand. "I'm sorry you have to deal with this." His jaw tightens. "I heard some of what Adam said to you. This is embarrassing—"

"I don't want to talk about that right now. I'm still pissed with Adam too."

"You don't know how close I came to choking him."

I cock my head. "How much did you overhear?"

"Enough. But when I realized where it was coming from, I decided not to kill him." He runs his fingers through his hair. "When you read the papers, it sounds like you're married to a fucking sleaze."

Now I feel guilty for calling his brothers disgusting.

I reach up and hook my arms around his neck, dragging him into kissing range. "You know that's not how I feel about you, right?"

He grabs my hips, holding me against him. "I heard you," he rasps, closing his eyes and resting his forehead against mine. "Love you so much."

"Good." I kiss his cheek and take a step back before we get sidetracked. "Let me call that guy right now."

Rock opens his eyes and stares at me. "Now? Seriously?"

I trail my fingers down his chest and play with the edge of his T-shirt. "I have this insatiable urge to claim my man."

He raises an eyebrow.

"So *that's* what we're going to be doing for the rest of the evening. Once I get this call out of the way." I glance at the kitchen. "I'd go down some fluids right now if I were you. Can't have you getting dehydrated on me."

He rumbles with laughter and sets me free. "Hurry. I'll be waiting for you in the bedroom."

"Pants off."

"Cock out."

I chuckle as I slowly work my way upstairs into my sitting room. I don't bother closing the door, it's not like I have to worry about confidentiality on this one.

So much for stepping back from my legal career.

I flip through pages of the lengthy petition until I find the phone number for Davis and Rich, PLLC.

"May I speak with Jim Davis? This is attorney Hope Kendall."

I've never heard of this attorney or his law firm before, but that's not so unusual. Empire's bursting at the seams with attorneys.

"Attorney Kendall, thank you for calling. I assume you received my petition."

"Yes. What is this nonsense?"

His mocking laughter only pisses me off more.

"Ms. Kendall," he says in that male-lawyer-condescending tone that reminds me why I hate lawyers so much. "I get that you want to fight for your clients and all, but you're aware they're part of a motorcycle gang, right? Most likely one of the named men is the father of my client's baby."

Now it's my turn to do the laughing. "One of those "named men" is my *husband*, Mr. Davis, I'm guessing Miss March didn't bother to tell you that, did she?"

The long pause on the other end is all the answer I need. "That's what I thought."

"Well, the court will order them to take the test. I can find several witnesses who will testify she had a relationship with one or more of the respondents—"

"Oh, let me save you the trouble, Mr. Davis. I'm well aware of my husband's *past* relationship with your client. All of my respondents are more than willing and ready to submit to a DNA test as soon as possible."

By the sputtering on the other line, he obviously expected a fight.

Inga must be either dumber or crazier than I thought. Who knows what she told this guy.

"Your husband too?"

"He has no problem taking the test. The sooner, the better."

"Well, it has to be a court-approved testing facility," he says in a snotty tone.

"You choose the facility and I'll have my guys there."

"Okay. Then we need to talk about support—"

"Hang on, if one of my clients fathered that child, you won't need to worry about child support. You'll be preparing for a custody case and perhaps a parental alienation suit as well—"

"My client's a resident of California," he blurts out, cutting me off.

I probably shouldn't threaten things I haven't researched in a while, but I'm too pissed to stop myself now. "Who hid the existence of a child from his father. She can live on Mars for all I care. She doesn't get to keep the father out of the child's life all this time and expect to waltz in with her hand out looking for a paycheck while still withholding visitation."

"Well," he says, backpedaling. "Let's cross that bridge when we get to it."

"Yes, let's." I call up my own mocking lawyer voice. "Also, let me be clear with you, this testing will be expensive. If it turns out that *none* of them are the father, which I'm pretty confident will be the case, I'm going to file a motion for costs and fees—"

"Just so you know, I'm a fantastic divorce attorney—in case your husband ends up being the father."

I don't even know what the guy looks like, but I can picture his slimy, smug smile.

It's amazing steam doesn't shoot out of my ears, but somehow I keep my cool. "That won't be necessary. I can round up plenty of witnesses who will testify she concocted this paternity test nonsense out of *spite* for losing her job due to her drug addiction."

He sputters for a few minutes before recovering enough to lob one final zinger. "I think we both know given her occupation and the candidates' lifestyles, there's a good chance we're going to win."

I'm too angry to be offended on behalf of anyone at his ridiculous comment. Underneath my outrage, there's an undeniable confidence lurking. I trust Rock with my whole heart.

My voice is cool and full of conviction when I answer, "I guess we'll see, won't we?"

*The story continues in **After Glow (Lost Kings MC #11)**.*

AUTHOR NOTES

Once again, I find myself in the position of having to apologize to you, my lovely, patient readers. I never intended After Burn to be two books. I've been writing it for close to three years now. First it was #6.5, then it was moved to #9, then #10.

But I had to get this story out. Many of you continue to write and ask me when or if Rock and Hope will have a baby. In my head, I always knew they would and I knew it needed to happen before Z's book. (Don't worry, Z totally agrees with me on this point.)

Then over the summer when I finally could buckle down and pour my heart into After Burn, I started to have concerns. I kept saying to Mr. Lake, "this is a really big story. It should probably be two or three books." He'd tell me to follow my instincts (and tease me for never being able to write short.)

Except, I had all sorts of reasons why it *couldn't* be more than one book. 1) I had promised my readers by the end of After Burn they would know who Grace *and* Chance were. 2) My readers *really* want Z's book.

But this story! There was so much to it! I actually wrote it in six parts. It was the only way to keep it all straight in my head (remember, I'm a pantser, not a plotter.) I could've written an entire book about the run to National and the Florida rally (don't think I didn't consider it!) I loved bringing in the Iron Bulls MC. I could've written about the two clubs mixing it up forever. Maybe Phoenyx will pick up that thread one day.

Honestly, I was worried that no one would buy another book about Rock and Hope let alone *two* more books about them. So, I went ahead and said it would be one book and one book only. That was the smart thing to do. The better *business* decision. I wrapped some duct tape around my creative brain and went about my business.

I had another freak-out late in the summer when the book Just. Wouldn't. End. But I had already revealed the cover for After Burn, and committed myself to another project (*Knight of Swords*, which you totally need to read if you want to learn more about Vapor and Juliet.) I didn't have the time and couldn't handle the stress of an additional book release. And I knew if I ended part 1 on a cliffy, I'd have to get part 2 out quickly.

When I turned After Burn into my editor it was complete. Probably the most complete book I've turned into an editor in a long time. I loved it, but I wasn't 100% satisfied with the ending. It felt rushed to me. It was over 116,000 words by this point and I knew I could either trim it down to tighten it up or unleash everything stewing in my head and make it the two books I thought it should've been all along.

I chose to pretend it was going to be one book and started cutting out scenes (which my crit partners can tell you is almost impossible for me to do.) The scenes I cut were some of my beta's favorite ones, so I hesitated again. I loved them too!

I was in Houston for a conference when I finally said, "Fuck it, this is going to be two damn books!"

Then I sat paralyzed with fear about announcing that it would be two books. I needed to arrange for a cover and a release date, editing, rearrange the blurbs (I hate writing blurbs!) and actually write the rest of the second book. I'd put myself in the same predicament as last year with Teller's books. Something I swore I wouldn't do again!

Finally, Mr. Lake pointed out that if I published After Burn the way it was, it would eat me alive that it wasn't the way I wanted it. He also gently reminded me that I was running out of time.

It was two books now. No going back.

By the way, at the time I'm writing these notes, I still haven't "officially" announced that it's two books. I put some info on my website and hinted at it here and there in my Facebook group. I spoke to another author who recently was in the same situation and told her I might just leave the note at the end of the book and run and hide. She wisely said, "don't do that."

This is probably the most cliff-hangerish book I've left you with, but I swear it's for a good reason. I think you'll understand why when you read After Glow (or is it going to be After Shock? I should probably figure that out.).And I figured since everyone accuses Slow Burn of being a cliffhanger anyway, "Why the fuck not?" Well, honestly I don't consider it either book a "cliffhanger." It's a romance. Rock and Hope are solid as a couple—no cliffy there.

You know what? I don't know what the fuck I'm doing anymore. Just know this, I love writing this series and these characters. I want to do it for a very long time. But also know that I try to balance that with my desire to meet reader expectations and make you happy.

Also, I'm an Indie author. For better or worse, it's just me making these decisions (Which by the way, I love! No publisher today would let me get away with writing six books about the same couple!) I think I can write a lot about Rock and Hope, because their story touches everyone in the club. I like interacting with each of the members through Rock and Hope's eyes. I also just love them. I love Rock's struggles between being a good president and a good husband and now a father (maybe to more than one kid!). I love that Hope's found her place in the club. And even though she's smart and respected, she still doubts herself from time to time (as we all do, or at least I do—I mean *hello*, did you read what I said up there about my struggles with this book?.).

So there it is. The story of how one book became two. I never like breaking promises to my readers, but I'd rather break a small promise than make you pay for a book that is not 100% of what I know it can and should be. Now you'll have two long books instead of one longer-than-average book.

Also know this decision didn't impact Z's book in any way. Whether

After Burn was one, two, or three books (don't give me any ideas!), Z's was never coming by the end of this year. It's nowhere near where it needs to be to see the light of day. Z's waited this long, his story needs to be told just right. He's waited patiently and I won't shortchange his story just to get a book out. I have a date in mind, but we all know how bad I am at planning stuff, so for now, I'll keep it to myself.

Hang in there for *After Glow* (that's the title I'm going with for now.) I promise you it's going to blow your fucking mind. You won't see it coming, but when it does, if you've been closely following the series, it will make sense.

Remember, I've been planning this book since 2015-2016. I started writing it as I was finishing up White Heat. It's been killing me to keep it a secret and now I have to keep it a secret just a little bit longer.

Thank you so much for reading!
Autumn

SOCIAL MEDIA

Visit my website autumnjoneslake.com to sign up for my newsletter. I'm also on the following social media platforms:

Facebook
Goodreads
Instagram
Twitter
Pinterest
Book and Main Bites

You can follow me on Book Bub or Amazon to find out when I have a new release or a sale.

Feel free to email me at: autumnjlake@gmail.com. I try to personally respond to every email I receive.

www.autumnjoneslake.com

The End

THE LOST KINGS MC

AUTUMNJONESLAKE.COM